The Prince who fell in Love with the Dragon

Jerry R. M.

First Edition:

December 2022

© 2022 by Jerry R. M.

ISBN: 979-8-9864080-2-6

Cover Designer by Jack Baker

Edited by Liz Gilbeau

Proofreader by Roxana Coumans

To my parents.

For believing in me before I did.

WRITER'S NOTE

The fictional story, culture, characters, worldbuilding, and everything related to the tale *The Prince Who Fell in Love with the Dragon,* are purely fictional. None is intended as a representation of any country, or culture at any point in history. In the story, you can find violence, combat action with different weapons, mild foul language, assault, self-destruction, bullying, gore, and death by dragons.

Contents

The Prince Who Fell in Love with the Dragon

A Stolen Kingdom Serie

Book I

PROLOGUE

Usually, the stories begin with, *"Once upon a time, there was a tall, handsome, and strong knight who bravely faced the dragon."* Sometimes the knights were firstborn, heirs to the throne, poetic, and often sang for the maiden. So, when he put on his armor to face the beast, it was the dragon that was afraid of him. Those adventures seemed to happen in every story except mine.

In my case, I didn't know of battle. I was the fourth son and didn't even know what bravery was. Therefore, the one who ran away was me.

ACT ONE

The Fire Competition

CHAPTER 1

For better or for worse, being chased by a dragon has been the most extraordinary thing in my life. When his gaze penetrated mine, I saw images of my life flashing before my eyes, wondering how the hell I got myself to that moment. I wanted to know where the mistake was. Perhaps it was at the moment that I decided to enter the ruins that were forbidden...

No.

It wasn't until later when I inadvertently provoked the dragon and had it there so close it was breathing in my face. *It was my fault,* I thought, running my mind back as its claws snapped into the cracked ground and a light began to grow from his throat. I'd never felt fear like the one that paralyzed me that day—when I heard the loud roar, a shiver tore through my bones, and my hair was wildly messed up due to its breath. It was more than fear. It was something I'd never experienced before in my life. My knuckles turned white from tight pressure. My breath held long enough to suffocate so the beast wouldn't hear me, losing my sense of balance as if my legs turned to jelly—I thought these were my undoing. But then it stared at me, at my *soul,* with those huge, yellow eyes, and I thought my worst mistake had been entering those ruins when I knew it was forbidden to do so.

Turns out, I was wrong. That was not my biggest mistake.

"Omhet!" someone yelled.

I cursed as I jumped, startled out of my sleep.

"I'm awake," I lied, rubbing my eyes while I sat on my bed.

"You're late," berated my brother, Cayetano, pulling me out of bed by my nightshirt. "Why do I always have to wake you like your damn maid?"

"I could stay sleeping." I loudly yawned but was interrupted by a sudden slap to the forehead. I hissed, "Would you cut it? I said I was awake."

"Just in case." He smirked, leaving the door to my room wide open when he left.

It didn't matter that I was eighteen years old, being the little brother came with the torment of being teased by my older relatives. It was a curse, to be sure, one that kissing a frog would not even break, it seemed.

I almost ran through the hallway while trying to put my dark parka on. I was grateful it covered most of my body. Living in the coldest of kingdoms meant having cold days basically every day of your life.

I was about to step into the dining room when Annally stopped me.

"Always in a hurry and never properly dressed." She clicked her tongue, pulling my clothes in every way to make me look like the prince I was. She was more than a maid. She was the one who raised me as much as my mother. "If you'd wake up when I order you to, this wouldn't be happening."

While she tried to better place the neck of my parka around me, I rolled my eyes. It wasn't like my family cared about how I looked. Hell, I didn't even think they noticed if I was there or not! I made a run for it, escaping her grasp as best I could. I heard her call my name as I walked away, but I ignored it. Dear maid Annally was getting old. There was a time in my life when I couldn't escape her at all. Now, she was losing her touch. Sometimes, I was glad for it.

I paused for a moment, leaning against the closed door and taking a deep breath before entering the dining room. I heard them before I saw them—my family was as loud and rambunctious as ever. Multiple conversations were taking place, noises of chairs being dragged, boisterous laughter echoing down the hall—for a royal family, it was not a conventional way to dine. It could be a tad complicated at times. But it was our family, and even though it got tiresome, it was how our little unit worked.

Honestly, though? It was chaos.

But it's my favorite chaos.

I finally took my place at the table between my little sister and Cayetano. Like I'd figured, they didn't even bat an eye when I sat because they were too involved in their conversation to notice. A fly would've bothered them more, honestly.

The grand table was surrounded by, first and foremost, the King of Glacier. Guillermo Espinho. You could tell he was the king by his flamboyant clothes, his neat, short hair, and spruced-up beard. He carried himself in a way that made it clear he was no ordinary man. Some would call him a loving father, but I'd say he was strict as hell.

My eldest brother, also named Guillermo, reminded me of our father in almost every aspect—almost. He was strict, loyal, and cruel. Personally, I suspect a witch took away his heart, or maybe our mother fed him vinegar instead of milk to sour him to the core. I chuckled at the image, and of course, he heard me. He raised an eyebrow and stared me down, which made me think he somehow read my thoughts. Maybe he didn't have to go there, though. I did make fun of him often, so it was natural to suspect I was doing so all the time.

I mean, the guy was twenty-five years old and hadn't even found a nice lady to settle down with. You didn't even have to wonder why, he was hard to handle after you got to know him and his difficult personality. I don't want to sound pessimistic, but it makes me happy that he's single. No one could stand a man like him. I know from experience.

Too much experience.

Perhaps what I will say is not possible for the future king of Glacier, but I wish he would never marry anyone.

"Don't start, Omhet," said Cayetano, nudging me too hard to be considered friendly.

I frowned, rubbing my side. I realized that I must have been thinking aloud.

"You know you'll end up marrying first," I replied. I loved to tease Cayetano because he was easy to rile up. But with his protective personality and charming looks, he really could attract any maiden he preferred.

Unlike my third brother, Rodrigo, whose vile attitude made anyone think he was planning the end of humanity while everyone slept. I leaned over and whispered this to Cayetano.

"You're cruel," he said, but then he chuckled.

"Call me cruel when the royal family is found dead in the middle of the night, and Rodrigo crowns himself king. You know what kind of intentions he's got by merely looking at him."

Cayetano almost spat his drink out when I said that so seriously—but it was true! He tried to hold back his laughter.

My sister, sitting on my right, made it worse when she said, "I think he'll do it with a knife."

"No," said Cayetano carefully, trying his best to avoid anyone overhearing, "I said he'd poison us."

"Poison?" I dubiously asked. "Usually, women use that tactic."

"Precisely," said Rodrigo.

We paused, tense. *Had he heard us?* He was staring at our father, who was addressing the whole table, even though most of us were barely listening.

Rodrigo turned to look at us and said, "And when people find out I'm the sole survivor, they'll think of me as the victim who survived, not the killer who did it."

While my sister shanked in her seat, Cayetano let out a boisterous laugh, no longer concerned about being heard.

"It was a joke," I grumbled, annoyed at getting caught.

It was our usual morning. Easy banter flowed back and forth between us. Father was trying valiantly to carry on with his conversation, Mother a silent force next to him. And when our plates were empty after the delicious meal, it was usually time to start with our daily duties. The King was always the first to leave, followed closely by the Queen.

But today, the King wasn't standing, and the Queen had barely touched her food.

I frowned.

Something was different, and only now had I caught on.

But just as I was about to inquire about it, my father's voice rose.

"We've received an invitation from the main Kingdom."

We stopped eating. We stared. An invitation, for us, from Andebeck? *Impossible,* I wanted to snark, but it would be unwise to interrupt now.

"As you know, in eight months, it will be a century since the dragon attacked." He paused for a moment and then quietly added, "One hundred years of a kingdom without a king."

Ah, yes, the legend that would never die. The story was shared everywhere for all to know and hear. As children, we liked to pretend we were the heroes saving the damsel in distress from the hideous beast that had trapped her. We all thought it was just a story, but the Kingdom of Andebeck claimed it was true.

A sorceress had summoned a dragon to interrupt the princess's wedding. The fire unleashed by the beast incinerated those gathered within the old castle's walls. The castle was destroyed, and the princess was kidnapped by the malicious sorceress, never to be heard from again. The only miraculous survivor had been her father, whose last words had been a decree: not a single soul would become king unless he rescued Laila Blume. Hundreds of brave men tried, but they never came back alive.

The ruins still remained high in the mountainous region of Andebeck. What had once been a beautiful sight to see was now a desolate, macabre reminder that no one dared to even look at for too long. Not unless they wanted to stir the beast back to life.

It was stupid, really, to think the princess was still alive and to suggest the dragon watched over her, even claiming they could hear its roars now and then!

Preposterous! Did they not remember the fact that it had been one hundred years?

It was too much. I shrugged, "They should give up the search. Find a nephew of the old king and crown him—problem solved."

Cayetano's elbow nudges my side again. I grunted, wanting to glare his way, but my father continued. "King Arien Lois Blume's last promise still stands—no one will be king until Princess Laila is rescued and the beast is slain."

"Rescued? It's been one hundred years. What if she's dead?"

Both Mother and Father stared me down, most likely wondering how I even dared to ask such a stupid question.

Father ignored me after that, continuing. "Which is why the Kingdom of Andebeck has decided to celebrate their legend by creating a competition: The Trials of fire!"

The trials of fire, I repeated in my mind. It had a worn-out ring to it, that's for sure. I said nothing, however. I did not want to interrupt my father, not when my curiosity had been aroused.

"All the kingdom and the seven courts will voluntarily offer a member of their family to participate in this competition." A proud smile graced his features, one we did not share. Everyone gathered around that table suddenly tensed, already knowing where this was headed to. "You'll be trained and sent to fight the dragon. Whoever succeeds will be crowned King of Andebeck."

No one was as enthused about the idea as he was.

Whose idea was it to make a massacre out of a *massacre*? Were they that desperate? And who would be brave enough to attend this farce of competition and win it by fighting against a *dragon?* If it were even there, to begin with!

My father was too excited about this whole ordeal. It was easy to figure out why, though. If one of us won, imagine the glory it would bring to our forgotten kingdom. Honor, riches, recognition, allies—it would solve all of Glacier's problems. When put like that, it sounded reasonable.

But not for me.

"If one of us has to go," I quickly said, "I vote for Guillermo." His eyes burned me on the spot, but I forged ahead, not caring at all if he liked it or not. "Don't get me wrong, it's not like I want you to die, but you are the strongest," I added sarcastically.

"Guillermo won't go," the king stated as if it was obvious. "He's the successor of the crown. I cannot risk it."

We stared at each other insistently. Who would be the lucky one to go on this mad suicide mission? Guillermo was safe. My sister was as well, she was still too young for this competition, according to Father. But for the rest of us? To be honest, I knew I was potentially out of the equation. Father never saw me as anything but the weakest, or as he liked to call it, *physically inadequate.* I slumped against the back of my seat, a bit bummed by the sudden reminder. Not that I wanted to fight a dragon, anyway.

I refocused on the heated debate as if the matter were of life and death. Maybe it was.

"I'm sorry, Father, but I don't even like to fight against my own brothers!" said Cayetano hurriedly. "This is ridiculous. I don't want to die in vain! I'm sure you'll find someone else to go in my stead." He pointedly stared at Rodrigo, trying his best to divert attention towards our other brother. It was obvious he was scared—Who wouldn't be?

"Cayetano is right," interrupted our mother, "exposing our sons for Andebeck's vile manipulation is unnecessary. They just want to create an army to rid themselves of the beast, is all!"

A hard fist fell on the table, silencing us all.

"An Espinho has to go," Father growled, "I will not be embarrassed by my cowardly sons. A volunteer will rise, or I will choose."

"Send Rodrigo, then!" Cayetano shouted.

"Why me?" Rodrigo yelled, bewildered.

"If something happens to Guillermo, I'll be the next in line!"

"And if something were to happen to *you,* I would be next!"

Everything got out of control. Father stood and yelled to try to stop the cacophony taking place in the usually loud but still dining hall. There were firsts on tables and loud accusations. My sister left the room with Annally. It was chaos. Only Guillermo and I remained relatively quiet. He was enjoying the show while finishing his breakfast now that he was off the hook.

I should have felt the same. It was a golden opportunity to laugh at the absurdity of it all, but something stopped me, and believed me, it was something stupid. Something crazy. Something I was trying to gather my strength for. In this impromptu battlefield, the king was searching for someone to represent this small, forgotten kingdom.

Small and forgotten—just like me. Small. Forgotten. Not even existing as an option for most things. So, unlike my brothers, they expected great things from them but never from me.

I stood and loudly stated, "I'll go."

The only thing that was heard after that was my brother's last bite being swallowed down.

That moment right there. That was my biggest mistake.

CHAPTER 2

I had not seen either king or queen exit their chambers for hours. I couldn't concentrate on my daily chores, solely thinking that maybe, just maybe, I'd done something wrong. I'd been staring out the window at the falling snow for heaven knows how long now, the grounds thickening with the beauty of my kingdom. The splendor of the snow was soft, like the silk that made the sheets of my bed. But to the touch, it was coarse, grating my skin—grating like my mother's screeches coming from inside the royal chambers.

"He won't survive!"

A sigh escaped through my lips. A thousand before it had already left me. Standing out in the hallway, awaiting my verdict, I couldn't help but get lost in the fight that had been going on for the last hour or so.

"He is no longer a child, and he needs this more than you think. You must learn to let him go!"

"Don't act like you know him because you don't!"

I stared harder at the snow, at every flake I could find, following it to the ground. The sound of a harsh sob broke me away from contemplating the enchanting village not far from the castle gates. Watching the snow fall through the window on the pine trees, meadows, and mountain ranges was not calming me at all.

"He won't be capable of withstanding the pressure of such a horrible kingdom!" the queen sobbed.

I was a coward.

Angrily, the king shouted, "This is the perfect opportunity for him to stop being a child and become a man!"

Weak.

My hands suddenly grasped at my hair, pulling hard in rising anxiety. I couldn't hear them anymore, I had to do something, I—

"If this is one of your stupid jokes, you better say so right now," growled Guillermo warningly. "You're taking this too far."

My brothers and sister were all there with me, in the hallway, wondering what would happen next. So was the whole staff, apparently, I hadn't even noticed them until now. Quickly, I shifted my sight back to my siblings, ignoring as best I could the worry that nagged the otherwise tranquil staff of the castle. Though honestly, this was so much worse. There was never a time when my brothers and I weren't joking around, arguing, or looking for any excuse to tease each other. I wanted to bring out a snarky comment from Rodrigo, to tease Cayetano, to hear my sister laugh —anything at this point. This absolute silence wasn't normal.

So, when Guillermo spoke, I dared him to continue —to argue or rage at me, but Cayetano sent me a warning glare when he noticed. I backed off, staring out the damned window again. Which, to be fair, had been the better idea. Guillermo, he—well, he was the firstborn, the one to inherit the crown. He was a very impersonal man. A great politician and tactician, yes, but what he had in spades he lacked in kindness. Emotions were a burden to him, it seemed. He'd been raised to be king since he was practically born, and I along with the rest of my family saw him as one. They demanded everything from him that can be expected from a great politician since before he even learned to walk. As if it were an act of punishment, I was the opposite. I'd been coddled and wrapped in protective blankets from the demands of the world. To be fair, next to him, I'd had it easy. I could see the hate in his eyes every time when he looked at me, for that and for reasons I didn't know if I would ever find out.

I didn't want any of this. I just wanted to show that I was also an Espinho as worthy as all of them, and capable enough to go to this competition and try for the sake of our kingdom. I may not be the best fit, but did I have to be the leftover crumbs from the royal family?

I softly groaned. How did it get to this?

Before I could hear anything else, the door was flung open and everyone in the hall froze. I straightened up and watched the queen walk out. Her eyes were red and swollen, and her neck was soaked with tears. By the gods, this woman looked as though she were already mourning over my grave. She looked at me, almost broke down again in a painful sob, but then noticed the audience that had gathered and managed to control it. She called for Annally, probably to go to the temple to pray to Krea.

I looked at my sister and gave her a nod that she understood well because she shot after our mother, grabbed her hand, and left with the poor thing. If anyone could help as much as prayer did, it was Estefania.

Hands on my shoulders snapped me back to the moment, jumping in alarm at the sudden touch. It was the king, and he held me tight while staring straight into my soul as if he were doing so for the first time in our lives. I stood still, staring so closely at my father's face that it felt strange.

His brown eyes lit up as he exclaimed, "Prepare yourself, for tomorrow, you'll be history in the making."

And that was it. Just as suddenly as he'd appeared, he left, followed closely by his guard. Baffled, I stared at his retreating back, and the staff were most likely doing the same I couldn't tell, not when my eyes were glued still to the now empty halls the king had vacated.

"You know," Guillermo said, messing up my hair. I pushed his hand away, beyond aggravated. I hate when he touches me. "I think you had us fooled there for a second. You'll be able to survive this ordeal."

I frowned at him, "Really?"

"Yes! You'll be the one found hiding by the end when everyone else has been declared dead."

"Guillermo!" snapped Cayetano. "He's scared enough. Will you stop it?"

"I'm not," I lied through my teeth, knowing full well I was terrified.

Everyone started to slowly disperse now that things had somewhat settled. I was the last to leave, trying to make sense of what the hell had happened ever since that morning. When Annally attempted to approach me, presumably offering me tea to calm down my nerves, my legs hastily carried me to my room. I was not in the mood to face anyone right then. I needed to be alone.

In my room, I fell against the door, heavily sighing. I was beyond exhausted. But the prospect of sleeping eluded me, so I made my way to the balcony. I was after the cold, the frigid wind embracing my thoughts until everything was clearer. Calmer. The night welcomed the four moons in the sky, where only the largest was seen more than the others. I clutched onto the railings and exhaled all the air I held, almost in a groan.

What have I done?

Why had I said yes to this?

If I stared closely, I would find the answer. After all, it was painfully obvious.

I wanted to be seen by my family.

Known.

Heard.

It hurts to be seen as nothing to them. I wanted to be... more.

"Is it true?" a whisper came from within my chambers. Startled, I turned, even though I knew who it belonged to. "Will you kill the dragon tomorrow?"

Estefania looked even more nervous than I did, so I tried, for her sake, to look like I used to. I smiled, a soft thing that bloomed whenever my sister was nearby.

"Of course not," I said, hugging her close. The fur of her wine-colored parka tickled my nose. "It will take quite a few months of training before that happens. Please, don't be afraid."

Not now, at least.

She almost smiled. Almost. Her eyes got lost in the thought while she stared at the horizon, at the village far away. Call it melancholy, but I stared at her and noticed how much she reminded me of our mother. Her beauty was parallel to hers, skin as white as snow and long, soft hair as black as night. I wanted to protect her and the innocence and warmth I knew this competition would eventually take away.

Then it hit me—she wouldn't be with me after tonight. I was leaving home. It made my breath hitch.

"I'll pray to Krea for you every day when we go to the temple," she promised.

Through the sadness, I smiled. "Trust me, don't be afraid. I rather everyone else doubt me but not you."

"I'll never doubt you; I never have. Just... promise me you'll come back home."

I swallowed hard.

"Omhet," she insisted, dragging my eyes to hers instantly when her entire body started to shake. It wasn't the cold making her shiver.

"I'll come back—I promise."

She nodded and, with a sigh, began to leave. I wasn't ready to go inside, so I sat on the balcony railing and looked at my kingdom one more time, saying goodbye to a place I didn't want to leave.

"Omh," she called out before she left, her feet stalling by the balcony doors. "Be careful with the dragon—I don't want it to suffer before dying."

That... was a strange thought to have. I simply nodded, not knowing what to say to that. Though I have to admit, it got me thinking the rest of the night. If it hadn't been for my sister, I would've completely forgotten that the creature was... well, a living, breathing creature. It was a dangerous, wild beast, but a living being, nonetheless. If it was still around after all these years, it made me wonder if it was tired and wanted its freedom. Perhaps it wanted to simply live and not be part of a witch plot to destroy and conquer.

I shook my head, wondering what was wrong with me worrying about a legendary creature that had no say in my life whatsoever. Though all this made me wonder if maybe that dragon was craving its freedom as much as I was.

Chapter 3

The sudden bang of the door opening brought me out of my sleep. I groaned when someone opened the curtains, and the sun's rays reflected on the snow, making my eyes squint. As I sat, I covered my eyes, rubbing them, when I heard Annally's voice. Was she talking to me? I started to answer when I noticed that, no, she was not.

I frowned, confused. Usually, Annally would be alone, preparing me for the day ahead with a warm bath and her choice of clothing. All the while, she would talk about my schedule, knowing that I would probably do half of it and ignore the rest.

She would definitely not be addressing other palace staff members or giving them orders in a way I was not accustomed to. My tired eyes took in the commotion inside my room, including the three guards that stood next to Annally, throwing me off. Were they wearing Glacier's guard uniform? I called out to her this time, wanting to know why she was explaining, in minute detail, my routine as well as my diet, my wardrobe, and my measurements, for heaven's sake. Who were they? Why were they here? And why were they privy to information only Annally knew by heart? They were the royal guard. They did not need to know what I wore to sleep. Right?

A knock at the door, followed by my father's smiling face, made me freeze.

"Good morning."

Now I was baffled. The king was inside my room, which was very unusual. What in the world was going on? Had he ever stepped foot inside my chambers before? I don't remember a time when he had. It was sad, really. I couldn't help staring at him like an idiot.

He curiously looked around at everything with one sweep of his eyes. "Your room is small," he commented at last, slowly walking to my bed.

I followed his gaze, glancing at the chimney in the small living room next to my dormitory, the dining room for two, the door that led to my private bathroom, and my study. True, compared to his or my brother Guillermo's room, it was small, but it was something I was used to.

Then I stared at him in casual wear, and I almost gaped. My vain and eccentric father was always a spotless man. To see him in just a thick shirt, and missing his usual jewelry and crown, would throw off just about anyone. The bed dipped with his weight as he sat next to me, his hand fixing his graying hair into an even more pristine state.

Immediately, I moved away to grant him some space and to give myself that same space. It was too early for me—I was still processing everything after seeing how agitated everyone was. Having the king sit next to me on my bed, as a father typically would, worsened the confusion. Food was the only solace that brought a sense of normalcy to the start of my day. My stomach rumbled at the onslaught of different scents.

The maiden left a tray on my bed, and my mouth fell open at sight. Were they trying to feed a battalion? There was baked bread, eggs, fresh fruit, and my favorite morning dish, sweet rice with cinnamon and dried grapes. *Am I dying?* I wanted to say, but I kept quiet. Now was not the time for jokes. And was I supposed to eat now? I hadn't even bathed.

A slight shove on my back startled me. "Eat well," said the king, reaching for a cup of coffee from the tray, "You have a long journey ahead."

I let out a small breath but did as told. And honestly, the food did look great, so I dug in while he stared at me.

"So much to explain," he suddenly mused, "yet so little time."

Between his words, the delicious meal, and Annally, concentrating was hard. But when she spoke to the three guards about preparations for the trip to Andebeck, everything clicked and settled badly within me. The reminder that I'd be gone from the only home I'd ever known made my stomach twist in uncomfortable knots. I dropped my fork as my appetite vanished.

My attention went back to Father, who spoke about Andebeck and how different it would be from Glacier. It was uncomfortably hot, especially during the summer. Their hostile culture was due to the immense fear that surrounded all who lived within the overpopulated metropolis. He kept describing what he could, which frustrated me because to think I knew so little of Andebeck. My tutors had been so focused on the folklore and legends that they'd forgotten to mention even an ounce of their real-life culture. I was lost enough as it was, and knowing that I knew the bare minimum did not help my anxiety die down.

"Do you know where you're going?" asked my father.

Annally and the working staff quickly packed and sealed my bags shut, hurrying out the door one after the other. When I noticed how distracted I was, I quickly looked back at the king, answering him promptly. "The Kingdom of Andebeck, the Union's Capital."

He nodded. "You will still be treated as royalty, but do note that training will be as rigorous as any warrior brigade training. Every kingdom and court will send their volunteers, don't let them see your fear, or it will be your end."

"I'm not afraid," I insisted, rolling my eyes.

He carried on as if I hadn't spoken. "Training will last eight months. I want you to be seen and remembered. I want everyone to remember that we exist up here in the mountain." He was enthused, I knew, because this was a perfect opportunity to expose our Kingdom to others once more. Glacier was, sadly, always forgotten when significant events took place anywhere in this world. "Make allies," he continued, "with the sons and daughters of the most prominent kingdom. Maybe even meet a lovely damsel, who knows? Court a princess, which would be better..."

"Your Majesty," I tried to interrupt, embarrassed.

"If you can't convince a princess to fall in love with you, then the daughter of a court nobleman will suffice."

My face felt close to bursting.

"Father, please," I interrupted, "I don't want to court anyone."

"You're handsome, like your father!" He nudged me playfully. It was an order disguised as a joke. "Just keep the jokes out of the equation, and you'll marry before Guillermo."

I huffed. "I'll take that into consideration just to annoy him."

We shared a bit of laugh but then sat in silence, staring at the empty room. So, it was real—I was about to leave.

The king's sigh surprised me a bit. "Never put our name to shame. You are an Espinho—no less than anyone else in the world."

I looked at him, swallowing deeply. If there was one main reason I was doing all of this, it was because of him.

Then I thought about what my father hadn't explained and said, "Father, you've told me about everything except the real confrontation. Aren't you worried?"

"Why should I be?" he said casually. "You're not going to face the dragon. You're not even going to see it." I frowned in confusion, not understanding where he wanted to go with all this. "Omhet, you didn't think you would face the beast, did you?"

I shrugged my shoulders, baffled. "That's what it's all about, isn't it?" I asked sarcastically, not disrespectfully, but because I was terribly confused.

"You don't have a chance!" he replied, patting me on the back hard enough to almost make my plate tumble to the bed. "Surely Ettezi kingdom will do it in a day. They don't need you." His tone made me feel like an idiot. "All I want from you is to keep your head held high while you leave a good impression for this kingdom."

I gaped at him, unable to answer. This could not be true.

"Enjoy your vacation," my father concluded, standing up, "and tell me all about it when you come back. I'm sure your brothers will be jealous of you by then."

He kept talking while he left my room, but I heard nothing. I was too stunned. I pushed the tray away from me and flopped back onto the bed. My appetite had been ruined.

"I look ridiculous," I grumbled, staring at my reflection in the mirror.

Annally berated me for my choice of words. But really, how could she not see I looked like an impostor in these clothes? Annally's great idea of lending me Guillermo's old guard clothing had backfired. They seemed too big on me. They used to belong to Guillermo when he was my age, but he'd been training since before he learned how to write, so he had muscles everywhere. Why did Annally think I'd fit in this uniform? For heaven's sake, this was laughable at best. The last piece to be added to the uniform was the soldier's official platinum parka with its turquoise and white interior—Glacier's official colors.

I rolled my eyes while I made my way through the hallway. It was time to go.

When I reached the main staircase, I found my family waiting for me by the two exit doors with serious expressions fixed on me while I descended the stairs. I noticed how Mother tried hiding her tears behind a handkerchief, which made me sigh. All this unwelcome fanfare of goodbye was making me nervous.

"It's not like I'm going to die, mother."

She tried to smile, but when words tried to come out of her mouth, she couldn't quite express them. She chose to stay silent, trying to keep her emotions in place. I was the emotional sort, just like her. I would've sympathized if I had the time to focus on that. The king held her still when she tried to hug me—he, too, knew how emotional we could be. This was not meant to be a teary goodbye. It was an honor to represent Glacier within the most powerful kingdom.

"Hey!" I turned to my siblings when Cayetano called out to me. "I won't be around to protect you." I sneakily glanced at Guillermo while he looked at his pocket watch, impatient for this scene to end. "Don't make enemies, don't be alone, but above all, do not do anything stupid."

"I know..."

"Omhet, I'm serious. I'm not going to be there. I'm—" he exhaled in frustration, "if something happens... *anything*, you're going to come back, understood?"

It has been so long since he used such a scared tone with me. I stayed locked in his gaze, unable to answer him.

I wanted to say something to the rest and at least embrace Estefania, but the king hauled me out and through the doors with nary a minute more sentimentalities. Immediately, snow started to stick to my hair even though its fall was soft and graceful. We quickly made our way toward the palace walls, where a carriage was already waiting by the exit. Four horses neighed quietly, calmly waiting for the orders to move. The whole thing reminded me of my imminent departure from all I knew. I couldn't stop the sudden urge to look back at my family and home, staring at Estefania's fearful, teary eyes as the gates closed behind me. *I'll be back,* I wanted to say to the one person in this world I'd miss the most.

I turned my attention to the carriage once more, seeing the king salute one of the guards I'd seen earlier in my room.

"Omhet, do you remember Cheikh?" He introduced the dark-skinned man, dressed from head to toe in royal guard uniform, with a gold medal I'd never seen on other soldiers, proudly gleaming on his chest. I remember him. He is the most important person for my father, after Guillermo.

"Sir." He saluted me. His impressive height and massive figure were intimidating. I nodded in return, feeling his dark eyes on my figure. I shuddered a bit.

"He'll be your most important asset and protection while you're in Andebeck. He's my right-hand man—the greatest general who ever graced Glacier." He smiled grandly, a hand falling on Cheikh's shoulder. "And my best friend."

Cheikh's stern face smiled briefly at the king's words. Then, avoiding his eyes in respect, he turned to his companions, pointing at them with his beard-covered chin.

"I'd like to introduce you to my companions." The other two, the same one who had also been rummaging through my room, approached us from the back of the carriage. "This is General Shin." He pointed to the man who eerily reminded me of my mother—thin eyes and straight, jet-black hair who nodded my way. "And this is Lucas." Then he pointed at the other man, whose light-brown hair was striking beside his bronze skin, and was distracted, cleaning his foggy glasses. "They are Glacier's best warriors, and from now on, we'll be your shadow—your guardians."

I didn't know if he meant that as a good thing, but I still nodded at them. At least Lucas's smile was welcoming. Maybe they weren't as strict as they appeared?

"Shin is a combat specialist, and his weapon of choice is swords," my father explained, making Shin nod. "Lucas is complicated," he said as a joke, making Lucas laugh. "He is a scholar—if you want to survive Andebeck's hostile environment, you best pay attention to what he has to say. He may seem like a nice fellow, but he'll be the quickest to act when danger arises."

My guardians studied me until all that remained were my bare bones, assessing, I presumed, the best way to deliver me to my destined trail. It would not be easy, especially when the king placed his son under their care. These men were the best at what they did, but even they recognized the importance of keeping me safe as if I were a fragile mission to endure for the next few months.

"I will not be the cause of trouble while we undergo this journey," I vowed respectfully. "May your lives be to protect mine, as mine be to protect yours," I said the pact of the Glacierian soldier.

They nodded, and I turned to my father, knowing it was time to leave but having no idea how to say goodbye. Even though I barely knew him, I respected him deeply. For everyone he could be the king of Glacier, but for me he will always be my father.

"I won't let you down."

"Come back home," he answered instead, taking me by the shoulders in a pleading gesture. "And try to behave like an Espinho. If you must, keep the jokes for when no one is around to hear them. All right?"

I frowned. "That doesn't make sense."

Then he hugged me, and that made even less sense. I froze, unable to move or act. Had time stopped? It certainly felt like it. I clenched my fists, holding myself still. I couldn't fathom why, but I was sure I would carry this moment with me for the rest of time.

"Please, whatever you do, Omhet," he pleaded, "do not face the dragon."

CHAPTER 4

I had never gone beyond my kingdom's limits, and getting to the train station was a churning experience. Everything happened so fast that I could barely process every moment. Cheikh led the way, while the other two never left my side to ensure no one got too close to me. I think none of us expected that there would be so many people saying goodbye to me.

"Prince!" They called from several places as I tried to focus on everything at once.

"Here, for good luck." One person managed to grab my hand and place a string bracelet in it. Someone threw a flower at me, but I accidentally stepped on it.

"Omhet," somebody said. That voice I recognized. I often visited his store with my brother when traveling to the city. "A cream for sunburn!"

I was going to ask why I needed a cream for sunburn, but Cheikh wouldn't let me grab it. He kept pushing the crowd away to break through. My people were so lovely and warm. It felt like they were saying farewell to a distant relative, not the son of a monarch. They wanted to give me valuable gifts that would serve me in Andebeck, but the train was about to depart when its whistle sounded a loud and clear message. I said goodbye as best I could and entered my cabin with my passport in hand.

We made our way through the cabins and didn't stop until we entered our private section. Only then could my guardians relax.

I looked around, surprised that the cabin was bigger than it seemed from the outside. I glanced down the narrow hall to find the sliding door where my room with a private bathroom was.

"You should've let me say goodbye," I complained to Cheikh as I went to open the window to wave at them.

Cheikh came behind me and closed the window before I could look out. I was going to protest, but he just glared at me without saying anything else. Safety above all, or at least that was his aim. I grumbled and flopped down on the first sofa I found with my arms crossed. These three were difficult to socialize with. I couldn't imagine what it would take to make them smile.

"How long will we be on the train?" I asked when it started too slowly but surely to advance.

"Three days," Lucas replied. The others seemed not to be paying me any attention at the moment.

I wanted to ask more questions, but Lucas took off his glasses, closed his eyes, put his legs on the table, and leaned back into his seat. Shin sat at the bar and began to speak in the old language with the train conductor, and Cheikh didn't even seem to intend to sit down. He stood on guard by the connecting door of the railroad car. I made a face—something told me that this trip would feel like an eternity with such a grumpy guy.

The first day on the train passed by slowly.

Looking through the windows at my city being left behind helped me release all the tension I'd accumulated since my father announced the competition. My eyes caught Glacier's beautiful yet familiar scenery through the window, accumulated snow, and in some cases, deer running through the woods. The journey was downhill because the kingdom was on the highest mountain ranges on this continent. It was why we hardly received visitors or supplies. It made things hard for us.

But it was my home.

I sat for hours in silence, fiddling with my new string bracelet on my wrist. I couldn't stop looking out the window, feeling melancholic as the train descended so low that the scenery began to change. The falling snow began to be substituted by rain, and soon I began to see grass instead of snow on the ground.

"The competition hasn't started, and two courts have already joined the kingdom in the desert," Lucas commented, reading a newspaper while he sipped coffee.

"*Mmm,*" was the only thing Shin muttered, sitting at the bar, looking out the window. He had a glass in his hand, but I had no idea what he was drinking so early in the morning.

"Which courts are left?" asked Cheikh, who was also seated at the bar.

"Daonna and Nova Cerise, though they're expecting another one to arrive."

Cheikh grunted, not particularly liking what he heard. "Daonna is problematic. Find out about Cerise."

Before Cheikh could move on, Lucas was already answering. "Nova Cerise is the only territory that practices magic in the academy. The Farhad family are the ones who have run the house for the last three generations, and the eldest daughter, Odette, is the one who is representing in the competition."

"Is she single?" asked Cheikh.

Really, Cheikh?

"No. She has been engaged for two years, but..." he stopped to think, with eyes closed for a brief moment, "*what was her name?* Oh! Yes, her younger sister, lady Adeline, is single and nineteen years old."

By the four moons! How does he know so much? He said it as if he knew each one by heart.

"Maybe I can make a connection," concluded Cheikh.

Hands inside my pockets, I reclined against the wall, trying to understand this game of kingdoms and courts. There were four invited kingdoms and seven courts throughout the land. It seemed allying to a court was a great benefit to have.

"Why not ally with a kingdom?" I asked. "Aren't we part of the Union? Isn't that the alliance my father wants?"

All three turned to me at the same time. The silence that followed my question made me feel cornered.

"It doesn't work that way," replied Cheikh after they finally seemed to notice I was there. "It's a competition, so a kingdom will not ally themselves with another. They will gain nothing from it."

"Of course." I nodded as if everything made perfect sense, but I was confused. Maybe I should've stayed quiet.

Cheikh exhaled, finding patience where he probably had none for a child like me. This was something I should've already known, or so it seemed. "Don't worry about anything, sir," he said. "We're already working on finding you an ally. Rest the matter in our capable hands."

Smile and shut up for the rest of the competition, is what he was basically telling me. Without waiting for an answer, they went back to discussing the courts like a game of chess. I sighed, feeling completely useless, so I turned around and locked myself inside my room.

I slept in my private room for hours and even stayed there for meals. My guardians refuse to have a normal conversation with me, so why bother? I sat on a quaint little table next to the lone window inside the cabin, finishing my food, lost in thought. They were so severe and rigid and only spoke to one another, telling me what was only necessary. Even my best jokes fell on deaf ears. That was cruel—vile even. Feeling a little lonely already, I decided to stay where I was for the rest of the trip to avoid them.

A sudden knock on the door announced that someone was about to enter my cabin. "We will arrive tomorrow. Have the uniform ready."

That was all Cheikh said, peeking through the door, not even fully entering my room. I hadn't even bothered to wear anything to sleep but pants. I got up to look for where I had left my uniform. Now that I didn't have a server to help me, I had to start being more organized, or I would mess everything up before my arrival.

When I suddenly realized that Cheikh was staring at me. No, not me. My back. I quickly put on the first shirt I could find and continued searching for my uniform without looking at him.

"Have you heard how I got my scar?" I asked casually.

Cheikh looked the other way. I think he was embarrassed, "I'm sorry if I offended you. I shouldn't have stared..."

"It's just a scar," I responded with a shrug. I didn't really care. It was a thick diagonal line across my entire back. As if someone tried to cut me open with a sword—because that's exactly what happened.

Cheikh started to leave, but he hesitated. "Is it true what the rumors say?" he dared to ask me, so I stopped and looked at him, "Is it true that the incident cost your life three times?"

I laughed. "Three times? Of course not. It was just a lot of blood and..." I tried to continue with my joke, but I got quieter as I remembered the event. I even looked in another direction. "I'm not good at sword combat. That was the first and last time I tried."

Cheikh nodded. Both he and I wanted to drop the subject. Why the first conversation together had to start with such a terrible topic? A situation that happened ten years ago when I was only eight.

"Get ready for tomorrow," he concluded and left.

The last morning on the train, I woke up sweating. It was boiling—the bedsheets were covered with my sweat as a result of how bad it was. Taking off my shirts until my chest was bare, I desperately ran to the window and opened it as far as it would go. I was drowning in this heat, breathless. How much heat could a human being withstand?

Then I noticed we weren't in the mountains anymore. I poked my head out the window, but I could barely see them because they were so far away. Only the tops covered in snow were visible. Everything else I could see was green. Green grass, green trees, green, green, *green*—and not a pine tree in sight. And the sky! It was so *blue,* with flocks of birds flying across clouds of white so pure that it rivaled the snow back home. How had everything transformed so quickly in such a short amount of time?

My smile and wonder faded when I saw a tunnel rapidly approaching. I screamed when it almost grazed my cheek and fell ungracefully on the bed.

At once, my three guardians entered my room, swords in hands. I would've laughed when Lucas tripped and almost fell had they not been looking for danger.

"Why did you scream?" Cheikh asked.

"That tunnel almost decapitated me," I wearily breathed.

Shin, grumbling, shut the window a little too hard, a silent warning for me not to open it again.

Cheikh lowered his sword, disappointed. "Are you looking for your fourth death or what?" His comment was supposed to be a scolding, but I considered it insulting. Cheikh had no idea how much it hurt that he used my past. He didn't understand it—nobody understands it, "If there's anyone that could manage dying before reaching their destination, it would be you."

"Was that your idea of a joke?" I asked, offended.

"I don't joke, sir. Now, *get* dressed. We'll arrive at our destination in an hour."

We made it to the Kingdom of Andebeck.

Excitement overtook me as if I had just made it to the best adventure of my life. Which, to be honest, it was. I could already imagine the metropolis full of all types of people and all kinds of cultures mingling as one. I also pictured their vendors, their stores, the famous academies they were acclaimed for, and their buildings. I couldn't wait to see everything, nervously moving around the room and waiting to get off the train.

Hurriedly, I searched through my bags for clothing, but all I found were long-sleeved uniforms and parkas. I frowned.

"Hey," I started, still shirtless when I slid through the door, "did Annally forgot to pack lighter clothes for the occasion?" It was hot, for heaven's sake—I needed clothing that would keep me cool under these harsh temperatures.

"You'll use your uniform at all times," answered Cheikh, who was as hostile as ever.

"You're not serious," I complained. He just raised a brow, making me grumble in aggravation. "Whatever."

After I showered, I stared at the ungodly uniform on my bed. I scratched at my head hard, still very annoyed. How could I survive this horrible heat? The train's whistle startled me out of my reverie, notifying its passengers of its arrival. I hurriedly put on my uniform as best as possible, but without Annally's help, it was more of an improvisation. But I would rather improvise than ask for help.

Just as I was about to put on my parka, Shin barged in and dragged me out of the room. Were we late?

"The welcome ceremony will be in four hours," I heard Lucas say to Cheikh while he stared at his golden pocket watch. "We'll make it in time with a carriage and escort. It'll give us a chance to attend lunch as well."

Cheikh nodded, then gestured at me to follow Shin.

The sun didn't bother me as much when I stepped outside, but I did pause to stare at the station. Unlike Glacier's, trains here did not need to arrive at an enclosed location due to the frigid cold. This one was located outside a building, encompassing a large portion of territory for the masses to walk through comfortably.

And by Krea, there were quite a lot of people.

"Don't even think about straying far, sir," ordered Lucas, sticking uncomfortably close to my side. "Don't stare, don't be rude, don't even try to communicate in a language you're not proficient in, and above all else, don't look like a tourist."

"But I am a tourist."

Cheikh rolled his eyes while he hurried us through the crowd. I was close to making another joke, but as soon as I stepped out of the station, my words got stuck in my throat. Andebeck was breathtaking, even better than what I imagined it to be.

Seagulls were roaming Andebeck's central since the city was on the coast. The buildings were nestled in close, and their terracotta roofs were a beautiful contrast with their yellow stucco exterior walls. My feet kept moving me through the cobblestone streets while my eyes gazed at all the sight, and my ears picked up at the distant sound of ships setting sail.

What made everything so special were the people. So many different cultures with different vestments made it hard to discern which was the traditional one for Andebeck. Some were dressed comfortably. The woman showed their legs, arms, and necks freely, and their hair was tied-up in different styles and adorned with jewelry. The man wore light clothing that I envied with fervor. Some dressed according to their occupation. I stared at the scholars, dumbfounded at their pristine and neat short robes. Fishermen, field workers, bakers, sailors—they all had their specific garments, making the streets a colorful explosion.

It was weird how they didn't look anyone in the eyes while hurrying past us to wherever they needed to be. Their tanned skin was proof that they spent most of their time underneath the sun, glistening with a livelihood that my own could not even compare to. Mine was as white as snow, to the point where you could see some veins. I wondered if my skin could withstand the heat waves like theirs could. And comparing what they wore to what I had on—a ridiculous parka in the middle of a kingdom that was not suited for it, made me seem like more of a tourist than anything else, including my accent. I crossed my arms, staring at Lucas irritated.

"This isn't working. I'm suffocating in these clothes!" I complained. "I want to dress like a pirate too."

"Omhet, for heaven's sake, shut up," Cheikh growled at me, looking around us.

"Do you want us to get exiled before we get there?" Lucas criticized me, pulling me by the arm to keep moving.

"Did I say something wrong?" I asked without understanding, noticing too late how other people stood still to glare at me.

"Do you know how easy it is to offend in this city? keep moving, and don't speak again," Lucas ordered nervously.

I didn't want to insult anyone. On the contrary, I admired what they wore. I had to bite my tongue and follow my guardians, almost pushing people in our haste. I felt that if I stared at the city too much, I would get distracted and lost, which actually didn't sound so bad. But the people didn't make me feel confident about the idea. I was so out of place among their people that they even stopped to look at me. Cheikh started walking faster.

"Is there a problem?" I asked, looking around me.

"You're still staring at them," Cheikh scolded.

We finally stopped where the carriages awaited, a loud commotion drawing our attention. There was a group of people who were visitors like me within these lands from the kingdom of the desert, Ettezi, I suspected. A carriage was getting ready for them. I noticed excitedly as my eyes looked at the union's strongest warriors. One young man stood out from the others in how he dressed and carried himself. I assumed he was a prince.

"Should I greet him?" I whispered, ready to approach, when Cheikh raised his hand, preventing me from even taking a step.

"Only if you want to lose your hand. In that case, please let me know so I can personally escort you to prince Karl," he said sarcastically.

I couldn't imagine the prince being more hostile than my guardians, but I kept that comment to myself. Instead, I stared back and marveled at the sheer power that radiated from them. Even their guards looked majestic while holding their spears, dressed in traditional dark-green and mustard uniforms. The group of soldiers was so massive that they had to follow behind the carriage on foot. They waited while the prince was led into the carriage. His height and strength were so intimidating that they made me feel very small. His bronze skin barely glistened with sweat, probably because he was used to the heat of his land.

Suddenly the carriage began to move forward, and I gasped audibly. It didn't have any horses attached to the front! It moved on its own, but how? What the hell?

"Andebeck's technology is incredible, isn't it?" Lucas said admiringly.

I couldn't answer. They seemed used to it, but I didn't even know what kind of sorcery this was. In my kingdom, everything was illuminated with oil and candles, transportation was on horseback, and we only had two telephones in the whole kingdom since no such technology was accessible to the community. I didn't know how to react.

"I need all citizens to leave! These are restricted roads," one Andebeck guard ordered.

"We have reserved transportation," Cheikh announced to the guard, showing his invitation.

The guards squared off, side by side, covering the entire path.

"We are not expecting another kingdom. The three kingdoms invited have already taken their transportation—" the guard started.

"Four kingdoms invited," Cheikh interrupted. "We are from Glacier, the fifth kingdom."

The guard looked at his partner, totally confused.

"The courts brought their own transportation," he tried to explain.

"I don't think they're a court either," his partner pointed to the invitation.

The guard snatched the invitation from Cheikh's hand, his face looking more confused than surprised.

"In any case, there are no more carriages, so you'll have to walk," he concluded and led the way. "Welcome—I guess."

It was as if some of them didn't completely believe that we were guests. They looked at our clothes, the suitcases in our hands, and the invitation as if we were impostors. I did not like this at all.

"Well," Cheikh said with exasperation as he turned to look at me, "it's a four-hour walk, maybe three if you can match our pace."

I swallowed hard. I didn't know how I would walk three hours carrying a suitcase and wearing clothes this warm, but it did not seem that there was another option. I looked around me, seeing that people began to gather again, not to look at me but to admire the kingdom of the desert fading away in the distance with their enormous soldiers trailing behind the carriage. They greeted them and pointed at them with admiration. They even pushed me by the shoulder to get a better view of the caravan.

"Whatever. I just want to get out of here."

The people were making it painfully clear that I did not belong in this place and that our arrival was nothing short of a nuisance.

Glacier was not welcome here.

CHAPTER 5

Walking toward Andebeck's palace was a suffocating experience that I swore was eternal. My excitement was gone the moment the heat penetrated every pore of my skin. The parka I'd worn hung over my shoulders, so it wouldn't drag on the ground. I was sweating enough without it on. Even my hair was matted against my face. It was ludicrous. The court's horses passed us by, and I swallowed the urge to yell at them for help and transportation. A mosquito bit my sunburnt face, and I swatted at it, irritated that, on top of everything else, I had to deal with that too. I was dying. No food, no water—I couldn't even remember when I had breakfast, and I was pretty sure it was already noon. I had no idea how my three guardians were talking, as if this was part of their training routine. I was already exhausted.

"Everything okay back there?" Cheikh asked, looking over his shoulder at me.

Each time I looked, I was farther away from the three of them.

"Could we at least throw away the suitcases?" I asked while I harshly breathed through my mouth. "These are no conditions for a prince."

I finally got to see the three of them laugh, but I wasn't making a joke. Unbelievable.

Lucas stopped and asked, "Do you have any idea of the training you're about to face?"

"Don't scare him," Cheikh interrupted. "I don't want him to run back to Glacier. Not yet."

They looked at the suitcases I was dragging as they laughed some more. None of this made sense. Why didn't I have the same privileges as the kingdom of the desert? I couldn't allow myself to be looked down upon. It was the last thing my king would have wanted.

For now, I dragged my feet toward my destination.

We left behind the coast, the vast academies, the docks, and the buildings. A lush forest took their palace—beautiful greenery pleasing to the senses. The roadside pathway we followed had several logs we had to go over, and the road sloped upward into mountainous terrain. It was so isolated. I wondered if the palace was built to hide from someone... or something.

I got the answer when I looked to my right. Beyond the forest, I saw a mountain, where there were no trees at the top, but there was a castle—no, some ruins. I stopped for a moment, my heart racing.

It was the first time I saw the ruins—where the dragon supposedly was.

"Keep walking," Lucas shouted at me, but I didn't react.

I could probably get there on horseback, but I didn't even want to imagine what the heck was up there. The ruins were isolated and plunged into the shadow that the mountain provided, making it scarier than I thought they would be. For now, I put it out of my mind, forcing myself to focus on the road ahead. First, I had to prioritize the mess I was in and how Andebeck had decided to treat me like I was just one more problem to deal with.

"Why are the citizens of Andebeck so indifferent to us?"

"Glacier was the last kingdom to join the Union," Lucas explained. He was the only one who waited for me. "Very few recognize our home."

"But we're here to help. It's not like I want to bother—"

"Why do you think our king insisted on finding allies?" he interrupted, not waiting for an answer. "Now hurry up and stop talking, or you'll run out of that little breath you've left."

I groaned in exhaustion as he grabbed me by the shirt to pull me along.

Despite Cheikh's calculations, the walk took over five hours because of me. Inside the very heart of the forest, we reached two iron gates with towers adjacent to each one. On the towers, guards stood at attention, beating their drums to announce our approach. I thought they would greet me with a more friendly greeting, but instead, guards armed with muskets came out of small doors at the base of the towers, ready to defend their territory.

"Stay back," Cheikh ordered, raising his hand with the invitation.

Nervously, I stared at the approaching guards with trepidation, noting how they treated us as strangers, as though we were invaders and not a kingdom they'd invited. Shin and Lucas stood before me with their weapons still sheathed but their hands close enough to grab them in case they were needed. But who do they want to impress with such defensive posture? The imperial guards had a bloody musket. A shot against a sword. I already missed Glacier and hadn't been in Andebeck for a single day.

"Why are you here? Who gave you permission?" the guard yelled.

Eight men gathered in front of us, with the general facing Cheikh. He ripped the invitation out of his hand, promptly reading it. A silence fell, and the only sounds I heard were those of birds and the slight rustles of the guards' armor. Then I noticed the watchmen on the towers, and though they still hadn't raised their long musket, it was still unnerving.

"All of the expected kingdoms and courts are undergoing the welcoming cere-mony," the guard stated. I clenched my hands, anxious. Had we made it so far for nothing?

"We're from Glacier, and we were invited," explained Cheikh.

The general processed this information and then spoke in the old language to his nearby companions. I couldn't understand what sort of conclusion they came up with, but once he nodded, everyone lowered their weapons and relaxed.

"Do you have a passport?"

I ground my teeth together. Why did I have to show my passport? I'm Omhet Guillermo Espinho, the fourth son of the King of Glacier. Come on!

"Prince, come closer," ordered Cheikh.

When I stepped forward, I tried my best to look as important as the King himself, but all I managed was to look like a fool. I was beyond exhausted, my clothes were in disarray, and I was sweating profusely. It made the guard before me stare at me as if I were a joke. I like to tell jokes, not to be one.

I showed the general my passport, and he scrutinized it once he had it. He studied me, then my guardians, and again the passport. He said something in that language of his to the rest of the men, and they all laughed. Were they making fun of me?

"Your Highness..." he said, stuck on my name, not being able to pronounce it.

And in a very cordial yet exasperated manner, I replied, "Omhet."

"Prince Omhet," he nodded. "Is this your battalion?"

Huh? Did he say battalion?

"Yes," I stated, voice firm. I am Glacier's prince, and I had to look the part for our kingdom's sake.

They had to finally get it through their heads that we existed, and that we were a kingdom. So, head held high, I stared at him with importance. It did not matter, though. The general still looked at me with nothing but laughter and pity behind his eyes.

He was almost as contemptuous as Guillermo.

"Very well," he said at last and signaled toward the towers.

The gates opened with an intense noise behind them, showing me a whole new world. I could finally take in Andebeck's palace.

As I slowly made my way forward, I found myself smiling. Everything was huge—Glacier's capital could easily fit in the area in front of the palace. It was, basically, their own city.

They couldn't offer us a carriage, but they could lend us some horses. We were finally blessed with a bit of comfort! There was one for each of us, and thank heavens, the general offered to escort us to the place we were supposed to be five hours ago. We galloped quickly through avenues, under bridges, and past buildings—all miles away from the palace itself. We made our way through the city as fast as we could. We were late enough as it was.

I couldn't stare at much, really. The wind made my eyes water, making it impossible to admire everything in our path. And when we slowed down and took a turn next to the palace itself, I couldn't take my eyes away from the most incredible and essential part of this competition: the training grounds. Hundreds of people gathered there, standing in front of a stage. I fought the sudden urge to leave, and Cheikh noticed, hauling me off the horse at once.

"Now is not the time to panic," he warned me.

I was forced to put on the damn parka again, and then we left our luggage behind as we made our way to the training grounds. Someone addressed the crowd from the stage, but I could not focus on them. I was having a hard time ignoring the heat that again invaded me from head to toe.

I did not know whether to feel excited or nervous, although I wanted to be here. I wanted to see each kingdom, visit each corner of the palace, and hide from my three nannies so I could enjoy this experience. But then, I started to feel trapped in the attention I gained the closer I got.

At first, I couldn't even tell which were the courts and which were the kingdoms. Their uniforms could identify them, I supposed, as their colors announced their domains of origin. And were they having a secret competition of who had more men in their ranks? It looked like no one had fewer than a hundred men. Then there was me, with my battalion of three nannies.

"So, this is what it takes for you to be quiet?" Cheikh said, guiding me to my place.

"I thought you didn't make jokes, Cheikh," I replied with pure sarcasm.

I was a mere mortal among gods of war. Whether I liked it or not, I had to position myself in the corner, next to the rows designated for each representative. Everyone in this place had experience with fighting or at least had the appearance of a warrior. I swallowed deeply. I hardly looked my age.

I don't know if it was my paranoia, but suddenly, I had the feeling that we had interrupted the whole ceremony. Head up, Omhet, head up, I heard my father's voice in the back of my mind say. Maybe I stopped listening because of my nerves, but there was an awkward silence as if thousands of people were watching me. It's in your head, Omhet, just breathe, I heard my father's voice again. It was the only thing that kept me calm.

Drums started beating, and I jumped involuntarily.

Shin glanced at me.

Lucas bit back a mocking laugh.

Cheikh sighed in disappointment.

I gritted my teeth, trying to pretend I was okay, but I knew I wasn't. This was not meant for me.

I settled into position with my three guardians behind me, in the front row, but isolated from view. We stood alongside rows of kingdoms and courts that intimidated me more than the idea of a dragon did. I focused on the stage, where the Andebeck soldiers were standing, and the drums were being played.

"Hail to the Minister of Andebeck!" the spokesman yelled.

I should raise my hand in greeting when suddenly, the soldiers from the kingdom of the desert gave a loud cry, making me jump back. After the shout, they positioned themselves in salute. Each representative made a different salute simultaneously until they were placed with jointed knees and hands at their side. It was a stiff and respectful greeting. My mouth still hung open in astonishment, looking at everyone around me, saluting in such an intimidating way.

Cheikh cleared his throat, drawing my attention. Then I saw my three guardians giving the salute of my kingdom. Legs parted, hands behind their back, torso straight, raised chest, and grim faces. I did the same before anyone could tell how slow I was. I didn't even know how to do a miserable salute! If my father saw me, he would be ashamed.

Eight guards climbed up on the high platform made of stone and sand and cleared the way for Andebeck's minister, a man with a thick dark beard and medium-short hair. His gaze was determined and royal as if his eyes could project his position. He was the closest thing to a king this kingdom had, and I could see it even in the way he walked. There was an equally confident woman in trouser uniform and long cape to his right. Her hair had been pinned up, and her gaze was rigid toward the crowd.

"Welcome, everyone," said the minister, with a deep and clear voice.

I struggled with the weakness that the heat had inflicted on me since coming here, making paying attention challenging. I felt sick—it felt like the sun was cooking me. I tried to hide it by straightening my legs and clenching my fists.

"Don't strain your knees," Lucas advised me, but I ignored him. My concentration was solely on what was happening on the stage. Or was it the heat that had me this agitated? Maybe both.

The minister got closer to the podium, and the woman behind him moved to the ranks of the guards.

"Today is a day that will be marked in history. Where the eleven territories are gathered in this courtyard..."

Twelve, I wanted to correct.

"It is a great honor for Andebeck. Today, the visiting soldiers will be distributed in different bases that we will provide, and they will have everything they need to begin their training.

"Meanwhile, each monarch will stay in our palace with designated rooms for the representatives and their guards. Your routine will be presented each morning, and we will diligently prepare for the competition to come. My best advice is the most obvious:" For a moment, he looked around the crowd without sparing a second on me, "Prepare for battle."

"You will have all the accommodations you are used to, but don't get too comfortable because you're not here on vacation," he paused. "You are the best of your families—the bravest and the strongest. But only one kingdom will be crowned champion of this orphaned place. Only one will be the greatest pride of their generation! And only the victorious will be honorably immortalized in the history of our world!"

His words, I must admit, made me want to bring him the dragon today on a silver platter. They inspired me to try my best to win.

Suddenly, my vision began to blur. Something was wrong, and I think it was the heat. For the first time, I missed being in inches of snow and not this terrible hell.

"The competition of fire will begin tomorrow," the minister continued, "Because on the first day of winter, we will attack the dragon, and once and for all, we will defeat it."

A massive roar of voices was heard throughout the courtyard. Emotions were heated, and people were ready to start training at once. And yet, here I was, panting like a thirsty dog. Not even a pathetic moan wanted to come out of my mouth.

"In eight months, it will be a hundred years of fear, but we can finally give Princess Laila a burial with the honors she deserves. In eight months, we will finish a chapter created by Tiara, and neither that sorceress nor anyone else will be able to stop us."

Tiara, I repeated in my mind. Was that the sorceress who caused all this?

People started clapping enthusiastically.

"Laila's memory will rest in peace, and Andebeck will be more prosperous than ever!" the minister declared.

The crowd all shouted, interrupting his words, clapping, and celebrating. I tried to raise my arms at least and join them in the celebration, but it was then that my eyes closed against my will.

The last thing I remember was hitting the ground with my forehead, falling completely unconscious. Cheikh yelled my name, people gasped in surprise, but I couldn't recover. All my senses were turned off. The heat had won.

CHAPTER 6

"That was pathetic," mocked Lucas.

I yelled in pain and anger when he hit my forehead with an ice bag. He'd done it on purpose as if the damn bruise weren't there beating with a life of its own.

"Gentlemen, who would have a bruise before training even begins?" Lucas asked my other two guardians. "Omhet Guillermo Espinho."

"Go to hell," I spat, falling back on the bed. Closing my eyes, I let the ice bag do its magic, pressed against my new bruise.

We were in what would be my room for the rest of my stay in Andebeck. I didn't know what had happened, how I'd gotten there, or who had taken off most of my clothes. All I knew was that I had a ridiculous bump and that my guardians stared worriedly and, somehow, at the same time, mocking me. Thankfully, it wasn't as bad as it felt, but passing out in front of every union member had been pretty ridiculous. I hope my father wouldn't hear about this.

"You hope he won't find out?" exploded Cheikh. I hadn't realized I said it aloud. "The whole event was being transmitted on radio. Every kingdom knows what happened."

"Seriously, what did you expect? I was frying in that stupid parka. How is it that nobody thought to bring lighter clothes?"

"We don't have lighter clothes," explained Lucas. "Besides, it was the King's orders always to use Glacier's uniform—"

"It's not working," I grunted, interrupting him. "I look absurd wearing it. I'll lose more respect wearing that parka with moose hair."

"Well," Cheikh said, in a voice so low I was surprised he was speaking at all, "at least you managed to get everyone's attention like your father wanted."

There was a short silence interrupted by Shin's sudden laughter. I hadn't even heard him speak that much, and there he was, laughing at me.

The door to my room slowly opened, and in strode none other than the minister himself with two women by his side. Shin's laughter evaporated, and they all stood tall, saluting the most important people who currently ruled over Andebeck. I was quick to act, shifting on the bed to get up and do the same, but the minister halted my actions. So, I sat back, tense, taking in their appearance and how immaculate they were up close. Their eyes were intense, as though with just one look, they could bid you to kneel and do as you're told, or else.

Their presence was awe-inspiring.

"It's hot here, huh?" he joked, and I smiled. Finally, someone with a good sense of humor! "You must be king Guillermo Espinho's son," he continued, bowing a little in respect. "It's a pleasure to meet you, Prince..."

"Omhet," I quickly replied. No one seemed to know who I was, but that was a given. My father only spoke of his firstborn. Even their names were the same.

"Prince Omhet," he said with a smile. "I assure you, you'll get used to the heat in the next few days. It was a bit rough, standing underneath the sun for so long, wearing those thick clothes."

"That's what I've been saying, Minister... am..." I strained my mind searching for the minister's name without success. "I'm sorry. What's your name?"

Cheikh cleared his throat, letting me know as best he could that I'd asked a stupid question. I should shut up now. It was a warning.

"My name is Marcus," he stated calmly, but the surprise lingered behind his eyes. He pointed to the blonde woman next to him, her face devoid of expression. "This is Brenda, my right hand and advisor." Then he shifted and pointed at the other silent force. "And this is my sister, Lois." Her dark hair and a smile so dry it barely reached her eyes. She looked a lot like him but *way* younger.

"You were the one to create the trials of fire," I stated, and he nodded. "That was an act of desperation to find a king. Why don't you take the throne, if you don't mind my asking?"

He frowned. The answer, apparently, wasn't simple enough. The tension between him and his sister seemed to grow, even though their faces barely betrayed their emotions. They were weird.

"Laila Blume's father decreed it before he died that his daughter would be the only heir to Andebeck," came Lois's dry response. Her deep voice surprised me.

"And what if Laila is dead?" I asked when I really wanted to say; *Do you realize it's been a hundred years already?*

"With the dragon's head in my power, we can continue to rule over this kingdom as His Majesty Blume would've wanted. In the meantime, we need to end the threat that cannot let my people rest," concluded Marcus.

So much superstition, so many fears. It must be overwhelming, both for him and for the entire kingdom. They needed to eliminate the dragon in order to close the chapter and put Laila Blume and the legend to rest.

I swallowed, imagining my kingdom under these circumstances. Living your life surrounded by a legend that could come to life at any moment and end everything in its path must be horrible.

"The union's courts have volunteered to participate in this grand venture. Even though they are not eligible to win the crown, making them your allies will be a big advantage. I suggest you try to win them over," Marcus recommended amicably, like a friend giving advice. "The more connections you make, your chances will be better."

There were seven courts and five kingdoms. If I could win even one of them as my ally or friend, my father would be satisfied. How hard could it be for me to make a freaking ally?

"Rest for today. Starting tomorrow, things won't be so easy." He nodded at me, then at my guardians. "It was a pleasure to meet you in person, Prince Omar."

I narrowed my eyes. "It's Omhet," I gritted out, but Marcus had already disappeared behind closed doors.

I fell back on the bed, beyond tired. Cheikh started to explain the routine I would start the next day, but I barely listened. I was too distracted trying to take all of it in. This room was a bizarre combination of flower patterns and striking colors that were pretty but a bit overwhelming. A huge mirror stood against a wall plated in gold. Potted plants and flowers were strewn about, giving the room a lovely aroma that did not bother the senses.

As pleasant as it was, deep down, I knew that this was not my home.

A sharp sting of melancholy squeezed my heart when I looked out the window and saw the absence of snow. After all the excitement had died down, my mind was finally processing the changes. Seeing the glaring sun hiding behind mountains instead of the grey clouds I was used to definitely left an impact. It was, however, a stunning red and orange that, no matter how strange it seemed, was so beautiful.

"Are you listening to me?" demanded Cheikh, startling my eyes back to him. He was pacing back and forth in front of my bed. "What was the earliest time you woke up back in Glacier?"

"A little before breakfast, sometimes right when it was served."

He suddenly stopped to stare at his companions, then at me, annoyance clear as day on his face.

"You do know that training starts before breakfast?" he asked, astonished at my laziness. "Your brother Guillermo and His Majesty the King always had busy days ahead of them. Training, meeting with the council, not to mention their regular visit to—"

"All right, all right, they're busy men, I know," I huffed, like nothing out of the ordinary had been said. I swore his eyebrow twitched in irritation.

He recovered his posture and said, "Well, your spectacular routine of doing nothing ends now. Tomorrow, you will wake before dawn. You will train, bathe, have breakfast with the rest of the kingdoms, and you *will* leave a good impression behind." *Was that a threat?* "The first phase of training will be resistance. Then you'll have training in strength. After that, you'll have—" He opened a little notebook, where he'd apparently written down my daily tasks. "Classes before lunch is served."

"All of that is before lunch?" I exploded.

"And dinner won't be until seven at night. Followed by your hour of prayers, as the Krea religion demands."

"My mother isn't here, Cheikh. I don't need to keep praying," I reminded him. "Besides, how much time will I have left to sleep?"

"You'll recover it in eight months' time," he concluded before snapping his notebook shut.

My body burrowed itself farther into the comfortable bed. "I'm not going just to faint. I'm going to die."

"Don't be so dramatic," snorted Lucas while he prepared some tea on the table next to the window.

"Will it kill you to treat me with more respect? You treat me like I'm a child," I stated. Am I not supposed to be the one who bosses them around? I felt like a kid and his nannies.

"We have custody over you," explained Cheikh, "as His Majesty authorized. From the moment you boarded the train, we're the ones in control of everything. We're like a family."

" If you are the father, I suppose one of these two will play the role of the mother. Can I choose which one at least?" I said with the same sarcasm Cheikh used. Lucas stopped imbibing his tea to kill me with a look. Shin simply snorted, hiding the laughter he could barely contain.

"Prince Omhet," Cheikh sighed, tiredly sitting by my side. "You must understand your purpose here for this mission to work."

"Easy. I have to train hard and participate in the battle."

Cheikh stared at me like a father speaking to a slow child. "No. You're here to earn Glacier's respect by at least making one ally. And if you're lucky, maybe you'll find a damsel to whisk away. That's all. You don't need to worry about the dragon. We'll protect you when that day comes."

Undignified, I said, "You mean to say you'll avoid, at any cost, me getting near the dragon."

"Correct," he nodded. "Eleven grand surnames in the palace control the whole union. They already have the tools needed to slay the beast. It would be unwise to risk your valuable life for something that, most likely, prince Karl will achieve in minutes."

I gaped at him, wholly offended now. I read between the lines the things neither he nor my father wanted to say. The prince from the desert kingdom, or perhaps anyone at all, was more capable than me. My only job in this place was to stand tall, proud, and look pretty. I needed to impress by doing nothing.

"Understood." I nodded, trying to hide my disappointment.

I walked through the vast, empty hallway of a castle I didn't recognize, where the portraits of past kings had no faces, and pitch darkness was all you could see through the windows as if shadows had swallowed the land. I looked both ways down the corridor but saw no end either way. This place seemed cursed.

My breathing began to quicken, as did my heart. I started running, but the scenery didn't change, and the hall didn't end. I was scared. I wanted to scream, but when I did, I yelled something I thought I had forgotten entirely.

"Tiara!" I called her several times until I heard her answer.

Like a specter, I felt something behind me, causing me to stop. Claws touched my skin, and I cried, closing my eyes because suddenly, her claws grabbed my head and began to crush me until I started to run out of air.

"How many times do I have to scream your name, boy?" Cheikh yelled at me, waking me up with a start. "You're late."

I repeatedly blinked, looking out the window. There were no shadows outside. On the contrary, it was light, and I could see some birds peeking out from the branches of nearby trees.

What a horrible nightmare. Why did I have to call that name? Or weirder still, why hasn't anyone mentioned that name before? The worst part was that I knew my mind would repeat what I dreamt about for the rest of the day, or at least until I discovered more of who the hell Tiara was.

"Forget about taking a bath. Get dressed," Lucas ordered, throwing my clothes at me.

I was so slow that they barely let me dress myself. I dressed in Glacier's training uniform, which sadly included long sleeves and snow boots. I looked at Lucas, infuriated.

"You have to fix this. I order you."

"I'll see what I can do," he said before he walked out the door.

The hallway was chaotic, with the servants and soldiers from different territories intermingled. I had to make my way among them, pushing them and feeling like I might lose myself in the crowd. I ended up entering through one of the service doors instead of the main corridor.

"Young man, where will your duties take place?" one of the servants yelled at me. "In the kitchen or the bedroom?"

"What?" Too late, I realized what he meant. "I'm the Prince of Glacier. Where is the dining room?"

But the servant started speaking in the old language to somebody else, passing me by, and never answering my question. I looked at Cheikh, begging him for help.

"This won't be easy," he said in a surrendered tone and passed by me.

I focused on following Cheikh. Luckily, no matter how many people there were in the corridor, none of them were taller than him, nor did they have the strength of his arms. I did not know how old he was. I imagined it was close to my father's age, but his face and skin looked younger than what time had demanded of him.

A trumpet played, and everybody moved aside and stuck to the wall. I did the same with Cheikh, not knowing what the hell was going on. Then, I saw a woman whose skin seemed to be painted by the sun. Dark gold, as if the desert itself were permeated in her being. She led her escort with footsteps that echoed on the tiles, making me stick closer to the wall, trying not to obstruct their space. Even her gaze demanded respect, causing there to be no other option but to let her pass.

"By the goddess," I heard Shin's voice whisper. I think she heard him because I could swear that they looked into each other's eyes for a mere second, causing him to lower his gaze.

"Why does everyone stop for her?" I was confused. She was terrific, but was it enough to stop everyone in the hallway?

"She's the Princess of Ettezi," Cheikh explained, and I snorted at his answer.

As soon as he passed by, I tried to follow her entourage to the dining room.

Then the whole hallway came to life again with people pushing past me, some going up, some going down, some just running. I stumbled, and I lost sight of my three guardians. I cursed in anger and then started pushing everyone like they had pushed me until I reached the main stairs and peeked down. The Princess of Ettezi had already descended all the steps, and I barely saw the end of her escort.

I was going to be late.

Too many people went up and down, so I climbed on the railing and slid down like a kid. Some gasped, others I accidentally pushed, but I must admit that I came down in perfect time, laughing a little at the end when I looked up and met Cheikh's stern gaze.

"I'll wait for you on the other side," I said, giving him a dismissal salute and then running to the dining room.

CHAPTER 7

When I got to the main dining room, it was empty, causing me to stop between the door and the hall. Some servants cleared the plates, not as if it were already done, but as if there had not been breakfast at all.

"Where is everyone?" I asked, agitated by the rush.

"They have all gathered in the arena. Training has begun," explained the server approaching me.

"What?" I asked, confused. "The schedule said that breakfast time was now."

"The schedule changed. Last night, each of the eleven territories were notified—"

"Twelve," I protested as I headed out into the hall again. "For heaven's sake, we're twelve."

I ran back to the opposite side of the palace. The problem with the palace was the size, making everything so far away that it felt like a stupid labyrinth. It would be helpful to have a map on every wall.

I accidentally went into the kitchen, went out into the inner garden, and finally went into the library.

"Shit!" I cursed, hitting the door with my foot, and someone inside the library told me to shut up.

I leaned against the door, trying to calm down.

"Are you lost?" someone asked, making me jump.

I recognized her face because Marcus had introduced her to me—it was his sister, Lois. She had black hair like crows tied knots sticking out from her scalp.

"I'm sorry, Your Grace, but I'm looking for my way to the arena," I explained, glancing around the corridor. The worst part was that even the servants had disappeared, leaving me alone. It was late. I could feel it.

"I'll give you a hint," she said, pointing to the windows. "All the balconies on this side of the palace have stairs that will take you directly to the outer courtyard."

I exhaled with relief. I bowed in reverence, and without saying goodbye, I ran out of the first balcony I found. Fortunately, it had the steps to the courtyard, where I could see everybody already in formation from afar as Marcus and his right hand delivered the morning message.

Call it a coincidence, but I felt Marcus looking at me in disappointment for a moment when I took my place. The gathered group bowed and began to move away to different areas. Before I could understand any words, the speech was over. Dammit.

"You've got to be kidding me," I said through my heavy breathing.

"You have to run with the Kingdom of Ettezi. You're in luck."

Lucas said out of nowhere, behind me.

"How did you get here first?" I snapped, turning around.

Lucas picked up a small package. "I found a new uniform for you. Wasn't that what you ordered me to do?" he asked proudly.

"Forget it, Lucas," I said, passing by him with an attitude. It wasn't until I saw his confused look that I realized I was venting to the wrong person.

Without asking anything more about the schedule, I had to run with one of the groups. I was able to get over to one in time to hear the coach finish giving instructions, showing on the map where we were going to run until we got back to the arena. It was funny to see everyone fresh, rested, and ready for the best run of the morning while I was already breathing through my mouth. One of the princes looked at me confused, and I tried to look energetic when really, I was already fatigued.

The signal to run startled me—a loud shot rang through the morning.

"Omhet, move!" Cheikh ordered. Where had he come from?

He pulled me by the shirt and made me run faster than I could. It was a relaxed routine for my guardian, but it took me two steps to get to just one of his.

"Your legs are long," I reminded him.

"Well, sir, those of the dragon will be even more so," he reminded me casually.

I huffed but tried to keep up.

The sun rose, welcoming us as we ran through the trees and over bridges in the gardens. The territory within the outer walls was large enough to get lost and even to give the impression that it had its own forest. I focused on not falling too far behind the rest that ran ahead of me, each monarch with its guardians around. They even laughed while jogging, as if it were such a simple exercise that it barely caused a reaction from them.

I had to get closer. I wanted to be part of the group, to identify all of them better, and to learn their names.

But then I tripped over a branch and fell face-first onto the path.

I was so tired that Cheikh had to pull me by my clothes to get me to my feet. "And this is how you want to make yourself known?" Cheikh asked, hearing me gasp for breath.

"I didn't even run when I was a kid," I replied, drenched in sweat.

I was a thin guy with more hair on my head than brain inside it. I felt like I should have exercised more. I felt so suffocated. I wanted to go back to Glacier. I wanted cold, to feel a real breeze and not the smothering steam that rose from the ground.

"Get out of the way!" someone yelled.

They pushed me hard, causing me to fall to the ground again. I wanted to get up, but the prince and his guards almost ran over me, causing me to drag myself out of the way. I recognized Ettezi's prince as the one who'd pushed me like it had been personal. I could feel the bruise on my forehead hurt more.

"You're starting to get famous," Cheikh said, stretching his arms and legs as if ready for another round of exercises.

"Not in the way the king wanted," I replied, standing up heavily. I shook myself as best I could and stared down the path through the trees as everyone continued on. "Not like this," I growled in frustration.

"Come on, run," he ordered, "You can't walk back. It would ruin your image."

What image? I wanted to answer, but I jogged again, following Cheikh's advice. The poor man even had to explain to me how to breathe in order to conserve my energy. How to place my hands and even how I stepped was very specific. Glacier's greatest warrior was teaching a boy to run. I could feel his frustration in his orders, as if he didn't want to be here, just like me.

When I returned to the arena, I couldn't see any of the kingdoms that had run beside me. I wondered how and when they split into groups with their guardians and had started with their training. I ran toward Lucas and Shin, who waited with a towel in one hand and a jar of water in the other.

Inhaling half my water, I poured the rest over me, then bent over and simply breathed. I had to calm down—was there a trick that could help with this too?

"Straighten up, you weakling," berated Lucas.

I stayed as I was, harshly breathing, my heart wanting to escape through my ribcage. I tried to do as I was told after a while of taking deep breaths, but I couldn't.

"Hey, kid," someone called behind me.

With the towel I was handed I dried my sweaty neck, turning around. It was the princess who had halted the whole hallway with her mere presence. She wore the same training uniform her soldiers did, the only difference being a medal on the right side of her button-down shirt. She fixed the errant brown curls that were getting in her face, and her brown eyes took me in with curiosity.

At least she looked kind, unlike most people I'd met so far.

"Me?" I asked. It came out at a higher pitch than I'd intended, so I cleared my throat and tried again. "Are you speaking to me?" That was better, more manly in tone, or at least that's what I tried to go for. It wasn't often that a beautiful lady with spectacular hips and gorgeous brown skin would address me.

I quickly looked at Lucas and almost pointed at him. If looks could kill, he would be murdering me right now. I stared back at the princess and introduced myself instead. "Prince Omhet, at your service."

"Where are you from, exactly?"

I felt all she wanted was to figure out who I was and not necessarily wanted to talk. Well, at least it was something. This was what my father wanted, right? To let everyone know about Glacier!

"The Kingdom of Glacier. It's located on Timantti, the highest mountain of the north hills," I said, trying to keep my chest puffed out in pride.

She nodded but frowned, eyes roaming over my body as if studying me.

"Have they forced you to come?" she asked, pity shining bright in her eyes. And even though the comment annoyed me, I remained calm. I opened my mouth, ready to respond, but she didn't even let me. "Do you need help? I can find a way to get you back home."

"What? No!" I smiled, trying to demonstrate that I had everything under control. "Everything is more than fine—don't bother even thinking about it."

"Are you sure? I'm still worried, you know, after I saw you faint yesterday during the ceremony."

I scratched the back of my head, "You see, I've lived where temperatures are always near freezing. Heat is new to me," I explained, eyes firmly on the ground, trying to hide my embarrassment.

Suddenly, someone pushed me again. This time I managed to grab onto Cheikh and not fall.

"The weather, running, exercise, even training is new for you," snarked Ettezi's prince, the same guy who had shoved me when we were running. He was just as stunning as she was, but the arrogance behind his eyes obscured his beauty. "What the hell are three nannies and their child doing here?"

My eyes narrowed. I was close to replying with hostility, but eight of his men stood behind him. They were tall, robust, and could easily win this ridiculous game of pride. It reminded me why they were the greatest warrior of the Union and how small I was in comparison. I took a step backward. I felt intimidated and trapped.

"Karl, stop it," pleaded the princess, "I just came to see if he was fine."

"Fine?" repeated Karl. "That sissy is nothing but adorable." He laughed along with his men.

My gaze darkened. How was it possible that someone else could utter Guillermo's words of humiliation toward me? I clenched my hands hard, anger suffusing me. When I was close to retaliating, Cheikh placed his hand on my shoulder, stopping me.

"I hope you're at least useful as bait for the dragon when the time comes," Karl added.

I did not reply. If I had, I'd still be the brunt of the joke because I lacked the tone of voice a man should have. I didn't even have a nice body like they have and lacked the words to say to someone like him. He'd hit me right on my weak spot—a painful reminder of how useless I could be.

"Forgive my brother," she apologized on his behalf, pushing him away from me. "Karl, move!"

"Let me see if he cries!" guffawed Karl.

I turned around, noticing that even Lucas was laughing. Of course, he was.

"Pay him no mind," someone by my side said. If it weren't for what was happening, I would've been surprised that Shin had spoken at all. Ever since we met, he'd barely done so.

I wanted to listen to his advice because I knew he wanted to help me, but the latest humiliation had made me defensive. Pretending words had no power over me was an ability I couldn't always control.

"Like I care," I angrily said, stepping away from them. I walked toward the first available station, feeling lost due to not knowing what to do or where to go. It seemed like I did not belong here. I'd never done any martial arts, weightlifting, fencing, and archery—and we were expected to train in all of them. It was easy to get lost on these training grounds, and too much was happening simultaneously.

Trainers from all over Andebeck organized the groups of each representative in different sections, but how could they accommodate me?

Other than my three nannies, it was only me. The other kingdoms had apparently brought their own trainers, their own military, and guides that could help them within each category.

I heard the princess's laughter, and I turned with curiosity, seeing her next to her brother while they were introduced to heavy weapons. They looked like they were born for this. She caught me looking, and I had to glance away as my face reddened at being caught scrutinizing them.

Embarrassment was the most dangerous of all the things that lived inside me. The fear I could fight, but embarrassment could make me give up.

"Omhet, from Glacier" a trainer from Andebeck called to me. "Have you completed your evaluation?"

"I'll do so right now." I nodded with respect, moving to the end of the line.

Standing behind every participant made me realize that I was the shortest in the group.

"Prince Alexander from Atsoc, twenty-two," called the trainer to the only blonde person in the line. "Lady Odette from the court Nova Cerise, twenty-four," called to the lady with white and long hair. "Princess Khloe from Ettezi, twenty." Then he gave the nod to the next one.

Once they started to call each of us by name and age, I also realized that I was the youngest. I swallowed hard—not one other person was a teenager. By the skies, this felt like a ridiculous mistake.

It was the desert prince's turn from the great, immaculate, untouchable, strong Kingdom of Ettezi. Freaking Karl. His evaluation included weights; from what I could see, they looked massive. Swallowing hard, I stared at my arms. My faith started to diminish. I almost rolled my eyes when the trainer announced that Karl had earned the title of the strongest man in the competition, since the weights he'd lifted had been the heaviest of them all.

So, for now, it seemed that Ettezi was the favored. But come on! It was barely the first day, did they have to be so hasty with their choice?

I waited until he left for my turn, but when I got closer to the trainer, he didn't even acknowledge my existence, preferring to stare at his little notebook in irritation. I was the last one there, so this should be done quick and easy. No one even looked at me because they were too busy with their next order of business. I stepped closer and cleared my throat.

He stared at me with disdain. "Prince Omar."

"Omhet," I grunted.

He barely nodded.

Of course, they all looked my way when the trainer called for me. Lingering for a few seconds, I waited for his command. He waited for me to get ready without any prompts, while inside, I was mortified. Couldn't everyone stop staring?

I gulped. In mere seconds I'd turned into the main attraction.

"The objectives of your training will be simple at first," he finally said. "Since this is your first day, I'll be testing your capabilities and strength to write you a routine for the next five weeks. Let's see what you can do so I can advise where you should begin your training process."

I nodded, ready.

"Let's start with pull-ups and see how many you can do," he commanded.

I stared at the station's bar, quickly browsing over the other tools and benches to weight lift. And as it always was in Andebeck, everything was done under the sun's harsh light. I prayed I wouldn't faint again, especially because I would be doing a pull-up for the first time in my life.

I took a deep breath, trying to concentrate. I took hold of the bar with both hands, and my legs were left dangling in the air. Good, good. Now onto the next step. I tried to pull myself up, using the strength of my shoulders, but I stayed where I was.

"When you're ready, you may begin," said the trainer, clearly waiting for me to do something. Did he not see that I'd already tried?

I fell to the ground and took another deep breath while I rubbed my hands with dirt, so I wouldn't slip. I tried again, doing all I could to lift my weight up. I growled more than I went up, but this time I managed to lift myself, though only a little bit. I dropped again, hearing laughter around me. I turned toward the crowd, seeing Karl with his sister chuckling without hiding the fact. This was not good.

"Do you have more to do?" I asked, trying to ignore them.

The trainer shook his head, writing his report. I stared around me again at the different training stations. Surely, he had something else I could do, like lifting weights or doing push-ups. After a few minutes, the man ripped the paper out of his notebook and handed it to me with undisguised pity in his eyes.

"Your evaluation is now complete," he quickly said.

"But..."

"Next!"

I clenched my fists around the paper. Thousands of things went through my head at once, causing me to groan through my teeth in anger at the unfairness of the situation. It didn't help that my audience doubled over with laughter, entertained by my failings and physical faults.

Unable to do anything about it, I turned and marched back to my guardians, trying to ignore everything and everyone. But it was impossible—the laughter grew harder and harder, becoming more the center of my focus.

It was like my brother's Guillermo laughter after he cut my back. I winced, feeling the scar on my back more than ever.

Chapter 8

I took a long shower the next morning, trying to prepare myself for everyone and the chaos I was sure to encounter. But even when I closed my eyes under the stream of water, all I could hear was the training rumbling in my ears. The clashes of swords against each other, the arrows being released, the weights being dropped against the ground, the grunts as people fought on the platform—it all mixed in my head. And what was I doing while the warriors trained? Simple resistance exercises. It was as if I was part of the competition and not at the same time.

I leaned against the wall, trying to calm down as if the water could magically take the thoughts away. It didn't work. What would I do if I couldn't fit into this place? I couldn't return empty-handed. Just imagining my father's and siblings' reactions...

The shame would be too much for me. I'd prefer not to go home at all, in that case. I am the fourth son. The one who will never inherit the crown or be an advisor to the future king or have a seat on the council. Guillermo would never allow it, anyway. The point is, that I was the one designated solely to marry someone who benefits my kingdom. And I didn't care, really. I used to enjoy being the leftover of my family. I didn't have responsibilities like my older brothers, and I took benefit of them more than I'd like to admit.

I used to attend every festival that Glacier celebrated with my brother Cayetano. My favorite was *The Kiss Festival* held every spring. It was fun—and quite intense. During my weekly routine, I would escape from my boring lessons with Estefania, and we would get lost in the city, not for hours, but sometimes for days. I know every store and many families in my entire kingdom as if they were part of mine. Sometimes we didn't have dinner with our parents because of the fuss we had in the city. My routine was not what my parents expected of me, and maybe they had gotten used to it. Perhaps they saw me as the irresponsible little Omhet who couldn't even compare to my brothers. I don't know, and maybe I never will. I accepted my fate and took advantage of it.

But now—I have found a *damn* purpose in my family, and I can't mess it up. By Krea, I can't.

When I came out of the bathroom, my clothes were on the bed, and I looked at them with disdain. It bothered me to even have the Glacier colors on, so I put on the neutral color uniform Lucas found. It was light and refreshing, and despite the long sleeves, I didn't feel hot. I wanted to thank Lucas, but I found myself alone in my room.

They left without me.

I stared around the desolate room for a moment, tempted to let my reluctance win. But no. Not today. *Not yet.*

For once, I knew where I had to go without getting lost, going straight to the dining room, but hesitating before entering. I could hear everyone inside settling in, and as much as I tried to remind myself that I was one of them, my mind screamed at me otherwise. *You are no less than anyone else,* my father had told me. So, with my head held high, I entered.

There was a large table in the shape of a *"U"*, and in the center were Marcus and his sister, socializing while everyone settled down. I sat on one of the corners, trying again to memorize the faces and, if I could, their names. It was like an exciting parade of cultures in front of me. We were all so different, and the only thing tying us together was the harmony and promise that we had to share an alliance. Each kingdom wore its colors and even its flags on its uniforms. I think I was the only one not wearing anything from home, not even a medal.

I tried to socialize and even laugh at some of the jokes I heard, but I felt like everyone was glaring at me. I gave up. Instead, I tried to focus on nothing specific, taking in what surrounded me and even looking at the ceiling. I sighed in frustration but kept looking around while fiddling with my string bracelet between my fingers. The golden curtains were opened, and the chandelier above our heads did not need to be lit because its crystals shone with the rays of the sun. I studied the textures of the tablecloths and the clay decorations on the table. This place screamed how exotic it was everywhere I looked.

I realized that I'd had enough. It wasn't when the servant began to serve everyone, but me or the conversation among my neighbors kept leaving me out. No, it was when the people sitting next to me moved their chairs away from me, leaving a large gap around me—that's when I knew I had enough.

Seven houses that didn't want to know me. Four kingdoms that stared at me like the plague. I couldn't blame them, though, because I sometimes wanted to get away from myself.

I set my table napkin down, got up, and left unapologetically. It was the complete opposite of what I had been taught in my kingdom, breaking so many etiquette protocols in less than a minute. Still, I didn't feel like being formal. I was aware that even Marcus had been staring at me, but I didn't care.

Nobody here expected anything from me either. I walked through the palace's corridors, admiring that there was a place like this, where the carpets were a deep wine color, and the ceiling was painted as if it were a massive work of art.

I went out on the first balcony I found to get away from the servants who hurriedly trotted through the corridors just to be able to get some peace.

"Father," I whispered, staring at nothing, "What would you do in my place?"

I got no answers to my prayer—I knew this was something I had to find out for myself. I breathed deeply, gazing at the faraway mountains. But, no, it wasn't exactly the view that had drawn my curiosity toward it. It was the ruins, hidden in the natural shadows cast by the mountains.

Eight months to train and invade that desolate place. My eyes focused, trying to find or see a bit of the fabled dragon or any movements at all. My heartbeat quickened in anticipation when I wondered what that place could be hiding. If only I could go and—

I shook myself out of those musings and left the balcony to disperse the crazy thoughts that wanted to take root in my head. For lack of a better idea, I went to the dining room meant for the palace staff, which for the time being, was being shared with the soldierly of each territory. This room had no luxurious table settings or long tables, much fewer lights hanging from the ceiling. The stone floor rang when people stepped on it, the only light source was the open windows, and everyone ate their food from wooden trays.

It was utter chaos. Not one single soul followed the appropriate etiquette. They were laughing, talking loudly, and using any and every available utensil for their food. I immediately loved it, feeling more at home here than in the stuffy room nobles had to eat in. Hands inside my pockets, I made it toward my guardians, who'd been sitting together finishing their meal. They didn't even notice me until I slightly pushed Lucas so I could sit by his side. They hushed as if I had interrupted their fun conversation.

"Omhet," Lucas greeted me, "are you all right?"

They weren't outright rejecting me, but I could see how they found it strange I was there. A prince amid the staff, guardians, soldiers, and everyone else who by birthright was not a monarch would seem weird to anyone.

He quickly got up and asked, "What would you like to eat?"

"I'm not hungry," I replied, having no appetite for anything right then.

Lucas stared at Cheikh and Shin. I think they noticed my reluctance. Lucas said nothing else and left. Meanwhile, I really did not feel like talking with anybody. I was merely waiting for hours to pass by so we could get back to training.

"This will cheer you up," said Lucas when he returned, setting a plate in front of me. "It's not the same as what you'd get at home, but it tastes incredible."

It was the closest it would get to Glacier's typical breakfast: sweet rice with cinnamon and dried grapes. I stared at him. Just feeling the smell of spices made me feel better. I was about to launch myself at the plate when a snort stopped me. I looked out of the corner of my eye and saw Ettezi's guardians saying something in their language as they pointed at me. The paranoia was getting the best of me, damn it.

As much as I tried to ignore it, I couldn't. What if everyone around us noticed how pampered I was being treated? I rather they would give me low-quality, cold, dry food in a can, with a spoon, like some of the soldiers were eating.

"If you keep treating me like my mother, I won't stop looking like a child."

"Look at it this way," he said, and with his elbow, he playfully nudged me, "at least you won't have to train on an empty stomach."

But I threw my etiquette out the window and dropped my face on my fist, exhausted from what had already happened in such a short amount of time. I needed a minute—just a moment to go back to being the funny and sarcastic Omhet.

"You need to get up," blurted Shin, sounding nervous.

"My head or my spirits?" I sarcastically asked.

"Both, *now*."

I couldn't understand why his undergarments were in such a twist, but then Cheikh spoke. "Your Highness, here, have my seat." He stood, letting Karl's sister sit in front of me.

These tables were small, so I drew my breakfast toward me, leaving space for hers. I couldn't look at her, instead pretended she was not there while I played with my food.

"Princess Khloe," she introduced herself.

My eyes rose to hers, and I nodded. Then I let them drop back onto my plate. She seemed to want to have a conversation, but I barely felt the need to make a joke—something new for me, to be honest.

"Does he feel all right?" she asked Shin.

Shin stared at her, but when their eyes met, he could not respond. Incredible—not only was he serious but shy too. Had he been paralyzed by her beauty or title, or was it because someone had dared to speak to him directly?

"Aren't you supposed to be in the royal dining room?" I asked so she would stop bothering my guardian.

She turned to me, noting how serious I was. Shin could finally breathe again when she took her eyes away from his. Poor guy, the princess got him nervous.

"I should be," she said. "But I saw you walk out. I wanted to know if you were all right."

Had she been following me around like a child? My grip on the plate tightened.

"Prince Omhet," she started, "may I ask why you're here in this competition?"

You can do it. Just answer casually.

"My king wanted someone to represent the royal family. I volunteered to be here. That's it." I went back to my breakfast or at least tried to.

"Do you want to be here?" she asked. Apparently, she didn't understand anything, or maybe me being the one representing my kingdom didn't make sense to her.

Or to anyone.

"Yes, I want to be here."

Liar! I heard Guillermo's voice. *Oh, no.* Not that voice. I preferred my father's, my own as depressing as it was, but not my brother's.

Do you really want to be here?

You should go home and avoid further humiliation.

You don't belong here.

"I may not look it, but surprisingly, I want to be here," I insisted, unsure if I was talking to her or the annoying voice in my head.

She nodded and even smiled a little. "I can help you," she offered, out of pity or something else I couldn't say. "We can train together after breakfast."

There was a sudden rush when my guardians ran and stood behind Khloe, silently waving for my attention and begging me to accept her offer.

She pities you.

I closed my eyes and took a deep breath. I shouldn't have left my room today.

What would a kingdom as powerful as Ettezi gain from helping you? She's playing with you, little one, Guillermo's voice insisted.

Shut up! I yelled at him, feeling my leg shake under the table.

"I'm fine," I spat, standing up angrily and leaving my breakfast behind.

"I can see your kingdom is not the only cold one," she murmured while I walked through the door.

Even though something inside me screamed to stop and to go back and apologize, I couldn't do it. I simply had to be far away from all of them.

Including my brother's voice—*Especially* my brother's voice.

Brilliant, Omhet, you blew it again, I thought in frustration.

I didn't go back because I knew I wouldn't be able to fix anything right now. I had to make up my mind first before trying anything else.

There was still time left until the representatives had to be on the field, so I took the opportunity to roam around the arena by myself. Station by station, I could see the tables set with weapons and exercise tools and a tent with manuals for survival. Who would've thought so much organization would've been done for a dragon that probably doesn't even exist. I grabbed one of the swords, but it felt uncomfortable in my hand, so I dropped it back on the table.

I remember what that thing did to me. I remember the bloodbath below me and my crying. There was no one to hear me. Nobody, except Guillermo, with the sword, dripping, watching me bleed. I thought I was going to die.

Enough! You swore not to think about it eight years ago, I reminded myself, burying my memories at the bottom of an abyss.

I wanted to get out of here when I turned around and ran into Shin. He was with me as if he had been watching me all this time.

I was surprised to see that he had followed me out here and was now reclining against a table nearby, contemplating the arena in a relaxed form. His sleek, black hair covered his thin eyes while he observed me. I stared back for only a few seconds. Why was he the one here? His seriousness was his shadow, and sometimes it seemed he disliked being near me. But his being here made that thought vanish.

"Let us help you, Omhet," said Shin, not out of pity. On the contrary, I could tell he was worried. "Every kingdom brought their advisors to this competition. Don't be stubborn—you won't be able to do this alone."

I didn't answer. I wracked my brain, trying to find a way for him to help me. It wasn't like they could grab me by the legs and make me do pull-ups or make connections for my kingdom by talking for me. *By the way, great job ruining your first chance with the princess of the desert, Omhet! Shit!*

"Do you want to make your father and your kingdom proud?"

"How?" I asked. "I can barely run fast enough to reach the slowest of all the kingdoms."

Shin sighed. He could see this wouldn't be easy, making me feel worse. "You're not supposed to focus on that, and you're here to—"

"Yeah, yeah, I know, to make allies."

Scratching his chin, thoughtfully, he gave me a look. "I don't know about you, but I think you owe Princess Khloe an apology."

I huffed. I knew that I'd messed things up with Khloe. "If my father had seen me a minute ago, he would have banished me."

Khloe had been the best ally I could've found, and I had just ruined it by being so stupidly hostile. I could imagine my father's voice full of excitement if he were to learn that Khloe, Princess of Ettezi, was my first friend. He would sway with emotion because Ettezi was one of the most important kingdoms in the Union. And I had just offended and ruined our chances to be allied with it without asking for forgiveness. It wasn't her fault that my insecurities and my lack of training had gotten to me.

Gods, I'd been so stupid!

"I've got faith in you." I chuckled, incredulous. He sighed again at my reaction. "Everyone here believes that the strongest will be the one to defeat the beast, but I think it'll be the smartest who will end the curse."

My eyes studied Shin. There was no trace of a joke on his face. He seemed like a philosopher with no real remedy—someone who used his pretty words to make me feel better.

And it worked. I smiled a little, silently thanking him for his words. It vanished once a trumpet sounded, making me jump. The representative entered the training grounds, wide awake and alert. Marcus stood once more on the stage, rehashing the schedule and officially beginning another training day.

I stayed where I was, taking in the kingdoms in formation and the words Marcus spoke. No one noticed the only kingdom missing in that information, of course. So, I simply chose to enjoy the moment where no one was looking for me, leaning against the same table as Shin.

While that was underway, I rummaged through my pockets for the paper the trainer had given me. Reading its contents, a grunt escaped me when my eyes took in what it said: only do cardio exercise and lift small weights to accommodate my strength. It was a logical choice, yes, and a great starting point. But was he forgetting we were to face a miserable dragon in eight months? This sack of bones needed more than just running and small weights. I needed a miracle, a strategy, something more productive than this.

"Come on, time to begin," ordered Shin when he noticed I was still at the table. Marcus had finished and left the stage, and everyone was already starting their day. Meanwhile, my body had chosen to stay where it was.

Frustration still coursed through me. Could I possibly move time forward and skip the next miserable months that waited for me? I wanted to go to a time and place where I was stronger, more resistant, with an army of thousand men and women at my command and not these three nannies at my disposal.

When my feet decided to finally move, I followed behind every representative to the first station that would offer their expertise. We were on our way to prepare for the greatest battle any nation had ever seen and to unite against the dragon, like brothers in arms to liberate Andebeck from its curse. Or at least that's how it was supposed to be since that sense of brotherhood was missing. In any case, we would start what we all anxiously waited for, hoping for a better future full of peace and harmony, unity, and camaraderie. We would become great warriors and change from children to men.

Finally, our great training would commence—

"Good morning. Please sit down," said the trainer.

By sitting at a desk?

After that epic speech in my mind, this lovely trainer had just doused me with cold water with the order that we sit like pupils in class under the white tent. I wasn't the only one complaining, but I was the only one not to take a seat. I was lost, I swear. Had Marcus mentioned this? Or had I been so distracted with my thoughts that I'd missed this part?

"Inside your desk, you'll find paper and a pen," he said. "Every day after break-fast, we'll take classes that'll last for four hours. We'll have warrior strategy and combat sessions, history lessons—"

"History lessons?" I repeated, dumbstruck.

"Do you have a problem with learning history, Prince Omar?" he asked.

Omhet!

I thought I'd whispered it, but apparently, I hadn't. I froze for a second. "My apologies for the interruption, Trainer..."

"Trainer?" he interrupted. "I'm General Mendez, second in command."

"My apologies, General," I said while the others kept laughing at my disgrace. Karl, naturally, was part of the laughing crew. "It just... I think it's useless to learn about history."

The general narrowed his eyes, fixed his glasses, and stared, trying to be patient. I could tell he wanted to throw me out, and we had barely even begun. "And what is useful for you?"

I cleared my throat, not knowing what to say. "Well..." I thought for a second and then said, "Weak points for the dragon, weapon handling, first aid, in case of third-degree burns—"

"Ladies and gentlemen," interrupted the general, pointing at me, "here we have the future King of Andebeck, who I believe will take control even before beating the dragon and winning the crown." His sarcasm was palpable. "Would you like to stand at the podium?"

I bit my lips and slowly sat. The last thing I wanted was to look like a Buffon—like I was doing now.

"Now that interruptions have ceased, let's continue with what's actually important."

The general began his lesson by briefly explaining Andebeck's culture and foundation. I barely noticed when and how he switched to the present and began explaining what each of us will be doing in his class and during training. He pretended our slight altercation didn't happen, but oh, how he droned on. The general liked the sound of his voice a little too much—he wouldn't shut up.

"In order to win this competition, you have to master each of the stations set on these grounds," he reminded us. "Following what has been stipulated in the evaluation phase, and with what the instruction is given afterward state, you will choose a station fit for your needs and will only switch to a new one when the first has been marked as passed." After a few hundred more words, he asked us to follow him back to the grounds. He turned back to us and said, "I wish you a good fortune during your training. And may the best kingdom win for the good of Andebeck."

The group saluted the general and then dispersed to their preferred stations. My eyes followed him, however, because I was still confused by the need to take history lessons.

Suddenly, Shin was there beside me. "Shall we begin with the easiest one?"

Every station was busy, so after my eyes were drawn to it, I approached the archery station. It embarrassed me to know that I'd never gripped a bow in my life. My curiosity sprang to life the moment I noticed the representative for the Nordem court training with the bow. I stared at him, and the excellent way he wielded the weapon. I didn't know much about him, not even his name, but at least I'd recognized the color of his uniform. Nordem colors were marine blue and black. They were said to be the best hunters around, and their favorite pastime was hunting in the woods.

"Lord Pierre, from the Nordem court," Shin reminded me when he noticed I was staring at him. "It would be of great help if he became one of our allies."

I nodded, mesmerized by the way Pierre got ready to draw the string. He looked to be around twenty-five, or so it seemed due to his massive beard—half of his face was covered with it. He swished his head slightly to let his ponytail fall behind his shoulder and got ready to shoot. He looked so sure of himself as his back straightened, his chest puffed out, and he took aim. With controlled breathing, he let the arrow fly. It hit the target right in the center. His guards applauded softly.

I gaped at Shin, surprised. Then I whispered, "He makes it look so easy."

Pierre huffed, "I've held a bow since I was four," he stated heatedly. "Of course, I can't say the same about you."

"My apologies, I didn't mean—" Shin shoved my back, interrupting me. When I glared at him, he was killing me with a look. I had said something wrong again.

Pierre stared at his guards. "Tell my trainer to find me a new challenge—I'm bored." Then, with an attitude, he left the station.

Scratching my head, I wondered what had gotten everyone in such a rotten mood that morning. I chose to ignore that, too and grabbed a bow. I was ignoring the recommendations written down for me by the trainer, but right then, I didn't care. The bow was heavy, wood, and coated in dark paint. I was fascinated by the beautiful weapon.

"Sir, need I remind you that everyone in this place has a knack for competition?" Shin said. "They're defensive and are trying their best to annihilate the weak and intimidate the strong."

"They don't intimidate me," I joked.

Shin gave an eyeroll. I knew he hated my jokes and that most of them were out of place. But I couldn't help it. I liked to make people laugh, even if just a little. I wanted to hear Shin laugh. All that seriousness had to be considered a sickness, I swear. Maybe one day I would. For now, my eyes shifted toward the target. I was a few meters away, but I had to close one eye to focus better, or at least I thought that was how it worked.

"Don't close one eye. Leave them both wide open."

I huffed but again aimed at the target.

"Lean your torso to the side with your arms toward the center of the target," Shin ordered. "Arch your back and breathe deeply before releasing the string."

Breathing deeply, I let the arrow loose. It fell just by my feet. I don't even adjust it properly on the string.

Shin closed his eyes. "Again," he said, pinching his nose.

Stretching my neck from side to side, I prepared for my next try. A sigh escaped my lips when the arrow did the same thing as before, joining its brother on the ground.

This would be a long day.

CHAPTER 9

Sunday became my favorite day because it was the only day I had to myself. I could see the representatives coming out of the palace gates from my balcony, noticing how alliances were forming for the benefit of their realms. I heard rumors that Nordem had joined Atsoc and Sierra Adaza with the great island of Puerto Escondido. It seemed like the only kingdom without an ally was mine. There had been no progress at all in these past few days, and as I watched everyone go off in groups, I could tell they were already feeling comfortable living here.

I went back to my room, leaving the balcony door open. And there were my three nannies, talking loudly while making jokes with each other in the next room. They had created a familiar relationship, while I didn't even have time to make friends. They interacted all the time... well, Lucas was the one who talked the most. Cheikh listened like a father, but Shin found unabashedly every chance he got to sleep with his nose stuck in the quilts. And strangest of all, he slept wherever he found a spot—currently, he was across his small bed with his head close to one edge and his feet hanging off the other.

I smiled a little and walked away from them through my spacious room. I spent some time sitting at my desk and opening my letters, reading them while fiddling with my string bracelet on my wrist. I never took off my bracelet, it was the only thing I had from my kingdom.

Several of the letters had arrived this week, and I took my time to read them and smile wistfully at each one. Everyone in my family has written to me—except Guillermo.

My father reminded me of every nonsense regulation I should always follow. My mother basically dedicated a spiritual poem to me on behalf of Kea to give me strength for the rest of my training. Cayetano begged me to return engaged to be married, or he would not allow me to come back home. I laughed a lot at his letter. Had he forgotten my age? What was the rush, for heaven's sake?

However, my sister's letter was my favorite.

My dear Omh,

I know your heart, and I know that you must be about to run away if you are not already on your way. If you need a reason to stay, read this letter as often as you want and understand that nothing extraordinary has come without sacrifice. Fight with everything, even if you can't anymore. Give up your strength, your emotions, and even your tears, but don't quit, because, in the end, you will regret it if you surrender. We are Espinhos. We do not give up. We are not less than anyone else.

Chin up, Ahnani.

Ahnani—That honor wasn't usually bestowed on your siblings. It was meant for the one you admired most and respected as much as your paternal figure. Estefania had never called Guillermo Ahnani, much less Cayetano or Rodrigo. It made me take a deep breath and close my eyes, trying to calm my emotions. I hadn't known how much I needed someone to tell me something like that. What a little faith did was extraordinary, so I took the pen and dipped it in ink.

Dear Estefania,

I can't lie to you, I want to give up, but I couldn't look you in the eye if I did. It is not about physical effort but the pressure of wanting to be seen like everyone else. I want to project Ettezi's pride, Puerto Escondido's confidence, and Atsoc's bravery, but it's as if I had personified Glacier's lack of visibility in the world. I will give my all, for you, the King of Glacier, and me. I promise you.

She was the only one I wrote a letter to. I folded the letter, sealed it with wax, and left it on the tray for a servant to take later. I sat for a while, leaning back in the chair and staring out the open balcony door, listening to a sporadic laugh from my guards.

Maybe I wasn't part of any group, but I could start with the simplest course of action—getting to know my guardians. So, I got up, slid the door open, and peered into their small private room. Shin was still asleep in the same place. Was he even breathing? Cheikh and Lucas, who'd been sitting on the floor, halted their conversation.

"Do you need anything, sir?" Lucas asked.

I sat close to them, with my back to the wall and my legs bumping into Lucas's because of the small size of the place. It was a small room—inside my room. So that they could remain close to me all the time, but it was their private space.

"The king told me that you knew a lot about the Union," I said in a pleasant tone. "I would like to learn about the territories I face."

There was a pause, and I feared he would not answer me.

I felt worse when Cheikh got up and left the room. I almost do the same. The last thing I wanted was to upset any of them. I shouldn't have walked in. I should have stayed writing letters—

"I thought you'd never ask," responded Lucas with a cheerful smile.

He loved to talk. He even settled more comfortably on the floor and continued without giving himself time to take a breath. In short, I had three courts available, and Lucas did his best to explain them to me.

"I think Nova Cerise is the best choice for you. It is the only territory that uses magic, but they are peaceful and have no intention of engaging in battle like you," said Lucas.

"I don't want to be pessimistic, but we are pretty useless as allies. What will two territories do together if we cannot fight in battle?"

"Oh, I assure you, there are many stations in a battle that don't necessarily need to be on the battlefield," Cheikh answered.

When he returned to the room, he had two hot cups in his hand and stopped next to me to offer me one. I stared at it for a moment to ensure the mug was for me. I took it, and he sat down in front of us.

He didn't leave to be away from me. He just went to make us a drink. It's... the nicest thing he's ever done for me. I bit back my smile, and even though I wouldn't say I liked tea, I drank it and even enjoyed it. When sweetened with honey, ginger tea was enjoyable, no matter how bitter the ginger might be, like Cheikh.

He interrupted whenever he could, correcting Lucas until they ended up arguing. I listened with a smile, realizing that these three weren't so bad after all. That's why I didn't complain about being in that little room, even though mine was much more comfortable. It reminded me of home. We used to sit on the floor, as close as we could get in the worst of winter so we could intensify body heat that, sometimes, not even the fireplace produced. So, I relaxed and enjoyed the afternoon like I used to do at home with my family.

Another day of crippling training ended me within and out. My lifeless body fell onto the bed at midnight, and I lamented that I would have merely five hours to rest. Sweat coated every inch of me, and I could feel my matted hair tangled in patches. I was filthy, but did I shower? Did I care? Not one bit. I simply closed my heavy eyes and tried calming my erratic breathing down.

At last, my first week in this hell had been over and done with. My body felt like it had been a month instead of a week, and every muscle in my lanky frame could feel the pain of overuse and overstretch. The noises from my guardians became distant—a first for me, but it was quite understandable. I could barely bother to take off my boots, why would their loud voices bother me?

The routine hadn't changed in the past few days. Every station remained the same; the only difference was their intensity and how creative they'd become—too creative, in my opinion. I couldn't go to bed until I finished with my daily objectives. The saddest part was not how everyone finished with the objectives every day. The saddest part was how everyone finished their tasks on time, and I was the only person who remained on the field for hours after they were gone. Mostly, the instructor let me retire out of pity and not due to my ability to finish because I never really did.

When the trumpet sounded the next morning, I didn't react. I didn't jump out of my skin. It was a harmless insect buzzing through my subconscious. Blearily, my eyes tried to adjust to the sensation of being up at an ungodly hour. I felt like weights had been placed on my extremities, and I could barely move. When my three guardians hurried me to get up, I tried—I really did. I trodden to the bathroom and took the much-needed shower my body begged for. My eyes closed underneath the spray of warm water, muscles lax and exhausted.

"Omhet!" Cheikh yelled, making me jump. I'd fallen asleep.

"I'm done, I'm done," I lied, eyes still closed.

With every training that passed by, my energy depleted. And I thought I would become stronger. This was ridiculous, and to think this wasn't the end of it. I wanted to cry out of frustration. It helped to imagine myself screaming at Marcus, *Let's kill the dragon now! Let's ambush it as a full army and split Andebeck among the surviving kingdoms. Why wait?*

The others were already halfway through breakfast when I made it to the dining room. Their voices were loud, sharing a camaraderie that stemmed from bonds made. Sighing, I sat on the farthest chair, as usual, waiting for the servants to set a plate of food on my side of the table. They never remembered I was there. Maybe it was because I was quiet all the time, or perhaps they'd chosen to ignore my existence, but they always took their sweet time in serving me. Yawning, I tried to catch their attention by waving at them.

Finally, one of the servants came to my side after ten minutes. Then he said, "I'm sorry, sir, but breakfast is over."

When everyone stood, my face fell in annoyance. *You don't say!* I wanted to shout, but I swallowed my words back. Instead, I also took my leave after I nicked an apple out of a nearby fruit bowl. Following behind the group, I suddenly felt that I'd gone from being a joke to being a ghost. Like a joke you constantly told so that it lost all its humor. I should be grateful for the reprieve but being invisible bothered me more. It spoke volumes about how important my presence was to the rest of them, which did not bode well for me.

It was so pitiful.

But it wasn't the only novelty of my daily routine. I could lift weights now! My muscle mass was responding, which was a positive thing despite what was happening with the rest of the stations. To know that I would be stronger than before gave me hope that nothing would remain the same.

I continued my training with archery. A lone arrow flew toward another station, sticking on the wooden column. Many people gasped because I'd been so close to hitting someone.

"Omhet!" they screamed.

"Sorry!" I said, embarrassed.

A little laugh was heard from afar. I didn't have to turn around to know that it had been Khloe. I thought she was laughing with me, so I returned her smile, only to have her glare at me. She kept walking with her guardians trailing by her side. No, she hadn't been laughing with me, she was laughing *at* me.

"When are you planning to make a new friend?" asked Shin. He stood by my side, nursing a cup of tea. He was always there when it came to training. To tell the truth, I'd gotten used to his presence more than the other two fools that always stayed by the tent, eating toast and drinking coffee.

My eyes drifted to Khloe, trying not to stare while she practiced martial arts. She appeared to be flexible, judging by those high kicks—I looked away when she caught me watching her.

"Don't you know about Ettezi? If I ask for forgiveness, she'll break my face," I replied while placing another arrow on the bow's string.

Back straight, chest puffed out, feet aligned, controlled breaths—I let the arrow loose and went straight toward the target, but it missed the center. Huffing, I felt the frustration that I'd yet to hit the center, but I was happy that I'd managed to hit anything.

"The more time passes, the harder it'll be to acquire an ally."

My hands held the bow in place, releasing the next arrow. It hit closer to the center, and I repeated my moves in my mind, wondering what I could do to perfect my skill. Shin raised my elbows and went as far as to correct my gaze, pushing my head this way and that.

"What do you suppose I should do?" I sarcastically asked, pointing toward the target as best as I could. "Should I go to her and bother her with my presence until she budges?" The arrow flew straight to the ground. Great. Growling, I grabbed another one.

"I want you to join her in combat."

"What?" I shouted. Distracted, I released my arrow and flew right to the center of the target.

I'd hit it perfectly for the first time ever. I couldn't help but let out a small cheer.

"Take that as a sign of confirmation," he said before taking a sip of his tea.

Sighing, my eyes looked to the sky. *A miracle, please,* I begged the beyond, as if it could solve all my problems with my desperate call. In the end, my brain concluded that, sooner or later, I had to make allies. I already established that I can't return empty-handed and face my father.

I would rather die from Khloe's hits when I asked her for forgiveness.

And while I hadn't strayed far from my desire to fight against the dragon, I decided that making allies was a thousand times better than training. With that in mind, I dropped the bow in its place on the rack and went toward the station Khloe had been at for a while now, going hand to hand with a trainer. Her clothes had been tailored for the exertion of exercise, and she had leather gloves protecting her hands. Sweat dripped from her brow while she ravenously fought. The woman had energy, that was for sure. She deflected her trainer and kicked him hard enough to throw him to the ground.

"It's done!" he yelled. "That was perfect, Princess."

She smiled as he bowed.

I grabbed a pair of black exercising gloves and donned them, careful to protect my hands from what would undoubtedly be a fierce fight. Without a word, I stepped on the platform, adjusted my gear, and stretched a little.

Khloe's eyes regarded me with a seriousness that chilled me while she straightened to her full height.

"People are waiting for their turn," she snapped.

This woman was rancorous. Ever since I mistreated her, she'd been avoiding me like a plague. I had to convince her that I was being sincere this time. That was what my father would've wanted.

"The dragon won't wait for anyone's turn come winter," I reminded her, posing for a fight.

She gaped at me, crossing her arms in annoyance. In her eyes, I was being an insolent little brat. When she figured out, I wasn't leaving that platform, she grunted. "Well, let's get this over with."

I hope that this would redeem my earlier actions toward her. I'd ruined it with the princess. *Here I am, miss, asking for forgiveness in the only way you understand.* My heartbeat quickened the moment she took her stance, adrenaline overtaking my nerves.

It wasn't the first time I had fought. I had plenty of experience with my siblings, especially with Guillermo. Nevertheless, it was the first time I fought against a woman. The respectful behavior I would normally display with her now waged a battle against my commitment to beating the princess in this fight, but I could not let this chance go. I knew that if I didn't go through with this now -thanks to Shin- I would never do it. I needed to win Khloe over, and I needed to remain centered on my tasks.

And honestly, I was anxious to mark my place in this competition! This would be a great opportunity to do that as well. I wanted to prove to the world that I, Omhet Espinho, was more skillful than what everyone believed. I just needed to demonstrate it with a little more enthusiasm, that was all. I was ready to do my best and face the challenge that the princess presented and show that I could win against her and anyone else.

Khloe raised a leg high and kicked me on the chin. I fell to the side, knee on the floor. How the hell had her foot reached my chin? How? I stood, rubbing my jaw as the pain radiated to my ear. A startled laugh burst through my lips. Khloe had surprised me. She remained severe, waiting for my next move. Incredulous, I stared at her. She was good.

But I could do this.

Nearing her in a fighting stance, I concentrated on any movement she might make. She kicked again, but I managed to avoid it. She did it again, leaving me no time to recover from the last one. Raising my hand, I held her leg in place, and without thinking and with all my strength, I threw her back on the platform. She tried to stand, but I quickly grabbed her to pin down her arms and legs. She grunted, trying to break free from my grip. I gripped harder.

"Tell me to let go, and I will," I said, agitated.

Without even a whine, she managed to free her arm and punched me in the nose.

I lost my grip and fell over. Gods, she did not give up. She wasn't merciful either, taking advantage of my predicament and sitting on my body as she slammed her fists on my face. I covered my head from her blows as best as possible, but she still found a way to land her punches. She split my lip, managed to hit my chin again, and made me see stars when her blows hit my temple. I had to escape her grip. But how?

I heard screams in the distance, and my name was called, but the voices blended, and my senses went black for a moment. Whether they were cheering me or discouraging me I didn't know.

Somehow, I managed to push her off me with my hips and I pinned her down when she fell beneath me. I was about to hit her face when I froze.

I couldn't do it, dammit! Her face gave me a painful reminder that she was a woman. How could I find the courage to do this when I'd been taught otherwise all my life? Her sudden burst of laughter startled me as she once more took the lead, thanks to my hesitation. Hitting the parts of me that were already bruised up, she forced my body to fall back, and a kick aimed at my chest knocked the wind out of me.

I had been weak, and she knew it.

"You've got a sentimental side, Omhet," she sarcastically said.

After inhaling a much-needed breath, I got up and miraculously avoided her next kick.

I didn't dodge her next punch, I caught her and wrapped around her waist, keeping her back against my torso. I wasted no time now that I had her trapped, but with my other arm I wrapped around her neck, squeezing. When she realized what I was doing, she hit me with her head to my nose, and we both fell. She was on top of me, and this time, I gave her no opportunity to recover, encircling her neck with my arms and holding on tight. I refused to let her go, no matter what she tried. She choked and lost her breath. No more than three seconds passed before she gave the signal to yield. I released her, smiling.

I stood and offered my hand to help her up. For a moment, I had been tempted to let her win. But then I noticed that half the people in this competition had stopped their own tasks in order to witness the fight as if it had been the best training they'd seen all day. I didn't know what was more surprising to them, the fact that I'd just fought against a woman in a most violent way or the fact that I had finally won a station.

Worry replaced my wonder at winning, so I had to ask, "Are you all right?"

She gave a slight smile, caressing her neck. "You won," she stated. "I think this is the first time you've passed a station."

I returned her smile, proud of my achievement. I did it! My first victory! Wanting to savor this moment, my smile widened, but soon it was taken away by a sudden hit to my face that made Khloe seem weak in comparison.

Immediately, I fell to the ground, out of my wits.

"Karl!" Khloe yelled.

A flurry of kicks fell against my ribs, over and over and over. Groaning, I spat in pain, sickened. What was happening? Why was I being attacked when my guard had been lowered? I heard Cheikh screaming and running toward me. Chaos erupted. My guardians raced behind Cheikh, but that was all I noticed through the dizzying pain.

"Don't you dare touch my sister again, imbecile!"

Managing to place my elbows on the ground to better look at him, I felt blood falling down my lip while I angrily stared at him. His entire army was behind him, ready to take me down.

"I followed the rules. I never hurt her."

Cheikh, Shin, and Lucas held me by the shoulders when I finally managed to stand, holding me back. They spoke together, a chorus, to get off of the platform, ask for forgiveness, to stop this at once. But I couldn't. I did not want to seem weak. And besides, I'd done nothing wrong. The one who should scurry away from the platform was Karl. So, I tried not to let his guards intimidate me, even though they all wanted to jump at me at his given signal.

"Let's find out if it's fair when we fight against you four, idiot!" he shouted, close to doing just that.

Had he just insinuated that fighting against Khloe was unfair? That woman was strong—she'd been close to breaking my face more than twice. She could hold her own, and this guy was definitely overprotecting her. She barely had a scratch!

"Khloe is more than a princess. She's a warrior!" I screamed back. "You should stop staring at the mirror for five minutes and see that she has more chance to win against the dragon than you do!"

He shut me up with another hit. He was not defending his sister now, he was defending his pride and ego. I couldn't see what had happened to my guardians, I could scarcely see anything through the chaos that ensued in the arena. I could barely see other kingdoms trying to stop the fight, and I could barely hear Khloe screaming, trying to stop her brother. It was the most unfair fight I'd ever witnessed or participated in—if participating was the right word for it. The whole kingdom of the desert against us four. I never even hit Karl because two of his men held me in place while he hit everywhere he could find.

"Karl!" Khloe desperately cried. Then she did something I was not expecting. She kicked his nose hard, making him tumble to the ground. "Stop it, you animal!"

A shot was heard through the grounds, stopping the mob in its tracks.

Nobody moved. We all turned to look in the direction of the palace, where Marcus followed by his armed guardians, was stomping toward us. His wined-color uniform harshly reflected the sun, and his fury was palpable even from afar.

Silence reigned when he stopped and fumed, trying to understand the situation. "Have you forgotten what this is all about?" he exploded. "I am not interested to know what happened—you're all adults and should behave as such. If this happens again, you will suffer worse consequences than an exile, understood?"

Karl gaped at him, incredulous. He said nothing.

"Understood, Prince Karl of Ettezi?" enunciated Marcus slowly through gritted teeth.

Fuming, Karl replied, "Yes, sir," slowly killing me with his eyes. If he'd been a dragon, he would be spitting fire through his nose.

Satisfied with his answer, Marcus shifted to me. "Omhet, come with me." He immediately started to walk away, expecting my compliance.

"What?" I angrily yelled. Why me? I had done nothing. I hadn't even touched Karl in the altercation that he started.

"Now!" shouted Marcus as he moved away.

Grumbling as I got off the platform, I left the crowd behind, followed closely by my guardians, who had been hurt in the unfair fight. They would surely let me hear it once we were alone tonight.

Today was not a good day, and I had little faith it would get any better.

Chapter 10

"For the third time, Prince Omhet, I believe you!" Marcus interrupted wearily while pinching the bridge of his nose. He reminded me of my father after I fought with my brothers.

If I kept arguing, we wouldn't get anywhere, so I was quiet for once. I had tried to explain to him that it wasn't my fault. I'd told him the story of my entire week from the beginning to the end. There was nothing I'd ever done to make Karl so abusive toward me. From the first day of training, he has pushed, detested, and mocked me. Did he hold it against me that I was from the smallest kingdom, or what? Why wasn't he fighting with someone his own size? Was it fun to make the weak suffer? I'd had enough of it, but Marcus calling me out was the last straw. It was humiliating for them to drag me off the field like a scolded child. I definitely lost the tiny amount of respect I might have managed to gain in the fight with Khloe.

"I don't think you understand that I just saved your neck," he said calmly, though I honestly didn't see how the hell Marcus saved me by humiliating me. "If I took Karl and gave him a punishment, it would be worse for you. Karl would never forgive you, and he would seek a way to get revenge and treat you worse every day of your life—and that's if he doesn't kill you first on the day of the great battle."

I snorted, crossing my arms and biting back a groan as I remembered how sore my body was. If it weren't for the fact that I was alone in his office, my guards would have beaten me for my impudence and for my rebellious way of reacting to the minister. His desk was the only thing we had between us, but it was so wide that if I murmured, he wouldn't hear me.

"You forgot to mention that you would never expel your favorite prince," I muttered as I wiped away the blood running down my face with my arm.

He narrowed his eyes but, in the end, nodded.

"Right."

I gritted my teeth when he blatantly admitted it. I didn't think he would hear me.

"Not because he's my favorite, but because he's the one with the greatest potential to kill the dragon. I couldn't lose him over such a stupid argument."

I could not answer. Anger boiled my blood. Seeing how Andebeck already had its favorite kingdom bothered me to the core. However, I kept quiet. In the end, this kingdom wanted to end the curse of the dragon, and I was the last person who could demand fairness in this situation.

"Unbelievable," I said, standing up, angry at everything and everyone.

Nobody in this place would be treated equally, apparently. And the more days that passed, the more the kingdoms mistrust each other, obtaining more men and weapons for battle. Now with this, and thanks to Karl, I could say goodbye to whatever ally I might have earned.

And to think that at last I had finally won a station, dammit.

"Prince Omhet," Marcus called when I opened the door. I stopped with my hand on the knob, not wanting to look at him. "Take the day off. Rest—you deserve it."

Marcus wanted to be nice to me, like I was the victim, but deep down I knew that all he wanted was to protect Karl and his untouchable kingdom of the desert. This time I did not respond and left the office without saying goodbye.

My guardians waited for me in the vestibule, beyond angry. They looked pathetic and in pain. Cheikh's eye was swollen and a tad purple. Lucas had a short cast on his arm, immobilizing his wrist. And Shin, with his hair a mess, had gauze around and over his broken nose. We looked like three messed up maids and a damsel in distress.

"They're waiting for you in the infirmary, Prince Omhet," said a woman who had been waiting near my guardians. Her cream-colored skirt, gray blouse, and hair tied up in a bun screamed nurse.

I shook my head as I walked past her. "I'm fine, thanks."

In my room, my legs took me to the bathroom. My body was clamoring for a long warm bath now that I had the rest of the day. After taking a shower, I stood in front of the mirror, staring at my horrid reflection. My nose was swollen, my lip was split open, and every time I took a breath, my ribs hurt.

Someone cleared their throat behind me. I guess I can't keep hiding from the inevitable. When I turned, I saw the three of them by the door, staring at me coldly.

"I know what you are going to say." I sighed, leaning on the edge of the sink. "You think I'm a risky fool, an infant who—"

"On the contrary," he interrupted, "you're finally behaving like your father wanted you to. My only advice is to know your limits. Karl is anxiously trying to find a way to kick you out of Andebeck."

The comment took me by surprise. When I found my voice, I said, "No one will kick me out of here." My eyes shifted, avoiding their gaze. "I have to say, though, I was a little scared. There were so many men against us, and something tells me they're not going to give up."

"Neither will we, and that's what bothers them most," stated Shin, and he almost smiled.

I dared to look at them again and saw their determined gazes. In an act of reverence, they bowed before leaving the bathroom.

"I say that it has been my favorite day since I arrived," said Lucas, but Cheikh looked at him disapprovingly.

"If it's not a bother, we'll also take a break. I suggest you stay here, in your room and get some sleep," Cheikh added.

Sleep? No one had to tell me twice.

But I couldn't—too much adrenaline still coursed through my veins. Lying on my bed, I whistled to ease the boredom—it was either that or my brain running a mile a minute, trying to find an easy distraction for my current problems.

The guards locked themselves in their room until the next day. I heard snoring mixed with whispered conversation. Surely it was Lucas interrupting the sleep of others. They were exhausted after a long day. What could I do? I couldn't leave the room without their permission.

Wait a minute!

If they were all asleep, they would never know if I left for a little while, right? Which meant—

"I'm free," I whispered to myself.

Excitedly, I sprang out of my bed, knowing that I finally had no one watching over me. I had to say, it was terrible of my guardians to forget that one of them was supposed to stay awake to stand guard. After what happened, though, they were not to blame for caving in to slumber, forgetting their only job.

Surely no one would miss me after what had happened with Karl. It had to be impossible to get in trouble twice in one day. What were the odds?

At least, I hope it would be that way.

Wasting no time, my feet carried me to my wardrobe, where I grabbed the most informal and fresh clothes I could find. Forget the uniform, I would not—could not, bother to wear that wretched thing on my free day! After changing, I quickly made my way out to the hallway, and in my hurry, my forehead chased against something, or rather, someone.

After we both winced in pain, I noticed it was Khloe in front of me, soothing her latest bruise as best she could.

"My apologies, I was in a hurry. Were you coming to my room?"

She nodded, taking my appearance in. After a sharp intake of breath, she whispered, "Oh, shit, I am so sorry! Look at what he did to you."

"I'm perfectly fine. And besides, thanks to your brother, my schedule has been cleared," I shrugged, and I immediately regretted it. Every move I made hurt.

Not being able to fathom why I tried to seem like an invincible guy in front of the princess—an untouchable person who had only been bruised and not beaten up to the point where it hurt to breathe.

"I couldn't look at my brother's face after what he'd done. We could've been banned from the competition," she angrily stated, playing with the end of her braid. *No, you wouldn't,* I thought, remembering how protective Marcus was over them, "For the gods, I'm so angry. My brother is so overprotective, but that does not excuse his behavior. We argued about it, and I assure you he won't do this again."

Sure.

It seemed their problems hadn't just started today, and she'd had enough. Silently nodding, I accepted her apology for what it was. Having brothers of my own, I understood where she was coming from.

Quickly, my eyes darted to both ends of the hallway, noticing it was completely empty except of us. An idea flashed in my mind, and oh boy, did I want to put it into action right then! Preferably before my nannies woke up and noticed I was gone.

"Let's get out of here," I said urgently.

She frowned, not knowing where I was going with this. Then she noticed my attire, and her sudden smile gave me hope that not all was lost and that maybe, just maybe, we could be friends after all.

"I see I was wrong about you." She chuckled, and a mischievous grin spread across her face, seemingly forgetting about her brother's transgressions for the moment. "Wait for me at the staff exit," she said as she hurriedly went back the way she came. "And don't let anyone see you."

I left through the staff exit, and then I anxiously waited for Princess Khloe outside the palace, hidden behind a pillar. Any minute now, she would show up. It had been half an hour, and I prayed that my guardians hadn't noticed I'd left my room. It was the first time in my life that I'd ventured on my own, far away from any adults. Outside my kingdom, I had to have guards trailing my every move, so this opportunity would not be wasted. At least for a little while.

I guess it wasn't so bad being away from home after all.

Khloe finally decided to grace me with her presence, quickly coming down the stairs, her wet curls bouncing behind her with every move. When I saw she wore her kingdom's formal clothing, it made me feel self-conscious about my casual clothes. Her long, light dress flowed with the wind around her ankles. It was a beautiful turquoise with white accents, and her sandals and golden jewelry accentuated her outfit.

I wondered where we were headed to.

"Let's do this before we get caught!" she exclaimed, taking my hand in hers. She pulled me toward the stables. Her eyes were set forward, so I looked back, making sure we weren't being followed. Someone had to do it, right?

Without saying a word, we each grabbed a horse and set off from the palace.

We looked like two escaped prisoners, riding as fast as the horses allowed us. My hands held on to the reins tightly. I hadn't ridden a horse with such speed before, so it was a bit tricky, yet amazing at the same time. Feeling the breeze whipping my face, seeing the green valleys in front of me without a wall to stop me—it was perfect.

We slowed down when we lost sight of the palace. I was just following Khloe, letting her lead the way. I looked over my shoulder and saw that we were not only leaving the palace behind, but that the coast was barely visible from where we were. I did not want to worry, so I tried to enjoy this time with my first friend. It was unbelievable that I had to let her brother smash my face in order to earn her trust.

Even though she spoke a lot more than I did, I didn't mind. She had stories to tell, and they were interesting. Compared to the life I had led, hers had been stricter. Through her captivating stories, I learned that Ettezi had not always belonged to the desert. They had been pirates, criminals who discovered the treacherous and arid lands of what they named Ettezi. It had been a terrain so bad no men would inhabit it. The group had come from the seas of Puerto Escondido and had been exiled for their transgressions. Without anyone expecting it, they had created the strongest kingdom anyone had ever seen. They expanded and conquered any tribe that tried to overpower them like the warriors they were. No one dared trifle with them once they made a name for themselves.

Ettezi was the only place in the world where the sand was red. Its culture venerated his warrior man more than anything else. She spoke of her family and how demanding their customs were. And was it me, or did she sound drained?

"It was a miracle they let me come with Karl," she said. "I was here merely for assistance in whatever he needed, like his maid. But he promised me that as soon as we were out of our place, I'd be as free as he."

My hatred toward him ebbed when she explained how much he'd helped her. It must have been hard knowing she felt forced to be a princess and not a warrior like she wanted.

"I sometimes fled when no one was paying attention to secretly train in martial arts, fencing, and lancing with Karl." She gave me a melancholy smile. "My strength came from his ever since I was a child."

Although I was a little embarrassed to tell Khloe how different my life was compared to hers, I want to tell her about my past. She basically spent her entire life trying to be a warrior, while I lived to run away from my family... from my brother.

"I was the opposite. I can't fight with swords. The only time someone forced me, I almost lost my life," I realized how aware she was of my story, so I changed the tone to a more cheerful one, "So, I learned about everything except how to fight. Our kingdom has never prioritized war or combat. We have a low population count, with a grave lack of resources and food that's driving the king mad. Every day, if snow allows, we have to import almost all of what we consume."

My life was an intense curiosity for her. It was strange, I assumed, to hear about the icy Kingdom of Glacier and how most people barely knew about us. It was far away, on the top of mountain Timantti, that, until now, I hadn't noticed how far it truly was.

"Interesting," she mused, eyes focused on the road. "We truly are rather different. Ettezi is in the middle of so many territories that what we collect on the borders of our frontier gives us plenty of everything we need. Our territory is very strategic. No one from the mountains can go to the coast without going through us and vice versa. We can't complain—money comes in by itself at this point."

I couldn't imagine how much money someone could have controlling those frontiers.

My horse slowed, tired from the rough road it had traveled. It was time to go back, especially now that the road had ended and what lay in front of us were hills. Khloe, however, dismounted and tied her horse to a tree. I looked the way back, noticing how far the palace was.

"Khloe, maybe we should head back—"

"Hey," she interrupted with a mischievous smile, "this was your idea. Now accept the consequences and get off that horse. We haven't finished yet."

Her relaxed way of talking made me trust her. Without thinking about it, I dismounted and tied my horse to the same tree as hers. I looked around, eyes falling on the grass before me and the palace behind me. To be honest, I was somewhat disappointed. I wanted to visit the city and sightsee, eat their native food, browse through the bazaar, and buy gifts for my family. I wanted to visit their beach and enjoy a quiet day on its shores. Now instead, I was on a boring hill with nothing but tall grass around us. At least I was accompanied by the best ally my father could ever imagine me having. I sped after her, almost running in my haste. She looked excited when she made her way up the hill.

"Khloe, wait! Where are we going?"

She didn't answer—she kept going and waited for me at the top. I caught up and stood next to her and took a deep breath, gazing at the view. It looked beautiful. It was the perfect place for a romantic date with so much splendor surrounding us.

Date? My stomach contracted. Yes, this was what my father wanted, but not me. However, this was what he had prepared me for all my life. I had to let go of what *I* wanted.

"It's—perfect," I whispered, looking at the great Kingdom of Andebeck. All I could see was the blue sea and the city on the coast. It was the perfect setting to be in this afternoon.

"That's not what I wanted to show you," she said as if it were obvious.

I sighed, relieved that my thoughts were just that. I turned around to see what she was referring to, dismissing the idea of a date completely.

What the hell—?

I was so impressed that I was speechless. Right behind me, in the shadow of a mountain made of rocks, was the dragon's castle—ancient ruins in the darkest place in Andebeck and a forbidden place where no one, absolutely no one, could be.

"Do you know the best part?" she casually asked, "We can go in right now and find out if the dragon truly exists."

For all the skies over Glacier!

Khloe gave a little laugh and stepped forward, walking where she definitely shouldn't be.

I realized that I would not have to wait seven more months to face the worst fear of this kingdom because my destiny was pushing me toward what was in front of me. For a moment, I even forgot to breathe.

Without planning it, without even wanting to, I knew—

I knew I wouldn't have to wait for winter to meet the dragon. The fateful day had arrived.

Act Two

The Legend

CHAPTER 11

Am I an idiot for leaving the palace with a girl I barely know? She'd planned a casual trip that could end up killing us. What was wrong with her?

"Are you crazy?" I screamed once I found my voice. I took a step back, my heart racing, with only one thing on my mind: run! If Marcus or any of the kingdoms found out that I was near or within the legendary ruined castle, they would kick me out of the competition without a second thought. They could accuse me of being a cheater or wanting to take advantage by approaching the dragon before anyone else.

Or I could die before any of that happened.

I hadn't even begun to think that maybe the sorceress was still alive. Tiara could already be watching me from the tower, or the dragon could have smelled me surely. No one has ever dared to approach it and lived to tell the tale. And here I was, trying my luck!

"I don't believe in fairy tales," Khloe admitted, looking at the castle excitedly. "I think that all this is a mere legend—a simple strategic competition for the benefit of Andebeck. We have to discover the truth..."

"No," I flatly interrupted. I was terrified. "I am lucky to be in the competition, and if they expel me, I will be the shame of my family and the kingdom."

"Okay," she agreed, rolling her eyes. "I'll go alone."

Then Khloe ran straight toward the castle, laughing.

She believed this to be a fun expedition—a child's game, a forbidden adventure. I looked back, debating whether to be a coward and run away on my horse or chase after her. I grunted, frustrated. I already knew the answer. I couldn't leave without Khloe. If something happened to her, they would put all the blame on me. I had to convince her to return, so I ran after her. This was no longer fun, and I even promised myself to find another ally. This girl was too dangerous for me.

There was no way to catch up with Khloe because she ran fast. It reminded me of when we ran the morning miles, and I was dying of exhaustion before matching her pace. The people of her kingdom seemed to learn how to run before learning to walk.

There came a point where I stopped looking at where she was running and instead focused on the castle, seeing how I was slowly approaching the huge ruins. It was hidden even from the sun, as the mountain's shadow covered it completely. The ground around it was rocky, the walls were barely discernible, and the front door was just a gap in the rocks. The only tower that was intact looked unsteady. It did not appear that there was anyone inside the ruins. It didn't even seem like a dragon could hide inside it without being seen from the outside. It wasn't merely a destroyed palace—this had been its own city. It was massive. I even had to stop to process it. Bridges were destroyed. Walls with evidence of fire were being reclaimed by nature, with roots and vines seizing everything from the bottom up.

I hid behind a collapsed wall, gasping as my heart raced. I peeked out, seeing the ruins in front of me. All I could hear was the breeze passing by, but for a moment, I thought I could hear the snores of the dragon. I shoot my head to clear it, telling myself I was hallucinating.

I swallowed deeply. I did not know where Khloe had gone. I was looking at the castle—all dark, abandoned, and depressing. What were once avenues were now scattered gray cobblestones, with weeds sprouting from all sides.

I held my breath and took my first step into what was once the castle's grand entrance.

Nothing happened.

I didn't hear anything. I took another step, slowly going through the gap in the main entrance. A dragon couldn't enter or exit. It was just too small. I decided to walk without stopping, somewhat confident from what I had deduced, but very slowly. I didn't have a sword! How did I agree to this? I'm crazier than Khloe!

It all made sense when I stood in the middle of the lobby. The hall didn't seem like enough room for a dragon, but the ceiling was nonexistent. When I looked above me, the light that shone through blinded me. I covered my eyes with my hand, and when it hit me —the hole in the grand vestibule's ceiling was the dragon's entrance.

Startled, I quickly stepped back until my back hit the wall. Paranoia coursed through me, gazing this way and that, waiting for the inevitable sigh of the fabled beast. However—and I was quite grateful for this, it was very quiet. I stayed still because I didn't trust the silence and didn't want to test fate with my curiosity's need to explore. Besides, I could see pretty clearly that everything was in chaos from my vantage point. There was a hall decorated with burned curtains, and what used to be windowpanes were now decimated holes of destruction. The stairs to the second floor were missing, making it impossible to reach it through the devastation that littered the grounds. The old palace had been grand and vast, but it was so dark I could barely see beyond where I stood.

When my hand was grabbed, I nearly jumped out of my skin, and a pitiful scream escaped my lips.

The flap of pigeon's wings rose from different corners, flying off toward the roof's hole. Khloe's laughter bubbled close to my ear, delighted by my fright. "I told you there was nothing here! Coward."

"Could you keep your voice down?" I furiously whispered. "It might be in there." I pointed to the darkest part of the castle. It looked like nothing was there, but it was suspiciously convenient that that hole in the ceiling—big enough for the beast to enter and exit freely, was so close to the darkness.

"There's only one way to find out," she said, pulling me by the arm.

Breathing harshly, I walked against my will toward our doom. It reminded me of that first day in Andebeck when I'd arrived and fainted in front of the world. We slowly but surely made it to the dark room beyond the vestibule, sticking to the wall for guidance. We had almost no visibility, so we had to adapt as best we could to the lack of light.

"Huh, it sure looks like a dragon's lair," she whispered.

The room appeared to have been a sizeable three-level library or grand ballroom—I wasn't sure, but it was huge. It was so tall and dark that we couldn't see the ceiling. The good news was that there were no dragons. So, I felt a little more relaxed. Apparently, this was the most prominent side of the castle, and there was absolutely nothing.

"I hope to find a witch at least," I admitted, still nervous.

We went through the area and found a door on the floor. Ahead was a wide corridor with its broken windows casting a dim light. At last, we could better see where we were going, so we continued walking. We stopped to look out a window because the entire city of Andebeck could be seen from it. The ruined castle had been built strategically—you could clearly see the whole town and the sea. If any visitor came or someone tried to attack, the people in this fort would be ready, and the distance would give them time to react. I stood at the window for a moment, feeling the gentle breeze while admiring the beautiful kingdom.

"You like this kingdom," said Khloe, leaning against the window.

"If the people here weren't so rude, I'd say it was perfect," I whispered with a smile.

She nodded, agreeing with my statement. "What do you think will happen now?" she asked while distractedly staring at the city. "The dragon is a mere legend—everything was a lie."

"I don't know," I admitted. "You can see Marcus has a preference for Karl. Surely, he'll pick your brother and crown him as the King of Andebeck. That's what I would do, I think."

She stared at me as if she were silently analyzing me for a moment. "My brother thinks you're here to manipulate people, to make allies, and then marry me."

Snorting without looking at her, I hid my red cheeks from her as best I could.

She continued, "But he was wrong. I don't see you as the sort to manipulate. On the contrary, you're always so genuine. It usually gets you in trouble."

"Well, I'll be! I'm flattered." My blush worsened when I finally looked her in the eyes. "But your brother is right—I'm here merely to make allies. I'm not saying I wouldn't want to marry you!" I quickly amended, making her laugh. "Forgive me. I shouldn't have said that." I couldn't look at her. I didn't know how to explain something so simple yet so complicated. "I assure you, I'm not doing it to bother you or anyone. I'm just trying to keep my promise to my father."

"What do you want, Prince Omhet?"

None of this.

I want to go home.

I don't want to marry.

I don't want to force anyone to want me as an ally... or anything else.

"I want to prove to my father that I can. Whatever it takes." I replied both to Khloe and the voice in my head.

"Thank you for your honesty," she murmured while sitting on the windowsill. "It must be a heavy burden to carry."

"You have no idea," I murmured back, staring at the city.

"Your father must be proud of you." She smiled, and I stared at her again as if she'd lost her mind. "You fight hard for what's best for your kingdom, even when I can see in your eyes how much you detest the idea of allies and forced marriages. I think you're crazy enough to do it just to satisfy him. And I think that's as brave as it is stupid."

"That's what I exist for anyway, isn't it?"

"And that is where you are wrong. That's why I ran away from Ettezi, because I wasn't going to fulfill a simple role of doing what they expected of me because I was a woman or because I was old enough to get married. I just... couldn't. And neither should you. I assure you that there is more within you than your father has asked for you. You just have to find it."

I couldn't help it, I smiled. I felt my shoulders lighten as I realized Khloe wasn't trying to convince me to follow my father's orders, but she was taking the load off me. If only it were that easy, anyway. To think that destiny exists and has something better for me.

"Khloe," I waited for her to look me in the eye, "I don't want to marry anyone. I want to join the others and face the dragon in winter."

Maybe I'm a little crazy, but I can't sit and wait to know if destiny exists or not. If there's something better for me, I'll have to fight for it.

"That's the attitude!" she nudged my shoulder with her elbow, and I bit back a groan. Does she forget that I have bruises everywhere? "Maybe you should try to win this competition. My brother would be a tyrant, I'm not kidding."

"I'd rather face the dragon than your brother, thank you."

I said, looking away while laughing.

Suddenly, my eyes locked with someone else's eyes.

It was a woman.

Deep green eyes behind a curtain of red hair stared at me intensely from the dark room. It wasn't a hallucination—I could see bare feet standing out from a tattered dress. Her hands tightly gripped the hinged door. She stood there silently warning me, quietly letting me know we were trespassing. I felt my breath leave me, petrified to the spot. Her eyes made my blood run cold; I was afraid even to move. What was I supposed to do?

"Omhet?" Khloe called, worried.

I turned to her, frightened. "Khloe." I pointed toward the door, but there was nobody there. "We have to leave *now*!" I grabbed her hand and pulled hard, making her trip when she tried to stand.

"What is going on?" she screamed.

"I just saw a woman," I breathed, running toward the hallway opposite of where I'd seen the vision. I could barely think or talk. We needed to find an exit immediately.

"We'll get lost if we keep going this way!" She kept running behind me. "Omhet, stop! We must go back the way we came!"

At the end of the hallway, an open door led outside, but when I saw the precipice waiting for us, I gasped and tried to stop. I would've slipped had it not been for Khloe, who pulled me back in by the shoulders. The bridge leading to the palace's garden had fallen. There was no way out in this direction. The other doors probably led to old dormitories or kitchens, making the only way out back where we came from, as Khloe said.

"Surely you imagine it. Please calm down!" Khloe loudly said.

My hands raked my face nervously. "Her look was a warning. We shouldn't be here!"

"What are you so afraid of? You wanted to face the dragon in winter. Well, here's your chance." And then she laughed.

Not like this, not like this—Not like this!

A roar made us scream, shutting up instantly. Our eyes tried hard to find the source, or at least where it had come from, but it was too dark. The end of the hallway was barely visible. We weren't able to see anything.

"Oh, *s*-shit," I stammered, trying my best to keep my voice down. "I think it heard you."

"It's not true..." she whispered, suddenly minding her volume. "Omhet, it can't be true..."

"I don't want to sound like a pessimist, but I think we're about to find out."

She said nothing. Her hand pressed against her heart as if she could stop it from beating out of her chest. We stayed quiet, knowing the dragon was some-where—anywhere, everywhere—waking up from its slumber.

We stared at the ledge we were standing on, gauging the gap between us and what remained of the broken bridge as well as the ravine below it. We knew if we jumped, there was a possibility of breaking our legs, and we would sorely regret it. We needed our legs now more than ever to run.

"Now what?" whispered Khloe.

I stared at her, incredulous. She was the one who had wanted to go exploring, not me. Why was she asking me what to do?

Another growl rebounded within the crumbled walls, closer than it had been before. As a scream left us, I almost retched when the beast's stench clogged all of my senses. We crouched low, trying everything to avoid the smoke that was visible through the grand room's door.

We were screwed.

"Maybe it's a trick. *M*-maybe it really doesn't exist, and Tiara is doing this to scare us," stammered Khloe.

The darkness was broken when a pair of yellow eyes opened and focused on us. My body tensed from the cold that shivered through me despite the infernal heat emanating from the open jaws of the dragon.

My body acted on its own, stepping away from the beast and toward the edge behind us that threatened to eat us just as the dragon did. Khloe's squeal was deafening when she hugged me close, trembling from head to toe. I barely felt it, my whole being concentrated on the only danger worse than the one behind me. And even though it couldn't get close enough—its body was too big to fit through the hallway. Its intimidating presence, larger than life, overpowered us from a distance.

"Oh, my skies," I whined, incapable of anything else to say or do. "It's real."

When the dragon roared again, it was as if time suddenly sprinted toward the finish line, and my body recovered. The dragon's heated breath prompted immediate action. Looking back, I knew we had no other choice—we had to jump.

Grabbing Khloe's hand hard, I pulled and pushed her to the edge. Her desperate screams echoed through the halls. With a death grip, I hadn't known I was capable of, I held her hand and coaxed her to lower her body over the edge. I slowly descended to the floor and lay my body flat to shorten the distance of the drop she dangled over.

"I'm going to let you go," I warned her while she frantically stared at me. "You'll fall on a bush. It won't be much help but try to flex your legs. I rather you damage anywhere else on your body than that."

She yelled, "What?! Omhet, no! you need to jump with me!"

"Don't wait for me," I ordered, then let her hand go.

She screamed as she fell. I couldn't see if she'd survived because I had to stand—

I gasped hard.

The dragon was in front of me.

It was looking into my eyes—penetrating my soul with his gaze. My mind told me to run like hell, but I froze for a moment. I was terrified, but also, I was—

I was fascinated.

I wondered if the dragon was as curious as I was—but it was not. It was the opposite. The dragon was settling for the worst, and I realized late when the smoke was already coming out of his mouth.

I immediately dive to the floor just inside the doorway. Fire flew through where I'd just dropped Khloe from. I tried to take cover, crouching low in what corner I found, screaming in agony when fire licked my arm. I had to rip off my jacket to put it out, feeling it eating my wrist alive. Once the flames were out, I ran and went through the first door open I found, coughing from the cloud of smoke that choked me.

I'd never run so fast, not even during training. It felt like I was flying through the halls while the dragon gave chase—a great motivator for exercise, joked a corner of my mind in its panic. I couldn't help looking back, wanting to see if the dragon was still chasing me. While doing that, I managed to trip on a rock, and my feet got tangled, making me fall. On a rock! Seriously? I gasped, seeing the exact moment when the beast noticed me. Like a freaking lizard, it ran toward me, though not very quickly due to the crumbling roof and tight walls, but it was still quick enough to outrun my weak body. So, I got up and ran without giving myself time to process what I was doing.

My feet slipped as I went, but I remained upright. I could swear the dragon was breathing down my neck, almost close enough to eat me alive. Shit! I wanted to shout, but nothing came out of my mouth except my harsh breaths when I took a turn down a hall. The dragon hit the wall where I'd been a second ago, its jaws snapping on air. Then I saw the dead end—no freaking way! —and without thinking about it, I started to climb the debris that blocked my way. The dragon was right there, but when it chomped this time, the force of its mouth pushed the debris so hard I went over the top of the pile and tumbled to the floor of an abandoned library.

My back hit the ground, and it took me a second to move. A second that seemed eternal. I dragged myself toward the first nook I could get to, breathing in the dust and feeling the scrapes of the stone and debris. I hid behind a bookcase as my eyes hurriedly scanned for the beast. The library was destroyed beyond repair, the roof split in two and open to the sky. Scaling the wall to get to the hole in the ceiling, however, would be impossible with how far the fire of the dragon's breath could reach through the gap I'd fallen through. I could stay here until it forgot about me, maybe find an exit in this broken labyrinth—

Or maybe the dragon would find me first, making it impossible to escape.

The dragon broke the rest of the entrance down when it wedged its body through, and I tightened my lips in hopes it wouldn't hear me breathing. I stared above, saying goodbye to my life and everyone I knew.

I closed my eyes, trying to control my breathing.

So, this is it? I thought, not feeling scared or sad. Surprisingly, I gave a tired smile. Come on! It's not over until it is over. It's not over until I'm dead.

I dared to peek at it while it lit a bookcase on fire on the other side of the room. Oh, it's pretty upset, I see. But sadly, I can't stay to apologize for interrupting his beauty sleep. Deciding against waiting out this morbid game of hide and seek, I slowly stood and edged toward where I'd come from. With my eyes glued to the dragon, I crept out, walking backward. I could feel the ground trembling with everything the beast destroyed, burned, and threw on the ground with rage. Then I saw its tail whip around.

Well, maybe running wouldn't be so bad.

I turned and ran back down the hallway. The problem, however, was that I didn't know where to go. Where the hell had I come from to make it here? Desperation screamed in my head.

The dragon heard me run away. It freaking heard me! Its legs thundered around the same corner I'd just turned, leaving me no choice but to hide behind a door I managed to open and close softly. I saw it sniffing the air through a crack, looking for its meal. I stood very still, waiting. Then it turned the other way.

I wouldn't be able to go back to the hallway, so I turned and, quickly surveying the area, saw a spiral staircase leading to a tower, and I hurriedly ascended them. I stepped through the door at the top of the stairs, adrenaline still running high. A small room greeted me, and after taking it in as fast as possible, I found what looked like a safe hiding place—a chest in a remote corner of the room. Opening it, I saw clean sheets. Grimacing because I was sure I was going to soil them, I got in and closed it.

I would finally wait until it went back to sleep to leave this place for good.

Chapter 12

This time, the hallway had no exit, and the doors didn't open. I could see a creature, but it wasn't a dragon or a human. It walked down the hallway even though it had no feet, or at least that's how it seemed to be. A dark cloud covered it like a specter from hell. I froze when I noticed I had nowhere to run as it walked toward me. Its skin looked like scales, and its eyes were yellow, but its body shape was of a very tall woman.

"Unpredictable," she said. It sounded like multiple voices speaking at once. I shuddered, but it was all I could do. "I don't like it."

Her yellow eyes penetrated mine, and I wanted to ask so many things, but I could only say "Tiara" in a whisper—more of a confirmation than a question.

The being abruptly stopped. "Leave Andebeck, Omhet," she ordered with such a terrifying tone of voice I wanted to scream. I gasped when the specter got closer, right in front of me. "This place is not for you."

"Get rid of me, then," I challenged, faking bravery.

She turned her face to the side in a frightening way, and I saw that her hands had claws as she began to reach for my neck.

It's a nightmare, I repeated to myself over and over. But no nightmare I'd ever had before restricted my breathing in a way that made this strangling feel real.

"You don't know what you're saying," she growled, digging her fingers into my skin. "You don't even have a clue..."

I couldn't breathe or defend myself. I tried to scream in my mind to wake up, fighting fear and sleep, until I hit my forehead against a wall. I moaned, stroking my forehead, and then I touched my neck and realized that none of it had been real. Was I obsessed with a legend? *Damn*, that nightmare was the most realistic I've ever had in my life.

I was disoriented by the darkness and the oven-like heat that permeated where I was until I raised my hands and collided with the top of the trunk. Slowly I realized that I was hiding from a freaking dragon inside a chest—of course, I was going to feel suffocated.

Wait a minute...

At what point did I lose consciousness? Why? How long have I been here? I raised the cover high enough to see, holding my breath, trying not to make a noise. I opened it a little more, looking at the room that I hadn't wasted time studying before. It was a circular room with a small door, a place where no dragon could be in or come through. I opened the cover and got out without making a sound.

I was about to leave, but then I wondered why the door was slightly open. I thought I had closed it. I looked around and saw another small door leading to a bathroom, and across the room, there was a table with a mirror full of feminine accessories. This room looked normal. It was clean, without any broken debris. It was as if it was not part of the ruins or, worse, as if someone lived in this place. I saw the window was open, with curtains moving slowly in the night breeze...

Night. *Shit!* They were going to kill me when I got back.

I leaned out the window and saw the entire city, beautifully lit, in the distance. Then I sensed a movement next to me, causing me to freeze. Closed curtains surrounded a bed. I watched the curtains for a few minutes but saw nothing move. But there was someone, and I could feel it. I stared at the bed more, finally seeing the curtains move slightly.

I didn't have many options, so I took the first one I found, grabbing a pair of scissors from the table. I began to approach the bed with the scissors raised. My breathing was controlled while my heart was racing in suspense. I could imagine Tiara, with yellow eyes like the dragon. I could even hear her voice in my mind.

I dared to place my hand on the curtain. I moved it and raised my improvised weapon above my head despite my nerves.

And then...

I didn't attack. Instead, I lowered my hand.

There was the woman I'd seen earlier, with hair the color of sunset flames and freckles all over her face.

I blew the air out of my lungs as if to expel all the fear that had invaded me. The woman was lying down, and I thought she didn't have any clothes on because I couldn't see anything on her skin except the silk sheet that covered her. She was asleep, but... she looked sick. She was fatigued, I could tell, and her reddish hair and skin were drenched with sweat as if she had a fever. I frowned, worried. I knew who she was. I had heard so many stories about her.

She was the most important person in the history of this kingdom.

"It's an honor to meet you, Princess Laila Blume," I murmured so as not to wake her up.

The beautiful woman was the lost Princess of Andebeck. Despite everything, I had to smile because she was alive. I knelt on the ground, looking closer at her. I even dared to place my hand on her forehead but withdrew it immediately. It was burning with such heat that it bothered my skin after I touched hers. Laila opened her eyes, tiredly searching for the person who had disturbed her troubled sleep. I held my breath in anticipation, waiting for her reaction. But I couldn't help myself. I had to say something.

"Hey," I whispered, my voice shaking a little. "Are you okay?"

Was that really the only thing I could think to ask her? It was evident that she was not. She looked at me, and her eyes widened with that little energy she had at her disposal.

"What..." she whispered, frowning. It seemed as if she believed I was a mirage because she reached out with her hand and touched my face.

I held my breath. Her hand was soft but so hot that it didn't seem normal. I raised mine and placed it over hers, squeezing it a bit.

"I'm real."

Sooner than I was ready, she immediately withdrew her hand. I could see in her eyes that she wanted to run away, but she was so weak she couldn't even sit up.

"I'm here to help you," I told her, trying to calm her down. "Don't be afraid. Please don't scream—I don't want you to wake up the dragon."

She closed her eyes and opened them again, forcing herself to stay awake.

"Kill me," she cried out in a strangled voice. "Please."

I frowned anxiously. This girl was not okay.

"May I carry you?" I asked, more scared of the dragon than of her. I didn't want her to scream and draw the dragon's attention to make me its dinner. "I can take you to safety—"

"No!" she yelled, causing me to step back. "The dragon will be wherever I am. I have to stay. Go—"

That was the last thing she said before she collapsed on the bed again, unconscious. The princess needed immediate help. I was afraid that she would die in front of me.

I wasn't going to leave her alone—I couldn't. The legend itself was alive. Was she going to be defeated by a fever after such a great miracle? At least, that's what I wondered as I started looking for something that could control her fever.

I closed the door to avoid any noise escaping the room. I rummaged through some drawers for anything that might help—medicine, food, or even a hand fan. I wanted to leave the ruins and take her to a doctor, but after her anxious words, I felt I could not move her until I knew what was happening. Would the dragon go wherever she went? Better to be safe before causing more chaos in Andebeck. They already had enough to deal with, and I had only added to the chaos since my arrival.

I went into the small bathroom and was surprised that everything worked. I filled a bowl with cool water. I opened all the windows and tied the curtains back as best I could so the breeze could come in and caress her skin. Then I moistened a small cloth in the bowl, kneeling next to her and wetting her forehead. She squeezed her eyes shut a little tighter but didn't wake up.

Under the calm I found while caring for her, my thoughts took flight. What had happened to Khloe? I did not know if she survived or was lying dead where she fell. I was worried about her—I needed to be certain she was okay. And what about the dragon? Such a large beast couldn't disappear as if it had never been in these ruins. It had to be around, looking for its prey. My body shuddered at the thought that that prey was me. I did not want to tempt my fate with what the tremendous beast was hungry for *everything*. I better stay here, where I could do something more than scream or run for my life.

I took care of the princess all night. I rewet the cloth every five minutes. It heated up as if her forehead was a burner. Even her breathing was hot as if she had boiling water in her mouth. This girl might not live to tell her tale—it was impossible for a human to endure such high temperatures. How could I leave her at the mercy of such an illness? I wanted to take her away from here and find a doctor but getting her out of the castle meant facing the dragon. I didn't want to push my luck, so I just accepted what little I could do and focused on doing it. That was more prudent, wasn't it?

I begged Krea to help with the speedy recovery of this living miracle. I hated the feeling that she was going to die in front of me. *For the skies*. After so long, I remembered my mother's religious, closing my eyes and saying a prayer she'd taught me. I never thought I'd give in to prayers but feeling closer to my family was the only thing that kept me at peace for the rest of the night.

The rays of the morning sun bothered me, but I tried to ignore them. I was so tired I wanted to keep sleeping. Besides, my head was too comfortable on the bed even though the rest of my body was on the floor.

The floor? I wondered as I startled awake, feeling like an idiot and the worst caretaker ever to exist. A great knight would've stayed up all night, maybe even killed the dragon and brought its head to the minister. I had simply fallen asleep in between desperate prayers. Brilliant.

I rubbed my eyes, looking for the damsel on her bed and then looking for her desperately all around her room. She was nowhere to be seen. All that remained on the bed were the sweat-stained sheets in disarray. As I stood, the morning rays shone through the windows, making me squint. In a vain attempt to find her, I rummaged everywhere I could, only to come up empty-handed.

But I did find a note nailed to the wall with a knife. Ripping it off, I read its contents.

Leave and don't return. I vow the dragon will not attack if you quietly exit the premises, but I cannot promise the same if you were to return. This will be my only warning.

I would've preferred she stayed and talked to me because I had so many questions I wanted to ask her. It was just my luck that she would disappear, leaving behind an ominous note. I wanted to laugh, but I held it in. I found a pen and wrote my own message on the back of her letter.

I cannot accept that this is your home and your circumstance. I could see the pain in your eyes. Let me help you. I will return, even though I'm scared of the dragon. I don't give up easily, especially when I know that someone needs help. If there's anyone who can recognize a call for help, it's me.

Omhet Espinho.

Getting out of the ruined castle was a confusing mission. Even though I managed to walk through the hallways without drawing attention, every little sound made me jump. Deep down, I kept hoping Princess Laila would suddenly appear. I stopped in the middle of the main vestibule and looked behind me one more time before leaving, waiting for her voice to stop me or at least give me a chance to introduce myself.

Nothing happened. "You're stubborn," I said with a little smile, "but I'm worse."

As if in answer, footsteps echoed nearby. Turning toward the sound, I expected to see her, but all I caught were the strands of her red hair retreating around a corner. That was enough for me. I smiled again, knowing perfectly well that I would see her again.

CHAPTER 13

Entering through one of the palace's main gates was out of the question. For that reason, I hid behind one of the bushes in the garden. Reaching the rose labyrinth was not so complicated but getting to my room would be the actual mission.

Hiding as best I could, the rose's thorns tangled around my arm, making me hiss. It was only a scratch, but it was in the same place where the dragon had burned me. I plucked the rose with attitude and threw it to the side. I immediately regretted throwing it on the floor. If anyone saw how I treated the native flower of Andebeck, I could get into serious trouble. The flower symbolizes its flag and the reflection of the Blume surname. The rose looked a deep wine-red color, but when you got closer, it looked white inside the petal—a unique and significant beauty.

There was chaos everywhere, especially on the towers, with soldiers armed with muskets and an annoying alarm that seemed to announce the end of the world. Even the kingdom's warriors were gathered in marching positions as if a war was about to happen.

I snorted mockingly, knowing this was all because they'd heard the dragon yesterday and were still expecting it to attack at any moment. Generals had ordered an entire cavalry to patrol the streets of Andebeck, and the most influential leaders were under surveillance and had constant security within the palace.

They were so distracted I was able to sneak up to one of the service doors. There was not a single servant in sight. It seemed they had been evacuated. So, I ran down the hall, holding my injured arm and praying that no one would see me.

It was weird to see the entire interior empty like a museum, but at the same time, I considered it a blessing because I got to my room and went inside, pressing my back against the door when it latched into place. I closed my eyes and recovered my breath. I needed a moment—

A harsh pounding on the door made me jump, and when I looked, I saw it was a knife that had been thrown next to my head.

"It's me!" I yelled, raising my hands.

Of the three guardians, only Cheick was there, and he stood in front of me with such a violent face that I was more afraid of him than I was of my nightmare about Tiara.

"I know," Cheikh said and pulled the knife from where it had stuck in the wooden door.

That answer didn't make me feel better.

Well, there went my gratitude for being alive. Just by looking at Cheikh, it was easy to discern that my death would not come through the beast of legends it would be brought by this nanny in front of me.

I tried to be polite and ignore the anger on his face. Or was that surprise? A bit of both? You never knew when it came to Cheikh.

"Hi." I greeted him with a smile. "How are you? Nice morning, huh?"

He didn't answer. Instead, Cheikh grabbed me by the shirt, shaking me with anger. "Where the hell have you been? We've been looking everywhere for you!"

Escaping his firm grip, a slight whine escaped my lips when I felt the wounds on my arm. I held it delicately against my chest, trying to protect it as best as possible while the agonizing pain invaded my senses. Honestly, I'd forgotten how badly I'd been hurt because the pain had been blocked by adrenaline.

"I-I was with Khloe taking a stroll—nothing else," I stuttered. Lying had never been my forte, so I knew he didn't buy it. But I said nothing else, simply choosing to observe him analyzing me.

He frowned and grabbed the arm I'd been cradling. "Are these burns?"

His question, a murmur full of things I couldn't decipher, paralyzed me. It was his eyes that made me fearful. "It was an accident" was the only thing my mind could come up with.

His eyes filled with surprise when he understood what I meant. "It was real?" I tried to interrupt him, but his strong voice beat me to it. "Omhet, you woke up the bloody dragon?"

I jumped from his yell, taking a step back, trying to steer clear of his fury. So that settled it—everyone had heard the dragon roar. Gods, now I really was screwed. "Cheikh, it was an accident. I didn't even want to—"

He cut me off. "Of all your stupid stunts, this has to be the worst! By Krea, Omhet, what is wrong with you? Do you even know what you've done?"

I couldn't answer—I merely stared at the ground in sudden shame. This was worse than when my father berated me.

"That beast could have slayed us all and destroyed Andebeck all over again!"

I couldn't defend myself if he didn't let me speak. I tried again, wanting to explain, but I got interrupted by knocks on the door.

Tensing, I held the knob so no one could come through. "You can't say anything to anyone!" I furiously whispered.

"Open the door," ordered Cheikh, but I leaned against it.

"No! No one can know."

"Omhet, I know you're in there. Open the door." It was Marcus, an order I knew I couldn't ignore.

I stared at Cheikh.

"What did you tell them?"

Marcus continued knocking, and I cursed through my teeth, eyes closed in despair. They were going to break down the door if you didn't comply.

"What was I supposed to tell them?" Cheikh gritted his teeth, trying his best not to raise his voice. "I told them you weren't here."

"Perfect," I said and ran off to the bathroom.

"Omh—Shit!" he growled, trying to decide between chasing after me and opening the door. "What are you—?"

The door banged open, interrupting him mid-sentence. I wasted no time as I heard quite a few people invading my room. I took off my clothes as fast as I could, and just before they barged into the bathroom, I managed to put on a robe.

"Minister." I bowed and then finished tying my robe in place while trying to look embarrassed. "My apologies, I was just finishing—"

"Where were you, Omhet?" he cut me off. There were guards behind his back, and his sister was beside him.

Swallowing hard, I tried discreetly kicking my clothes behind the bathroom door. I couldn't wash my hair or face properly, so the least I could do was hide the rest of the damning evidence. This was a disaster already.

"I was getting ready to take a bath..." the threatening way Marcus looked at me made me shut up, clear my throat, and start over. "I was in the infirmary last night. I fell asleep because of the sedatives they gave me. I'm sorry..."

"In the infirmary?" repeated Marcus.

One of the guards said something to Marcus, but it was whispered in Andebeck's old language, which I didn't fully understand. I know he said something like "was searched" and "infirmary" in the sentence, implying that they had looked for me everywhere. I tried to look casual, but Marcus's sister glared at me with piercing eyes, which made me nervous.

"Everybody out," Marcus ordered, raising his hand to interrupt his guard.

His sister turned and glared at him.

Marcus looked at her more calmly, with obvious affection and respect.

"Ele e ympozlol," she said.

I repeated her words in my mind trying to translate them.

"Trust me," Marcus replied. It seemed as if he didn't want to argue with her in front of me.

"Mo-zompyo," she concluded, and with a wave of her hand, she ordered the guards to follow her out. She bumped her shoulder into Cheikh without pausing to apologize. She was furious.

Marcus waited and then cleared his throat when he saw that everyone had left except for Cheikh.

"I'm not going anywhere," Cheikh said.

Marcus looked irritated for a moment but quickly made his face neutral again. Cheikh was overly protective, and it seemed unnecessary to me—Marcus didn't look like a person who would kill even a fly. I tried to be patient because I knew I deserved this and more. I just hoped I could control my mouth because I didn't want anyone to know what I had discovered.

"It stinks—" he started. I blinked repeatedly. Was he trying to offend me? "Like ashes and dust. A peculiar smell, don't you think?" I swallowed deeply, looking for any answer, but he raised his hand, interrupting my thoughts. "I'll give you a minute," he concluded, leaving the bathroom and slamming the door.

It took me longer than a minute, of course, and half the time I was under the stream of water, I wondered what the hell he would say. I examined my arm, seeing the burn from the elbow to the wrist. It didn't look too serious, but it was red and burned like hell due to the water. I put on a long-sleeve shirt and buttoned it up, moaning a little when I felt the fabric brush against my skin. When something caught my attention, I even looked at myself in the mirror, confirming that I had just a few minor cuts and bruises.

Finger marks across my neck.

I leaned closer to the mirror, not believing what I saw. No one had grabbed me by the neck in the last couple of days, not even Karl. I touched it, noticing that the finger marks were thin and long, like a woman's...

As if the nightmare had been real.

"What the hell..." I whispered, feeling my heart pound.

"You have so much to explain, boy," Marcus said behind me, making me spin around.

I hadn't heard him come in, much less get so close to me.

" I can explain everything except this," I said, closing the top buttons of my shirt. "I don't know where the marks came from—it was just a nightmare. She must be real... Tiara..."

"Tiara ceased to exist a century ago, so please avoid any more superstitions, understood?" I wanted to contradict him but kept quiet. "Come with me."

I left the room with him, and Cheikh followed behind us. I didn't know if I was more intimidated by Marcus or Cheikh. I thought Marcus would lead me to a torture room or whatever terrible madness existed in this place, but no—he led me to a balcony with a small round table for two, with tea and appetizers already set out for us. I got so confused that I remained standing near the door even though Marcus sat down and pointed to the seat across from his.

"What are you doing?" I asked. No matter how hard I tried to understand the minister, he was a mystery that made my mind crazy with so many questions.

"They have to see you with me, or they'll think it was you who caused all this," he said, gesturing to the edge of the balcony.

Then I saw the courtyard full of guards, kingdom representatives, and servants moving from one end to the other agitatedly. Some stopped to look our way as if they had been expecting me.

I sat across from Marcus, so stiff I couldn't feel comfortable. I started fiddling with the string bracelet on my wrist—

"Relax," he told me, preparing his tea calmly. "Make yourself a cup of tea. I'm curious to know how they drink it in Glacier."

I blew out my breath, trying to relax, and looked at Cheikh for help. He stood in the doorway, his stiff face watching me like he wanted to punch me for the mess I'd made. I stopped looking out over the balcony, noticing that the more seconds passed, the more they stopped gawking. So, I began to speak, at first babbling but then more clearly. I explained that tea was rarely made in Glacier because the king was addicted to coffee instead.

"Guillermo sounds like a very admired man," Marcus commented.

How did he manage to hide his anger with me so well? I could sense it in his eyes but not in his voice. My eyes strayed beyond the balcony railing again, noticing how they seemed to be whispering about me down there.

"Look at me," Marcus scolded and then drank more tea. He took a deep breath and continued as if nothing had happened. "Relax your shoulders and drink the tea as naturally as possible."

I tried, but it was not as easy as he made it seem. I felt he was expecting more from me—maybe more stories about Glacier or coffee—but I couldn't keep talking about nonsense. I wanted to end this. I wanted to go back to my bedroom now. His presence overwhelmed me.

"Let's get to the point, then," he said, putting the tea on the table, and straightening up. "Yesterday, shortly after noon, the roar of the dragon was heard. We haven't heard that sound since the festival of the lost princess.

The festival of the lost princess? I had no idea when that occurred, but I didn't ask for more details. I didn't want to imagine the terrible fear that must have invaded the city when they heard the dragon yesterday.

Marcus continued. "The streets of Andebeck were evacuated, with the vast majority going to underground shelters. And here in the palace, all the kingdoms readied for a fight. We thought we would see the dragon at any moment, and without a doubt, it would be our end."

My mouth fell open, not knowing what to say. I just knew that I had to say something.

"I can imagine," I agreed, trying to be sympathetic and hide the guilt I felt when listening to how his night went.

"Yes, you have to imagine it because I doubt you remember it—You weren't here." His face, in an instant, changed. He placed his arms on the table, leaning closer to me, his low voice filled with rage and stiffness. "We ran a tally in the courtyard for everyone present—kingdom representatives, courts, maids, soldiers, everyone! And do you know who was the only one who didn't show up?"

"Let me guess—"

"I've been trying for days to prevent everything from getting out of control with your shenanigans, and now this?" He took a knife in his hand and saw Cheikh slowly move his own toward his sword. I squeezed my hand on the cup in front of me. But then Marcus began to put jam on a piece of bread with his knife without looking at me. "Everyone thinks it was you who provoked the beast. So, explain to me if this is true because I am trying to prevent animosity from happening against you and your kingdom, but the evidence is not helping you."

Amid my disbelief, I laughed from nerves and fear. They were all correct—everybody. This was not looking good for Glacier or me. What could I do to prevent this disaster from happening? Well, the only thing I could do was deny everything. So, that was what I did.

"Sir, I... was sleeping."

I'm a dead man.

Marcus raised his eyebrows, took a bite of his bread, and chewed it slowly.

"Sleeping?" he repeated as if trying to confirm the statement.

"I was with Khloe at noon, walking with her through the garden. You can ask her if you want to. Then I visited the infirmary due to Karl's beating me up and fell asleep on one of the gurneys."

My nerves got worse the more I lied to him, but I had to keep going. If I stopped giving him a plausible reason for my absence, the whole story would be in vain.

Marcus looked at Cheikh as if searching for the truth or the lie in his eyes, but my guardian was closely watching me, close to shaking his head in disappointment.

"With all due respect, minister," I said, trying to make him believe me. "Do you really think I could face a dragon and survive? Maybe Karl could, but me? It sounds a bit... silly."

I didn't say anything else after that. If I hadn't convinced him, then I would accept what was to come. But I couldn't say any more. I was already burying myself in my own grave with this mess.

If the people in the city found out that I had awoken the dragon, they wouldn't expel me. They would kill me!

Marcus's silence lasted so long that I thought I hadn't been able to convince him, but then he sighed, finally nodding.

"It's not me you have to convince," his statement caught me off guard, but I didn't dare to question anything. "That's reason enough for me to consider the matter done." Then he stood. It was evident that he didn't believe me, but at the same time, he seemed satisfied with the explanation. "Just recite it in front of the mirror until it sounds better."

"Minister?" I called, getting up from my chair.

I followed Marcus, but he seemed to be done talking. I felt more confused than at the start of our conversation. It seemed more dangerous to me that he knew I was lying and took it so calmly than the fact that the lie had convinced him.

Something very strange was happening.

"I won't be able to protect you from the beasts that stalk you," he said, placing his hand on the door. Before he left, he looked at me once more. "But please let me know when you find the courage to tell me the truth. I'll be looking forward to it."

I wanted to insist on my story, but he raised his hand, interrupting me. "If you don't want to, I understand, but remember, Omhet, you are here to save Andebeck and nothing more."

I swallowed deeply and nodded.

"When you trust me, I'll be waiting for you, and maybe next time, I'll prepare that coffee you talked about so much."

Without saying anything else, he finally took his leave.

"You are in grave danger, young Omhet," Cheikh said, standing beside me. "All of Glacier's soldiers won't be able to protect you from what you're causing."

I turned around and looked at him, determined. "So be it," I replied with an attitude, "but nobody will scare me out of here—no matter how much they try to intimidate me." I touched my neck with my fingers, and it felt cold as a corpse where whatever had touched me and left these marks...

Incredibly, it seemed that the dragon was the least of my problems.

Chapter 14

"We have to talk," Cheikh told me.

"I need to see Khloe first," I interrupted him.

"She's fine," Shin said, "but she hasn't left her room since she returned to the palace."

I angrily released a breath. I knew absolutely nothing about the princess other than she was safe and remained out of sight. It was frustrating—how had she returned to the palace? I desperately needed to confirm what had happened when I let go of her.

"Omhet," called Lucas, "let me see your arm."

So much happening at the same time.

I sat on my bed, took my shirt off, and showed Lucas the wound on my arm while ignoring Cheikh. He explained there would be no scar left behind when it healed, partly thanks to the shirt I'd been wearing. It had taken the brunt of the burn. In any case, I needed it to recover quickly to avoid anyone seeing it, which was why I easily complied when Lucas applied salve on the burn. With nothing else to do, while waiting for his task to be done, my eyes trained on Shin, who was pacing back and forth in my room. Nervously and exasperatedly, I let my head fall on the deb frame with a sigh. My guardians were worse than ever.

"Stop pacing," I growled.

"They're all talking about you out there," Shin replied. "And do you want me to calm down??"

I didn't know how I would return to training the next day. I was scared people would start asking questions that would make my lie crumble into dust. *It's not me you have to convince,* Marcus had said, and with every minute that passed, it made more sense.

"Your nervousness won't be of any help," I argued.

"I said we have to talk," repeated Cheikh, and this time we all stared at him.

The three of them looked agitated. It was then that I realized that the least I could do was give them an explanation.

Getting comfortable in my bed, I took a deep breath. "All right, I'll tell you everything."

With them getting comfortable around me—Lucas at the foot of my bed, Shin on a chair he'd dragged from the table, arms and chest resting on the back of it, and Cheikh reclining against the bedpost, unwilling to sit. I told them everything from start to finish. Even the part where escaping with Khloe was my idea, thinking about how innocent and convenient it would have been to have Khloe as a friend. Or so I'd thought before Khloe decided she wanted to explore a myth to confirm it was true. What had begun as an incredible plan to become allies ended like an expedition to hell. I was still processing what had happened—a scared princess lying sick in her bed. A dragon that had, out of nowhere, appeared. A race through the ruins and a nightmare as real as life itself. My hand caressed the dark marks on my neck when I spoke of it. Even Lucas shifted slightly away from me, and Cheikh tensed when the story unfolded.

"Tiara?" Lucas said, frowning. "No one ever speaks that name. We've all been told that she disappeared after the dragon attached."

"Maybe she's not as real as you and me, but when I stepped foot inside those ruins, it all felt sufficiently real to me," I shuddered. How else could these marks on my neck be explained?

"You're making it up," said an incredulous Cheikh.

I huffed and let my hands fall back on my lap. When I finally told the truth, they couldn't believe me.

"Oh sure, I also burned myself with my own hands."

"How does Laila look? Like the old paintings?" Shin was the only one excited by everything, it seemed.

It took me a moment to answer. I looked at the open balcony door, losing myself in the ruins that could be seen in the distance. I described how her red hair looked like a soft summer sunset that painted the sky a deep orange mixed with the sun's rays.

"Oh, so he's a poet now," Lucas joked, interrupting my description.

"I'm trying to explain that she's real." A small smile crossed my lips. "The painting is nothing in comparison. Did you know that she had freckles all over her face? How do they miss something so crucial? And... and her eyes—her emerald eyes—it's impossible to look at anything else when she looks at you." I hushed when I noticed their looks. "What?"

"I've never seen Omhet's eyes shine bright for a girl," Lucas chuckled, but before he could say something else, I kicked him hard enough to make him fall off the bed.

"It's not like that! I'm not talking about her in that way."

"In what way?" Shin playfully added.

I blushed and avoided their eyes. Better to stop describing her more than necessary before they get the wrong idea. "She's not going well. You should've seen her—her clothes and appearance, her eyes—she looked... tattered, and with every breath, she seemed to be wishing for her death—"

"That's enough," Cheikh shut me up, moving from the bedpost.

We looked at Cheikh, waiting for him to say something, anything. Still, he remained quiet for a while, analyzing the situation. He seemed overwhelmed by emotions he could not put into words just yet, and I couldn't blame him. They were all still angry with me, and of course, I knew why. I couldn't imagine how they felt when they woke up and noticed I was nowhere to be found, immediately followed by the roar of a fabled beast. It must have been alarming to have their only and most important responsibility—to keep an eye on me and protect my hair's breadth from failing. I couldn't imagine what it felt to wonder if I'd been dying to a dragon's raging fire. Cheikh had probably been close to calling the king to tell him he'd failed, and that his son had disappeared thanks to a nap. It must have been a daunting experience for them to go through.

"You..." Cheick began to say and paused. I could feel his internal struggle with all the emotions and thoughts clouding him. "You've woken the most feared beast this city has ever faced, fooled death, put Ettezi's princes at risk—"

I had de audacity to try to interrupt him to explain that it was Khloe's idea, not mine, but he gave me no space to do so.

"And you managed to survive facing the dragon with a mere burn. To top it off, you've seen the ruins of old Andebeck and the sorceress in your dreams. Why the hell are you so special?"

I shrugged, "Why does it matter if I'm special because I survived? Princess Laila is stuck there." I pointed out the window where the ruins could be seen.

"And that's where she'll stay for seven more months," he stated while I gave a dazed look of bewilderment. "We're not going to talk about the princess, or the dragon, or the sorceress—"

"Cheikh—"

"That's an order!" he yelled, getting closer to me. I couldn't look anywhere but at him. "Or else I assure you I'll be the first one to let your father know and have him pull you by the ear out of this place."

I tried to answer. I opened my mouth, intending to argue, and closed it again. That was a low blow—the lowest of them all.

"You can't—"

"Give me one more reason to, Omhet Espinho," he growled, forgoing my tittle—a silent yet powerful statement of how much respect he'd lost for me.

He finally moved away from my face. I don't know if he did it when he saw the surprise on my face or my inability to answer him because of his abruptness.

Oh, I'm not done with you. I got up and pasted my other two guardians, chasing Cheikh into his small room. "What am I supposed to do then? She is the priority of this nonsense competition."

"Omhet," Shin called me. Although he didn't say anything else, it was a warning. I needed to stop, but I couldn't.

"Your life is my priority. Andebeck is responsible for the lost princess, that beast, and everything else in between. Understood?"

I couldn't reply—I merely tightened the grip in anger. No, I couldn't agree with that. I couldn't just abandon her, or ignore her existence, not after I swore I would be back. Wasn't I here to help? I did not, in fact, understand.

"If it had been me stuck in those ruins, you would've come to rescue me," I angrily spat.

Lucas put his hand on my shoulder, trying to get me out of the small room. The two behind me desperately wanted me to shut the hell up.

"It's been ninety-nine years—a few more months won't hurt her." He stepped in front of me, so close that I took steps back.

"But—"

"But nothing," he growled again, stopping next to the door to his room. "Thanks to your exploits, you verified that the legend is true, right? If you really want to save her, now is the perfect time for you to train harder. But above all, stop being a *damn* headache for the ministers, especially me. Now go fulfill the only thing your father has asked you and get a fucking ally!"

And just like that, he shut the door, almost hitting my face.

"Seven months is absurd," I muttered to myself. *Especially knowing how sick she is.*

The princess didn't need a knight in shining armor to rescue her in seven months. She needed us *now* to save her from her doing. The crown didn't matter, and neither did the prize. Why couldn't Cheikh understand the urgency of the matter was of utmost importance, more than this competition was?

I couldn't just stay here and do nothing.

Standing before the dining room door, I could hear chairs being dragged and muffled chatter beyond it. It was dinner time, and while it seemed things would carry on normally, the very air was tinged with fright. Guards for each kingdom stood near every window and through the hallway, ready and armed for anything.

Oh, by the gods, this is my fault, I thought, hesitating between going in or not.

"If you're trying to hide your guilt, you're doing a terrible job," Lucas criticized me.

I steeled myself for a few moments, then went into the dining room, trying to act naturally. The conversation halted, and those who were about to sit stopped to look at me. I ignored everyone and sat in my place, in the far corner, as usual.

"Shall I serve you the evening wine, Your Highness?" the waiter offered while I settled in.

I was at a loss for words for a moment. Since when did they serve me first? He didn't let me answer before pouring me a glass. I tried not to look around and act with the same distance as always, but I felt so many curious glances at me that I almost swallowed half of the wine in one swig.

Marcus stood up and caught everyone's attention. I looked at him, seeing that he and his sister still looked stiff despite trying to look calm.

"May this day serve as training for everyone," Marcus warned. "The adrenaline we all felt today will be nothing compared to the day of battle. Last night, the end seemed to come with a mere dragon's yawn." *Did he just try to make a joke?* Some laughed, except for me. "I hope this will serve as a learning opportunity to intensify your training and your prayer to the gods if you believe in any. Because no one knows how much time we have left, much less if we will make it to winter." The tension increased at the table, and I knew I was not the only one desperate to go and kill the damn dragon. "May the blood of the beast coat our feet."

"And so, it will be!" many agreed at once, raising their glasses while Marcus sat down.

I toasted with them and drank, thinking more of the princess than the dragon itself.

"Lord Pierre," I said to the lord on my left, and he looked at me. I thought the great man, warrior of the bow and arrow, would insult me for having called out to him, but he looked at me curiously. "Have you seen Khloe?"

"If you don't know where she is, why would I?" he answered with an attitude.

Only Karl was here in the dining room. There hasn't been a moment that I've looked in his direction, and he hasn't been looking at me. This was not a good sign, but for now, I had to ignore it. I needed to be patient and rid these men of the idea that I could have been the cause of the dragon's roar.

If one thing was clear, I was no longer invisible in this place. I couldn't decide if this was good or not. Marcus looked at me across the table and gave me a friendly smile, which felt more like a reminder than sympathy.

"Have you tried the soup?" someone asked me suddenly.

It took me a moment to confirm that it was me they were talking to and not Pierre.

"No," I said, looking at the woman to my right: Princess Alanis of Puerto Escondido.

"It's the best dish in this place," she said before eating a spoonful of the pumpkin soup.

Of all the volunteers, kingdoms, and courts I have met, I can admit that Alanis of Puerto Escondido is the easiest to recognize. Her jovial accent projected joy as if the bright sun of her island radiated into every part of her personality. Her hair entirely up allowing her face and lovely brown skin to be appreciated as she deserved. I don't know if it was a coincidence, but her skirt looked like petals from her native flower, colorful and so vast that the edge fell scattered on the floor.

"The most popular dish in Glacier is soup," I said, surprised that she was talking to me. "To not waste any wood in the stove, a cauldron was created for families to cook in chimneys." I leaned back in the chair to explain better. "Glacierian s are creative. I don't know what special gifts they have, but they make the best soup ever." I got excited as I spoke. I missed talking about Glacier. "Don't tell the king I said this, but they really are the best when cooking in cauldrons because it's the only thing they have—"

I was interrupted when I heard a laugh. Looking to my side, I saw that Pierre had been listening. Maybe I was talking too much about my kingdom. Surely, they were bored with me already.

"That's smart," said Pierre, sticking his fork through his fish without looking at me. "They created a popular dish by saving some firewood."

Alanis nodded at his words, and I realized that a quiet, normal conversation was happening between us. I didn't grasp that others were listening to the exciting chat I was having until I saw Karl suddenly get up and leave the dining room. He was angry, and I knew without a doubt that I was the cause.

"He's jealous," Alanis said.

"He always needs attention," I teased, making them both laugh. "If you'll excuse me..."

I got up too, noticing that perhaps it was attracting attention, which was the opposite of what I wanted to do right now. I couldn't help it. I had to go after Karl, especially now that I could finally talk to him alone.

"Where is she?" I asked in a firm tone, causing him to stop in the middle of the hall.

I felt him sigh as if preparing for a fight. When he turned toward me, he was not volatile, just simply annoyed. "You fractured her foot—what did you expect?"

"It was an accident—"

"I know exactly what you did, little one—you don't have to explain yourself. Khloe has never lied to me and never will," he frustratedly growled. "I owe you one for saving Khloe's life."

It had been hard for him to say that I could tell, so while I felt odd about it, I stayed still as he approached me. It was then that I noticed my guardians stepping behind me, wanting to protect me from the guy who'd attacked me yesterday.

"Could I be left alone?" I asked while they narrowed their eyes at me. "That's an order."

Without Karl noticing, I winked at them, holding back the smile that wanted to escape. I just wanted to seem more intimidating for once. Cheikh sighed but signaled Shin and Lucas to leave me be.

"We'll wait for you in your room," he stated after a quick bow.

I waited until they left to look back at Karl. "I want to see her," I told him. "I need to speak with her—"

"Oh, you misunderstood," he interrupted. "I won't allow you to ever speak to her again. I don't approve of anything that comes from your mediocre kingdom, Omar."

Omhet, dammit! "She's my friend."

"You don't need her anymore," he grunted. "Attention is all you wanted, and you got it, right?"

I didn't answer. It was true that was what my father expected of me, but that didn't mean I would abandon Khloe, especially after what had happened.

Karl snorted disdainfully. "Keep your filthy kingdom away from her, Omhet. Don't make me regret promising to pay the debt I owe you."

"You can't choose for her," I gritted out angrily.

"I'll win this competition, and you know it."

I narrowed my eyes at his words but said nothing. Before he turned to leave, he spat, "The last thing Khloe needs is a hindrance like you near us."

"You're not her owner," I said, but he kept walking. "And you very well know that if Khloe wins, it'll be you kneeling before her."

Karl halted near the stairs, wondering if it would be worth killing me on the spot. However, he continued on his way up the stairs angrily. Karl wouldn't take the lead—I wouldn't allow it, especially if it meant he would take control over Khloe's life.

And I knew there was only one way to solve all these problems, and that was by saving Laila Blume.

I ran to the infirmary and knocked on the door several times, but no one answered. Looking both ways to confirm I was alone in the hallway, I hurriedly went inside and closed the door. Turning on the light, I ran to a cabinet full of medicine, and after I grabbed a nearby bag, I filled it with everything I could find in just a few seconds. I barely had time at my disposal because Cheikh would eventually come looking for me. With that in mind, I took what I thought was necessary: gauze, fever medication, preserved food, a canteen full of clean water, and clean bedsheets. Closing the bag as best I could, I took my leave not through the main hall but through the service door. It led me to a narrow corridor, and unlike the rest of the palace, it was lit by candlelight. Hearing nothing behind or in front of me, I ran, noting how slippery the stairs were and how humidity painted the walls as if this were a tunnel headed underground.

The exit led to the courtyard, and I made my way to the stables. Mounting a horse without a saddle, I escaped.

Cheikh wanted me to understand that my priority was not to save a ghost forgotten by life, like Laila Blume, but for me, she was the answer to all my prayers. If Laila could return to Andebeck, the competition would be over. She would not allow Karl to win, and she could save Khloe from his clutches. If she could do me a favor, I could get rid of Marcus and his followers once and for all. I didn't trust him or his whole facade. Thinking of that, I guided the horse through the night in a hurry until it could go no further. It wasn't about competition or training. It was about something much more complicated than all of this—a part of the story that I was not understanding and that appeared more complicated than it seemed. And I was willing to challenge my fears to find out.

I reached the ruins but didn't enter them—I wasn't completely crazy.

I ran to one of the trees in front of the ruins and placed the bag in front of it. Then, I quickly wrote a clumsy note.

I brought you medicine and supplies. If you need more, please do not hesitate to ask. If you don't want my help, leave me a message here. I will come again on Sunday.

Omhet.

I left everything by the tree and turned to look at the ruins, realizing that it was ten times more frightening at night than during the day. I bowed and said the prayer my mother once taught me to take care of the princess. Then I mounted the horse to leave again with some excitement. Breaking the rules was not so bad after all—I would rather try than give in to indifference.

I need to try whatever it takes. By the gods, I had to try.

CHAPTER 15

An exhausted Cheikh entered my room, not even surprised to find me awake and getting ready for training an hour before the morning alarm rang. I don't know where he was so early in the morning, but I didn't ask him. I was more energetic than ever.

"Good morning," I said while I tied my boots. "How's everything?"

He rolled his eyes. I see that he still hasn't forgiven me.

"I just finished a call with our King," I stilled, eyes wide. *What? What did he say to my father?* "Due to what happened with the dragon, your family is close to personally escort you back home. However, I managed to convince them that the story they read in the newspaper was exaggerated. I've forced myself to lie for you," he gritted out, "I told them you're safe and that no dragon has been sighted."

"That's not a lie—not really. I'm safe now." I tried to joke.

"Omhet," he interjected with a tone so profound I bit my lips shut. "Don't *ever* do this to me again, please." As he pushed past me, he added, "I need to fast and have an afternoon of prayers to say for Krea. Shin and Lucas will be your companions for today." With nothing else to say, he stormed to his room. I knew I couldn't see him for a while—he looked miserable, though it was easy to figure out why.

He never lied.

My guardian was like my mother, loyal to his faith and applying that commendable trait to what Krea's spiritual laws demanded. I admired that in Cheikh. His outer strength was remarkable. That was why his mood had plummeted—my father would believe anything this man said to him because Cheikh had never been a liar. Not until now.

For once, I couldn't joke around when I peeked my head inside their room. Shin and Lucas were getting ready for the day, focused on their shoes and belts. Cheikh knelt before his bed with his hands clasped and his forehead resting against them, praying quietly in the old language of Lwz. I understood little, no matter how much my mother tried to teach me. I felt so bad seeing him so defeated. Staying away from him would be best, so I didn't even bother to go inside. I merely waited for the others to come out. The last thing I wanted was to break Cheikh's spirit. During his thirty years of working for the king, no battle or training had gotten him so frustrated, I'm sure. Everything changed when a teenager with an insecure personality and desperation for his father's validation became the focus of his life.

I'll make it worthwhile, I vowed in silence, taking my leave with my two guardians and feeling like something was missing. It wasn't the same without Cheikh.

"Will he be all right?" I asked, going down the stairs without the usual crowd of bustling servants due to how early I was.

"Only if we go back to our usual routine," answered a serious Shin. "The faster we can leave this foolishness behind, the better."

That sounded more like a warning than an explanation, but I ignored it. Going back to our routine meant I had to forget what had happened. I could still hear the dragon's roar and feel the weight of its body stomping as it ran toward me.

The dragon *exists.*

Laila Blume is still alive.

No. Worse than alive—Laila is cursed as though she has a strange disease consuming her. I had to do something, and that peculiar impulse felt like a shot of adrenaline, motivating me to take my training seriously. I ran that morning with an energy I didn't know I had.

Today I wanted it to be different. Today I wanted to beat all the courts and kingdoms. I tried to imitate the experts who ran as if it took no effort, even though it hurt to breathe. I don't know what unusual vigor Princess Laila had sparked in me, but I managed to catch up with the group. Maybe I could win for once. Perhaps I could get to the finish line before everyone else, even before the Prince of Ettezi.

But the race was completed before I even caught a glimpse of Karl ahead of me.

"Breathe through your nose," Shin ordered, appearing next to me. "Damn, how the hell did you get in fourth place?"

I couldn't speak. I had to hold onto my knees, drowning in my own air. *I have to run, I have to be better than everyone else, or I won't be able to save her,* I wanted to say, but I couldn't, not right now. I needed to learn to control my breathing and suppress my weaknesses, so I would not pass out again. If I wanted to be around these warriors, I had to act like one.

"Pay attention to your position," yelled Shin, and I lowered the bow until I found the perfect place.

This station was fun, but Shin made it feel like everything I did was wrong. This time I didn't protest. I simply aimed and pulled the string.

"Breathe one more time."

Doing as I was told, I stared at the red center halfway across the field. I fired, but it didn't hit the center. Cursing softly, I grabbed another arrow and placed it on the bow. I could feel other archers staring at me, but my focus was centered. I could barely hear what was going on around me.

"Exhale," said Shin calmly. "The bow is not a tool. It needs to become part of you."

I felt the string, assimilating each movement, thinking of what I'd be facing in a couple of months. I stared at the target and let it fly. It wasn't perfect, but it was my best shot so far.

I took another arrow and released it. Then I did it again and again. I couldn't stop, not even to make one of my silly comments.

"Objective complete!" the trainer screamed, making me blink out of my concentrated stupor and lowering the bow.

Lucas laughed. "The boy has finished his station early in the day. I'm impressed."

"The dragon changed him from a boy into a man," chuckled Shin.

I turned to Shin, "I liked you better when you didn't talk."

My comment made them laugh harder. I ignored them. I was not in the mood to joke today—Wait. What's wrong with me?

I went to the next station, where tables and barrels full of weapons waited. I have to pick one of the weapons, like katanas, scimitars, knives, daggers, or sabers. There were so many.

"Prince Omhet, welcome," said the instructor behind the table. "You've never made it this far in stations before."

I gave a step back and bumped into Lucas.

"I'm sorry," I said, without taking my eyes off the weapons.

"Well, what are you waiting for? Pick up a sword," said Shin.

I tried to answer, but suddenly, I couldn't speak.

"*I*-I can't."

"What do you mean you can't?" yelled Lucas in confusion.

I looked at everything around me, feeling my heart race even though I wasn't running. There was a round arena for combat weapons, men clad in armor, trainers screaming, and swords clanging.

But I was not here, not entirely.

"Wake up, you little shit," Guillermo ordered me, but I was already awake.

I had learned the sound of his footsteps approaching, and the way he carefully opened the door so no one else would hear. I had already been waiting for him, looking out the window as my entire body trembled under the covers. *Don't show him fear. You're just feeding his morbidity,* my father had scolded me for all the times I hid in my mother's bed when I heard Guillermo come to my room.

Ten years have passed since this event, and I have it more alive than any present memory.

I sat up in bed and looked at him with false bravery.

"Go away," I yelled at him.

"I will be your king. You will have to obey me. Or do you want my first order to lock you in the dungeon and have your eyes gouged out?"

"What do you want of me?"

"Today, we are going to train. Now, move!"

I chased after him wondering what kind of training he was referring to. Today he wasn't suffocating me with a pillow or pulling my hair down the hall. I thought it meant that perhaps my older brother had finally let go of the immaturity my father said he had. Because that was what my brother is, immature. Right? A fool who likes to threaten my life with words... and actions.

When he opened the door to some stairs leading down, I stopped. It seemed like he was taking me to the bottom of a dungeon or hell.

"Hurry up. We're running out of time," he yelled.

He grabbed me by the shoulder and pushed me down the stairs. There I began to fight, shouting. I did not want to go to the dungeon to have my eyes gouged out.

Guillermo pulled me by the arm as if he were going to tear it off. He was seventeen, with the body and muscle of a man. I tried to calm myself when I reached the underground field where Glacier's guardians trained. The only thing that illuminated the circle were torches. The rest were cold stones. Even the ground was slippery with ice.

"You're already crying, and we haven't started yet?" Guillermo yelled and kicked a barrel, throwing all the practice swords to the ground. *"That's why you're the family's disgrace because you're weak!"*

"I want to go to sleep, please," I begged.

Guillermo picked up a sword from the ground and pointed it at me.

"If you turn your back on me, you're a dead man. Grab a sword and fight!" He roared, *"fight, Omhet! Do not be weak."*

My hands trembled as I reached for the sword, but I didn't have time to raise it when he bellowed and lunged at me.

I had to raise my sword and stop his. I was terrified. I remember yelling, *"I don't want to fight you,"* so many times that I started crying. Fear filled me from head to toe.

What did an eight-year-old know about fighting a seventeen-year-old? He was superior to me in everything, in body, in the fight, in experience. Guillermo was an animal with swords, as once my father was in his youth. And I was good at school subjects and nothing else. They never required me to be good at physical training because having Guillermo and Cayetano was enough. That's why they called me the weak and the coward.

"Fight!" Guillermo shouted, watching my tears mix with my runny nose as I yelled for help.

Guillermo's sword hit mine so many times it went flying. I tried to run out to look for it because I had a feeling that if I didn't defend myself, he would kill me right there.

"I told you not to turn your back on me!"

And it was at that moment that I felt the cut. The scream that came out of me was the loudest thing I've ever cried. Guillermo tore at my back until he ripped at my clothes. In the middle of a scream, I fell into the middle of a pool of blood. I didn't move. I stayed crying weakly, waiting for my death. Guillermo turned me with hostility, looking me in the eye with the sword in his hand. I covered my face, afraid the blade would cut at my neck to finish the job.

"Too bad I can't legally kill you," was the last thing he said to me before walking away and leaving me abandoned in that room to die.

"Prince!" yelled Shin.

"Shit! Don't yell like that!" I jumped, trying, for goodness' sake, to avoid the memories. Everything returned with an overwhelming force I couldn't ignore for the first time.

"What is wrong with him?" asked Shin looking at Lucas.

"Nothing!" but I was yelling again. I took a deep breath, trying to calm down. "I don't like... this. I don't need to learn about fighting with swords. I need to learn how to slay a dragon from a distance. A sword would only tickle a dragon."

"I have news for you, Omhet," Shin told me, making me grasp the sword in my hands. *Oh, skies.* "You'll have to learn to fight humans as well."

Shin pushed me to the arena. I think they're waiting for me.

"Wait!" I turned around, and Shin pinched the bridge of his nose, taking a deep breath.

"I got this," said Lucas and took Shin's place. Lucas placed his arm on my shoulder, and his serene face almost calmed me down. Almost. "You are stronger than you think."

"It's not about that. You don't understand—"

"Omhet," he was going to say something, but nothing would help me on this. *Nothing.* "The only way to confront your fear and your past is to face them."

"What are you..." I tried to ask and looked at Shin, but he was too far to hear what Lucas was telling me.

"Guillermo is not here. You're safe."

I couldn't answer. I think I was shaking.

He knew...

"We're here. We'll always be here with you."

I nodded but couldn't look him in the eyes. He knew about my past, and I felt so embarrassed. But my father didn't want me on the battlefield, and if I wanted him to change his mind, I had to overcome my fears first. *Krea, help me.*

Several trainers were waiting for me. They started putting protective armor on my arms and abdomen and even shoved a helmet on my head that I could barely see through. *You're not suffocating. It's in your head*, I repeated it a thousand times. The sword felt so... so heavy in my hand.

I closed my eyes and remembered those emerald eyes—*she needs me.*

I opened my eyes and felt different. I was not going to run away this time.

In front of the circle was the prince of Atsoc being prepared. A prince with blond hair who was significantly taller than me. But that means nothing. Even Khloe is taller than I am.

Shin approached me like he would give me some last piece of advice before the duel, but his voice was harsher than I expected.

"You are not going to face any dragon," he reminded me in my ear. "We swore to the king that you would return safe and sound. Do not forget that our lives are in your hands. If something happens to you, we will pay—understand?"

"Where did this sudden threat come from?"

"Just a reminder that meeting the ghost with emerald eyes changes nothing."

We'll see.

He didn't wait for an answer before he left, but my guardians weren't idiots. They could feel my determination in everything I was doing. I even glanced toward the palace and saw Cheikh watching me on the balcony.

I can't stop now, I thought, swinging the sword in my hands, craning my neck, and moving to the center of the arena. My opponent did too. I couldn't see his face, but I could feel he was focused, swinging his weapon naturally. *He's not my brother. It doesn't intimidate me—the dragon is bigger,* I thought, feeling my heart race.

I bent my knees and positioned myself at the proper angle, with my sword parallel to the ground. Whatever I did, I couldn't let my guard down—not again.

The duel began when the general gave the signal, and before I had time to react, my opponent was the first to attack.

"On guard" Shin yelled. I'd almost forgotten to act defensively. His scream saved my skin.

My opponent's guardian was also yelling at him in his native language, more energetically than Shin, but it didn't matter. Shin's calmness was the only thing keeping me focused.

He attacked me from above. I held the sword with both hands, lifting it above my head. Not only did I stop his attack, but I also pushed him away with my shoulder. Then I hit back, but he dodged. *Oh,* he's fast. I bellowed and lunged again.

This is painful to watch, said Guillermo's voice.

Shut up! I screamed in my head.

"Defense!" Shin yelled. As soon as I heard his order, I stopped attacking, and my opponent's sword almost cut into my abdomen.

I didn't know how to keep track of his blade, movements, and strange dance that made me dizzy and doubt each attack.

Everything was spinning around me. I felt buried as if everything had turned dark in the middle of the day. I couldn't breathe. I can't do this... What was I thinking?

I was with Guillermo again. I could see it in front of me. I could feel the pain in my back.

I couldn't focus, so I was hit with a surprise blow. With his fist, he punched me so hard on the helmet that it flew off.

Shin hissed in frustration. I was losing not to the prince of Atsoc but failing to myself.

I wiped the blood from my lip with my arm and kicked the helmet with attitude.

"Come on, love," my opponent taunted me, and I could see his crooked smile through his helmet.

It's enough! I'm not going to fight my fears. I'm going to fight with fear.

I wasn't sure what rage was eating me up inside, but I didn't hear Guillermo's voice again. And I wasn't going to let him come back.

I moved the sword several times, studied his posture, and focused.

How heavy his armor is, I thought, studying him slowly, moving around the circle. I knew he couldn't fully see around him or turn with agility, but he was quick with his hands and strong with his fists. He could rip my head off if he were facing me...

I moved, pretending to attack him from the front, and he lunged right for my head. Shin screamed, probably thinking I was doing something stupid. Maybe I was, but my trick worked because I cut behind his legs instead. He dropped one knee to the ground.

It wasn't enough for me to win, but when he tried to get up, it took him longer than it should have. I think he was angry. As if it were an act of revenge, the prince lunged at me so aggressively that I couldn't hear Shin's shout anymore. The sound of blades clanging and battle grunts overshadowed everything else.

I didn't give up.

I didn't even show fear because I didn't have it anymore. I envisioned the dragon, which filled me with an energy I hadn't had before. I was motivated. I had the challenge of trying to be as strong as everyone else. I had a reason to be here. I wanted to save Laila more than I wanted to kill the dragon, and I did not care about the kingdom or the reward. I want to help her and the hell they had put her through. I counterattacked, swinging my legs and pointing forward with my blade. I hit my opponent square in the chest.

The tricky thing was that every time I got close to having a certain advantage, it was as if a beast inside him woke up because he attacked me so hard that my wrist started to hurt. He struck over and over. He kept hitting me and was about to throw me out of the circle.

Shin had told me that it wouldn't be the strongest who wins but the smartest. Easy for him to say when one of the strongest was one step away from taking me out of the damn arena.

He would win. I was convinced. His posture and style had an experience advantage that I couldn't compete with. If this battle were real, he would have already killed me. But it wasn't real—not completely. So, I waited for the end, when my opponent raised his hand to begin his fiercest and crucial attack. I stood my ground, noticing his helmet and asking myself why the hell did we have so much protection for such an informal practice. It wasn't that serious.

I smiled at him with amusement and dropped my sword. Shin screamed my name above all other sounds. I dodged the blonde's attack and hit his helmet. I didn't want to take his helmet off with a fist. I wanted to flip it over and take away his ability to see.

"What the hell..." he yelled and dropped his sword to remove his helmet.

Before he could finish, I kicked him in the center of his chest so severely that the poor thing flew for a couple of seconds before falling out of the circle.

"Victory for the Glacier Kingdom," the general proclaimed.

Thank you, Laila, I thought, exhaling the air from my lungs as I closed my eyes. Who would have thought I would learn to overcome the worst moment of my life thanks to her?

I knew that my father was not going to like the idea that was growing inside me. The desire to do the right thing, even though it contradicted what my king expected of me. Perhaps he sent me to Andebeck out of sheer self-interest, swearing that I could make allies on his behalf and expecting me to return home without ever having seen a dragon.

Maybe he didn't believe me capable because of what I experienced in my past. Well, he was completely wrong because I had changed my mind. I didn't want to just follow my father's orders. I didn't care about making connections or allies.

I, Omhet Espinho, of Glacier Kingdom, would dominate all the training stations because the one who would kill the dragon would be me.

Chapter 16

I knocked on the door with my knuckles, looking both ways down the hall to confirm that there were no Ettezi guards around. Then the door was opened by a soldier, so I ended up facing one anyway. As soon as she saw me, she became aggressive, placing her hand on the blade she had at her waist.

Lucas pulled me by the shoulder, and Shin drew his sword before it could even occur the guard to threaten me.

"Enough," I ordered my guardians—they had to calm down, for heaven's sake. "I'm just here to visit the princess."

"No, you know very well that you shouldn't be here," she said in her accent.

"Then, at least let her be the one to reject me," I demanded, placing my hand on the wall.

Khloe appeared behind her guard and ordered her to withdraw in their native language, and then she leaned against the door frame, looking at me with a scowl. My shoulder relaxed as I looked her up and down. She was in perfect condition except for a bandage on her ankle.

She didn't even look like she'd been running for her life a few days ago.

"Finally," I breathed out, relieved. "I thought you were dead—why are you hiding from me?"

Khloe had an attitude that I didn't recognize, looking at me like I was her enemy. Even Shin whispered to me to get away from her a bit, as the situation was unpredictable.

"Easy, guardian, I won't bite," Khloe said to Shin.

"You won't, but I will," Shin replied. Lucas and I looked at him in disbelief.

Khloe hid a smile and looked at me again.

"I liked him," she said.

"Are you okay?" I asked, narrowing my eyes.

"And why wouldn't I be?" she said casually without answering the question.

We just ran away from a mighty dragon and almost died, I want to answer, but I couldn't with so many people around.

"Oh, I don't know. Maybe because you're avoiding me," Khloe frowned at my sarcasm. "Can't we go back to how we used to be?"

"You mean the part where we didn't talk to each other? Yes," she responded, winning to my sarcasm. She was impossible. "Omhet, I don't mean to offend you—it was fun, but my adventure with you is over."

I crossed my arms.

"You are my friend, and if someone has threatened you—"

Her laugh interrupted me.

"You live in a fantasy world, don't you, little one?"

I hated... hated being called that. I couldn't even answer her.

"Omhet, come on," Shin ordered me, but I kept glaring at Khloe.

"Go," she pressed, "your paranoia has you thinking stupid things."

"You're acting like Karl."

"I'm an Ettezi! And I can't walk around with you all the time," she effortlessly offended me as if she had planned all this. "My brother was honest with me and warned me that if I kept hanging out with you, everyone would think my kingdom has allied with yours, and we don't want that. I'm sorry, but you'll scare the other allies away."

"Since when does that matter to you?"

"Since I got into so much trouble for a mere outing. Don't you realize that wherever you are, there are problems? Now go. You'll be late for lunch."

She went to close the door, but I placed my foot in the way to stop it. We stared at each other once more. I tried to find what she was really feeling, but she was hard to read.

"What did he do to you, Khloe?"

I thought I saw a flash in her eyes, but it was so brief I couldn't be sure.

"Don't pretend to know me," she concluded, kicking my foot. "I'm not your damsel in distress."

She closed the door without saying anything else.

I walked to the dining room, feeling angry with her. She wasn't usually like that, or maybe I didn't know her at all. I was so confused.

"We're in a competition," Lucas said, trying to cheer me up. "Everyone lies. Everyone plays with the kingdom like a freaking game of chess. Don't fall for every person you meet."

"I don't think we should abandon her like that."

"Khloe of Ettezi is stronger than she appears," Shin said with such confidence that I didn't dare to contradict him.

"When she's ready, she'll look for you. In the meantime, you should focus on one problem at a time. Don't you think?"

Whenever Shin spoke, he made me feel like I didn't know anything. So, I decided to try having a relaxed lunch by myself. When she's ready, she'll look for me, I repeated several times, feeling unsettled.

I looked at every representative at the table, from Marcus drinking wine with his sister to Karl socializing with his allies. Everyone acted as routine demanded, but as much as they tried to pretend nothing was happening, it felt like the opposite. Focus on one problem, I reminded myself, relaxing as best I could. My problem was the dragon and what I had discovered about it, nothing more for now.

"Good duel, love," someone told me as he sat in front of me.

Neither Pierre on my right nor Alanis on my left spoke to me. It was someone who'd never talked to me before.

"Prince Alexander of the Atsoc Kingdom," he introduced himself.

I just looked at him blankly, forgetting my manners.

"You just beat me at the last station," he said in a confused tone because I didn't recognize him right away. "Congratulation, you fought well."

I drank water from my glass slowly, looking at him. It was not common for these people to congratulate me for doing something good. I felt something was up. Maybe I should be less spiteful and try to make as many allies as possible, but I couldn't trust anyone in this place. Everyone around me was so competitive that I highly doubted they could be pleasant to me out of the blue.

"Thanks, I guess."

"Were you able to sleep after Karl beat you up?" he asked me, laughing a little.

"Like a baby," I replied with the same smile.

He nodded, and I waited for more. I knew he wasn't done with me. I could feel it.

"Did you hear the dragon?" he blurted out. "It sounded terrifying."

Aha! That was what this was all about. He wanted to know if I was really involved with the beast. If they discovered I was the one who woke it, surely the kingdoms would return me to my home in little pieces.

"I was sleeping—the pain meds are a bit strong, you know," I said casually.

I was looking at the waiter approach one by one, looking anywhere but at Alexander. He was making me feel uncomfortable.

The waiter placed the first plates of food in front of us, and although everyone ignored them, I always said thank you in the language of Glacier. In my home, the servants were part of the family because their lives began and ended in our service. Treating them with familiarity was the least they deserved.

Rice. Another day of rice. I found it a fascinating experience that in Andebeck, they ate rice all the time. The colors changed, the size of the grain, and the companions, but there was always rice.

"He has one fight with a muscular jerk, and he considers it painful enough for medication, huh?" he scoffed, making Alanis laugh.

"When you pierce your own hand with an arrow, then you'll know what pain is," Pierre replied, showing me the center of his wrist where he had a mark.

"When your body gets tangled in jellyfish tentacles, then you'll know what pain is," Alanis added, reminding me that her island was surrounded by dangerous sea.

When your arm gets burned by the flames of a dragon, then you can talk to me about pain, I thought and laughed a tiny bit, noting that Alexander was staring at me with his intense blue eyes. I had to drink water to cover up my private joke.

"You should come with me after lunch," said Alexander. I almost spit out my water. "We'll do the next station together."

"Do I have a choice?" I asked, feeling threatened.

"You are the youngest in this competition. I don't think you have a choice at all."

Pierre was laughing, and Alanis had a provocative smile. I felt cornered.

"You three are cruel," I said, shrinking in my seat.

I ran along with Pierre as fast as possible, trying not to trip over invasive roots, bump into bushes, and get my face tangled in branches. If I slowed down just a little, Pierre would yell at me like he was my trainer. I wanted to take a break, but when I got to the top of the hill, I found Alexander a couple of meters in front of me. I raised my bow and shot an arrow at his torso. I had no idea that a person could be so fast that he could cut an arrow in two with his sword before it could touch him.

"What the hell?" I bellowed with heavy breathing.

Pierre shot from behind me—his arrow was so fast that Alexander couldn't stop it and was knocked to the ground as the arrow snapped into his shield. Alanis came out of nowhere with two long blades in her hands, jumping out of a tree. He cut Pierre's belly, but I drew my blunt sword, hitting one of her hands. She groaned as one of her knives fell to the ground. We began to circle each other, waiting for the best moment to attack. Sweat was running down my forehead, and I was so focused that I wasn't even strategizing.

Alanis screamed as she lunged, causing me to duck to counter her with my sword. I don't know how, but she got behind me, climbing on my back. She was about to place her knife on my neck, but I raised my hand and held hers. We fell to the ground, trying to take it from her.

Unable to shake her off like a parasite, she got a lock on my neck that I couldn't escape.

I couldn't breathe.

In front of my face, I saw Pierre and Alexander looking down as if hoping I could get out of such a lock. I gave a sign of surrender, but Alanis squeezed harder. I coughed out of desperation and couldn't even keep my eyes open.

"I don't know, guys. I don't think it was him," Alexander commented, setting his hands on his hip.

"Maybe he's pretending," Alanis said and squeezed harder. I frantically kicked as I tried to breathe.

I asked for help with my hands, eyes, and every sound that came out of my mouth. I really started to panic when I saw that no one was doing anything, even though they were watching me.

"Mmm..." Pierre made a gesture as if he didn't care.

"Do you really think that someone like him could have really provoked the dragon?"

"If he escaped from the dragon, he will manage to escape from Alanis. Just wait a little longer," joked Pierre.

"I don't know—I'm not convinced. I think that's enough."

My mind went blank as my hands fell helplessly. I was losing this duel—not this duel, this trap.

"Alanis," Alexander scolded.

"Don't trust his innocent face..."

"Alanis," Alexander insisted.

"Fine!" she growled and released me.

I breathed in a violent gasp, throwing myself aside. I tried to get up and fell to my knees again, coughing so hard I thought I was going to throw up.

"It's okay, just breathe through your nose," Alexander told me, but when he raised his hand to touch me, I crawled away until I collided with the tree trunk.

My chest heaved, and I couldn't find my voice for a moment.

"Don't touch me!" I managed to scream, dragging myself away. I sat on a log, holding my neck and trying to breathe. What the heck just happened? "You were going to kill me," I said, trying to look at her—all of them simultaneously.

"Of course not," Alanis said, crossing her arms. "We were just testing you."

"For what?" I bellowed, but my voice cracked.

I wanted to close my eyes and breathe slowly to calm myself, but I was scared to close them in front of them. It was not good to show so much terror to my opponents, but there was no one around who could help me. My guards were waiting for our training to end back at the arena, the trainers were nowhere to be seen, and the three were fully armed. This was a stupid ambush, and I fell for it.

"He will be a dead man in the first five minutes in battle," Pierre grumbled as he started to leave.

"Come on, Alex," Alanis said, chasing after Pierre. "We need to finish the stations."

Alexander stood in front of me, looking at me with... I don't know. Pity? Curiosity? He held out his hand, but I didn't take it. I didn't trust him. I didn't trust anyone anymore. Everyone was being needlessly cruel.

"Are you coming?" asked Alexander.

I looked at Alanis and Pierre, who stopped and looked at me with contempt.

"Don't waste your time," said Pierre.

"He doesn't pose a threat to anyone. What is your problem?" Alexander argued, turning to them. "We confirmed that it was not him who provoked the dragon. Can we leave him alone from now on?"

Alanis and Pierre looked embarrassed, but that only lasted for a moment. They turned away from not only me but Alexander as well. That meant only one thing—Alexander was about to lose his allies.

"Don't argue because of me," I said, getting up. "You have much more to lose if you do."

Without letting him respond, I stomped off. The forest was perfect for training in group fighting station, but it was easy to get lost in. It was a private forest in the middle of the walls, and it took me almost an hour to find my way out. The trek helped me calm down, but my anger was soon replaced with frustration. The kingdoms were all suspicious of me because of what happened with the dragon. They almost came close to destroying me because of it. I didn't know what to think—I was able to survive this ambush, and my weakness seemed enough for them to rule out that it was I who provoked the dragon. However, it didn't make me feel better.

I thought I was about to have allies to make my kingdom—no, my king—proud of me, but I realized that I had caused the opposite.

"Omhet," Lucas called, running to me, "are you okay?"

I tried to act naturally when my two guards ran to me with a towel and a canteen of water.

"Excellent," I said casually. "I got lost like a fool."

Shin glared behind me at Pierre and Alanis, they were under the designated tent, but they kept staring at me and not in a friendly way.

"You should have let us go with you," Shin said as if he could read the fear I felt in my eyes.

"What for?" I protested as I walked through the stations, trying to escape my humiliation. "Tell me, who needs bodyguards to protect them from all the kingdoms?" I didn't let him answer. "Just me."

"The competition is getting very personal," Shin reminded me, looking around defensively.

"It's always been," I mumble.

It was a competition, not a game. I had to expect the worst, which was the hardest part to accept.

I sat in the study tent before the others got there, drinking water, recovering from the ordeal, and grateful that I was alone for a while. It was nice to be done with all my stations on time for once—it meant I could go to my room at sunset and not at midnight. One more class and my afternoon was over. It was a useless class where I learned nothing that could help me kill a magical beast.

Someone sat down next to me, and I breathed in annoyance. I had chosen a chair in the back corner to be alone, so I glared at Alexander.

"I'm not spiteful," I said with an attitude. "If you are looking for forgiveness, you have it, but please, don't take me as an idiot—"

"I don't see you as an idiot," he interrupted, tying his long hair back with a ribbon.

"What do you want from me then?" I asked. "Be honest, say what you want to say, and then leave me alone."

"You can't be alone," he said at last. "Yes, it was my idea to ambush you, and I'm not going to apologize for that. But I had to ensure you're not a traitor with an innocent face."

I looked at him, more confused than before.

"Omhet," he continued. I was surprised that he knew how to pronounce my name. "All the kingdoms are convinced that you went to the ruins to get an advantage. It's easy to believe that you did—you are weak, you are alone, and you look quite desperate."

"Thank you," I said, narrowing my eyes.

"I offer you my alliance—"

"Wait, what?" How did we get to this point?

"I swear it on my descendants and my kingdom," he said, making me straighten up in surprise. "In return, I ask for the truth."

Oh shit.

I couldn't trust anyone, much less the person who had just ambushed me. *It's not me you have to convince*, Marcus had told me, because he wanted me to lie. Lie until credible, I told myself. My voice shook when I tried, so I looked anywhere but his eyes.

This was what my father expected of me. There was nothing more important than this moment because it was the purpose of my trip and an opportunity that would make my kingdom—especially my king, proud. I had to either share what I had discovered about Laila with this stranger or make my kingdom a priority and do whatever it takes to make an alliance.

"Well, this is new," he said after my long silence.

"What?" I whispered, still unable to look at him.

"Being rejected. I'm not a person who begs. Mostly it's the other way around," he said with a crooked smile.

I tried to stifle my giggle and surreptitiously covered my mouth, but then I burst out laughing—the irony. The prince with blue eyes and long blond hair tried to convince me to be his ally. Of course, they all begged him. By just looking at him for too long, he can persuade you to do anything.

"I want to reject you just to have the honor of being the first," I said after speaking through the laugh.

"The only one," he corrected me.

"You are the most idiotic prince charming I have ever met. Your smile may work with all the damsels you try to convince, but not with me."

"Noted," He nodded, and I dared to look at him. Alex fixed his eyes on the coach, who had just arrived and arranged his things on the table.

Ah, curse you and your sad eyes, I thought, exhaling with irritation.

Alexander stood up, and I closed my eyes while I said: "It was Khloe's idea," I finally said. Alexander's gaze widened with such surprise that he couldn't say anything. "And I was desperate, not to meet the dragon, but to have an ally. That's why I followed her, and we almost lost our lives."

Alexander sank into the chair slowly and looked away. He said absolutely nothing.

"Now I've lost her as a friend, and everyone looks at me as a target," I concluded, but he said nothing. "Alexander, please say something."

He looked at me again and took a deep breath. "What is it like?" he whispered.

I remembered the dragon's eyes shuddering. I didn't want to keep talking about it, but now I couldn't back down.

"Terrifying," I said, unable to look at him. "The problem isn't just the fire. It's also its speed. Its legs move like a bloody lizard."

Alexander laughed, but he seemed nervous.

"Omhet, you can't tell anyone, and you'll have to train better if you want to have a chance in seven months."

"I'm working on that."

"Let me help you. It will be valuable for me to hear from you what you discovered about the dragon, and it will be beneficial for you to have protection when the battle comes."

I thought about it for a moment. I knew that soon I'd have to drop the subject when the seats began to be taken by the others entering the station.

"I told you a serious secret. You will have to stay as my ally, or I will have to kill you."

We both burst out laughing. If telling him my secret was a mistake or not, only time would tell. For now, I tried to convince myself that maybe sharing little secrets could work to give me the ally I needed and that my father demanded so much. I just hoped it wouldn't affect anyone else, especially Laila.

"Let's welcome a new student," the general sarcastically said as he pointed at me. "The Glacierian was finally able to finish his stations in time to join our class."

I gave him a fake smile but held back my response because I knew he wouldn't like it.

"Today will not be a combat or survival class," he began, sitting at his desk, dropping his general's jacket, and rolling up his sleeves. This class promised to be extended. "After what happened with the dragon, I want to talk about the last festival that took place in Andebeck. The festival of the lost princess. When the dragon attacked the first time, it was in the middle of the wedding of Princess Laila Blume, but everyone knew that already. The princess disappeared, and the dragon destroyed the entire castle, killing almost all the Blumes."

The general had arranged images on the table. The first one he picked was a drawing of a princess and a prince named Rafael. They were at an altar, dressed for the wedding. I exhaled slowly, frowning at all the questions running through my mind.

In the drawing, both seemed in love.

And now... she looks so devastated. Why—what the hell happened?

An elbow made me hiss, nearly knocking me off my chair.

"Guess where Prince Rafael is from," Karl whispered to me so as not to interrupt the general.

"I'm dying to know," I replied between clenched teeth.

"From Ettezi, of course. Or do you think he was going to be from your court?"

Don't answer him. Do not dare to answer.

Although I kept quiet, I did wonder why Laila would choose someone from such a place. She deserved better. Not a kingdom that looked at the woman as her object. Laila deserved a prince who would kneel before her and promise her safety. Who swore her unconditional love—

"Maybe the dragon did her a favor and saved her from your kingdom," I whisper, barely moving my lips.

"You little shit..."

"Is there a problem?" the general asked.

I hid my smile. Karl was in trouble. He stood up without saying a word.

"Stop provoking him, or you're not going to make it alive to battle," Alexander scolded me.

"I'll do my best," I smiled crookedly.

"As I was saying," the general continued, "a year after the unfortunate wedding, a festival was held in the city in honor of Laila and Raphael, the grooms who perished in that terrible wedding. It was a celebration where the memory of the tragic couple was honored—the largest in the history of our territory. There were statues, works of art, feasts, dances, and revelry. There were even visits from kingdoms that were not part of the union."

He showed the following image of the festival. One with burned corners.

I couldn't imagine a festival of that magnitude in Andebeck, as the city was boring, and its people did not seem like the type to throw parties. They were so scared and lacking in friendliness that I could not even imagine them dancing.

"The dragon arrived without warning," he continued in a more serious tone. "The city, the homes, the entire bay, and the people were engulfed in flames. The screams were heard throughout the kingdom, the buildings burned to the ground, and the beast devoured everything it could grab. Since then, the city has never hosted another festival or guests from other kingdoms. There were no longer any signs of the beast—until last Sunday."

I lowered my gaze as soon as the general looked at me when he said the last sentence. I felt so guilty.

"Moving forward, your assignment for this class will be to read Andebeck's story, listen to the citizens you meet in town, and understand that this beast will not be easy to destroy. It will take more than stations and classes to defeat it," He took a deep breath, looking around at everyone. "I wish you all luck because you are going to need it."

Although everyone seemed focused on teaming up with their allies, understanding the story, and planning ways to kill the beast, I couldn't even react. Laila was going to get married, and she lost everything in one night.

Laila, I can only imagine how you must feel. To lose everything and be alive to remember everything—every single day.

How could Cheikh dare to ask me to ignore this? It was pure torture, not for me, but for her.

Something is wrong with this competition, and I can't take it out of my mind.

"Do you want to talk about strategy?" I asked Alexander, trying to pretend the story didn't affect me.

"Not here," he said, looking around. "People can hear us, and we'll have to pretend we don't care."

"Easy," I said, trying to relax.

The rest of the groups huddled together, dragging chairs, and planning the great battle to come. It was really going to be impossible to use this time to do anything productive. Not when I felt the constant gazes on me. Especially the harsh murmurs between Pierre and Alanis. At this point I don't think they were upset with me, but with both of us. I saw jealousy in every gesture and look they gave me.

"I want to invite you to a gathering on Sunday," Alexander said, and I knew he was trying to distract me. I can almost taste the violence in the air.

I didn't want to feel excited to finally be invited to something, but I was. I, Omhet Espinho, had officially managed to make an ally. I wasn't sure if I should take it with such glee after his friend had almost mercilessly strangled me, but I decided to trust him. He projected such confidence it was easy to forgive him. It almost seemed silly for someone like me to be around him, but I could tell he didn't want to belittle me. In the end, I could be that sidekick he needed—the companion that every hero needed, whether to make him laugh when he needed it most or help him if emergencies arose.

"Why does something tell me this party of yours is not allowed?"

"It's allowed as long as Marcus, the general, or the kings don't find out," he said casually, making me laugh. "The event starts when night falls. I won't take a no for an answer."

"Fine, I'll go."

"You're getting used to being begged. I don't like it. Who do you think you are?" he joked.

"Omhet Espinho, fourth son of king Guillermo and prince of the high mountains Timantti."

"Whatever you said," he punched me in the arm, "I'm starting to regret this alliance."

"No, you are not."

I accepted his invitation. For once this week, I wanted to have fun.

Then I realized that he'd said the gathering was next Sunday. My smile starts to fade, my eyes looking at nowhere. Oh, no. I already have a promise to keep that night and didn't want to abandon the princess. Worst of all, I was hearing my father's voice in my head, knowing that if I asked him what he would do in my place, he would choose the ally above all else.

CHAPTER 17

You are not going to the ruins, you are not going to the ruins, I repeated in my mind as I paced back and forth in my room. Everything was finally starting to get better, and I could spend time at my stations and training with Alexander. He felt more like a friend than an ally. I couldn't—for any reason—screw this up.

But Laila's situation seemed just as important.

"Hey, Shin," Lucas called out to Shin from his desk, "Do you think these words sound like Omhet? I apologize for my absquatulate dearth of constancy in responding my letters. You all shall be dumbfounded at the resplendent announcement of my new affiliation with the Prince of Atsoc—"

"By the skies, Lucas," Shin interrupted. "I'm not sure he even knows half the words you just said."

Shin and Luca were trying to write a letter to my family under my name. I honestly hadn't felt like writing letters, so I ordered them to. So far, Lucas has been doing a terrible job. Shaking my head, I peek at Cheikh's room. He avidly listened to the radio, getting annoyed when he got interrupted by anything or anyone.

"The protests in the capital have intensified, and the crowd has tried to reach the minister at any cost. There are rumors that Puerto Escondido brought ships to the coast, but the minister has yet to confirm or deny these claims. What can Andebeck expect if the competition gets out of control? Is the battle just against the dragon or against their people as well?"

I wanted to keep listening to what they were saying, but Cheikh turned it off when he finally noticed I was standing by the door.

"They're getting angrier, huh?" I commented, trying to have a normal conversation with Cheikh.

"Fear is turning into violence," he explained. "They are afraid that at any given moment, history will repeat itself if this competition keeps provoking the dragon." He settled against the back of his bed, arms crossed. "Marcus, however, seems calm. In the last interview he granted, he dared to admit that he did not fear his citizens. Of course, they are not a threat, not like the dragon."

"Everyone here is willing to die for the crown rather than the princess herself," I answered, unable to hide my irritation.

"Destroy the dragon, and you'll win the kingdom. Or save the princess and lose the crown. Tell me, Prince Omhet, what would someone choose in a competition?"

I was ready to argue with him, but I heard the chair behind me being dragged. Looking over my shoulder, I saw Shin and Lucas stop what they were doing, looking concerned.

I relaxed my shoulders and exhaled slowly, "I'm not trying to argue." Cheikh raised an eyebrow. "Lucas will send a letter to the king to calm them down. Surely, when they find out I've made an ally, they'll stop calling you so much."

"Krea hears you," he grunted while standing. "Now, let's pray for the night. I don't want to tell your mother how you flee from your routine every chance you get."

"Speaking of routine..." I said while scratching the back of my head.

I followed Cheikh back to my room, giving him a minute to make some tea at the table with the other guards as I sat on the bed, not knowing how to ask him the question.

"I was invited to a gathering with Alexander," I said calmly.

"A gathering," he repeated. Again, he raised his eyebrow. That was not a good signal. "What type of gathering?"

"He is privately meeting with other allies, and I've been invited to..." I stopped talking when Cheikh took his notebook out of his pocket and began to check it. "No, Cheikh, you will not find the event on the schedule. It's kind of... informal."

"Informal as in clandestine?" he asked, closing the notebook.

"Clandestine is a very strong word," I said, but already Shin and Lucas had turned to me as if they were three parents analyzing their adolescent's escape. "He invited me, and I think it's a great opportunity for our alliance."

Cheikh said nothing and drank some tea, still looking at me.

The wait made me desperate. I'm supposed to have the privilege of giving orders, to get dressed whenever I want, and leave without saying a word.

But who am I kidding? They had me in their hands.

"I haven't used my formal uniform for a lavish dinner in a long time," Cheikh agreed.

Lavish dinner?

"Oh no, you're not coming."

"Sir, I remind you that you don't go alone anywhere," when I tried to interrupt, he raised his hand. "Take Shin with you then."

I was going to interrupt. This was absurd.

"Don't make me regret it," Cheikh concluded. He took his cup of tea to his small room and slid the door closed. I knew that now he would kneel in front of the bed and do his routine prayer to Krea before sleeping. I looked at Shin with a raised eyebrow, but he seemed angrier about the situation than me.

I dressed in my best clothes—dark jacket, ironed button-down shirt, boots, and combed my dark-wavy hair. I needed to see myself as equal to the other kingdoms. Nothing could mess up tonight, or so I intended. I slid my gaze to the window, seeing the ruins as the sun fell behind the mountain. Focus, I growled to myself, looking away.

I was ready to go, but Shin was in the same place I had left him, with his regular uniform on. I wanted to leave, and he looked like he wanted to ruin my night with indifference.

"Shin, by Krea, tell me you're not going dressed like that."

"First, I don't believe in Krea. Second, I'm your guardian. Third, I'm not a guest," he reminded me with attitude.

"The point is to try to be a part of their group, and going with a chaperone is basically the opposite," I argued. Still, Shin looked at me so unbothered it made my blood boil.

"Take it or leave it," he concluded. "Do I have to keep reminding you that you are the only minor in this place?"

"I already look like one!" I screeched, feeling cornered as if they were my parents. I was already treated like a child by the other representatives. What could be more humiliating than walking in with a chaperone?

There was a knock on the door in the middle of the terrible discussion. I had no choice but to go out with Shin, and I preferred having Shin as a shadow than not going at all.

I hoped my guardian was a ghost, invisible enough not to turn this vital opportunity into humiliation. I have had enough experience with that. Also, I had never looked so elegant, and I needed to take advantage.

When I opened the door, Alexander was waiting for me with his arms crossed, leaning against the wall. His long hair was not tied back, noticing that it was longer than it appeared. The prince's attire ranged from turquoise to white, with gold trim. I loved and hated that Alexander only had to exist to look like the perfect prince who could effortlessly save your life.

"You're bringing your nanny," Alexander accused me.

"No, Shin is... my friend," I tried to nudge him playfully, but Shin pouted and stepped away from me. Shin! Pretend for once.

"Sure. Or maybe your general doesn't trust you," he said referring to Cheikh.

"Why wouldn't he trust me?" I asked, shooting Shin a threatening look.

"Maybe out of fear that you might escape to go look for the dragon," Alexander said as a joke.

I laughed out loud—the fakest laugh I could come up with, but it really made my hands sweat. Shin looked at me, knowing that Alexander was right.

"Alexander the comedian, huh?"

Shin rolled his eyes irritably, but at least he didn't answer. How serious my bodyguards were!

We didn't take the main hall but instead snuck through a door so small that I had to duck. We followed the narrow path lit by torches. I thought we would reach some dungeons where another ambush would await me. It was hard to hide how nervous I was when I couldn't find the end of the hall. Until Alexander opened the last door and the breeze outside hit my face and nearly blew out some of the torches.

"Not a chance. We're going back," Shin ordered when he saw a waiting carriage. "You're not allowed by Cheikh to go outside the palace limits. Especially with the protests happening in the city."

"I'm not going to get in trouble. Trust me," I replied while following Alexander in a hurry.

"Omhet, I swear..."

I stopped short and turned to him. "I promise you we will return without question if any danger arises. Better?"

"No, not at all," but I already was stepping inside the big carriage. "Cheikh is going to kill me."

"First time in the city?" asked Alexander.

"Can you tell?" I responded sarcastically.

I was with the window open. If I could, I would get half of my body out because I wanted to see it all. I was impressed even by the little things like the wagon moving without horses, poles with electric lights, and a cobblestone road with no snow and no horse smell. The roofs of the houses were terracotta, the wooden windows varied in striking colors, and the sea's smell began to intensify as we approached the bay. It was a beautiful city, but at night it was even more so.

"There are too many people. I don't like this at all," Shin commented, peering next to me.

"Calm down, guardian. Protests are only seen in the mornings. On Sunday, there is no civilian who wants to lose a day off in such stupidity. Everyone is looking for an escape, like us," said Alexander. He was reclining with his legs up, taking up all the space of three.

We got off in the middle of the street, and I looked around excitedly. The sky was starry today, and the four moons lit our way. The houses were dark as everyone was asleep, but I could hear music in different parts. The nightlife had begun.

I walked next to Alex, talking about unimportant things, except the competition. We were just two friends running away from our lives for once. I hoped I wouldn't regret it, but above all, I hoped I wouldn't get in trouble.

"Don't get lost, guardian," joked Alexander, looking over our shoulders. Shin was having difficulty staying close to us, with so many people bumping into him.

"I want to see the ocean," I said, sniffing the air, almost tasting the salt in the breeze. "I have never seen the sea."

"And it won't be today," Shin managed to apparated to my side, his breathing heavy from the rush. "Neither of you can go near the bay. Obviously, you are unaware of how dangerous Andebeck is at night, especially on the pier."

"I will not allow anything to happen to you or Omhet. Nothing has ever happened to me when I visit *The Twin Moons* tavern, and I don't think today will be any different. Why so afraid?"

"He's paranoid..." I tried to answer for him.

"No, I'm not. You have no idea how easily this guy gets in trouble," he yelled, pointing at me. "In Glacier, there's a rumor that Omhet is so fragile that he died three times the first moment he tried to train with swords."

"Tell me you're lying," laughed Alexander so hard I blushed.

"Shin! That's enough!" I tried to interrupt.

"I can spend the rest of the night explaining why bringing Omhet out of the palace is a terrible idea," said Shin, now both leaving me behind while they enjoyed the conversation at my expense.

"The rumors are not true. I didn't die three times. That was exaggerated. Can we change the subject?" I beg. This guy was ruining my night.

Shin stopped, making a circle of people who began to walk around us.

"So, it's just an old rumor, then?"

"I was eight years old!"

"My sister beat me when she was six," Alexander said with a laugh.

I stared at Shin with a glare. I couldn't believe he was doing this to me.

"I wasn't training," I explained angrily. "Guillermo took me in the middle of the night—"

Shin frowned. "Guillermo? That doesn't make sense. For what?"

I couldn't answer. My voice shook as I tried to explain that it was an accident. Maybe Guillermo got up on the wrong side that morning... and all the previous ones.

Alexander put his arm around my neck in a friendly hug. He was so tall that I almost lost my balance. "All siblings try to kill their younger brother at least once in their life. As a big brother, I can assure you, it's part of our role."

But Shin was petrified as if he had discovered a secret that no one knew.

"Omhet," Shin whispered. "I didn't know—I..."

"It was nothing," I tried to yell at him, but it was barely a whisper. "Just old rumors and stupid put-downs that haunt me. Any other rumor you want to share, Shin?"

Shin tried to reply, but he bit his lip and shook his head.

We didn't talk the rest of the way anymore. What was I going to say? Shin brought up stupid events that everyone thought were jokes. Alexander probably thought I was an idiotic, weak, useless kid who allowed his older brother to use him for years at his whim. But I was worse than a rag doll to my brother. I was his perverse joy.

"So...," Alexander said. "I see you don't have a good relationship with your older brother. I shouldn't be surprised. You're a magnet for chaos."

I think he was trying to cheer me up.

"I have a good relationship with all my family except Guillermo. It is not a big deal, anyway," I *really* want to drop the subject.

"Isn't he the one who will be the king of Glacier? If he's so bad now, I can't imagine when he gets to the throne."

And though I've never admitted it to anyone, I've had nightmares all my life about that day.

The Twin Moon tavern was huge.

At Glacier, the taverns were one floor, one bar, and we all knew each other's names.

Not in Andebeck. It had three floors! In two different corners of the first level, there were two bars. In the middle a round stage, with the musicians playing instruments with such energy that I was barely going to be able to hear my own voice. It was packed, every floor except the third.

The third level had dozens of doors as if it were some kind of inn—but inside a tavern? Why would there be rooms on the third floor of a tavern?

"What's on the third floor?"

"Don't ask," Shin interrupted and shoved me by the shoulder. "Don't lose sight of Alexander, don't get distracted, don't walk away from me—"

So many instructions made me snort. Shin was frantic.

The place was crowded. I thought I would lose sight of Alex until he stopped in front of a hallway with stairs to the basement.

"Welcome back, Your Highness," a woman greeted him. One that lifted her hand and caressed his face. If someone touched me like that, I would have blushed all the way to my ears, but Alexander acted like it was normal. He motioned for me to walk ahead of him, and Shin placed a hand on my shoulder, I think he tried to stop me, but I brushed it off. I went downstairs and entered the only door at the end of the corridor.

Upon entering, I found a private room. Red carpets, its own bar, and waiters in uniform. It was fancier than the rest of the tavern on the main floor, but here were for guests only. And everyone who was here I could recognize.

Especially Karl.

"Welcome to our little escape," said Alexander entering behind me.

I exhaled. I'm just glad it was not an ambush.

"Why did you bring him?" Alanis asked.

She approached with her usual wide skirt and a short top, which showed part of her belly. This time, she didn't have her hair on top of her head. Instead, she had it curly, free, and with a flower above her ear.

"Don't," said Pierre. "He's Alex's guest."

As if that meant something, Alanis did not protest further. That was good, but it made me stay close to Alexander in hopes of feeling safe. No one seemed to dare look at me too much when Alex was with me.

Not even Karl. He was not only with his guards socializing with his courts, but Khloe was with him too. As soon as Karl noticed me, he positioned himself closer to her. Worst of all, she didn't stop looking at me for more than a second before she continued socializing with the other guests.

A sigh caught my attention, and I noticed how Shin was staring at her. I couldn't blame him—Khloe had on a dress where the translucent fabric fell to her ankles, but there were high slits open to the thighs. I had to nudge my guardian, and he turned his flushed gaze away.

"Someone is excited to see an old friend," I commented.

"If someone hears what you're implying, Sir, I'm a dead man," Shin blushed, and I held my laugh. He was right. I shouldn't had said that. No one was allowed to touch an Ettezi woman without permission. Much less someone as ordinary as Shin, or they could sentence him to death for just looking into her eyes.

"Omhet," Alexander called me. "I want to introduce you to the daughter of a powerful High Lady. This is Sani from the court of Sierra Adaza." He pointed to the woman in front of me, whose dark skin glowed in the candlelight.

I did not recognize her at first, I was used to see her in training uniform. She moved toward me with delicate grace, as if she didn't have a huge cloth headdress with gold designs that matched the fabric of her garments. Her attire covered most of her skin, but her earrings and accessories made her look like a goddess.

"My lady," I made a short act of reverence to greet her. "Is the Sierra Adaza court as beautiful as you? If so, it would be a paradise."

When she smiled, she was even more beautiful.

"You and your family are welcome," she told me joyfully in her musical accent. "As you are familiar with small territories, mine is the second smallest in the union."

Without causing any problems, I was able to have a conversation with Sani, getting to know her culture and court. It was interesting to discover that hers was a country primarily connected with the desert near Ettezi, but they also had a coastline. Even more interesting was when she told me that Ettezi and Sierra Adaza had decades of warfare before joining the union as allies.

"History is written in lies by their hands. They convinced the world that they were pirates who adopted the red desert, but it's their most vile lie. The red desert was ours. Now, we are cornered by the sea."

Waiters passed us by with trays of hors d'oeuvres and drinks in glasses. I was so wrapped up in her story that I didn't dare to look at the Ettezi across the room. Surely, they could feel that we were talking about them.

"In theory, are Sierra Adaza and Ettezi friends or enemies?"

"We're at peace," she concluded, but I noticed how her voice stumbled a bit. "Ettezi is not to be trusted, Omhet. I know you have seen yourself as a friend with Khloe, but you must be prudent."

"Khloe is different from Ettezi. She doesn't want to be like them," I insisted.

"Perhaps, but she's part of it and has to behave like them. She has no other option," I surreptitiously glanced at Khloe, seeing that she was acting like an Ettezi. Unlike how she behaved when her brother was not around. "We had the desert until they invaded us. They were mere pirates before starting their wars, and we managed to defend ourselves. They are here now, trying to conquer the capital with their pretty faces."

I stared at them. Karl and Khloe dominated wherever they were because that was part of who they were. They conquered with their presence and destroyed whatever it touched. They acted like they could conquer the world with their arrogance.

"My court is allied to Puerto Escondido, and I want to win this competition," Sani continued. "But mostly, what I want is to take our lands back from those conquerors."

I looked away from Karl when he caught me glaring at him.

"Every culture can change. You only need a small flame to make a big explosion," I commented, thinking about Khloe because I knew she detested the unfair part of her culture as much as I did.

"Pray to your god that Khloe of Ettezi will win, then," she concluded. "Because, if Karl does, she will not be happy either."

I wanted to hear more about Ettezi, but Sani broke off, looking over my shoulder. It wasn't until that moment that I realized someone was approaching me, and I knew who it was by just hearing his steps.

"Don't you dare," Sani warned.

"I come in peace," Karl said.

I turned around without showing any fear. We stared at each other with the usual seriousness.

"Interesting choice of word because until recently, the word 'peace' didn't exist in your dictionary," Sani replied.

"We are natural warriors, which is why I have dedicated my entire life to being the best. I'd rather have the enemy afraid of me than become his prey."

"We are rational beings who have learned to forgive as well," Sani said, waving her hand for her guardians to move with her. "Don't forget your mercy, Prince Karl—you can easily lose control."

Sani joined another group as far away from Karl as possible, but I had to take a deep breath. It was my turn to deal with him.

"I know just by looking at you that you have no idea you're in front of the leader of this competition," Karl began, crossing his arms. "You must feel like a rodent in the middle of a parliament of owls."

I wanted to answer him like we were having a normal conversation, knowing there were people around who could defend me. But then I found myself alone as Alexander followed Alanis to enjoy dancing, without realizing that I was cornered. Then I looked at Shin, but he had left my side, leaving to go...

Over to Khloe? He touched her shoulder, and when she turned around, he said something to her that made her laugh. What the heck was going on?

"It's actually three territories that are dominating," I responded to his comment, trying to focus. "It must feel terrible to know that it is no longer just you."

"It's good to always have your opponents close," he replied with a shrug. "The more you know them, the better."

"What a disappointment for you that I'm here with all of the favorites of this competition, huh, Karl?" I scoffed.

"Oh, make no mistake," he said, grabbing a few grapes from a nearby table. "Do you think being Alex's shadow makes you have a powerful ally?" He laughed. "You have something valuable that they want. If you want my advice, be careful."

I looked at Alex. He was having a wonderful time dancing with Alanis, and I couldn't answer, feeling that the drama in this place was too much for me. Especially since I didn't see evil in them—in Alexander. Or maybe that was his specialty—to manipulate with his charming personality. He already did it once, it wouldn't be strange if he did it a second time—

Stop overthinking. Don't listen to Karl!

"You might act like the biggest idiot here with your pretty, innocent face," Karl whispered to me, coming up behind my back to speak in my ear. "But everyone knows that you had the balls to get close to the damn dragon, and that's why they're hanging out with you—to steal all the information they can..."

"I have nothing to offer," I protested. "What happened was an accident."

"You're in a bloody competition, and by mistake or blessing, you've surrounded yourself with allies and enemies, but can you identify which is which?" he asked, and I heard him popped another grape into his mouth.

I wanted to defend Alexander. I wanted to say that I knew who my allies were, but while I looked at him, I knew that I didn't know anything about any of these people.

"What does it matter to you, anyway?" I said, trying to maintain my attitude.

"I care," he said, getting closer to my ear. I could feel his huge body almost pressed against my back. "Because I want you for myself, Omhet." All the sounds in the background, music, cacophony, and chatter, disappeared as the rage took over me. "I don't want any enemy to touch you before me because when I become a king, guess which kingdom I'm going to conquer first."

"You can't..." I turned with attitude, moving at least three steps away. I couldn't let his closeness intimidate me.

"Or what? What's a coward like you going to do? Cry?" He turned and left to go back with his people.

I clenched my teeth and my fists. I grew up as the youngest son, constantly mocked, and I had to learn to defend myself continually. So, I had a natural urge to fight Karl. I wanted to jump on him and bust his face. He couldn't get away with taunting me like that, so I started walking toward him as soon as he turned his back on me. I pulled him around by the arm, and before he had time to react, I punched him in the face so hard that everyone gasped in surprise. Even the musician stopped.

"You're not going to intimidate me," I shouted. "You can mess with me, but don't you ever threaten my kingdom again."

His allies began to approach and surround me, but Karl waved them off.

"How dare you touch me in front of..."

"I don't give a fuck about your ego," I spat, approaching him more.

I waited for him to hit me back, and I saw him getting ready.

Alexander came to stand behind me, followed by Alanis and, finally, Sani.

"That's enough!" Alexander ordered.

Karl looked at me and those behind me. Without saying anything else, he grabbed his things and opened the door.

"Khloe," hollered Karl.

"I'm not done," she said and took a glass of wine from a passing servant.

Karl was furious. He reminded me of the look Guillermo used to give me when he would go into my room and pull my hair into the hallway. I shivered, remembering it.

But he didn't say a word and stormed out the door without her.

I thought I had ruined the night and would get in a lot of trouble, but when I looked to find the useless Shin, he was leaning against the wall next to Khloe, sipping beer with a victorious smile.

Did he leave me alone on purpose?

"He won't sleep happily tonight," Khloe said to Shin, and they laughed.

I couldn't control my breathing. I was furious. Not even a small victory makes me feel better.

"Relax," Alex said from behind. "Everyone here is celebrating with you. I promise there will be time for consequences later," he said, and when I turned, he offered me a glass of wine.

I nodded, listening to the laughter around me at Karl's expense. When the music played again, it was more energetic than before.

I tried to return my attention to the group to enjoy the rest of the night like the rest were doing, but Karl's words stayed with me. Deep down, I knew Karl was right about a lot of things. I didn't know who the hell was my ally or my enemy. Or if there even was a difference in this competition.

For the moment, I tried to enjoy what was left of the night. I could smile for now because I had won this round. I had won the massive warrior of the desert kingdom.

"You are very protective of your kingdom," Khloe said.

I was surprised that she had dared to speak to me, but now that her bodyguards weren't there or her brother, I saw the same Khloe I first knew.

"It's all I have," I murmured in response.

"Becoming Ettezi's enemy with a kingdom as vulnerable as yours is risky," she said, sitting on a stool, resting her back against the wall.

"That's why he can't win this competition," I insisted and drank from my glass of wine. Bitter, just like tonight has turned.

"Everyone knows it is becoming more difficult to compete with him. He has Rustilla and Or-Mua on his side..."

"On Ettezi's side," I clarified, and I declined when a waiter offered me an appetizer from the tray. "You are an Ettezi, and you're in this competition just like him."

She laughed bitterly and hid it with her glass as she sipped her wine. "Leave your risky comments for those who really have an army to fight." With her eyes, she pointed to the others enjoying their night. The real heroes of the trials of fire.

We didn't say anything else and kept our distance. One that seemed like we hated each other, but on the contrary, I felt comfortable having a normal conversation with Khloe once more.

When Shin returned with two new drinks, I was about to thank him because I had run out of mine...

If it weren't for the fact that it was one for him and one for Khloe. I dropped my hand. He turned his back on me to talk to her, causing me to move further away from them.

What the hell got into him? He never laughed at my jokes, but he was giggling like an idiot as she tucked her hair behind her ear.

I was about to interrupt his insolence when someone pulled me by the arm.

"Let them breathe," said Alexander.

"If anyone sees him near her..."

"There are many rules in this room; one of them is that there are no titles. In other words, what happens here does not come out of here. Don't worry."

"Yes, but Karl—"

"Do you think you'd be in one piece if it weren't for the rules that protect us here? Karl would have murdered you as his culture demands. You publicly humiliate him."

"Don't *you* think I should have known these rules before arriving?" I asked, noticing he was pulling me closer and closer to the dance floor.

"You were supposed to smile and enjoy the night. How could I know that you were going to end up provoking the most violent guy of the competition?"

I snorted. "Smile and enjoy. You talk like my father."

"For a reason!"

I tried not to, but I was laughing when he looked at me. I think I'm starting to understand why my father doesn't want me in the upcoming battle.

I stopped at the edge of the dance floor, with people to the left and right. Alanis kicked off her slippers, and the music adapted to her movements.

She thrived in her dance. Drums and guitars filled all the sounds as she moved her skirt. I found it fascinating that her movements controlled the music and not the other way around.

"Can you dance, prince of the high mountains?" Alanis asked me.

"Not like that," I instantly said.

"Let me show you."

She offered me her hand, and I hesitated. Alanis was the last person I trusted—

But Alex pushed me, and I took her hand in my stumble. Alanis rejoiced at my forced acceptance, and I danced. Of course, I danced. I was never a combat person or a scholar, but if I have experience in something, it's in the nightlife.

If the battle to come were about dancing, my life would have been easier.

So, I laughed as I danced with dozens of guests, losing myself in this pleasant sensation. Even Alexander grabbed me around the waist while we imitated Alanis's movements. Besides being drunk, we were unbearably happy.

Or so I wanted to be until I saw one of the guests with reddish hair dancing among the others.

It seemed unfair to have to disappoint some people to make others happy.

CHAPTER 18

"Okay, that's enough. You're drunk," Shin ordered, pulling me by my shirt.

I tripped over the waiter and knocked over several glasses. I tried apologizing through my laughter, but I kept making it worse.

"Take him home, Shin," Alexander yelled, with Alanis on his lap.

They both look like the gods of this room, sitting in a chair the size of a throne.

Khloe drank every last drink behind the table as if it didn't affect her. Sani was dancing, and Alexander seemed too busy with Alanis to talk to anyone else.

"I'll see you on the battlefield, my friends," I said, bowing as if finishing an act.

Shin pulled again out into the hall. This time I stumble up the stairs, pushing and getting lost in the crowd. Until we were outside, and the four moons greeted us.

"Throw up in the gutter, where I don't have to see you," Shin ordered me.

There was no longer a soul in the streets or alleys of the city. It was deserted. It must be past midnight, and ironically the city looked more beautiful than ever.

I straightened up, pushed my hair out of my face, and adjusted the jacket in its place.

"I'm not drunk. I was just pretending to be," I said in a hurry. "Now, let's go before it's too late." I started walking down the street in the opposite direction of the palace.

Shin looked at me, confused. I think my change was too drastic for his understanding. "Where are you going?"

"I have one more place to go," I said, speeding through the alley. "Laila is waiting for me."

"What? Laila! Omh—Omhet! Come back!"

Shin yelled my name several times, but I outran him past the alley, now exiting the city limits. I was going directly to the paths through the woods because I was going to the ruins.

There was a horse station where the avenues ended, and the endless streets outside the city began. They were mainly near the inn for tourists to rest, which I was looking for because I was going to *borrow* a horse.

"Omhet!" Shin shouted, catching up to me at last. "We must go back to the palace, or Cheikh will kill me..."

"Cheikh, the king of Glacier, Marcus... how many leaders are above us?" I answered with an attitude while entering the horse station. "There will always be someone telling me what to do. Power is exhausting."

There weren't many horses in the corrals or any guards. I had to be quick, so I grabbed the saddle and sprinted to the first horse I found.

"Sir, if you were king, you'll understand all those leaders have to do to keep a kingdom at peace," he scolded me.

"Peace?" I repeated, pausing for a moment before opening the corral. "Kings look only at their own interests and the prosperity that suits them. Don't be naive, Shin—not everything is black and white."

I put the saddle on the horse as quickly as my fingers could move. I jumped on the horse and started toward the exit. Until Shin stepped in front of us, preventing my escape.

"Why are you doing this?" he asked, dropping his arms. I had never seen him so frustrated.

"Because this is what we're here for," I replied in a hurry, trying to get past him.

"Not this way! Wait—" he ordered. "I'm not going to continue indulging in this stupidity. Sooner or later, someone will find out what you are doing—have you thought about that?"

"Who is going to tell them? You?"

He let out a moan. "Omhet, you're playing with fire, and you're going to burn me with you."

"You have two options," I said, fully determined. "Go and run to tell Cheikh or Marcus. They will notify our king, banish me from Andebeck, and in the end, I will have you removed from your post and rank." Shin took a step back in shock at my threat. "Or be quiet, fulfill your mission of guarding me as the king would have wanted, and help me save Laila Blume," he shook his head. "Is the only thing that matters!"

"Don't make me choose between you and my duty. Don't do it."

"Has your heart ever contradicted reason?" his eyes widened, but he didn't answer.

I did not say anything else and ordered the horse to run.

Maybe it was the wine, the adrenaline, or the desperation, but having taken everything out so harshly on Shin made me feel like crap. I wouldn't be able to fire Shin. My father would first dishonor me before allowing me to ruin my guardian's life.

May your lives be to protect mine, as mine be to protect yours, I vowed, and today I just spat in his face the worst thing I could've said.

I was desperate. I couldn't allow him to tell Cheikh. If my father takes me out of this competition, it would all have been for nothing. In Andebeck, they were killing themselves for a crown, while a woman was desperate to be helped in the ruins. If someone found out what I knew, it could be worse—they could use it as an excuse to finish off the dragon.

Laila was not only the answer to this competition but to all of Andebeck's problems but mine as well. I had so many questions that only she could answer, so that's why I hurried my horse down the path that I was already learning by heart.

I got off by the same tree as last time, tying up the horse and looking at the dark and silent ruins. I didn't hear a murmur, so I circled the tree, looking for any notes or signs that Laila had been here. Sure, she should at least have left me a message of thanks or rejection. Whatever it was, I hoped for an answer because if I didn't hear from her again, I would go crazy.

I looked where I had left the bag of supplies but couldn't find it. That meant Laila took the bag but left me no answer to my note, and I didn't know how to feel about that. I knew it would be better to simply forget what little I had discovered, but my heart raced in contraction. What the hell was wrong with me?

I was about to climb up the tree to look for any other possible signs when I heard a hiss, like a cat stalking prey—a big cat. I froze, lowering myself back to the ground, not because I was afraid of a wild animal but because the horse had reacted with such terror that it made me nervous. That was my signal to get out of there now. So, I dropped to the ground and turned to run back...

A gasp left my lips as I abruptly stopped when I met the gaze of some familiar yellow eyes.

I stepped back and collided with the tree trunk. At that moment, I forgot how to breathe. The dragon must have been close to me all this time, hidden in the shadows, as if waiting for me.

"Good heavens," I whispered.

Ignorantly, I thought the dragon would not come out of the ruins and that perhaps the beast was as trapped as Laila. There it was in front of me. I could see its tail moving, feeling the gusts of wind that it made just by moving. One flick of that tail could split me in two. Maybe I should have reacted. However, I could not stop looking at it without moving or breathing. The dragon began to show its teeth, exhaling air so strong through its nose that it emitted smoke.

"Eat me now, roast me if you want, because if you don't, I'll destroy you and Tiara. Laila Blume will be free one day, whether you like it or not," I said with a strong voice. I didn't want to show fear. I tried to look strong, but my tremors didn't help much.

The dragon growled as if it understood every word I said.

Interesting...

"Why haven't you bathed me in fire?" I whispered, more out of curiosity than surprise.

Like a much larger cat, the dragon opened its mouth and bellowed loudly. Its hot breath hit me so hard I felt like I'd opened an oven. I tried to stay calm, even though my eyes burned.

I detached myself from the trunk and took a step toward the dragon.

It took a step back.

I smiled. It had moved away from me instead of eating me.

"You won't be able to scare me," I said, taking another step and looking into its eyes. "You are a creature—" I tried to find the right words, but as I got closer to it, only fascination remained in me. My shoulders relaxed as my posture became more comfortable in front of it, and a smile crossed my lip as I watched it. "You are a beautiful creature."

His yellow eyes were no longer violent, his teeth were hidden, and I could even appreciate the soft reddish color of his scales.

It did something I didn't expect—it lowered its head to my level, looking at me face to face as if it wanted to eat me and was ready to tear me apart, but it did nothing. I raised my hand, looking into its eyes, calm and fearful at the same time.

The dragon growled at me, so I stopped. But then I tried again. I raised my hand and slowly brought it closer.

I took a deep breath, held it with all my might, and took another step.

I touched the dragon—right on its cheek, as it looked at me, grumbling in a warning. I did not take my hand away. I expected death, but nothing happened.

I blew the air out of my lungs.

The dragon was still looking at me, but now it looked confused.

"No," I said, responding to its curious gaze, "I'm not afraid of you." At least not so much, I corrected. My fascination outweighed any fear. It was a beast, a huge animal, but it was beautiful. I got closer. I wanted to put my other hand on its thick skin. I wanted to touch the strong scales.

Its wings spread with such force that I fell to the ground. They were enormous, and when they flapped, I had to grab the grass under me because the breeze almost dragged me across the ground. I did not have time to move because, out of nowhere, the dragon flew in the direction of the ruins. It was going to hide, but why so suddenly?

I laughed, lying on the ground, watching the dragon zoom away from me. I was definitely drunk or completely insane. I couldn't stop my smile and fascination. I felt like I'd been locked up in Glacier for too many years. This was unbelievable! I wanted to see it again. I wanted to be able to earn its trust. I wanted to ride it and soar through the skies. I wanted... I wanted things to be different.

I have to kill it in winter, and the thought irritates me. Why not just find it a home where it can be free from the witch and Laila? The dragon was not to blame for the curse, and deep down, it seemed like a good creature.

"You're the craziest guy I know," a voice said behind me.

When I looked up from the ground, I saw Shin crouching behind a tree. He was so scared I thought he was going to collapse.

"It was you! You scared it away," I accused, standing up. I didn't wait for an answer as I ran toward the ruins. I had to see the dragon again. I had to touch it again. It had such curious eyes, showing its aggressiveness and merciful side simultaneously.

"Omhet!" Shin yelled, running after me. "No, Omhet!"

I ran tirelessly for once in my life, leaping over rubble and destroyed steps until I reached the castle's entrance. I peeked inside without making a sound. The dragon was there, clawing up the walls, destroying everything in its path. It crept through a gap in the wall until it disappeared as if it were its nest. I hadn't noticed that hole the first time I'd been there.

Shin came up behind me, leaning out with his sword in his hand, looking around.

"We have to warn Marcus and the rest of the Union. We can ambush it and cut off its wings and head and..." I glared at him, and he went silent. "What?"

"What's wrong with you?"

"No! What's wrong with you?"

"Lower your freaking voice, Shin. Do you want to die?"

"Do you?" I rolled my eyes. "Can we leave now?"

"We're not here because of the dragon—"

"Laila's ghost?" he yelped, and the echo bounced around us.

"Come on, coward, we're through the hardest part."

"Is it me, or do you sound sure of your words?" he yelled while I left him behind. "It's a dangerous beast. You can't know if we're through the hardest part. Perhaps it's waiting for us on the other side. Perhaps we are its damn dinner."

I went down the hall where I had walked with Khloe while Shin whimpered behind me. He wouldn't even let me concentrate as I tried to remember where I had run to find the door to the tower.

I knew it was close when I walked through a double door and found the destroyed library. I couldn't even see beyond the first shelves because of the darkness of the night. Our only help was the light from the four moons that came through the broken window, walls, and ceiling.

"Did you hear that?" Shin whispered, crouching down.

Yes, I could hear a growl, as if the dragon was in pain or snoring. I wasn't much of an expert on beasts, so I stood at the library entrance, knowing it was close.

"We passed the tower entrance," I said, returning my steps. "I remember that I turned down one of these corridors."

"This place is three times the size of Andebeck palace—we'll get lost," Shin yelled. The fear had utterly overcome him.

If he'd just shut up for a moment, I could have explained that I knew what I was doing. I could have shown him that the first time I ran from the library to the main hall, somehow, that desperate run had led me to the steps leading to a tower. At least that's what I wanted to explain, but when I turned down the hall, I found those emerald eyes that I'd been thinking about so much.

Laila...

She was holding onto the wall and stopped just as if she had been looking for me. I could barely see her because she was using the shadow to hide.

Shin gasped and held me. He reacted not as if he had seen a ghost but a demon.

She closed her eyes, holding onto the wall for support.

I tried to step toward her, but she moved away from me.

"I warned you..." she said in a weak but angry voice, "not to come back."

Shin looked terrified. I thought he would pass out as I had on my first day at the competition because he was so pale.

"Do you really want me to go?" I asked in a soft voice. "I don't want to intrude—I just want to help."

She moaned, and I wanted to run to her to see what was happening. It seemed like a terrible pain was pounding her head because she held it with her hands.

"Why don't you understand..." she began to sound weaker and weaker. I tried to get a little closer. There was sweat on her forehead, part of her tangled hair was covering her face, and her knees bent as if she was about to fall from weakness. "I am trying to save *you*?"

Me? She's trying to save my life when she's the one who needs help?

Her eyes were closing as she started falling. I knew it was coming. I dove to the floor next to her to break her fall so that her head would rest on my chest.

Shin crouched close to us and brushed the hair from her face to get a better look at her. He flinched when he realized that she was real. Coward. He was brave to face any enemy, but for ghosts and dragons, he almost vomited from his nerves.

"She's alive," he whispered and looked into my eyes. "What the hell have you gotten yourself into?"

"This is not the time for this," I said in a hurry. "Shin, forgive me for threatening you, *for...* for acting immature, but this is what I needed to show you. I need someone to help me—I can't do this alone. She needs us, and I—I need you."

Shin nodded, even though he didn't seem convinced.

"Okay, for today, I'll help you."

"Thank you—"

"No. Don't thank me. I'm going to tell everything to Cheikh as soon as we get back, and you will not ever threaten me again. Do you understand, Prince Omhet?"

Everything?

I knew the outcomes would be horrible after this, but I didn't hesitate to answer. "I will assume my consequences, guardian. And I will never threaten you again."

I got up with her, surprised to find that she seemed to weigh almost nothing. She was so light and thin that I was able to carry her and even trot up the stairs to the tower without a break. I need to bring food immediately... wait. Can she eat?

When I released her into her bed, I could finally see her clearly in the night light that came through the window. Her breath was gasping as if she was struggling to stay alive. Her dress was tattered, and her cheeks were red. I wasted no time and began looking in the drawers, the corners of the room, and even the bathroom for the bag I had given her.

"Omhet," Shin called me urgently, and I turned around. He was next to her with his hand on her forehead. "She's not looking good."

I moved to the side of her bed and touched her soaked forehead. It was so hot I had to move my hand. I looked at Shin nervously.

"We can't let her die."

The bathroom had a shower without a tub, so I couldn't fill anything with water to the brim. I cursed. Only one thing occurred to me, and that was to turn on the shower. Then I took off my jacket and shoes so I wouldn't get more soaked than I needed to. I ran out of the bathroom and approached Laila again.

"I think she's dying," Shin said. "She's speaking in another language, and her eyes..." he couldn't finish, but he didn't have to.

I stared at her for a moment, feeling her life slip away.

"The fever is at a level I've never felt before," I said as I lifted Laila, leaning her face on my shoulder.

Without thinking further, I got under the cold shower water, yelping when I felt the ice water on my body. Laila started to slip from my grasp, so I lifted her better, hugging her against me, with her back under the stream of cold water. It may sound absurd, but I felt her temperature burning my skin like a stove would.

Shin peeked around the door frame, looking at me in shock. No one expected this night to end with me hugging a girl tucked into a cold shower.

Laila opened her eyes and finally looked at me. She didn't try to stand on her own. She didn't even move. She looked as if she was torn between being asleep or awake. She must be so confused.

"Don't be scared," I whispered, tossing her wet hair out of her face. "You are safe."

She laid her head back on my shoulder, this time willingly closing her eyes.

"No one is," she whispered.

I smiled because I could tell I had managed to lower the fever she had.

I slowly returned her to her bed, and it no longer looked like she was going to die at any moment. She looked like she was sleeping. There was nothing left to do but to let her cool down in the night breeze and finally rest. I dropped to the floor, leaning my head against the wall, staring at Laila silently beyond exhaustion. I looked out the window, realizing that the sun could start to rise at any moment.

"This is crazy," Shin said, sitting in the far corner. "What if the dragon appears? Or the sorceress?"

"If there is a sorceress, she doesn't live here with Laila. I think she's cursed to live here with the dragon, but I don't think there is anyone else."

Shin nodded and didn't comment further on the matter. It would not make sense for a sorceress to live here in such a horrible condition if she was alive. If she was as powerful as the legend says, I was sure she was in another part of the world, enjoying the good life, not in this terrible, tortuous place.

"What are you going to do, Omhet?"

"For now..." I whispered and looked at her, feeling lost. "For now, we have to wait."

I know Shin was wondering about the whole mess, and so was I.

Would it be wise to continue to help Laila?

How am I going to hide it from all our leaders and kingdoms?

What would I do now that I had touched the dragon and seen that it wasn't a complete monster?

What would I do if everyone found out and threw me out of the competition or accused me of betraying the trust of the ministers?

What was I going to do with all my responsibilities to my kingdom while playing with fire without feeling the slightest bit of regret?

The worst thing about the whole situation was that deep down, I didn't care at all.

"I have a little sister," I whispered, watching Laila sleep. "She made me tell her tales of knights and damsels in distress. Especially your legend. You're pretty famous, you know?"

There was no answer. The only sound was Shin's soft snoring when he fell asleep. I kept talking, waiting for Laila to reply. To do something. Anything. I desperately wanted to see some sign of life besides her faint breathing.

"In every story, the knights were handsome, tall, strong, poetic, and often even sang to the princess." I rolled my eyes. "I had none of those qualities, of course," I looked out the window, immersed in my thoughts. "I remember Estefania's smile whenever I read the part where the knight saved the damsel, rescuing her from the evil witch, and her reaction gave me the courage to try to be like that knight she admired. For Estefania and—" I inhale deeply, "for you, I'll turn myself into what I'm not. Because I know what it feels like to wait every day for a miracle—for *someone* to save you, but on the contrary, every night a demon enters your room instead of a hero."

I hated to talk about my experience with Guillermo, but it was the first time I was able to talk about it without stuttering.

"There are people that kill your hope, and that is worse than death, I think. My older brother...um..." I closed my eyes. "He killed my hope once. I didn't speak for a whole year. My mother thought that I would never say a word again. And my stubborn brother Cayetano... he saved me."

"Omhet, please, talk to me," I remember Cayetano's tears while I just stared at the snow falling in the window. I didn't cry or argue. I was dead and alive at the same time. The three deaths, rumors said. If only they knew they were in separate times because Guillermo did not want to stop. No matter how many punches Cayetano dealt him or my father's scolding, he was always protected as the future King of Glacier.

And I gave in to fear.

I couldn't speak.

One day Cayetano forced me to look at him, and I pushed him violently. I didn't want anyone to touch me. I just wanted to stay hidden behind the heavy curtain, sitting on the window sill, watching the snowfall.

"Damn it, you can't let him defeat you. You're more than that," I couldn't respond. After a year, my back was healed. No injury held me from speaking, but I couldn't even look him in the eyes. *"Forgive me for not being there,"* he whispered, and I noticed his voice trembled. *"The gods know that I would have killed him if I were. You are the craziest, most daring, and cheerful boy in the family. You can't let him steal that from you. You can't let fear defeat you—come back. Please... please, come back, little brother. Say something. Anything!"* He sobbed. *"Talk to me, please. Omhet, please, talk to me—"*

"Laila," I called her in a soft whisper. "Please, talk to me."

CHAPTER 19

The light of the dawn woke me slowly, and there was enough light to see the room better. I felt the effect of last night's alcohol in a negative and heavy way, but above all, I felt exhausted. I closed my eyes again, groaning at the stab of headache. What a night...

Sleeping for two hours was not nearly enough. I squeezed my eyes and looked quickly to my side.

And for the second time, Laila was gone.

I banged my head against a brick wall in frustration. How the hell does she get up from the dead and walk away without saying goodbye? I was definitely not good at being a knight, and Laila was even worse at being the damsel. I looked in front of me, finding Shin asleep in the other corner. I moved, grabbed my shoe beside me, and threw it with all my strength at Shin's head. He gave a startled cry and drew his sword at the same time he woke up. I would have laughed if it weren't for the exhausting night I'd just had.

"Where is she?" I asked, looking around.

Shin threw the shoe back at me angrily, as the shock had left him in total confusion, even after understanding that he was in no danger.

"How should I know?" he grumbled. "Did you expect me to stand guard for her as well?"

I sighed and started to put on my shoes and jacket. After I had gotten out of the shower, I hadn't put my clothes on. Honestly, I was a complete mess.

"We must go before formation starts," Shin said, getting up sleepily. "Cheikh should have figured out we're gone by now, but if Marcus finds out, we're doomed."

"I can't believe this girl," I commented, ignoring Shin's concern. "Again, she disappeared as if I had imagined her."

Shin looked at me like I was an idiot.

"Omhet, I saw her too. Whatever is going on, it must stop here, now."

"I thought that when you saw her, you would understand that she needs help."

"What are you going to do exactly? This will get out of hand sooner or later."

"Look around you," I said, exasperated. "Do you think it's easy to pretend that I didn't find any of this and forget about her?"

"It's not," he agreed. "But it's not something you and I can fix. If you keep interfering, I assure you that there will be more problems than solutions. Leave this to Marcus!"

"No," I protested, clenching my fists. "I don't know if you've noticed, but Marcus's interests are far from this reality. The only thing that matters to him is the kingdom and getting rid of the dragon for his own benefit. If I tell him about Laila, it might make things more complicated."

"You don't know him—"

"And you are blind! You will always see the best in your leaders because that is what you've been trained in your whole life, but I know... I have *seen* what they can be when no one sees them. And I have a hunch that Marcus is not as good as he appears to be. Give me a chance. I know I can fix this."

Shin restlessly fidgeted while he shook his head. "I already told you I'll help you with this, but that doesn't mean I'm happy with the decision," he finally answered.

The bathroom door opened, startling us. I was on the verge of being defensive because it did not occur to my tired brain that a dragon that big would not fit in such a small bathroom.

"Who's Marcus, and what exactly does he want to do?" Laila asked with attitude.

Shin and I were stunned for a moment. Laila was standing in front of us in a long, clean dress. Her face looked much better and more alive, although her eyes still looked tired. It was the first time I'd seen Laila looking like a normal person—alert and strong. How the hell did she do it? She had gone from being deathly ill to suddenly acting like nothing was wrong. Was it part of the curse? A normal girl with a terrible attitude during the day but delirious at night.

Shin nudged me, trying to get me to talk. The two of us were stunned at seeing the beautiful princess in front of us.

"Are you okay?" I asked, forgetting what she had asked.

Laila looked right into my eyes, making me feel... nervous. Not the kind of nervous that made me run away, more of a I can't believe you're real kind of nervous. A whirlwind of questions came to me. I wanted to know who she really was, if it was true that she had been locked up for almost a century, if she knew where we could find the dragon, and what we could do to break the curse. Good heavens, too many questions—I couldn't think straight.

"Yes," she answered, her face somber. "Thank you."

There was an awkward silence. We had her in front of us, but we didn't know what to say.

"Thanks for the medicine, but it won't help me at all."

"What's happening with you?" I finally asked, taking a step toward her—and regretting them immediately because Laila took a step back.

"No matter what happens to me, I will survive," she said. She didn't want this conversation. I could tell by the way she avoided looking at me. "I'm not going to die... I can't die."

Shin and I looked at each other. I didn't understand exactly what she meant.

"Are you—immortal?" I asked, choking on my own words.

She rolled her eyes. "Do you think I can live a century and still be alive or at least look eighteen?"

Shin snorted. He was annoyed by her attitude.

"We're just trying to help, you know," Shin growled.

"And I can't be helped," she replied in the same tone and looked at me. "You should listen to your friend and stay out of my life, Prince... whoever you are."

"Omhet," I introduced myself, feeling like an idiot. "And you must be Princess Laila," if she'd said it was Tiara, I'd have thrown myself off the balcony, I swear.

She nodded. I could see that she wanted me out of her life. She didn't want any help, and this visit irritated her. This is not how I thought this was going to end. It was driving me crazy!

"Where is the dragon?" asked Shin.

Laila closed her eyes as if something terrible had been mentioned to her. She even hugged herself as if she had gotten cold.

"Hidden," she answered, suddenly shy.

"Where?" Shin pressed.

She shivered and flattened herself against the wall. She clearly didn't want to answer, and I know that feeling very well.

"Shin," I yelped. "Enough."

"Why won't she give me a straight answer?"

I looked at Shin impatiently.

"Go outside—that's an order," I snapped, already fed up with his attitude.

Shin looked at me like he couldn't believe what I'd said. Without saying anything else, he opened the door and slammed it shut on his way out.

"You should go with him," Laila said after Shin was gone. "There is nothing you or anyone else can do to help me."

How she averted her gaze, crossed her arms fearfully, and forced an angry tone of voice were painfully familiar. She had given up. Laila didn't want to hope, and she was trying to save me, not from the dragon—

Laila was trying to save me from herself.

"Okay," I finally nodded. "I will respect your decision and will not try to help or visit again."

She raised an eyebrow. "You're going to ask me for something in return, aren't you?"

I held back a smile. She already knew me, and for that simple reason, my heart raced like crazy. "I want to know why you're pushing me away."

Her shoulders slumped. "Isn't it obvious? I'm cursed forever. I can't have anyone near me. I don't want you to get hurt again. I know what the dragon did to you, and I don't know if next time I—if that beast—I can't protect you..."

"Hey, I'm sorry, I'm sorry," I ran close to her and held her hands. By Krea, she was shaking. She looked me in the eyes, and I think I was not the only one stuck. I couldn't look at anything but her eyes. She squeezed my hands over hers, and I smiled a little. "Princess," I was so close I spoke in a whisper, "I don't want to leave you unless you say you despise me. Otherwise, no beast will stop me from being here."

She closed her eyes and took a deep breath. "Your presence doesn't bother me, but I don't intend to be responsible for your death. So, you'll stay for one short conversation. *One*, and then you will go."

I smiled widely. I think my excitement made Laila blush. I could see it on her cheeks and how her beautiful freckles radiated on her skin. "It's all I wanted."

She rolled her eyes, but she wasn't angry anymore.

"You were right—you are more stubborn than me."

The entirety of the castle might have been destroyed, but I was surprised to discover something new each time I visited. This time I came across an indoor garden that was growing naturally where once there had been a ceremony room. I could see the broken glass mosaic on the ceiling, and when the first rays of the sun hit it, the room lit up with rainbows. I walked through the center, seeing how the vines and wildflowers took over the walls and the tile floor was cracked. Even though it looks like overgrown and out of place, it was now my favorite room in the entire castle. I whistle in surprise.

"It seems small now," Laila said, leaning against the arch of the entrance. "It was once so big that balls were held here."

Like your wedding to Rafael? My mind screamed almost immediately, causing me to blink as if that would take my thought away.

I disturbed a small butterfly clinging to a nearby vine to see if it would perch on my finger. "I want to ask you so many questions. I don't know where to start," I admitted, seeing the butterfly opening and closing its wings. I let it go and then turned to Laila, putting my hands in my pockets. "I want to know what really happened."

"I'll start by explaining that if you've heard anything about me, it's probably not real," she began. She seemed to hate talking about this. "Or at least, not the correct version."

I nodded—I already suspected that.

"Tell me," she said with a soft voice. "What do you want to know?"

"Where is Tiara?"

I looked into her eyes, expecting something terrible—but she just shrugged.

I think my disappointment showed on every part of my face.

"The great and terrifying Tiara, so despicable that she brought a dragon to ruin a joyous wedding." She rolled her eyes. "I looked for her and invoked her to remove this curse, but she disappeared like the worst fairy godmother who ever existed."

I laughed unexpectedly, so I covered my mouth. Imagining Tiara as a coward was surprisingly funny.

Laila almost laughs. Almost.

I must see you smile before I leave. I just have to...

"Well, she doesn't sound like the great sorceress I was expecting," I said. I was going to ask why Tiara would be afraid of what she created, but Laila interrupted me.

"My turn," she said and started walking in my direction. She was barefoot, and her hair was messy, but at the same time, she looked like a nymph in the middle of a fairy garden. It was hard for me to focus for a second. "I don't recognize your accent or your elegant garment. Who are you, and where do you come from?"

I bowed as if I was introducing myself to her for the first time.

"Omhet Guillermo Espinho of Glacier." I responded as my king would. "And I have come at the invitation of the minister Marcus, the last of the Blumes."

"Marcus?" she repeated. She seemed pretty far from all the palace issues. "Is Glacier a court—?"

"A kingdom, Princess," I interrupted. I couldn't hide my tone. "In Timantti, the highest mountain of the Union."

"I'm sorry. I didn't mean to offend. When I was a little girl, there were only two kingdoms," she explained, walking distracted around the room. "I only remember visiting Ettezi and the beaches of Puerto Escondido."

"I'd like to take you to Glacier one day," I invited her immediately, and she stopped to look at me. I looked down, a little flushed—did I sound too forward? "My kingdom loves visitors."

She almost smiled, but she was still keeping distance. That's why I keep my hands in my pockets, so that she wouldn't be afraid of me and that the distance from me would make her feel safe.

"I can't," she said as her sad look returned. "I can't get out of this castle. I never have and never will."

I was going to ask for more details when she turned and left the room. I wondered if it was my fault that her terrible mood had returned, and I was willing to drop the subject of her condition to try to make her smile. However, I had to remind myself that I was here to learn as much as possible about her, and I still felt like I hadn't gotten anywhere.

I ran after her, back into the unsteady corridors with broken walls.

"Princess," I called, but she didn't stop. "Laila!" I yelled louder, and this time she stopped. "I'm not here to take advantage of you or give you false hope," I began to approach her slowly. "but I want your permission to come back."

Laila turned at last, and I saw the pain in her eyes.

"Dear prince, I'm the one who doesn't want to give you false hope," she said, walking to me. "If a hundred years have passed without a solution, why do you think now will be any different?"

"Because a hundred years ago, I didn't exist," I said, totally joking.

She covered her face, and I thought it was out of anger at first, but then...

She laughed. It was a soft giggle, but it was enough. At least for today.

"Oh, Omhet, you are insane."

I clenched my hand back in my pockets. I wanted to feel Laila's hands in mine again.

"A little." I laughed with her. "What do you say?" I asked nervously. "Will you let me visit?" She shook her head, but she didn't say no out loud. "I promise to bring your lizard a bone when I return."

"The dragon is not a dog," she exclaimed.

"Give me a couple weeks. I'll tame it anyway."

Something about my comment made her blush, and she lowered her eyes.

"Are you always this funny?"

"I'm trying to control myself, just to make a good impression."

She shook her head. She was having fun with me even though she tried to hide it.

Just when it seemed that Laila was finally feeling comfortable with my presence, I heard Shin whistling at me from outside. I leaned out the window and heard him yelling, but I couldn't understand. From his agitated state, I knew I was in trouble.

I took a deep breath because what awaited me would not be pleasant.

"I have to go."

I started to rush past her when she took my hand. She caught me so off guard that I didn't know how to react when I turned around.

"You can't leave," she told me, and I felt like I was willing to reject my last name and whole kingdom just to stay with her infinitely. "You haven't told me what you're doing here and what Marcus wants."

"Then let me visit," I plead. "I know it's hard to trust a complete stranger who invaded your ruins but believe me, I am here for the sole purpose of helping you."

"I trust you," her words unleashed a whirlwind in my heart. "But if something happens to you, I'll never forgive myself."

I wanted to insist and persist. Tell her that I already touched the dragon, and it didn't attack me. That I would find a way—by Krea, I would find a way to visit her, to control the dragon—to save her from her curse. But when I heard Cheikh's voice near the ruins, my mood came crashing down. *Oh, shit! Not him—not Cheikh.*

The situation worsened, and I didn't want to involve the princess. I had to leave, *immediately.*

"I'll come next Sunday," I said in a hurry. "I'll tell you everything."

She squeezed my hand a little more. "Do you promise?"

"Have I ever stopped bothering you with my presence?"

Her smile was answer enough for me. What are you doing to me?

When she let go of my hand, I started to run, but I had only taken two steps when I stopped.

"Oh, I'm sorry—me and my manners," I said, returning to Laila.

I grabbed her hand, gave it a respectful kiss, and after a quick smile, I ran away.

"I'll wait for you..." I heard her whisper. I think she was speaking to herself.

And I'm not going to let you down. I'll see you again. I swear I will.

Chapter 20

I stopped the horse with such force that it rose on two legs, almost letting me fall. I was in front of the labyrinth garden, closer to the arena. When I turned to run to the training arena, I saw Cheikh getting off his horse and stomping toward me. I had to escape from him, desperately searching for an alternate route.

"Omhet Espinho!" Cheikh roared at me.

"I'm sorry, but I'm late," I excused myself and ran off.

Cheikh had gone looking for me in the ruins, and I was sure this would only bring me more trouble that I couldn't face right now. I needed to get to the arena and start my first station.

It didn't matter that I had barely slept or was wearing the same clothes as the night before. Or that the garment was damp from getting in the shower with Laila—

I'm screwed!

I ran down the garden, the stone path, past guardians, and all the main entrances until I reached the training arena. They were all gathered in front of the stage, in their formation rows, while Marcus addressed all the representatives. Which meant that I not only missed the morning warm-up but also breakfast in the dining room.

As usual, I slowly positioned myself at the end of the line, glancing over my shoulders, seeing that my guardians stayed behind and, worse, didn't dare to approach. This is a terrible sign, I thought, just when Marcus fell silent.

"Shit, shit, shit..." I said in an inaudible whisper.

"Prince Omhet," Marcus called from the dais.

I took a deep breath and looked forward again. Everyone had fallen silent, and I realized they had made room to let me onto the stage. I found the courage to walk up to Marcus, repeating in my mind that I hadn't done anything wrong because everything I did was for a good cause. Too bad I couldn't explain any of it, so I pressed my lips together, trying to form an impromptu lie I could use.

"Come closer," Marcus ordered as I stood at the foot of the dais.

I climbed the concrete steps and was in the last place I wanted to be—in front of everyone. It was packed with soldiers, Marcus in front, his adviser Brenda on one side, and Lois on the other. I was surrounded.

"You're a little late," he criticized, and I heard snickering from the crowd. "You should have bothered to at least change your apparel."

"We can talk about it in private," I suggested immediately. This humiliation was unnecessary.

"Not this time. My patience is over, young Glacierian . Your appearance is unacceptable—I can smell the wine from here."

"I can explain," I tried to interrupt.

"You act as if I don't know what happens to you and each of your movements," he accused me. I widened my eyes in astonishment. He couldn't rat me out in front of everyone. If he did, I was lost.

Being surrounded by all of them was embarrassing enough, but knowing that I was being humiliated in their presence felt like I was going to be burned at the stake like a witch. I didn't dare look at any of their faces. I could feel the representative approaching the stage as if it were a public trial.

"A child among adults can make the decision to act maturely or highlight his idiocy, and you know very well which once you're doing," he continued. "Crumpled clothes, the smell of alcohol, red eyes—this boy escaped the palace last night, and as clueless as he is, I know he didn't do it alone."

I expelled the air from my lungs in relief. He didn't mention a dragon, and that was enough for me.

"Tell me here and in front of everyone—who were you with last night?"

The silence deepened with all eyes on me. I scratched my head, looking around and seeing that even Alexander widened his eyes in fear.

I shrugged, more relieved than I should have been. "I don't remember."

I think I heard laughter in the crowd, but I saw Marcus's brow furrowed in anger. Nothing could be as terrible as I imagined it would be if he knew about the dragon. Laila and her secrets were well-kept.

Lois huffed, "You don't remember?" she repeated.

"Not a bit," I said with a shrug. "Alcohol does that sometimes."

Marcus looked at Lois and back at me. It seemed like he really wanted to behead me as punishment.

"Listening to you is a waste of time," he said furiously. "Ladies and gentlemen," he turned to the crowd. "I know some of you escape to go to forbidden places. I already caught one of your honored guests today," he said sarcastically. "And I will give him a punishment that will continue until he tells me the truth about where he was last night."

When he looked at me, I knew we were no longer talking about my escape to the city. Marcus can be many things, but an idiot is not one of them.

"Minister—" I tried to interrupt, but he raised his hand, silencing me.

"Expelling you from the competition would be an abysmal embarrassment to your king that I want to avoid," he continued in a loud voice for everyone to hear. This was not a simple punishment—this was a public trial.

I think I speak for everyone when I say no one has ever seen him so angry.

"Miss Brenda," Marcus called, quickly approaching his counselor. "You will supervise the boy and show him his new position: a palace servant."

I blew my breath, looking at him as if he had insulted me. Expelling me didn't sound terrible after all—It was like he was taking it out on me for all my mistakes with one punishment. Among the audience, I could hear laughter and gasps. I couldn't even react. I looked around for my guardians to beg for help, but they were nowhere to be found.

"Miss Brenda will provide you with your new uniform and bedroom," Marcus continued. "The punishment will last until the end of this month, young Omhet."

Young Omhet? He took my title from me.

"This has to be a joke," I said, too stunned to defend myself.

"Do I look like a person who makes jokes?" he said, looking at me sternly, and drove back to the crowd. "Whoever dares to try to ridicule Andebeck or me, I will punish him three times worse." Having finished, he turned and walked off the stage with his sister and his guards.

General Mendez ordered the representative to return to their formation to prepare for training, and I desperately searched for my guardians. I felt a soldier from Andebeck grab me by the arm when I tried to go down the steps. This was not looking good.

"Cheikh," I called when I spotted him. He was at the far edge of the crowd with Lucas and Shin, watching me as if they hated me. I asked them for help with my gaze, but Cheikh said something to my guardians without flinching and backed away.

It had to be an exaggeration. If I didn't see Laila again in a week, I would be failing on the most significant promise I'd ever made. There had to be a way to get out of this mess. I had to see Laila again, or the grain of trust I built with her would go to waste as if everything that had happened in her life wasn't already bad enough.

The servants' quarters were a world apart from the rest of the palace. I had no idea that going down the service steps, I would find corridors, lounges, and even lodging where all the palace staff resided. There was no color on the stone walls or floor tiles. Dozens of people in uniforms were jogging frantically from one side to the other, pushing me on the shoulder so many times that I had to flatten myself against the wall. There wasn't room for two people in the corridor, but they were experts at getting around—three passed me at the same time, and they didn't even touch one another.

I think I discovered I might be claustrophobic or was about to be. It felt like the walls were shrinking, and to make matters worse, there was hardly any light. There was no electricity, only oil lamps on every wall. The ceiling was low, and so many doors that I felt like I was in a terrifying maze.

"Move over, mister Omhet," Brenda ordered, stopping several steps in front of me.

The counselor looked at me sternly with an attitude that beat my older brother Guillermo's. She was blonde, with her hair tied up so tightly that she didn't have a single strand loose. She was wearing the soldier uniform but with a skirt and heels. It made me wonder if maybe she was a soldier before. Her age was difficult to decipher, with a face without spots or wrinkles, but her gaze was so rigid and ruthless that it made her look older than she probably was.

I had to get going, trying not to hit anyone else, but I almost tripped when a waiter walked past me with a tray in his hand, pushing me in his haste. I was going to end up with a bruise from the blow, I was sure.

Brenda opened a door for me, and when I tried to go through first, she slammed the door, causing me to hit my forehead with the edge. I hissed, taking a few steps back. What the hell was that?

"You already failed," she scolded me. "Hold the door for me, and don't look me in the eyes."

"You're unnecessarily hostile," I criticized, holding the door for her.

Brenda finally entered, and I followed her, finding a room with round tables and so many people that the noise was deafening. However, when Brenda stood in front of the room, they all shut their mouths, straightened up like soldiers, and silence reigned. They were terrified of her.

"Intendant," greeted an older man with gray hair, wrinkles even on his hands, and a neutral voice out of respect.

"Geronimo, I have a task for you," she said and gestured with a finger for me to come closer. "This is mister Omhet. He needs a uniform and must be assigned to one of the teams." The man looked so confused when he looked at me. "The young man has lost his title. Now he is your responsibility. He will be a servant like any other. I order for him to be treated as such. Dress him and teach him everything you know. You are now responsible for everything he does—right or wrong—do you understand?"

Geronimo opened his mouth, but he didn't say anything. I could tell he wanted to ask many things but couldn't.

"Of course," he said, bowing to her.

I looked at Brenda, annoyed. I couldn't believe it.

"This is ridiculous," I said, laughing, but not because I was happy.

"You can leave if you want," she said haughtily. "Get your things, get on the first train to Glacier, and get the hell out of Andebeck—what do you think?"

I raised an eyebrow, looking at her with the same attitude.

"You wish," I replied. "I'll stay here whether you like it or not. Your miserable hostility will not—"

Before I could finish, she slapped my face.

I was surprised, raising my hand and feeling my cheek get warm. What the hell was wrong with everyone in this place? Had they gone crazy or what?

"You will address me as intendant," she reminded me, getting so close that I had to take a step back. "You are nobody right now. I can put you in the dungeon if you dare to disrespect me again, insolent child."

How dare she touch me?

"When I get my title back, you'll regret—"

She didn't let me finish.

She slapped me again.

There were gasps of surprise from many people around us. They'd undoubtedly never witnessed a grumpy woman hitting a prince with no power or title.

"Do you want to say something else?" Brenda asked. "Or would you rather talk to me from the dungeon?"

I swallowed deeply. I closed my eyes, trying to hide the anger and embarrassment.

"No," I growled through my teeth. "All clear."

She dared to grab my face under the chin and pulled me close to look me in the eyes.

"All clear, Intendant." she taught me.

I gritted my teeth and didn't respond, but I felt her nails grate against my skin. I wanted to push her, at the very least.

"All clear, Intendant," I finally said, my voice choked with anger. I had never felt such rage.

She was able to control her hand and move away from me.

"Better," she said and even tried to smile. "Now that you know your place, I hope you can behave. All yours, Geronimo," She concluded and left, slamming the door shut.

I was so furious I could not control myself that I kicked a chair, crashing it against the wall.

I sat at a table, slowly closing my eyes, and massaging my temple. I am Prince Omhet of Glacier Kingdom, I repeated to myself, trying to overshadow my humiliation. If my father found out about all this, he would surely defend me, but he wasn't here, was he? I had to get out of this one alone.

For me.

For my kingdom.

For Laila.

CHAPTER 21

When I was sixteen, I kissed Lady Mishka, a guest from the Daonna court. I kissed her good. I left marks on her neck and her swollen lips.

I remember that we were all at the table, both the guests and the entire Espinho's family. They discussed the possible arranged marriage between the young woman and my older brother Guillermo.

No one had noticed the marks, and I was getting impatient—

Until I felt Guillermo change seats with my brother Rodrigo to be by my side. I hid my smile as I drank wine.

"You, little shit—"

"Careful, brother, you don't want to interrupt such an important meeting about your future wife," I whispered.

Families laughed together, servers brought more food, and musicians played typical Daonna court songs. Nobody was paying attention to us yet.

"My future *wife* can't stop staring at you," he accused me in the same whisper. "Tell me you didn't make those marks on her neck."

"Mmm..." I thought about it for a moment. "You should see the one I left on her breast. Probably you'll see it on the honeymoon—"

Guillermo hit the table hard, and when he got up, the chair fell backward.

"There will be no wedding," he bellowed, and everything went quiet. "I'm not going to marry that whore."

"Guillermo!" exclaimed the queen, rising to her feet.

The chaos began immediately. My mother ran after my older brother. The guests began to argue and leave while my father chased after them, apologizing, and Rodrigo took Estefania out of the dining room.

Lady Mishka smiled at me as she rose. "Thank you," she whispered to me and left.

When I went to leave, I was startled by the intense gaze of Cayetano next to me. "You went too far this time."

"It was just a kiss," I shrugged.

Cayetano was going to say something else when the bellow of my father shouting my name echoed off the walls.

Cayetano patted me on the back.

"I'm sorry, little brother, but I can't protect you from him," he told me sadly.

When I got to his office, he was looking out the window with his arms crossed. My father was huge, thanks to his arms and broad back. I closed the door, leaving myself alone with him.

"What excuse do you have this time?"

I swallowed deeply. His tone of voice was stern.

"I saved her life. You should see how happy she was—" when he turned around, the look on his face silenced me. "Guillermo didn't deserve her, and no one wanted to listen to me, so I did it my way then."

"You are playing to be a king. Is that what you are trying?"

"*Wha*—No!"

"I'm not good enough as a king or father, it seemed. Do you want my crown, Omhet?" he threw his crown to my feet, and it broke when it hit the floor. Seeing the crown on the floor hurt me more than my father's anger. I went to my knees to pick it up. "Don't you dare to touch it!"

I got up immediately. My father started to approach me, causing me to look up slowly.

"This war between you two has to end—"

"Nothing I've done to him compares one bit to what he's done to me."

"I don't care!" his scream silences me. His words hurt more than an insult. He knows what my brother has done to me and has never done anything about it.

Because he didn't care.

"Right. I'm sorry, Your Majesty, I forgot my place," I said, trying to contain my frustration. He was my king, after all.

My father shook his head, and without saying anything, it was he who took the crown from the ground.

"This thing does not represent Glacier or my status. It's all of us who represent the Espinhos, including you. Why can't you behave like one of us for once?"

That hurt me, my eyes watered, and I looked away. *Like one of us,* I repeated.

"Father, with all due respect, I know you don't understand my behavior, but you must know that I'm trying to make you see—" he tried to interrupt me, so I yelled. "Guillermo cannot be king! He's an asshole!"

He raised his hand. He was going to hit me.

I took steps back from fright, bumped into a table, and fell with everything and coffee cups. It was a disaster. Cups and containers were broken.

The king stepped over the broken pottery and grabbed me by the shirt to bring me closer to his angry face.

"To prevent Guillermo from being a king is admitting that I was a terrible leader, father and king. Do you want to see Glacier in the ruins?"

"Of course not—"

"He will be king whether we like it or not. There is nothing I can do to prevent it. We must accept it. So, stop acting so immature, stop this nonsense, and don't ever embarrass me like you just did, Omhet. I'm warning you," he threatened me and then turned around, leaving me on the floor.

I wanted to get up from the mess but hissed when I realized I had a piece embedded in the palm of my hand. I tried to take it off and hissed again.

My father poured himself a cup of wine and wandered over to the window for a moment. I didn't dare to move. I was shaking. My father had never behaved violently with me before.

"Once we were nothing," the king spoke in a controlled but severe tone. "We were a mere territory of Andebeck—a piece of land that was exploited until no more gold or kalica stone was left. The enslaved people revolted until many were killed, and the rest of us were left with mixed bloodlines." He drank some of the wine but still didn't look at me. "When we finally won our independence and created our own flag, my grandfather found it difficult to be recognized as a king, and it still is. Do you know what happened in these lands to have our current privileges?" I didn't answer because I did not know anything. "The enslaved people, natives, refugees, and allies joined, and we took out the oppressors. We are not mixed bloodlines. We are one country."

He finally turned and began approaching me, kneeling in front of me. I flinched, thinking that he would try to hit me again.

"And today, you embarrassed me in front of my guests," he told me, looking into my eyes.

I had a small victory against Guillermo, but at what price? We rarely had visitors from other territories, and the enmity I had with my brother was ruining our lives and the kingdom. If this affected Glacier, I was never going to forgive myself.

"Father," I whispered, looking down. "I'm sorry."

But my father lifted my chin and made me look into his eyes.

"Don't look down," he ordered. "Not at me or anyone else. You are a Glacierian , my son, and you are greater than you think. Do you want to win your enemies? Don't act like them, be better than them. And above all things, do not ever again dishonor your only home in front of anyone."

"Yes, Your Majesty."

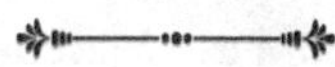

The experience with Brenda echoed in my memories. That first night, I was so upset that I couldn't sleep, so I stared at the oil lamp, fiddling with the string bracelet on my wrist. Getting slapped by Brenda made me remember that day with my father. I prayed to Krea that he would never find out what happened today. Everything that happened was the opposite of what he had asked me to do.******

The room was so small that I could touch both walls if I stretched out my arms. I had nothing except a small bed with no sheets and a table with drawers where I was supposed to keep my uniforms. At least they left me a kerosene lamp. I kept the flame very low and tried to preserve as much oil as possible because, to top it all off, I had the bad luck of getting an underground room without windows. I didn't even know what time it was—it could be noon or midnight, it didn't matter.

I would've liked to have the letters my family sent to reread them and find the courage to overcome the problems I put myself into. I would give anything to have the chance to make a call to the king for just one minute. I wanted to hear the voice of someone from my family or get some wise advice from my mother. I took a deep breath, crossing my arms. Deep down, I knew that even if I had the option, I would prefer the dragon eat me before seeing my father's face if he discovered what had happened to me. Not only did I fail to make my kingdom proud, but I was also dragging my family name down lower than I thought was possible.

I needed to get out of here. I needed to talk to Marcus and explain—but how exactly? Should I admit that I ran away again and spoke to a princess who should've been dead a century ago? By Krea, this problem was bigger than me.

I heard someone put the key in my door to open it. It was Geronimo who unlocked the door, poking his head in, and ordering me to get up quickly. I clenched my jaw, trying not to say anything sarcastic for once. The worst part was knowing that I could quit—I could ask Marcus to take me to the train station, and he would do so without question.

But since that was what everyone expected of me, it was just the opposite of what I was going to do.

"Hurry up," Geronimo ordered.

"It's not like I can even step in this little place without tripping over something."

Geronimo threw clothes at me as I got up, and I barely caught them in the air. He ordered me out into a hallway that looked like a city avenue. Everyone was running everywhere. I assumed then that it was the middle of the morning, the busiest hour of the day. Geronimo shouted many instructions at me as we walked quickly down the corridor, but I couldn't listen to him because there was so much noise in so little space.

We stopped in front of a door I didn't recognize because they all looked the same. I felt like we were going around in circles.

"Five minutes to clean up, put on your uniform, and get back out here."

I walked in and instantly came back out.

"There are naked men in there."

He massaged his temples impatiently.

"It's the male's bathroom, mister Omhet."

Prince Omhet, I would have liked to correct it.

"So, you want me to get naked and get in there with all of them?"

"Be thankful there are showers available. In the afternoon, you'll have to share it with even more guys," then he pushed me inside.

I tried not to look at anyone, but they just stared at me when they recognized me. This was so hard. I looked for the farthest shower from the others, and still, my hands shook when I started to undress.

Someone whistled, then boisterous laughter followed.

I had to remember my family more than ever if I wanted to survive such embarrassment. I tried to keep my eyes on the floor when I got under the shower. But then I choked on a high scream as I felt the rush of cold water hit my naked chest.

The man behind me laughed even louder.

I searched among my few things for my new toothbrush—a thin wooden stick with a weak bristle, soap, and a straight razor. I had never shaved my face without a mirror or much less under five minutes while doing the rest.

"Hey, friend," someone yelled, but I ignored it.

I groaned when I cut my cheek, trying to shave as fast as possible. I wanted to get out of there and never get a shower for the rest of my punishment.

Someone wrapped me around the neck in a hug, and I shoved him away with a bellow as I bumped into someone else behind me. I ran back to the opposite side, realizing that I was being surrounded. I hold the razor, just in case.

"Could it be that the dragon gave him that scar on his back?" one asked.

"Omhet, the dragon's slayer," joked another one.

"He's not the dragon's slayer. He's the dragon's bitch," all of them burst into a laugh.

"Get away from me," I ordered.

"Says who?" asked a third one.

I was no one to them. The morbid smile made me realize I was in danger.

Without thinking, I pushed between them, grabbed my clothes, and got dressed while running away from the bathroom: cream button-down shirt, dark red pants, gold-trimmed jacket, and black boots. I felt so stupidly uncomfortable.

"Late," Geronimo scolded me as soon as I found him. "You just missed your chance to have breakfast."

"Impossible," I protested.

He hit my fingers with a stick he carried hidden behind his back.

I hissed, shaking my fingers.

"I'm not your friend. I'm your supervisor, and I deserve respect."

"But—"

"You will speak only when I say so. Otherwise, I don't want to hear your voice. Is that clear?" Geronimo asked, but I didn't answer. "Much better," he said more calmly. "Now, follow me."

When he turned around, I rolled my eyes.

Freaking bitter old man. I couldn't talk, I couldn't eat, and I couldn't even choose my job for the day. I tried to ask if I could at least run with my training group, and he smacked my hand with that damn stick without replying. When I asked what time I had my break, he hit me again, and this time, it left a mark on me.

The first place he took me was the main dining room. There was no one there, just a massive mess on the table that someone had to clean up. And that someone was me.

"We will prepare the table for lunch. We only have a couple of hours, so let's get to work."

"I have no idea how to set the table," I admitted, grabbing a tray of cheese and rolls and then eating them without asking permission.

Geronimo tried to scold me but gave up when he saw how ravenous I was. The food would likely go to waste anyway. Besides, he wouldn't be able to get me to do anything if I was famished.

"Start picking up this mess, or I'll make you clean the servant latrines with your bare hands," he threatened.

When Geronimo came looking for me the next morning, I was already dressed in uniform. I only needed to clean my face with a hand towel and all the soap residue after shaving.

"What do you think you're doing?"

"I already showered."

"How? I left you locked up."

I gritted my teeth. I knew I was locked, I tried to escape all damn night, and nothing worked.

"With the canteen water. I'm never going back to the public bathroom again."

Geronimo looked at the ceiling, and I think he said a prayer.

"You're disgusting. Hurry up and get out right now."

Another morning I cleaned up tables, but I had a team while Geronimo supervised closely. I can't say that I learned to prepare the table correctly, but I worked silently, imitating Geronimo as much as possible. Besides, I dined with these settings every day. I should know the placements just as well as the others.

He smacked my hands, causing me to withdraw them with a hiss.

"Does the cutlery look perfectly vertical to you?" he scolded me.

"I assure you that there will be no prince who will notice—" he raised the stick to hit me. "Fine! I'll keep quiet."

Geronimo didn't actually do anything. He just supervised the workers and hit them if he had to— which he had only done to me so far today.

When I heard the door open, I straightened up, expecting either one of the representatives or, better yet, Marcus. I needed to talk to him and convince him to stop this stupidity. This punishment had to be a joke just to annoy me because it seemed impossible that I could be forced to do this for the rest of the month. But the person who entered was just another servant passing through.

"Move," Geronimo ordered.

I needed to talk to Marcus. I wanted to get back to my routine and my guards. I was going to find a way to escape this punishment—I was determined. I was sure I would find a way out by Sunday.

"Will I be allowed back to the arena for training later?" I asked. Geronimo and I had gone outside to tend to the flower labyrinth.

"You can't be trusted, and I'm keeping you away from the other representatives," Geronimo explained. "If the representatives go to the dining room, you will work outside. You can return inside the palace when they return to the arena."

The old man annoyed me. He had me cutting specific flowers in the garden and pulling off the leaves and thorns to keep me away from everyone I knew in the dining room. I snorted in annoyance.

"You won't be able to hold me prisoner, forever. You know as well as I do that this is ridiculous—" he had hit my hand again. "Enough!"

"Why is it so hard to get you to shut up?"

"Let me talk to Marcus," I pleaded, turning to him with the flowers in my hands. "If I can't convince him to get me out of this hell, I'll serve the rest of my sentence in silence."

Geronimo crossed his arms. He looked exhausted.

"I'm surprised at your nerve trying to negotiate with me. I've gotten locked up in dungeons for less than this."

"There's not much you can do with me—not without Marcus's permission," I reminded him. "At the end of the day, I'll always be a prince. It's better for you to let me talk to Marcus so I can get out of your hair."

I went back to cutting more flowers.

Geronimo looked at me sternly, and I don't know if he was frowning out of anger or if he just looked that way because of his countless wrinkles. He was thinking about it. I could see it in his eyes. I knew he wanted to get rid of me. Perhaps it was pride and the desire to reject my proposal that made him hesitate automatically, but in the end, he knew I was right—getting back to my routine was best for both of us.

"Follow me," he finally said, and I let out a breath of relief.

For once, I followed him without protest. He led me through the narrow service corridors, past the public dining room, and down past the lodging and showers. I trusted Geronimo to help me talk to Marcus. He hated the idea of having me around as much as I did.

Geronimo opened a door at the end of the hall. I found it suspicious that it was the only door in the hallway, and it was so dark inside that I couldn't see past the door frame. I felt isolated. There was no one in this entire section. Even the silence felt terrifying.

"Come in," he ordered. I hesitate. "Here you will find the answer to your proposal."

"A dungeon?"

"No, Omhet," he said, rolling his eyes. "It's not a dungeon. I cannot lock you in one without your king's permission." I leaned inside the doorway and covered my nose when the smell hit me. It was a horrible stench—it even knocked the wind out of me for a moment. "But latrines are not a dungeon, are they?"

"No!" I turned around, but Geronimo pushed me inside and closed the door.

It took me a second to understand this was the servant's latrine. It was so dark and unbelievably disgusting.

"Geronimo!" I yelled, banging on the door. "What the hell do you think you're doing?"

"You won't get out of there until they're all clean," he said calmly. "I hope you have fun. I will come back for you—maybe tomorrow."

Maybe?

I bellowed and kicked the door.

"You can't do this to me!" I yelled. "Your kingdom can't take my title away from me—no one can! I am the—"

"Prince Omhet," he interrupted me. He seemed amused by the situation. "Perhaps you're important in your small and useless kingdom, but look around you! There is no difference between where you are and what your kingdom represents."

Oh, good lord. I did kick the door harder. Nobody insults Glacier!

But as much as I screamed, he left me in that terrible place. It was so disgusting in there I ended up crouching and throwing up on the floor, realizing too late that I'd have to clean that up too.

"Once, we were nothing," my father had told me, without the slightest idea that we were still nothing in everyone else's eyes.

CHAPTER 22

When they finally opened the door, it was difficult for me to get up from the floor due to the excruciating pain in my abdomen. As I'd attempted to clean the latrines, I had continued vomiting periodically until I lost count of how many times it had happened. The effort had drained every ounce of my strength.

A soldier I didn't recognize pulled me out by my shoulder. I had to hold on to the wall, aware that my skin was as green as a corpse. I couldn't even get angry when I saw Brenda and Geronimo in front of me.

"His silence is music to my ears," Brenda commented triumphantly.

"That doesn't make sense," I answered, groaning while holding my belly. I felt the urge to vomit again, but I had nothing left in my stomach.

"Perhaps next time, you won't speak out of turn. Don't fail any more of the orders you're given, and the time you have left with us will be more enjoyable for you."

I straightened as best as I could while still holding my abdomen tightly.

"Whatever you say, Intendant," I said, clenching my teeth so hard my jaw hurt. I had no desire to be locked in the latrine again. I preferred to let her win—for today.

"He looks better," Geronimo said to Brenda.

I wanted to ask what part of me looked better. Was it because I looked weak, bowed down, and submissive?

"Give him a bath and lock him up for now," Brenda ordered calmly. "Press day is too close to let him mess it up."

"Of course, Intendant."

I was curious about what event they were talking about—I hadn't heard of press day before. I wondered if it was a new event, but I couldn't ask. I let Geronimo escort me to the shower without protest, so I could rinse the vomit off and put on a clean uniform. I did not refuse to go to the public showers. I didn't care at all at this point.

"For having been locked up for almost two days, you don't look so bad," Geronimo commented as he escorted me to my room.

I stop in the middle of my room, turning to him and slowly reacting to his words. "Two days?"

"Have a good night," he concluded and closed the door.

I flopped down on my bed, taking a while to comprehend what he'd just said, feeling that time was going by absurdly. I couldn't see if it was day or night. I didn't have a radio to hear what was going on. I couldn't even interact with anyone.

This was not a usual punishment for disobedience—I was a prisoner.

I resolved that when I found my three guardians, they would pay for this—for leaving me alone, not doing the impossible to get me out of such humiliation, and not even looking for me to confirm that I was okay. I felt they abandoned me when their only job was to be by my side. I was furious. I didn't know what day it was, what was going on in the competition, or anything outside my daily duties. They had me running through the service tunnels nonstop, whether helping the endless kitchen scrubbing or in the food pantries—any place with no exit door to the outside. To top it off, Geronimo was always where he could see me. Didn't he have anyone else to supervise? His mistrust was so great that he never left me unattended. Although I had spent several days in a row pretending to cooperate and be polite, I knew nothing would convince him that I had accepted my punishment.

I needed to escape, and I think Geronimo could see it in every part of me. He wouldn't even allow other servants to speak to me directly. Everyone stuck to their routine no matter what, as if they lived to serve their whole lives. They may say that Andebeck did not have slavery like in Or-Mua or Ettezi but lacking free time and working for such a depressing salary was almost the same thing.

"You have ten minutes," Geronimo told me, handing me a bowl of soup.

I sat on a stool in the corner of the locked kitchen. My hands were dirty, my hair was greasy, and my back ached. There was so much that had to be done in this place that it made the time pass quickly, at least.

I gagged when I tasted the soup. I choked down as much as I could stand, leaving half of it in the bowl.

"Typical ungrateful prince," Geronimo said, throwing the bowl in the sink.

"How can I be grateful for such terrible food?" I protested. "Why do they give the representative all the good food and leave the servants with the crumbs?"

"I suppose your kingdom perfectly distributes the food among the monarchs and their servants," he said sarcastically.

"Why not?" I protested. "They can give the same food to everyone, and when winter comes, the rations are cut for all of Glacier. We are all citizens of the same realm..."

"Save your philosophical discussion for the kings." He threw me a canteen that I caught in the air. At least they gave me clean water. "Glacier isn't a real kingdom—you're a mix of exiles trying to convince everyone you're a country," he said.

I stand up slowly. "You should be thankful that my king is not here to hear you," I replied, trying to control my rage. I couldn't hit him like I had with Karl.

"Give thanks to your god that you will never be a king," he snapped. "I will give you some advice: quit and walk away. No one in this realm needs you, and you know it. Take your useless and desperate kingdom somewhere else."

I watched him go with a wave of anger that throbbed inside my head. I let him go, controlling my impulses and understanding that arguing with him was pointless. His thoughts were not just his, but also everyone around here, including the minister.

My strength didn't come from his comments or his insults. I knew who I was, and his humiliations wouldn't bring me down. But I would be lying if I denied that I wanted to quit. I was ready to go home and never speak of this humiliation again. It would be so easy to give up...

But I wasn't here for them, the ministers, or Andebeck. At this point, I wasn't even doing it for my father.

There was someone else who desperately needed me. So, I thought of Laila and prayed I would find a way to return to her.

For now, I obeyed Geronimo's orders for the rest of the afternoon. I had to try to convince Geronimo that I could behave.

Honestly, I thought it wouldn't work, but eventually, he pulled me out of the service tunnel and assigned me to a new job near the main dining room. The sun blinded me at first, and it felt strange being near the window after being underground for so long. I was hoping I might run into my guardians while I was in the open, but I didn't know if I would hit them—or hug them at this point.

"You will polish each piece of cutlery and silver tray with the polishing cloth," he ordered, opening the stockroom door.

Each silver utensil was kept strictly and organized, and I first wondered why they had so much cutlery. I didn't complain because at least I wasn't scrubbing dishes or cleaning latrines. I imitated what Geronimo was doing in silence, taking the utensils from boxes in a row, one on top of the other, gently polishing them, and then placing them in specific drawers. I had to organize them by size, which was not too difficult.

Several times, Brenda peeked in to give Geronimo information, and she was making him impatient. Something told me it had to do with the famous press day she mentioned so much. I didn't ask what it was about, and eventually, Geronimo left me alone in the stockroom, under threat and instructions.

It was the first time he had left me alone, and I didn't want to let him down.

I hummed as I polished a spoon, planning an escape in my mind. If Geronimo was too busy for the next few days to keep watching me, I could use the time to look for Marcus. I had to find a good explanation of where I had been the night I was in the city. Telling him about Laila was out of the question. But what could I say to make him understand, or at least forgive me, and end my punishment? I knew I wouldn't be able to endure this situation much longer because that was what they wanted—for me to give up, and the worst part is that it was working.

Don't you dare give up, I yelled in my mind, breathing deeply. *You got this. Everything will be alright.*

"Hey, servant. Your service is required," someone called.

When I turned around, there was Khloe from Ettezi with a mocking smile.

I felt overwhelmed with emotions. I was so excited to see a familiar face at last. Her hair was tied back, with curls on either side of her face. She was still in her workout uniform, which meant she would be getting ready to go to lunch after completing her first station. Then disappointment and coldness invaded me, and my smile disappeared. She had cut me out of her life like our friendship had never mattered or like everything that had happened was my fault alone. I didn't trust her, which made me angrier because I wanted to. She doesn't trust me, or she's afraid, but what or why?

"Your Highness," I greeted as if I were a servant. "What can I do for you?"

She didn't like my greeting when she realized that I wasn't faking it—on the contrary, I was playing my part as was expected of me. Khloe approached, snatched the cutlery I was still holding from my hand and threw it into the closest drawer.

"I just polished that!"

"Stop this nonsense. You're Prince Omhet—don't be absurd," she scolded me, placing her hands on her hips. "When your punishment is over, you will return to the routine, stay away from troubles, and above all else, stop provoking Marcus."

"If only it were that easy."

"Why not?" she pressed, and before I could answer, she closed the door behind her. "Tell me you were so drunk you got lost in the city. Tell me you maybe fell asleep in the alley, but please, tell me you didn't go back to the ruins, Omhet," she approached me suddenly, and I raised my hands to try to calm her down. "Tell me."

"No offense, but I don't trust you."

Khloe growled.

"You're unbelievable!" she yelled, waving her hands aggressively. "I knew there was something strange with this punishment. It's because Marcus knows—"

"Khloe, stop yelling," I tried to interrupt, motioning for her to lower her voice. If Geronimo found me locked up with her—I didn't even want to finish that thought.

"Even Alexander's begs didn't help get the penalty off you because it's about nothing but the damn ruins..."

"Wait, Alexander tried to help me?"

"...After everything that happened, you went back for more?" she continued without hearing a word I said.

"Because I can't abandon her!" I blurted out, and for once, Khloe was silent. "She needs us."

"She?" she repeated softly.

I took a deep breath and looked into her eyes, wondering if telling her would be a mistake.

"Laila is alive," I finally said.

Khloe leaned back against the wall. I thought she'd say something, but she didn't.

"This competition isn't about us or the dragon or Marcus, or even your brother. There is something more complicated than all that."

Khloe covered her mouth and turned away for a moment.

"Are you sure it's her?"

I exhaled all the air, dropping my shoulders. "Look where I am, Khloe. Do you think I wouldn't be completely sure?"

He nodded but was still processing all the information.

"Who could've guessed that out of all the representatives, you would discover such a secret?" she finally spoke.

"Thanks," I said, rolling my eyes.

"Listen to me. You must get away from all this," she ordered me with great concern. "Leave it to Marcus to deal with—"

"No," I said forcefully. "Nobody can find out about her. I don't even trust my shadow."

"How can you take on such a huge responsibility? They're going to crush you. Think about your kingdom." She scolded me severely.

"There are plenty of people who think about every single realm of the Union, but nobody thinks of her. Kill the dragon, and win the crown, the rest is basically bullshit—"

"Stop caring about her!"

"I can't!" the silence that followed made me realize how angry both were. I could hear it in our agitated breaths.

I remember how hopeless I felt while lying in my own bloodbath. I thought that of all Guillermo's attempts, that night was the end of me.

Until Cayetano arrived shouting my name.

My father covered for Guillermo, saying it was awful game on his part, and simply ordered him never to come near me again. My mother blamed me for following him, for being such an idiot. I should have known better.

But Cayetano entered the infirmary shouting Guillermo's name and punched him and punched him *and punched him*—I thought he would kill him if the king hadn't gotten in the way.

Maybe I didn't speak for a year, but Cayetano never gave up on me.

"Sometimes you only need one person. Just one to make all the difference," I whispered.

"Omhet, please—"

"I just need more time," I explained, feeling the desperation in me growing. "If I could convince you and my guardians to help her, I know we could—"

"No," she interrupted me. "Don't even think of dragging me into this. I can't do anything that will make my brother suspicious, not after what happened in the ruins. You're on your own," she concluded, reaching for the doorknob.

"Khloe—"

Before leaving, she stopped once more, looking at me. Gods, she was so angry.

"Everyone wants to step over everyone else for the crown of this kingdom, including you and maybe even Laila. If you think that finding her solves your problems, then you have no idea what this competition is for." She turned and left me alone in the storeroom.

My heart was racing, and the desire to keep doing my assignment as asked went to hell. I closed the drawers angrily and resolved to do nothing but think. I've been so distracted for the last few weeks by what's happening in the ruins that I haven't been paying attention to what's happening around me.

"By heavens," I whispered nervously. "Laila, what am I going to do with you?"

CHAPTER 23

*Y*ou *know you should never have left Glacier. You are not enough and never will be,* Guillermo's voice returned, and I tried to ignore it. So, I shut his voice in the back of my mind as I hurried through the narrow service halls.

My mind liked comparing itself with my brothers. So, I ignored the demons in my head—those damn voices trying to crush me. But some days were easier than others.

While my father trained Guillermo to be the future king, Cayetano concentrated on being a great politician and the future right-hand of the crown. He was terrific with words. I always told him that. He could recite any speech in front of anyone and look as natural as if he was born to be admired for his wisdom. He basically got everything he wanted without trying hard to convince people—a trait he had inherited from our father.

Rodrigo is a separate case. He was introverted but listened and knew everything happening as if he had ears in the walls. My father loved bringing him along for complicated consul meetings. If there were someone who could solve any problem, no matter how difficult it was, it would be him.

Then there was me.

It's incredible how I never got the time or the need to analyze all this until the morning I volunteered for this competition. I thought if I could manage to make my king proud of me, I could fit in with my three brothers.

Maybe I don't fit in anywhere, and I've rushed to try to satisfy everyone at once. I wanted to believe I would find my place in this journey without comparing myself to my brothers or other people around me. But somehow, finding Laila changed me completely.

I don't want to be Alexander's sidekick or anyone else's. I am ashamed to have even thought such a thing—it was mere contempt on my part to believe that I could be the second man in this story. I no longer wanted to be just the simple jester who makes the hero laugh.

I am more than this.

"You will have breakfast in the servants' dining room," Geronimo ordered me.

That morning, he was in more of a hurry than usual, and I was thankful because I didn't have to take my breakfast as a prisoner in my room.

I stood in a long line behind the others. They all had the same color uniform but with different styles. The fanciest were those who served in the main dining room, wearing gold-trimmed jackets and gloves, while the others could wear plain button-down shirts and dark wine-colored pants.

By the time I managed to grab my tray, I only had three minutes left, making me feel frustrated. I was used to taking the whole hour allotted for each meal, not this mess and rushing for everything.

"Thank you," I said to the lady that gave me the tray. What I got back was a glare.

How can a kingdom live in such hostility? It's overwhelming.

Looking for a space to sit in the busy mess and occupied tables, I looked at my breakfast with relief. It was freshly cooked food.

I thought that morning would be more pleasant without Geronimo breathing down my neck, but then I spotted my three guardians at one of the round tables, having breakfast and looking relaxed. I gripped the wooden tray so tightly in my hand that I thought it might shatter.

I walked past the tables, accidentally bumping some of them, and when I got to my guardians' table, I dropped the tray, scattering food everywhere, drawing their attention. They had been chatting with the guardians of the Atsoc kingdom as if they were comrades.

"Good morning," I said, gritting my teeth, trying not to explode like I wanted to.

The three were silent for a moment—even the Atsoc guards sat back with concern when they noticed my aggression.

"You look better," Cheikh began and returned his gaze to his plate to continue eating his fruit salad. I swear my eyelid began to twitch out of sheer anger. "The punishment has done you well—you look submissive."

I had to take a deep breath—this was not going to end well.

"Now you're a servant, aren't you?" Lucas joked. "If I ask you to bring me water—"

I grabbed the first jug of water I found, and poured it over him, then slammed the pitcher on the table with a loud thud. Lucas gasped, getting up to shake himself, noticing how the people around us gradually fell silent.

"Too early for jokes," Shin said to Lucas as he drank tea without flinching. "You deserve it."

"*Joking*?" I burst out, "I've been underground for days—where were you?" Cheikh tried to answer. "You were supposed to be here for me."

When I didn't let him speak, Cheikh got up from the table, wiping his lips. Then, he grabbed me by the shoulder so hard I couldn't resist when he pulled me out of the dining room. Everybody was watching intently at the most entertaining show of the moment.

"Let's start with the thank you part, shall we?" Cheikh began, pulling me through the halls like I was his child. I tried to get him to let go of my shoulder, but he didn't. "You only got a short sentence for being late for formation—imagine if I had mentioned anything about being in the ruin? Twice?"

"Keep your voice down, Cheikh," I bellowed at him. We were passing dozens of people at once.

He finally let go of me in the middle of the busy hallway.

"You need to lose your attitude," he replied, pointing his finger in my face. He was as angry as I was.

We were being watched from everywhere as we were about to be run over by the crowd.

Without saying anything else, he motioned for me to follow him. It took me a second to decide if I wanted to go or not but to be honest, going back to Geronimo was worse. Grumbling, I followed Cheikh, praying that he could find a way to release me from this penalty. The only task that mattered to me was to be with Laila on Sunday. I couldn't break that promise.

We walked out the back door, taking us to the west wing, between the labyrinth garden and the training arena. The sky was so gray it appeared like it would rain at any moment, with loud thunder and relentless gusts of wind. It's been a while since I last saw the skies, and even more surprisingly, was to see the volunteers training in such unpleasant weather.

They were all training at different stations. I could see General Mendez in the tent giving the classes while a group ran through the paths of the forest and the rest divided into the rest of the stations. I can't believe I missed being there.

"That's where you should be," Cheikh said. "Not cleaning latrines."

"Please tell me no one knows about that," I said with embarrassment.

"It came out in every single newspaper, dear prince."

I breathed uneasily. I didn't know how to explain that I was not too fond of this situation, but I didn't regret it at the same time because I still wanted to run away again.

Cheikh was going to kill me.

"Cheikh—" I got stuck on my words. "I have to see her again, and I need your help," I finally said, and Cheikh spun around, looking like a soldier about to go to war. "Sundays are the lightest days of the week for training, so it shouldn't be difficult to escape for a couple of hours—"

"Are you listening to yourself?" he interrupted me. "Haven't you learned anything?"

"I'm doing what I should do," I explained, trying to convince him. I was desperate. "There is a decree signed by the last King of Andebeck that says no one can touch the crown except his daughter, Laila Blume. Let's save her life, and all the drama will be over. This useless competition will be over!"

"Marcus will find out that you are breaking all existing rules, and not only will you get in trouble, but Glacier too. If you dare to put our kingdom in disgrace, your father will never forgive you."

"I'm doing just what he would have expected of me. He doesn't let me fight the dragon, and I'm obviously no good at making allies. What could be better than ending the trials of fire before the battle to the death?"

He couldn't sit still, waving his arms and pacing back and forth. "I won't argue with a teenager in love," In love, did he say? "If there was any connection between you and your ghost, you should know that it ended two days ago." Before I could ask what he meant, he blurted it out to me ruthlessly," Sunday has already passed. You failed your promise. Now, finish your punishment and forget about going back to the ruins."

I turned around and tried to swallow the news. It was not possible. I thought I had marked the days and counted correctly. In my mind, I had been in my stupid prison for four days, not nine.

Maybe it was because I had stopped focusing on the noises around me, like the training, Cheikh's voice, and the horses in the far stables, that I felt the air get more oppressive. The breeze whistled, and I could even swear that the thunder sounded louder. Even though there was no rain, I felt the weather coupled with my inner storm.

"Omhet," Cheikh called, but I was about to lose all control. "I can talk to Brenda right this instance and order her to take you to Marcus, and then you can return to your training. We can start from scratch—"

"You could have done that all this time?" he exhaled, which means a yes. "*Why*—why you didn't do it?"

He hesitates for a moment. "You broke the most important promise that we, as Glacierian soldiers, have. May your lives be to protect mine, as mine be to protect yours. You threatened Shin, exposed him to the worst danger, and forgot your promise to your King Guillermo. I was deeply disappointed in you—"

"Cheikh, please, let me explain—"

"And I still am," I couldn't interrupt. Every word of his hurt me more than I thought. "But I believe you have suffered enough. Come back to the training, but never mention Laila's name again. And I promise you that I'll forgive everything you've done."

General Mendez began to scream as the first drops of rain fell. He said something about the press day. I don't know. He was too far away to hear it, and I wasn't part of whatever was going to happen next.

"My father lives disappointed in me, too, because I do the stupidest things I can think of. But the thing is, he never listens to me. And neither do you. My place is to obey like a puppet, and I have tried. I swear that I've tried, and I'm tired of it. I need you to trust me for once—"

"I'm sorry, but I won't," my shoulders fell in frustration. "Your only place is to obey and to do what your King and the ministers ordered you—"

"I'm sorry, general. But sometimes, doing the right thing is wrong. I don't expect you to understand that, but I'm not going to submit to this bloody morbid competition of crowns," I concluded and walked past him angrily.

If I explain it to Laila why I broke the promise, maybe she'll understand, I thought, with my heart racing. I had failed Laila—hasn't her life had enough disappointment for an inexperienced teenager like me to fail her too?

I ran down the path that led to the stables, feeling Cheikh chasing after me. He was welcome if he wanted to go with me, but I was determined to go to the ruins, and no one would stop me. I would face the dragon and even let it attack me if it wanted. I had to see Laila, I had to explain to her, I had to tell her—

"Omhet!" he yelled at me. His speed was unbeatable. He stopped me in a few long steps by just standing in front of me.

"You're not going to stop me, so don't even try."

"If you go into that stable, everything will be over," he threatened me. "Marcus won't give you another chance, and I won't lie for you anymore. You need to decide what's more important."

I found myself at a crossroads, looking at the stable and then the arena. The training area was empty of representatives. They had all left for an event I was the only one not to be a part of. Only I was missing, stuck in a stupid limbo where I had failed Laila, my king, Andebeck, my guards, and myself.

"Boy, listen to me," Cheikh said in a softer tone. "Focus on His Majesty Guillermo." When he said the king's name, I couldn't help but look at him. "Your father expects certain things from you, and you're doing the opposite. You must remember who you are and what you're doing here."

"Failing Laila doesn't feel right," I whispered, feeling anger replaced by sadness.

"If she's real, she'll be strong," he insisted. "She's been waiting a century—she'll be able to take a couple more months. How can you help her if you become a traitor to Andebeck with what you're doing?" I let him place his hand on my shoulder. For once, we weren't screaming at each other. "If you want to help the princess, you'll have to be smarter than this. Going to war with Marcus hasn't helped you, has it?"

"I can't ignore her. Let me at least talk to her one more time—"

"No," he flatly denied me, "the topic of Laila is over. You will be the representative our king expects you to be, and I promise you it will be worth it in the end," Cheikh concluded.

I wanted to think that I had the option to choose between my duty and my will, but there was nothing to choose from.

"Shit!" I spat out the bitter words, closing my eyes in frustration. "Fine."

I went back to the palace with Cheikh in silence, feeling that I hadn't just failed Laila. I'd also failed myself. And I was never going to forgive myself for that.

Laila, I'm so sorry.

The increasing raindrops did not bother me. My conscience bothered me more. This was wrong.

As we reached the service entrance, I saw Geronimo and Brenda waiting for me from afar. They looked furious. I groaned, slowing my pace. Was this really better than going to the ruins?

"Let me do the talking," said Cheikh.

"Good luck with that," I responded, looking down. I was already shaking.

"Hey," Cheikh called me, but I ignored him. "Chin up."

"Not today."

"You are a prince of Glacier. Chin up, I said."

I gave a sad smile. "Didn't you hear? I'm no one—"

Cheikh stopped me when we were almost at the door, and he didn't say anything until I looked at him.

"What?" I asked, annoyed.

"Who are you?"

"A disappointment," I joked, but neither laughed.

"Who are you?"

I sighed. "Cheikh, they are waiting for me—"

"Who are you?" he started to yell. "Say it."

I looked at him and shook my head. "I don't know anymore."

He was going to say something else when I felt them. Both of them started to surround me.

"Mister Omhet," said Brenda, and I closed my eyes. Here we go again. "You should not have left the walls of the palace.

"The prince and I were having an important conversation," Cheikh explained directly to Brenda.

"I don't care, general. The young man is no longer your responsibility but our property," Brenda interrupted him, and I saw how Cheikh got defensive. Was it me, or was he moving his hand closer to his sword? I immediately got nervous because Brenda probably had no idea who Cheikh was.

"For your sake, ma'am, I hope you don't give the prince unnecessary punishment," Cheikh said, moving so close to Brenda that Geronimo took a step back. Brenda looked small with Cheikh in front of her face. "For you, he's just another young man, but for me, he's Prince Omhet Guillermo Espinho, and the consequences, if you harm him, will be severe. Like it or not, you need to respect that."

Brenda was slow to respond, trying to hide how intimidated she was.

"I'm in charge here," she dared to say. "Only Marcus can say otherwise."

"I won't repeat it," Cheikh pressed, and as if he had summoned them, Shin and Lucas appeared next to us with an attitude that I hadn't seen until now—they were my guardians. "If I hear that you penalized our prince beyond what Marcus ordered, I will call for Glacier's sentence for you, and believe me, you will not like it."

"You have no right to threaten me."

"It's not a right. It's the law," Lucas said in a firm voice. "Choose your next words well because I'll send them to the Glacierian King."

"Since when is a minister more important than a king, anyway?" Shin asked. The three of them had her cornered between them and the service door. "Or have you forgotten that you are holding a desperate competition because your people don't have an overlord to protect them?"

"I'd say this is the most vulnerable realm. Don't you think, Cheikh?" Lucas asked.

"A kingdom without a king is a weak one," Cheikh agreed. "If I were you, I'd be careful. It would be so easy to invade your land. It's laughable."

Brenda's lip trembled, but she bit back her words. I never thought the leaders of Andebeck could shut down by three Glacierian, and damn, that felt so good. After offending me at every opportunity they found, they were now trembling like children. I was amused when she looked at me, waiting for her following words.

She exhaled and looked at Geronimo. "Take him—"

"Take who? I'm sorry?" interrupted Lucas, getting closer to her.

She glared at Lucas, but without option, she looked at me. "Geronimo," she tried again. "Take Prince Omhet to Marcus immediately," Brenda said at last, and I felt relief wash over me. "Let him wait for him in the press room."

Geronimo bowed for me and pointed the way, treating me not as a servant but as a prince, letting me go first.

I looked at my guardians once more and smiled respectfully at them.

"Thank you," I whispered to them. They had no—no freaking idea how much I missed them. "Don't ever leave me alone again, I beg you."

I wish I could express to them how sorry I was for everything I'd done. I want to show my guardians how much they meant, and what they have done for me today will never be forgotten.

"We'll be close, my prince," Cheikh replied.

I started to leave but felt Cheikh place his hand on my shoulder.

"I'm sorry about all this," he told me before letting me go. "I won't turn my back on you like that again."

I nodded and left with Geronimo.

I would finally talk to Marcus, and I hoped that this time, I could find a way out of this stupid sentence.

CHAPTER 24

The palace library was just as one might imagine. It had three stories, tall windows, and shelves on the second and third levels with infinite books. On the first level was the main meeting room. It was interesting how they prepared it for reporters by setting up wood tripods. At the same time, others prepared typewriters on a long table. As I entered, one of the reporters setting up the cameras looked at me and signaled to another. Confused by his interest, he didn't give me time to react as he snapped a picture of me walking next to Brenda and Geronimo. They were not easy cameras to handle—they were boxes with lamps so heavy that they had to use a tripod just to get an uncolored image in a newspaper.

"No," Geronimo stood in front of me. "There will be no interview or photographs for this young man. He is not part of the event."

I was so confused that I used Brenda and Geronimo as a shield as people with notebooks and tripods began to surround us.

Across the room, I saw Marcus escorted by the soldiers. They sat at a table at the front of the room, where they started taking questions from the reporters.

"Is it true that the Glacier kingdom has attacked the dragon?"

"Is the punishment permanent?"

"Is it true that the Glacierian King sold his youngest son for his debts?"

"How can you assure the battle will succeed if there's no control over the volunteers?"

"Omh, zela ezpwlzapo?"

They asked in several different languages, making me realize that they weren't just newspaper and radio press people from Andebeck, but reporters from every realm, including Glacier. I could see the difference in technology, some with cameras that could be held in a person's hands, and others that were older and needed tripods. I recognized Glacier's journalists by their light parkas and by their style of reporting, which two people did as a team—one asked the question, while the other wrote in her notebook without speaking.

"What's going on?" I asked, taking a step back.

"If you want to talk to Marcus, you'll have to wait for the event to end," Geronimo said, leading me away from the questioning.

We went to the second floor, and I leaned against the railing, admiringly peering at Marcus. He looked like they he had the situation under control and didn't even seem bothered by the tricky questions.

The minister had made himself comfortable at the table while the reporters waited to ask questions. Marcus made himself some tea, sitting tall and attentive to everything happening.

Karl and Khloe entered the room with their formal uniform and controlled expression as their culture demanded. They kept their eyes always looking forward.

The reporters went wild with questioning, and some even tried to get closer to both.

"With one month now completed, are you worried that other kingdoms may learn from you during training and take your place?" asked the first journalist to Karl.

Karl laughed, making my stomach turn.

I hated him.

He was so pedantic and arrogant that he seemed as if he believed that the crown rested on his head already.

"My opponents can train and admire my virtues," he answered with a booming voice. "But the only one here who was born fighting was me, and for that, there is no training to help them."

I gazed at Khloe, begging her to look at me, hoping I could urge her to speak. She had better things to say, and I was sure that if Karl had any chance of winning, it was only because she was here with him. However, Khloe remained silent the whole time, as if she was just his decoration.

"Princess Khloe," one of them spoke to her at last. "What is your routine to look so good in men's clothes?"

I gritted my teeth. What kind of question was that?

Khloe laughed but didn't answer. I think she was as annoyed as I was.

"Is it hard to concentrate with so many men around you?" asked another.

Khloe was able to answer questions as a warrior just as well as Karl. Why were they asking her those kinds of questions?

He whispered something in her ear, and she nodded as her smile dropped. Whatever Karl had said to Khloe made her get up, apologize, and leave.

"Since when are these interviews held?" I asked Brenda, who was standing next to me.

"They will be done once at the end of each month. This is the first one," Brenda responded without looking at me.

There was laughter in the press. As I turned around, Alanis made her entrance by saying something funny, making everyone laugh. The room got full of colors with her wide skirt and native flower in her ear. She was born for attention and carried it extraordinarily. Even the minister was smiling.

But when Alexander entered, it was the opposite. Silence reigned. His hair, clothes, and figure made everyone wait for him to say the first words.

"Don't be nervous. I haven't started yet," Alexander joked, making the women giggle.

I laughed a bit. He unnerved every lady in the entire room.

"Is it true that you have a secret relationship with Alanis?" They asked the first question.

Alanis laughed out loud. "He wishes."

Alexander looked at her with a mischievous smile. "I am what she says I am."

Questions and more questions. I wondered if they remembered what the real urgency was in this competition. They all seemed more interested in their relationships and internal conflicts than the trials of fire.

"We're good friends," Alanis said at last. "There is no time for personal relationships. There are more important things."

"You can enjoy on days off. It helps to relax," Alexander joked, making Alanis blush.

"Alex," he scolded, and Karl rolled his eyes. Without any effort, the two of them had taken away all of Karl's attention.

Marcus stood up, and out of respect, there was silence once more. "Dear guests," Marcus addressed the interviewers directly. "Let me officially introduce you to the heroes of Andebeck."

The three kingdoms rose and bowed. The interviewers let out everything they had and started clapping and clapping for several minutes nonstop.

"You didn't bring me here to talk to Marcus—you brought me so they could see what I've become," I accused Brenda, the clapping drowning out all sound.

Her eyes lit up maliciously. "Your kingdom will see you wearing a servant's uniform in every newspaper while the other realms are effortlessly revered. If I were your king, I'd get you out of here to avoid further shame."

Son of a—

I clenched my rage into my fist. If I lost control, it would be like indulging this hideous woman. That's why I looked back at the reporters, but I could no longer listen or pay attention to anything.

"You demand respect, but you don't give respect," I finally replied, penetrating her with my angry gaze. "What kind of leader are you?"

As if my words offended her more than I expected, she didn't answer me but turned and walked away, leaving me with Geronimo. She had nothing more to say to me because the damage had already been done.

The interviews arranged all the representatives together to take pictures, with Marcus in the center. I should have been frustrated that I was omitted, but instead, I was relieved. The whole absurd way of conducting the interviews made me feel that this was a spectacle I was glad not to be part of.

A loud clap of thunder shook the windows, seeing that the storm was finally upon us. The deluge spread throughout the kingdom, and lightning began to light up the sky.

"They don't care," I whispered. Geronimo looked at me, but I wasn't speaking to anyone in particular. "This isn't about the dragon. This is just a power contest."

"Sir?" he asked.

I could see many flashes going off that bothered my eyes from where I was. They were all having a great time. At no time did they talk about the dragon, only about themselves.

"What have I done?" I whispered. I looked to the window again—I looked at the ruins.

My heart was pounding. I was disappointed with myself for pretending I was part of this—this mistake.

Everyone wants to step over everyone else for the crown of this kingdom, including you and maybe even Laila, I remembered what Khloe had told me in the storeroom and repeated it until I got tired of thinking about it.

"I need to go," I finally said, my mind clearer than ever.

"If being here bothers you so much, I can take you to your room," Geronimo offered, pleased.

No, I didn't give a damn about the event. On the contrary, it opened my eyes. They have clear goals, and mine will never be the same as theirs.

I was tired of pretending I was just like any of them.

Explaining that to Geronimo would be a waste of time, so I pushed past him. I was trying to hide my desire to run away, so to avoid drawing attention to myself, I began slowly walking across the meeting.

"Omhet," Geronimo called to me, trying not to shout.

I just have to get through the library door, I thought, trying to resist the urge to run. Not caring if I was attracting attention, I reached for the door, yanked it open, and ran faster than I was in training. Geronimo couldn't reach me even if he tried, so I left without looking back. I ran down the corridors, passing soldiers and servants who stared at me curiously.

I crossed the beautiful main stairs, where I got lost for a moment because it had been a long since I'd gone to my official room. It felt so good to go in and close the door, locking it behind me.

"Cheikh! Lucas!" I yelled, shaken by adrenaline and haste. "Shin!"

I took off my stupid service jacket and rolled my sleeves up to my elbows. I was in a hurry, not because of the bad weather, but because someone would stop me.

I rushed into the private room of my guardians. They were not here. I cursed angrily and leaned against the wall for a second.

I was going to have to go without them.

I took a deep breath, holding back the urge to jump off the balcony to save time. The first thing I did was change my appeals. I tore off my shirt, flying off the buttons, to grab one of my guards' uniforms—Glacier's guardian uniform. When I was tying my laces of my black boots, I noticed a weapon next to Cheikh's bed. I got up slowly and took his sword in my hands.

As my fingers trembled, I tightened my hand around the grip. I am not a brave knight, I thought, But I am a mad prince, I answered, laughing at my own joke. Fear was not going to control me—not today.

As I tied the sword to my belt, I went to my room and almost screamed when I saw Marcus's sister sitting on my bed as if she had been waiting since before I entered. Does she have a master key? I didn't even hear her come in. It's the first time I've seen her in formal garments, probably because of the event. She wore a dark dress, split mid-length, and her straight black hair fell like a curtain down her back.

"Everybody in this palace is busy today with the event, and probably nobody noticed you left. You picked a good time to do the crazy thing you're about to do," she commented, crossing one leg over the other.

"Aren't you supposed to be busy as well?"

"Calm down, my dear prince. I'm not here to stop you," she said, but I kept looking at the door, waiting for an ambush at any moment. "I came to know your intentions," she explained, rising with the grace of a gazelle. "Depending on your response, I might be able to help you."

"How?" I asked defensively, no longer trusting anyone.

"I can get you the privilege of going to the ruins every Sunday."

I snorted. *Sure.*

Did she think I was an idiot? Honestly, it would be a sweet deal for me, but I know she'd want something ridiculous in return. From my little experience with Marcus, they seemed like people with ulterior motives in everything they said or did. I had to be defensive, or at least appear to be.

"What do you want in return?" I immediately asked.

She moved closer to me, and I could smell the scent of lavender on her skin.

"I want you to swear to me that you will kill the dragon when the times come."

"If you can convince the king to allow me to be in the battle—"

"Done," she interrupted me. "Anything else?"

So, it is done, then. I'll be in the battle in winter.

"That's it? That's all you ask? That's easy," I said, sensing something was missing from this deal.

She bit her lip as if she was hiding a private joke.

"It is, just not for you," she said. There was something else in her eyes. "But unlike the others, I want to give you the opportunity."

"You want to give me the opportunity," I repeated sarcastically. Nothing she said made sense to me. "You just admitted that you don't think any of this would be easy for me, as if I were weak—"

"No, not weak," she interrupted and placed her hands on my chest. "You're vulnerable, but from here."

My heart pounded in her hand, and I knew she could feel it. It was a puzzle that she wasn't putting together for me.

"You'll have to excuse me, but I don't understand," I said. Her closeness made me nervous.

"Prince Karl has an advantage in this competition with his obsession with power. Alanis dares to fight with her life for what she believes in, and Prince Alexander has the perfect appearance to rule. But your strength is in your sensitive heart." I was going to ask why, but she continued. "I'm just unsure if you'll have the courage to face it."

The image of the dragon came to me, and I shuddered.

"It's just a beast," I whispered.

"A beast in the eyes of others." She smiled and looked deep into my eyes. "But not for the prince who fell in love with the dragon."

I didn't answer because I was trying not to laugh. How could a person fall in love with a dragon?

I looked at the ruins beyond the balcony as the torrential rain poured on, and then Lois started walking to the door to leave. I was more confused than ever before. The conversation had only made me sure of two things: the kingdom leaders were obsessed with having the dragon's head at all costs, and they were both simply irrevocably insane.

"I want to make one thing clear," she said before walking out the door. "The day you decide to defend the beast, you'll become my enemy, Omhet. Don't take this favor lightly."

I nodded, unsure if it was a threat or just a reminder.

"I don't know if you're my fairy godmother or if I'm your prisoner, but I agree."

CHAPTER 25

The horse trotted over the potholes caused by the deluge, splashing mud on my pants. I could hardly see with the drops of water hitting me in the eyes, but I didn't slow the pace. I couldn't go slowly.

I did not want to.

Lightning and thunder unnerved me, but I was more terrified that it was too late to return and receive, instead, rejection from her. My heart was racing with anticipation, and I couldn't stand the wait any longer—the road felt eternal. I tried to speed up the horse more, but it didn't respond. Paranoia was driving me crazy. My mind screamed at me that the Andebeck guards could be after me or that Lois could be allowing my escape as an excuse to kick me out of the competition. I looked behind me so many times that I almost lost my balance. I didn't want anyone to follow me. If they caught me this time, I would fight.

I was almost there—I could see the tree where I usually tied the horse when I visited. I was so close until lightning struck near me. I couldn't see it, but I could feel the vibration, and the thunderclap was so intense that the horse dropped me as it reared up on two legs.

"Coward!" I yelled at him, brushing the mud off my clothes.

The horse almost ran away. I quickly got up and grabbed the reins. He yanked me back, but I didn't let go, slamming my boots into the dirt and pulling hard. Maybe I didn't know how to fight with swords, but controlling a horse couldn't be that hard.

"You're trained to battle, but you can't handle being near a damn lightning bolt," I yelled at it in frustration.

I tried to pull and control it, but the horse kicked me in the face, and I fell back on the ground, watching as it ran down the road path. I moaned, covering my mouth. A damn horse beat me.

"Brilliant," I said, standing up.

Ignoring the torrential rain, I walked the rest of the way irritated. I was here to face a dragon, but I couldn't even stand up to a horse. This is not how I read in the books that it usually happened.

When I reached the main entrance, I spat out the blood from my broken lip, thanks to the stupid horse, and drew my sword more confidently than I really was. I peeked through the doorway and walked in.

"Laila," I called out bravely, but nothing happened.

I walked carefully, looking around, expecting the beast to appear at any moment.

After half an hour of walking through the main corridors, the destroyed hall, and the ballroom, I realized that no dragon was in sight. I lowered the sword, put it back on my waist sheath, and went up the steps to the tower.

I got nervous when I got to the top. My clothes were a mess, strands of my hair were in my face, and dripping with rainwater.

"Laila," I called, laying my palm on the door. She would have heard me clearly if she had been in her room.

She didn't answer me.

I opened the door a crack and peeked in. The room was empty, and all signs of Laila had been removed. The last time I was here, there were personal belongings throughout the room, but there weren't even sheets on the bed this time. It was as if she had left the castle.

What if the sorceress had returned?

What if Laila was in some other sort of danger?

What if it's too late?

My head ached from so many possibilities. I ran back to the main level, in front of the broken stairway and the hall with the hollow ceiling.

"Laila!" I yelled, looking everywhere. The thunders competed with my screams, and the rain accumulated at the level of my ankles. I didn't care. I yelled her name again. "Laila, please—"

But I didn't know why I was imploring for.

To give me a sign.

To forgive me.

To give me one more chance.

To come back.

Shit.

To—please, come back to me.

But I heard no answer. The last place I entered was the library, not intending to look for her, but because I had completely given up.

Feeling hopeless, I leaned against the destroyed door and looked at the abandoned castle. This room was boisterous because several streams of water were pouring from the ceiling like waterfalls, falling on the shelves and destroying what was left of the library. I walked around the room feeling frustrated that I had failed the only person who trusted me.

Deep down, I knew I had to get out of there and probably never come back. If it kept raining like this, the first level would be flooded. I could see the marks on the walls where the water had reached during previous storms. I looked around curiously, feeling like I was in a haunted bookstore. The walls had vines with little flowers that had consumed the stone blocks until they hung from the ceiling, the destruction cracked the floor, and it would be a miracle to find a book in good condition. I even tried to pick one up from a shelf above my head, and it crumbled in my hands like dry leaves.

I heard a noise and turned around with my hand on the grip of my sword. But I saw nothing. It must have been the sound of shelves shifting as the water level began to rise.

Or it could be her...

I relaxed and took my hand off the grip.

"The first time I came to this place, I thought it was horrible," I commented loudly. I was talking to Laila and prayed she could hear me. "But it's like entering an alternate world. I could swear that fairies or ghosts could dance here, and it would be perfect."

I stroked the little flowers on the walls and stopped in front of a broken mirror on the wall. I looked at my face and raised an eyebrow mockingly. My lip was swollen, and fresh blood was dripping from it. I wiped it with my arm and kept walking.

"Sometimes I feel like I can hear music come out of these walls," I continued. "There has to be a grand piano somewhere. I can imagine you playing it while your siblings were studying—did you have siblings?"

Despite getting no answer, I didn't stop talking. I felt like somebody was listening, even though I had no proof.

There was a hole in the floor in the middle of the library. I went to the edge and peered down, but I couldn't see the bottom. I wondered if the dragon had created the hole or if years of exposure to the weather had made it grow slowly over time. I took steps back to gain momentum before jumping to the other side, slipping a bit. I almost fall back into the hole.

I went through an archway to a different part of the library. The room seemed infinite in size because it was six stories high, and the ceiling was completely open. I whistled in surprise. It was beautiful, despite how destroyed it was.

I walked over to the far wall, where there had once been wooden steps to the other levels, but now there was nothing left. However, there was a painting on the floor with the royal family's image.

My hand shook as I touched the art with my fingers, feeling strange about seeing the Blume family for the first time.

"So, you did have siblings," I said in a weaker tone. I could feel the smile in my voice.

There was a man—King Arien Blume, with dark hair. Then there was Laila's mother. By heaven, they were the same. She had ginger hair and green eyes. Next to her, Laila sat with a wider smile than people usually have in paintings—for an artist to paint the royal family, they have to stay still for hours. Which had to mean Laila was smiling the whole time. I looked at her two younger siblings—a boy who must have been less than ten.

"Are you the oldest? Oh, you and I can't be friends," I said jokingly. "I'm the youngest, and you know what that means, right?" I laughed. "I'm the nuisance of the family. You're the oldest—the one who scolds and demands silence from the little ones."

I took a deep breath, backing away from the painting. I was suddenly feeling sad. I couldn't stop looking at her.

"I miss my family," I whispered. "I can't write that to them because I'm afraid they'll think I'm weak." I sighed. "I don't want to imagine being what you'd been through—alone for so—so long." My voice trembled a little. I wanted desperately to let Laila know she doesn't have to go through this alone. I might not be cursed, but I can understand what alone feels like. "Laila, forgive me for failing you." I took a step away from the painting. "You are the last person I wanted to disappoint, but I did."

I forced myself to turn away from the painting, feeling a wave of disappointment when I didn't find her behind me. I brushed my hair off my face, even though it was pointless—the water was coming in everywhere.

I took a few steps back and jumped back across the hole to leave but slipped on the water and almost fell through the gap. I had to dig my nails into the floor, holding on to the cracks, hissing when I felt no ground under my feet. Well, surely it was a mistake to have explored so much, I thought, trying to drag myself against the stream of water pushing me toward the hole.

I clawed hard and pulled as best I could until I managed to get my knees out of the hole and crawl away. I sat against a shelf, watching the current of water gain strength.

I exhaled the exhausted air in my lungs and gently banged my head against the bookshelf behind me. A book fell, nearly hitting my head. I couldn't help but laugh because I was such a mess. I closed my eyes and let my mind wander for a moment, wondering how I ended up here. Small decisions accumulated one by one, until I was pulled from a privileged life in a humbled kingdom to some dark ruins where a dragon hid. Something told me that when I returned home, I was not going to be the same person, and for that reason alone, I did not regret it at all.

"You're a divine mess," she whispered to me.

Laila...

I bit my lip to hide my smile. Laila was here—the whole time, she'd been listening. But I didn't open my eyes because even though I felt her so close, I was afraid that she would disappear again if I looked for her.

"You come with a sword and courage, but the one who seems to carry the curse and the confinement is you," she told me. I can tell a humorous tone when I hear it—was she making fun of me?

I grinned when I opened my eyes and saw her standing in front of me. Her hair was longer now that it was soaking wet, and her dress was plastered to her skin as it dripped.

"Hey," I greeted her tiredly.

She kneeled on the floor in front of me. She looked at my face like she was worried. Without saying anything, she placed her hand on my face, and I flinched. Her perfect emerald eyes studied my face as she touched my lips. I had a second of confusion until I noticed that she had wiped some blood from my lips.

I raised my hand and held hers—her skin was softer than I remembered.

"It's nothing," I told her when I saw her forehead frown from concern.

Even though she stopped looking at my wound, she didn't remove her hand from mine.

"I waited for you," she said, and I could feel more sadness than resentment in her voice. "I had never before allowed anyone to set foot in these ruins in a hundred years, but I did with you."

I noticed the tremor in her voice and wanted to hug her so badly—but I didn't dare.

"Laila, I can explain—I tried..."

"You failed me," she withdrew her hand abruptly. "Why didn't you come back when you said you would? Why did you come here now?"

"I tried to escape, but the ministers did not allow me. I didn't even know I missed Sunday until it was too late—"

She laughed, and it wasn't a cheerful one. "I can't believe you," I looked at her, so confused. "You had all this time to create an excuse, and this is the best you got?"

She was going to leave. Oh, not this time. I held her hand and brought her back in front of me. "I am not lying—"

"Well, you should've," she yelled, closing her fist angrily. "Try again, prince. But this time, tell me something more exciting, at least. Tell me the dragon injured you on your way back to the palace, or even better, that you were cursed by a witch and fell asleep all this time. At least I would have enjoyed hearing any of those rather than this pathetic excuse."

I was going to reply when I saw a tear running down her cheek. What have I done?

"I am so—*so* sorry. I admit that I thought it would be easier to escape—"

"Escape what, Omhet?" she yelled and pulled her hand away from mine. "What could possibly be worse than this?"

She stands up, pointing out everything—the ruins, her life, herself, the damn curse.

I stood up slowly because I didn't want to scare her away. "I have rules that I must follow to prevent being kicked out of Andebeck. I would have come the next day if it wasn't for that."

She looked into my eyes. I saw her struggle, wanting to reject me or, worse, kick me out of her life forever.

"If only you knew how hard it is for me to trust people," she said in a shaky voice. "I can't do it again. I can't fall for this again—"

Then she started to go down an aisle between some shelves.

I immediately started to follow her, but she wasn't there when I turned down the first aisle. I continued to the next row of shelves, following the sound of her footsteps, but the place was like a maze of fallen shelves, and it was difficult for me to find her again.

"I convinced the minister's sister to allow me to visit you every Sunday, and she agreed!" I exclaimed, chasing her in the direction of where the echo of her footsteps had come from. "I convinced her to end my punishment and be able to visit you more often. I know I can help you get rid of that damn dragon—"

I jumped over a cupboard and caught up as she stopped between two shelves. She turned around with a confused look on her face.

"Punished?" she repeated. "What kind of punishment?"

Thunder interrupted me when I went to speak. I exhaled. How do I explain so much like this? "I know this will sound stupid, but they took my title and locked me underground. I tried—by Krea, I tried to escape every night, but I couldn't."

"Nobody can take your title away," she said, and I couldn't look into her eyes. I felt so embarrassed. "And much less, lock you up like a criminal. Is all that because you visited me?"

"Is not your fault. It just—" my though were all over the place. "I couldn't tell them that I met you. I tried to lie, but those people are rude and violent as all hell. I hated how they enjoyed every moment of my misery."

She came closer, now anger replaced by worried. "Why didn't you go home?"

I went quiet and gave another step closer to her.

"I will if you come with me," I said and took her hands softly. "I'm not leaving you, Laila. I never wanted to."

I thought she would push me away when I felt her fingers entwining mine.

"I can't," she said, noticing how hard it was for her to say. Her tears accumulated and her voice cracked.

"Then I'm staying here with you," she shook her head, but I almost saw a smile. "I'll put a name on the dragon," she made a tender sound like a laugh and sob at the same time. "Even do some renovation to the ruins. But I'm not leaving until I find a way to break your curse."

She got closer, and we barely had space in between. I couldn't say anything else, now looking at her lips—her *eyes*! Looking into her eyes.

"I'm still trying to figure out how a crazy person like you ended up here in my ruins," she whispered and raised one hand to leave it on my chest. My breathing quickened. "Since the moment you showed up in my ruins, I'd been unable to think of anything but you—so, please, I beg you, don't—don't give me false hope."

"On the contrary, princess. I'm here to end this curse. I promised to explain what is happening, and I will," I said calmly. I saw her surprised eyes widen as I respectfully dropped to one knee in front of her. "Your Majesty, I have come all the way from Glacier to volunteer for the trials of fire. I have sworn to submit to the rules and the training and to face the dragon at the beginning of winter on the exact date that marks the century of your curse. In your name, so shall it be."

Laila exhaled, and for a second, I thought she would never breathe again.

"Competition?" she repeated. She sounded choked up. "You—and the whole union are here to kill the dragon—? Oh, no." She said, closing her eyes as if she were trying to control panic or anger. Her hand began to shake, and her breath hitched.

I got up, searching my mind for a way to calm her emotions. She seemed on the verge of collapsing.

"It's good news," I explained, trying to sound optimistic. "Five kingdoms and seven courts had united to end this hell. On the great day of battle, the dragon will be killed. We have come to free you."

"Whose idea was this?" she demanded. "Was it this Marcus that you mentioned so much?"

I wanted to ask why she was trembling, but I nodded, confused by her rage.

"What's wrong, Laila?" I asked, feeling like I had said something terrible.

She backed away from me, pressing against the shelve as if she needed them for support. She tried to speak, but what came out was a painful moan.

"Leave," she ordered without looking at me.

"You shouldn't be afraid," I said, approaching her again. "This time, we won't allow the dragon to hurt anyone else, especially you."

"Run, Omhet!" she yelled at me. She grabbed her face as she fell to her knees.

"Laila," I called, dropping one knee in front of her. "Let me understand why you're so upset! Let me help you," I exclaimed, gently taking her by the shoulders, trying to make her look at me.

"It's going to kill you," she cried as if something was hurting her. "The dragon is coming—"

She couldn't say anything more because a shriek escaped her lips.

Feeling the horror in her voice, I understood what she meant, so I drew my sword and turned around, looking everywhere for the beast. I wouldn't let it touch her or even come close. I would try to take her away from here if I could. I wasn't afraid of it anymore.

Or so I thought.

A chill of horror ran through me when I heard the dragon bellow from behind me.

I slowly turned around as if understanding what was happening was too much for me. I lowered my sword and refused to believe what I was seeing.

"Laila," I called to her.

She fell utterly, clutching her head as she panted exaggeratedly. As if she was dying, or—

"Where is the dragon?" I shouted.

She raised her head, and when she looked into my eyes, I didn't scream, but I felt fear invade every part of me. I took a few steps backward until I hit my back against the shelf.

"Run!" she yelled in a voice that was no longer hers.

I couldn't react, not even when her eyes were no longer green but yellow. Reddish scales rapidly appeared all over her skin.

"Laila, no—" I shook my head in denial. "You can't be—"

She tried to say something else, fighting against what was growing inside her body.

Her dress tore into a million pieces, her skin flared, her shoulders expanded, and her head distorted in a sickening way. I had no choice but to move away quickly, but I refused to leave.

I stared in horror as I watched Laila's terrifying transformation into a dragon.

Act Three

The Curse

CHAPTER 26

The thud of the shelves crashing against the walls woke me more than the roar itself. I was sure that everybody from the palace to the coast of Andebeck must have heard the beast.

I had to run when its yellow eyes bored into mine.

The dragon was scrambling, clawing, and roaring wildly, which I used to my advantage. Its lack of self-control made it trip over everything and break whatever got in the way, giving me time to run. I jumped over the hole in the floor, but there was no door or windows, just some destroyed stairs that previously led to the other library levels.

I had to turn around with my sword in my hands, wanting to put up a good fight at least. But before I could see it, its tail hit me in surprise. My entire body rolled across the floor until the wall stopped me, and my sword slammed against the wall. I couldn't move. I could only open my eyes weakly, seeing the animal hissing violently. At that moment, I saw the light come from its mouth. I gasped in fright. I flailed around, trying to escape, but it was too late. Almost instantly, I got out of the way, but the fire ignited my arm, consuming my skin.

I bellowed in pain, kneeling as I tried to get up. I had to jump, not to put out the fire, but to protect myself from its teeth. It almost bit me and ripped my face off, so I dove into the hole I had tried so hard to avoid. For some reason, my mind preferred to die from a fall rather than be chewed up.

I screamed for a second before falling into a deep pool of rainwater that put out the fire.

I was so disoriented that I felt everything running in slow motion as I sank deeper into the pool. I could see the eyes of the beast as I closed mine, knowing I would have nightmares about this moment—if I even survived. I tried to swim but had trouble sensing which way was up until finally, I managed to surface in a violent and desperate gasp of air. I looked through the hole and saw a furious dragon that could not fit its enormous head inside. It tried over and over to stick its head through the hole with rage that had me paralyzed. It opened its mouth to bellow, shooting out flames again. I gasped again, diving under the water, feeling like I hadn't gotten enough air this time.

This is the end. I'm going to die, I thought, but I kept fighting. I didn't understand how I had gone from talking to a sweet princess to running from a monster. I refused to accept that she and the beast...

For the skies, for my god, Krea, and for my kingdom. What am I going to do now?

I swam to the surface again, coughing and spitting water, holding on to the pool's edge. I looked up and saw the dragon clawing at the hole, trying to get its head in with desperation, and I felt terrified. Its desire to devour me was impressive. I tried to stay completely still for a few minutes, weirdly hoping it would make me invisible.

"Laila!" I yelled loudly. "Please, stop!"

I don't know why I tried to beg her—it was clear that she wasn't there.

Or so I thought, because the dragon hissed as if fighting against itself. It banged against the walls and shelves. Something seemed to be forcing it to move away from me because it was screaming and howling with pure pain.

It walked out of my sight from the bottom of the hole, but I could hear it smashing everything in its path, hitting itself as if it wanted to self-destruct.

I knew I should stay where I was and patiently wait for it to leave or for someone to come for me, but who was I kidding? It only took a minute of silence for me to start climbing, groaning as I forced my injured hand to grab hold of the cracks in the wall. As dangerous as the flooding had seemed earlier, it ended up saving my skin.

When I reached the hole's edge, I screamed in pain as I rolled over and finally saw my burnt arm. I ripped my shirt sleeve off and hissed as I saw blisters growing all over my arm. This wasn't a mere burn—by the sky, I had almost lost my arm from the elbow to my fingers.

"Shit," I muttered, feeling horror at what my arm had become. Now I wasn't going to be able to hide it.

With pain all over my body, I forced myself to get up, finding the dragon closer than I thought. Its body was hidden in the shadow of the most remote corner of the library. It was curled up in a ball. I could hear its breathing, like a soft, violent bellow.

I held my arm, slowly approaching it, never taking my eyes off the dragon. I couldn't even see the color of its scales in the darkness. It was trying to hide from me, or worse, it was trying to control itself.

I stopped when it bared its teeth at me. The best I could see now was its yellow eyes half-closed in the dark. It growled a warning, and I waited a long time until the dragon closed its mouth again.

I walled once more, unable to hide how terrified I was.

"Forgive me," I whispered, looking into its eyes. "I didn't want to hurt you," I explained with a raised hand. I took another step toward the dragon. "Please, Laila, come back to me."

The dragon bared its teeth a bit but didn't bellow.

"Laila," I repeated her name. "I will have to draw a line with your dragon. If I ask you out on a date, it can't come, okay?"

Why the hell was I making a stupid joke in such a situation?

I took another step, but the dragon had had enough of me and lashed out with its tail. This time, I managed to duck out of the way, but when the tail smashed the shelf, it fell on top of me.

I didn't know if it was the books or the wood crushing me to the ground, but it was too much for me.

I tried to drag myself out, but before I could call her name one more time, I lost consciousness and surrendered to fate.

Laila, I whispered in my dream, come back to me.

"You finally figured it out," a voice said. *"It took you longer than I expected."*

I thought that a paradise would be revealed as my mother had taught me about what would happen after death, but instead, I stood in a meadow, listening to cries of pain. There were dead bodies of warriors around me, all with faces that I recognized well.

I walked away, trying not to step on any corpses, but I couldn't—they were everywhere. It's a nightmare, control yourself, I yelled at myself, trying to stay calm. The sky was red, smoke was rising from the burning ground, and screams were coming from the town of Andebeck. From a distance, I could see that every house and building was engulfed in flames while the dragon flew overhead, destroying everything in its path without mercy.

The palace where I had trained was no longer standing. There was nothing left. It was the end.

"Let me tell you a secret," the voice continued. *"This is how it will end if you keep her alive. The dragon needs to die."*

I turned around, seeing the same specter I'd seen in another dream once—gray face as if it were a corpse, completely yellow eyes, and long black hair like the shadow of the night. It was Tiara appearing in my mind once again, which meant this was no mere nightmare.

"Then tell me how to break the curse—"

She laughed sarcastically. *"Stupid prince. Do you really think you can solve everything your way?"*

"I might be stupid for risking my life the way I did," I argued haughtily. *"But it wasn't me who caused this."* I pointed at her. *"It was you."*

Like a blink, she disappeared and reappeared in front of me. I gasped in fright but didn't move. She wasn't real, was she?

"You don't know anything about me," she bellowed, sounding as if it were several voices in one. She was terrifying. *"And I doubt you'll ever understand."*

"Try to enlighten me," I challenged her. *"What are you, and why don't you release Laila from her cursed?"*

"I can't free her from something she did to herself," she answered, leaving me even more confused.

"What—" but I shook my head. It did not make sense. Laila would never do something like that on purpose. *"You're lying! This was all you—"*

"Ask her then! And understand that nobody can break the cursed but her own self."

Don't listen to her. I just need to find her and destroy her, I thought, feeling so confused.

"Who are you?" I yelled. *"Face me in my world."*

She laughed and then disappeared from my sight. *"Even if I showed in front of you, you wouldn't recognize me—"*

Like the nightmare itself, her voice began to fade as I woke up with a loud cry of pain.

When I opened my eyes, I found myself squeezing a sheet between my fingers while clenching my jaw so hard that it ached. I realized that I was screaming, so I tried to take a deep breath and control myself. I was disoriented, lying on a hard bed with a broken window nearby. It wasn't raining anymore, but it was cloudy, with distant thunder in the middle of the dark night.

"Cheikh," I cried, trying to move my arm, but the burning hurt so much that I immediately stopped.

"You're going to be okay," I heard a whisper. "Just—stay with me."

I felt so relieved to hear her voice.

I turned my head, fully waking up when I saw her tearful emerald eyes. Laila held my injured hand in hers, trying to heal me. I flopped back onto her bed, wondering how she could have dragged me here.

I had a terrible headache, so I closed my eyes again.

"And the brave knight was finished by a tail blow," I moaned, holding my head.

"It's not funny, Omhet," Laila cried. I didn't know if she was angry or sad—maybe both.

Laila dabbed my arm with gauze, and I pressed my lips together tightly.

"To torture me, you're supposed to tie me up first, love," I reminded her and then yelled involuntarily as she pressed the gauze on my arm.

"Omhet, by your god, if you tell one more joke..."

I chuckled through the pain. I looked at her, and my smile was replaced by sadness. Slowly I wiped a tear from her cheek with my good hand.

"It's not your fault—"

She stopped what she was doing and squeezed her eyes shut. "I thought I lost you," she pressed her lips. I think she was trying not to cry. Why was she so hard on herself? "I thought I killed you. I lost my mind when I saw you under the shelves." I tried to interrupt her, but she didn't let me. "I told you to run."

"I know, and I'm sorry. I should have listened to you—"

"Now, hold still, or I'll tie you up."

I nodded, taking a deep breath. Her mood hadn't changed at all, so I let her clean off the dead skin, the bits of cloth stuck to my arm, and the dirt covering my wounds. I sat on the bed, pressing my back against the wall. I shivered when I felt the cold stone, realizing I didn't have my shirt. Which means she took what was left of it—

I managed to control my screams, though not my grimaces.

"Laila," I said, biting back the urge to moan again.

"If I don't clean it, it will get infected," she answered. "Almost done, I promise."

She threw away the dirty gauze, and I saw the bag of medicine I had left for her on the bed. The irony. The one who ended up needing it was me.

Finally, she wrapped a cold compress around my hand and sat at the contrary end of the bed. She didn't look at me—she didn't even look like she wanted me there.

I ruined everything, and I didn't know how to fix it.

"Say something, please," I begged. Even though we were sitting next to each other, I felt her so far away.

Laila took a deep breath. She couldn't take her eyes off my arm, as if she had burned it herself—because that's precisely what she did, I thought, not knowing how to handle the situation. For now, I just decided to be patient.

Laila was wearing a robe with no design or shape. Her hair was tousled as usual, and her face was sweaty. She had a fever again—I could see it in the red on her cheeks, the sweat on her forehead, and her tired eyes.

"I usually sleep for hours until I can recover," she explained. "I can't think straight. Everything hurts—"

Now I understood why she never managed to wake up when I found her, because all the time I had interacted with her, she had just come out of her dragon phase. I had so many questions. If she was the one who murdered her father and her entire family, where did Tiara come from? Can she control the beast, even a little?

Well, that last one was obvious—I was alive to tell about it, right?

The whole world was alive to tell the tale, really.

Laila closed her eyes, and I put my hand on her shoulders when she started falling. She was not okay.

"It would be better if I gave you space—" I said, crawling out of bed. Laila needed the bed way more than I did.

"No," she begged and grabbed my hand immediately. "Don't go—not yet. Every time you leave, I don't know if you'll come back. Would you stay with me tonight, Omhet?"

I held my breath, knowing she was waiting for an answer, but I got timid. I didn't know where this nervousness came from, so I just nodded. Side by side, we lay in the same bed. I liked lying on my stomach because of the pain in my arm. While Laila was staring at the ceiling. The lights of the moons shone on her face, startling her beautiful freckles.

I felt her fingers, and then she looked at me. I watched as Laila slowly played her finger around my good hand until I caught hers myself and intertwined my fingers with hers. The silence didn't bother me. On the contrary, I looked at her and smiled a little—tired, in pain, confused, with a thousand questions running, but still smiled.

What were we doing, holding hands, lying in the same bed, and looking at each other the way we did? The breeze blew through our hair, and time rushed through my mind, reminding me that I shouldn't be there. But I stayed, looking into her eyes when silent tears fell from her cheek, and I wondered if it would be too much to give her a hug. By Krea, I don't know how long I've wanted to do it.

"Omhet, *I*—I'm so sorry," she whispered, closing her eyes.

"It wasn't you," I reminded her.

"It is me," she explained with pain in her voice. "I can feel the blood in my mouth from my victims. I can feel the urge to want to kill for no reason. Although my mind screams otherwise, I can barely control it."

I took my hand out of hers and brushed her tears away—caressing her skin and her cheek, and—

She opened her eyes, and I froze my hand in her face, slowly caressing her with my thump. It was not a hug, but it was enough for me.

"I'm not going to judge you. Sometimes I want to burn some people myself—"

"Omhet—this is serious."

"I know."

"I've killed—"

"I know, and I'm not afraid of you," she bit her lip to stifle a soft sob. "I'll stay here, and we'll talk about your situation when you feel better. For tonight, let just—" I shrugged. I'll do whatever she wants to do.

"You say you're not afraid, but I can feel your hand shaking in my face," she said, placing her hand on mine.

I gave a nervous sigh. "You—" how can I explain what I don't understand? "Laila, you make me nervous when I'm so close to you. *I*—I don't know how to explain it, but at least I can assure you I want to get closer to you, not farther."

She didn't say anything; I thought that would be my end. I said too much. I should have stayed quiet—

But Laila got up and started to move towards me. I had no idea what she was going to do, but she was getting closer and closer—I held my breath, almost closing my eyes, when she lay on my shoulder, using me as a pillow.

I was petrified. I didn't know how to react.

"Does it bother you?"

I finally moved, turning around to accommodate her better on my shoulder—and my arm went around her until I hugged her.

I was hugging Laila.

"No," I answered in a weak whisper.

"I have never slept with anyone in the same bed. It feels good not to be alone for once in this eternity," she said, feeling how every part of her body came closer to mine. I just wondered how I would sleep on my own again after tonight.

"*God*, Laila, you are so warm."

"And you are so cold," she said, hugging me back, "It feels—nice."

Her skin was my delirium, and I wanted to submerge in her. To be closer, to press my lips on her hair...

I wanted to take her curse and take her place if I could.

I took a deep breath, watching how she shuddered. Her tremors from her sudden illness drove me to despair.

"Tell me what to do, for God's sake. I can't stand seeing you like this," I said desperately.

"Sleep," she whispered weakly. "I'll be fine in the morning like nothing happened."

I watched her as she fell asleep amid sobs and moans of pain. It was not until I felt her calm and without fever that I allowed myself to be carried away by her tranquility and fell asleep.

Chapter 27

I could have sworn I felt caresses on my head, making me fall into such a deep sleep that I had difficulty waking up. I could even smell her scent, familiarizing myself with it. It reminded me of a spring morning filled with soft drizzles and delicate flowers opening at the feel of the sun.

I must have been dreaming, though, because I was alone when I opened my eyes. I sat on the bed and rubbed my face, feeling a little disoriented by everything that had happened so quickly. The dawn was sneaking through the gray clouds, welcoming a new day without rain or thunder. Although the clouds were still opaque, the sky finally cleared up.

A sudden nauseous sensation invaded me as everything that had happened came crashing down on me. I had an arm burned by a dragon and a horrible wound on my head that might have given me a concussion.

"Laila is the dragon," I realized aloud, and I rubbed my face in the middle of a confused exhalation.

I had explained to her that a battalion of people would come to kill the beast—to kill her.

How the hell am I going to return to the competition with this information? If the others discovered this secret, would they help her or use it against her?

When I tried to fiddle with the bracelet in my hand, it wasn't there. My string bracelet was gone, probably burned.

I exhaled hard and let my head hit the back of the bed while closing my eyes.

I can't free her from something she did to herself, Tiara told me. Although I promised myself not to believe that demon, her words repeated themselves in my mind.

What happened? Why is she cursed to a dragon?

"I recognize that face," Laila said, interrupting my tortuous thoughts.

She entered looking like nothing as last night. She was wearing a turquoise dress with sandals, and her hair was tied in a ponytail. She looked better after sleeping. I glanced at my arm, and it looked worse. I guess the bright side of being cursed is the ability to self-heal.

Laila carried a plain wooden tray with a tea set on it.

"What face?" I asked and noticed my voice was hoarse from so much screaming the day before.

In a relaxed manner, she poured tea into each cup and then offered me one. It smelled so sweet and lemony at the same time. The cup was missing a small piece, and the tray was just a piece of wood, but the tea was some of the sweetest I had ever tasted. I can guarantee that this has been the only tea that I have liked.

Laila sat on the bed in the corner farthest from me. She seemed wary of me—like she was afraid I would run away.

"The face I made the first morning I woke up understanding that this curse was real," she explained in a controlled whisper. "I looked like that."

I covered my scared eyes by drinking tea. I did not want it to be true—like it was just a terrible nightmare.

"You've always been the dragon," I finally said, and she nodded. "How do you invoke it?"

"By emotions," she said calmly. "Anger, sadness, fright," she shrugged. "Anything negative."

I nodded and swallowed deeply.

"Noted," I said in a jocular tone, trying so hard to cover my true emotions.

The following silence was awkward. I think she expected me to say something, but I didn't know where to start. I must admit that I didn't want to provoke her again, and none of the questions on my mind seemed like they would prevent that.

"I have a question," she said eventually while I drank my tea. "Do you still think you can tame the dragon in a couple of weeks?"

She reminded me of one of the bad jokes I told her the last time I visited, causing me to choke on the tea and cough uncontrollably. She flashed an amused smile and drank her tea like it was nothing. She almost drowned me.

"I didn't mean to refer to you that way," I said, blushing. Rarely did someone manage to defeat me with my own words. "I didn't know that the dragon and you—" I shook my head and stayed silent. She laughed a little—I could tell she was trying to ease my nerves.

"I know," she said and got up with her tea. "I prepared clothes for you. Everything you need can be found in the chest. I'll wait for you downstairs."

I nodded. I was grateful for a moment alone, even if it was to shake my shyness. It was difficult for me to accept so many things simultaneously, and I think she could tell.

For now, she left me to clean up in her bathroom, and I let my mind wander for a moment in freedom. I told myself that I wouldn't be shy about starting my questioning when I got downstairs.

Before someone else discovered her big secret, I had to find out if her curse had any way of being broken.

This was a disaster, but it would be worse if this information fell into the wrong hands.

I walked down the steps slowly while pulling a robe over me that didn't wrap tightly around my arm. It was enough to protect me from the cold in the morning but loose enough not to touch my skin. My arm ached constantly. I couldn't move it, I couldn't even open and close my fingers. I needed urgent attention, but I ignored it for now.

I wasn't sure which way to go until I heard some noises. I realized they were coming farther down the tower stairs, so I continued to an area I hadn't visited. Honestly, these ruins were as massive as a small city. I knew that it would be difficult to fully explore the castle.

At the bottom of the steps, I found a door ajar, and peeking in, I found the best room I'd been to so far. There was a small wood stove taking up a large part of a seating area and a fireplace at the other end of the room. The leather couch took an entire corner, plants were hanging from the ceiling from ropes and vases, and a working table where I saw a sewing machine. This wasn't just a room—it was her home.

Of all the rooms in the castle she had at her disposal, it did not occur to me that she would choose such a small part to live in, but it was so lovely. And warm. Laila was in the tiny kitchen, putting something in the oven like a normal person. Yesterday seemed like the end of the world, but today, she acted like nothing was happening.

My head ached, and I resisted the urge to hold it.

I walked to a hole in the damaged wall and peered out, seeing the sunrise coming up the mountains. The cliff the castle was perched on was so high I could barely see the bottom. The wing of the castle did not have a view of the city; instead, infinite mountain ranges were interrupted by the cloudy sky.

"I'm sure I can find a door in another room and make it fit here."

"I prefer it open," she replied, too busy to look at me. "It's easier to jump if I start to transform."

My stomach clenched. Omhet, this is no time to be weak.

"Sure," I tried to control my tone of voice. "Sound logical."

I felt her approach and pretended I was focused on the mountain ranges. I was afraid that she might see in my face all the questions that gave me such nervousness.

"Omhet," she said sadly. Gods, I couldn't fool her. "You know you can tell me anything." Are you sure? "If you want to leave..."

"I want to be here," I stated firmly. I didn't want her thoughts to go that way. So, I turned around, facing her with whatever courage I had left. "I'm torn between the reality of what's happening and the thousand questions in my mind."

She nodded and leaned against the wall in front of me. "Start with the first," she said as if talking about this was normal. Wasn't she the one who nearly whipped me to death for telling her there was a competition? I had to be careful with my words.

"The first," I said. "I thought you were immortal, so why do I see a kitchen full of food?"

She exhaled, and I saw a bit of life come into her eyes.

"Omhet, that's not..."

"It's a genuine curiosity," I said with a shrug.

Laila narrowed her eyes.

"Okay," she said and went back to the kitchen. She seemed annoyed at the fact that I didn't ask her a more relevant question. "I don't think the term immortality is correct." She opened the oven, taking out some tart that smelled better than anything I'd eaten in Andebeck's palace. "Every morning, the event where I transformed for the first time is repeated in my nightmares, and I wake up with the marks of blows as if they were recent, and I feel hungry only for breakfast all the time. I think it's because it was the last thing I had done before falling into this curse."

Laila placed the plate full of jelly tarts on a table with two chairs near the broken wall.

"You're frozen in time."

"I'm stuck in time," she corrected. "I have new memories of everything I do every day, but if I don't keep track of them, a hundred years haven't passed. For me, it's like I destroyed everything yesterday."

I nodded. I was able to understand that part well.

"I can feel hungry," she continued and grabbed a tart as if it weren't hot. "I can sleep, I can bleed if I cut myself, and temporarily, I can die." She looked at the tart in her hand as her voice weakened. "I just wake up at any moment craving breakfast and the vivid memory of having destroyed everything without control."

She took a bite of the tart and nodded like she enjoyed the taste. Her calm was contagious.

"Okay, we made it through this part, and no dragon in sight," I said, relieved.

She smiled wistfully.

"I try," she admitted, chewing on the tart.

When I went to get a tart, it was so hot that it slipped from my hand, but Laila ate it unaffected.

"Oh, and I'm not affected by the heat," she concluded. She flashed me a sweet smile with tart residue on her lips.

She was incredibly adorable, with a curse that horrified me. What am I going to do with her? My mind was screaming at me that I should have listened to everyone when they warned me not to get into this situation, but even though I was terrified and panicked by all this information, I didn't want to allow it to scare me off. I couldn't leave. So, I laughed in disbelief at her honesty, wanting so badly to wipe her lips clean with my fingers.

I put my hand in my pocket to control my impulses.

"So—" she said as if she was now preparing for her part of the question. "How much time do I have left? Until winter, right?" I nodded carefully. "I don't know what intrigues me more, the fact that the ministers can convince the entire union to be easy food for a dragon or that someone like you has agreed to be part of it. You don't seem like a prince who likes to belong to something so violent."

"The first part is easy to answer. Every kingdom wants the crown, Kill the dragon, and win the crown. But the truth is, the battle is mandatory. If I resign, they will bring someone from my family in my place."

She waited for me to say something else, but I didn't.

"And you, prince? Why are you here?"

I swallow slowly. "It's complicated."

"Do you want to win the competition? Do you want the crown?"

"No," I said louder than I needed. "Sorry," I took a deep breath. "My father wants me to find an ally or to marry someone." I rolled my eyes. "I want—I'm here... because I wanted to be useful. I had no idea what I was getting myself into."

"So that's why you were with that girl the day I met you..."

"Yes, with Khloe—"

"...Because you wanted to marry her."

"NO," I yelled, and she laughed. "By Krea," I looked away, totally blushed.

"Omhet, I've been holed up here long enough to know what two young individuals want to do when they come to the ruins to be alone."

"I can assure you, my princess, that if having an ally is a challenge, convincing someone to be with me is even more impossible," I joked, but when I looked at her, she was not laughing.

"No, it's not," she said severely. "Why would someone reject you?"

"Again, it's complicated," I looked away once more.

She stared at me as if analyzing every part of me. I felt exposed. I was getting nervous.

"Who was him?"

"Who was what?" I asked, confused.

"The name of the person who gives you that look."

"Laila, I'm so confused right now."

"You are scared of something," she got closer, and I gave a step back. "What's his name?"

"Of whom?"

"Your brother..."

"I have many brothers—"

"The one who gave you the scar on your back. What is his name?"

I froze. Maybe Laila remembers the story I told her while unconscious and saw my scar last night. She's connecting the dots, and I was not ready for this.

I took another step back but got stuck with the stove.

"Can I be frank with you? I don't feel comfortable saying my brother's name to a dragon."

"I'm not going to kill him. I'm just going to scare him," she told me with a mischievous smile.

Oh, Guillermo is so dead.

"We are not here for me but for you. Forget about me. My problems aren't half as complicated as yours, okay?"

She giggled. "You're so cute when you're nervous."

I relaxed my shoulders and smiled back at her. "Fine. Let's solve your dragon situation, and then I'll tell you about my life. But I promised you, it's not really that interesting."

She exhaled. She seemed disappointed that I didn't want to tell her about myself. As if she wanted to know every part of my life. My heart raced just seeing how intense she looked at me.

"Well, I don't want to be pessimistic, but the minister is wasting time in the most ridiculous way."

"Yes, I realized that last night." The comment slipped out, and I closed my eyes in regret. I didn't want to admit that seeing the dragon in action was the scariest thing I've ever experienced. "It'll take much more than arrows and swords to stop it, huh?"

"They can cut me into pieces," she said. I shivered—this conversation was too much for me. "They need to realize that at dawn, I will reappear, and I will surely swallow whoever is still here."

"Sounds fair," I said, scratching my head. She was ruthless behind tender eyes. "Didn't the sorceress say something before she cursed you? Anything?"

"No," she said with a shrug. "The cursed doesn't break with true love's kiss if you're wondering."

I raised my eyebrow. "Have you at least tried?" She laughed but looked away, blushing all over. "We must cover all the bases," I continue. "Kiss a frog, find true love, sacrifice a fairy, ride the dragon and fly with it—"

"Omhet, by heaven, do you think I'm in a fairy tale?" she interrupted, amused with my jokes. "It's dark magic—it can't be easily broken."

The smile started to fade. "So, it can be broken?" Tell me right now. I'll do anything. How hard could it be?

Her smile faded slowly as well. She left the rest of the tart at the table and looked at me. "Are you ready?"

When she asked me that question, I thought of so many possibilities that I had to look away. Would she use me as a frog for practice or what? I'm ready—Omhet, control yourself.

"What for?" I asked, suddenly feeling nervous.

"To tell you what really happened," she said determinedly. "I'll tell you everything from the beginning."

No, I'm not ready.

"Start, then," I answered, looking into her eyes. "I want to know what happened and above all, how we can break the curse."

Chapter 28

LAILA

One night, I went to sleep and had my first nightmare. It was so horrible that I was frozen on the bed as if I had been paralyzed. It was Tiara—I saw her in my dreams, and it was such a terrifying image that I tried to learn to live without sleep for the next few days. How could a girl explain to her parents that she saw a monster that seemed so real? How could I make them understand the danger I witnessed without sounding like mere childish imagination?

My mother held me as I cried, and I told her about my nightmare, and as much as I tried to convince her that what I saw was real, she just told me that it was not real. It was just a nightmare.

But I knew it wasn't just a bad dream because nothing was ever the same afterward.

My home used to be so joyful, but then I noticed how everything began to change. My father, King Arien Lois Blume, transformed as if he had been replaced. It was so sudden that his own advisers were muttering behind his back that he was sick in the mind. But I knew it was something else because I had felt it too, a strange presence, invasive and dark as mist in the middle of a terrifying forest.

What could others do when the king was in complete control of everything in the kingdom? No matter how cruel, insensitive, and violent he became, they continued to obey him instead of looking for a way to help him. Only my mother tried to stand up to his madness; I must admit that it was her biggest mistake.

"Anni," I yelled for my mother in Andebeck's language. I was just a little girl.

I banged on the door again and again until my nanny grabbed me around my waist and pulled me away from the door. She knelt in front of me, patiently lifted my hands, and placed them over my ears as if she could shut out what was happening in the other room.

"If you don't hear it, it will be easier to forget," she told me calmly.

But I heard my mother's screams and the blows hitting her body. I sobbed, feeling the hottest tears I'd ever had, running down my cheeks.

"Stop it," I begged my nanny. "Save anni."

"Everything will be fine, little pejy," she comforted me, using my nickname, which meant face with freckles.

I continued clutching my ears as she hugged me so I wouldn't run out the door. She sang to me and calmed me down, but she didn't do or call anyone else to stop the fight in my parents' room.

When my father finally came out, he had blood on his clothes and hands.

I stopped breathing.

"Tell the council that Her Majesty the Queen has taken her own life," my father ordered his minister.

His coldness was not natural. He was no longer himself—I could see it in his eyes without having any idea that this was the beginning of the end.

Everything progressively got worse in the years after the queen died. The king even remarried the woman who had been my nanny.

The kingdoms began to unite as allies, the courts were created, and although the king stopped being seen publicly, his orders were severe even when no one could see him.

That was not my father, and although it took me years to find courage, I forced myself to be strong for the memory of my mother and my siblings. I had to try to understand this being whom I once called my father. I tried to find answers—I read his diaries, books, and letters to other realms and even eavesdropped on his meetings with the council. But nothing could explain his transformation.

To this day, I still do not understand how he changed so drastically.

He went from a father who smiled and loved everyone to a cruel monster who murdered the mother of his children in such an inhuman way. I had to find an answer and snooped as much as possible in every corner of this castle.

If there was one thing I was sure of, it was that there was a being greater than anything I knew who controlled the king like a puppet. I could feel it, but I had no evidence. The king did not smile anymore, as if he had no life. The person he had been wasn't there anymore.

Spies from other kingdoms were involved in plots to reveal the kin as a traitor. After they were caught, I saw their trials, where they were sentenced to death. They were burned alive in front of the people while shouting, "the king is dead!"

I believed the spies—my father no longer existed.

I think all the people knew it, but no one dared to confront him.

"A new kingdom has joined our allies: the great kingdom of war, Ettezi," the king told us one evening while we dined as a family.

It was such a silent moment that I clearly heard my siblings' cutlery scraping their plates.

"What did they ask for in return?" I asked in a harsh whisper. I was eighteen and dedicated my entire life to understanding this kingdom, desperate to uncover my father's senses. And I knew that hearing about Ettezi was not going to end well. "They always want something in return," I added.

My father says nothing for a long moment, just staring at me. It was so painfully obvious that my eyes started to fill with tears. Tears of rage.

"I thought it was evident," my father answered and drank some wine.

My siblings stopped eating, slowly noticing the change in my mood.

I took a deep breath, trying to control the way it hitched noticeably.

"You cannot—"

"It is done." My appetite went to my feet, looking my father in the eyes without blinking. "They have asked for the hand of my firstborn, and after the ceremony, you will have to leave to Ettezi..."

"No!" I bellowed, standing up. "You can't kick me out of my home—I'm the heir of Andebeck!"

"Not anymore," he said as if all this meant nothing. He pointed to his wife next to him. "She is expecting an heir, and he will be the one to whom I will give the crown."

I looked at my sibling, seeing that they lowered their eyes as if they had already known. He spat at the memory of my mother and the claims of all her children, basically. It was too much to take in. Since when had that woman been pregnant? A woman who used to be my nanny. A woman who heard what my father did to my mother.

Sometimes I wondered if I was still stuck in that nightmare I once had because nothing seemed real.

The king got up after finishing his dinner, and without waiting for anyone, he began to leave. I was tired of being the fool who silently followed the impulses of a mad king.

"I will not do it," I told him, walking toward him with great courage. "You are not going to take away my right to the crown and give me to a kingdom that I do not know."

"You have been taught to serve. You must keep your mouth shut and submit to whatever your husband tells you to do."

"To hell with that," I spat out angrily.

Before I could continue, he slapped me in front of everyone. I started at the wall, holding back my angry tears.

My father grabbed me by the shoulders, and I looked into his black eyes in the middle of a frightened gasp.

I didn't cry, not in front of him.

"You have to go away, Laila, or you'll end up like your mother," my father concluded with no emotion in his voice.

"You are not my father—what did you do with him?" I screamed, but he left without answering.

When I was alone, I cried, not because my father was abusive but because he was indifferent. Something had been done to him, and I couldn't figure out what or how. I only knew that everything had changed, and I couldn't find a way to save my poor brother and sister or myself.

I tried to run away with my siblings. I tried more than once, but the guards dragged us back to the castle by the hair. It was a shame for the kingdom because all the citizens saw the spectacle. We try to escape hidden in cargo wagons. We got on vessels going to Puerto Escondido. We tried to run after the train but couldn't even make it to the kingdom's border.

We tried, and we tried and tried—for months before my wedding. Before the end. I couldn't stop fighting for our lives, but nobody cared.

I knew what the citizens said about me, the mockery was in the newspapers, street puppet shows, and even in tavern songs: the rebellious princess who didn't respect her father. The fool who didn't care about the kingdom. The coward. The one who tries to steal her siblings instead of saving them.

I tried to convince someone in the castle, any guardian, even a citizen. If someone—anyone, could believe me and help me—

The only person who listened to me was my guardian Julian, but as soon as my father found out that he tried to help me escape, they murdered him in front of my siblings and me.

After that, the king locked me in my room like a prisoner.

I didn't see my siblings again until my wedding day.

"This is Rafael of Ettezi," my nanny—the new queen introduced me, along with the king.

I didn't make an act of reverence, and my father's eyes darkened.

"Princess, I have longed to meet you," Rafael said in a deep voice. He was so tall that I had to tilt my head slightly to look at his face. He had broad shoulders, a shaved head, and a beard. I didn't have to look very closely to know that this man was twice my age. His skin was stained by the constant sun they received in the desert, and his eyes did not seem to have compassion, even though his voice was calm.

As soon as I met him, I knew that man would destroy what little I had left. I'd already had enough experience with my father's coldness. My end was near. I could feel it, and there was nothing I could do to stop it.

"I know that your kingdom has no religion, but you will understand that I do," I commented to him later while they served us a private dinner in my prison—in my room. I thanked heaven that the table was long so I could keep him away from me. "I wish to have my own space and room for that very reason."

"When you become my wife, you will have no religion," he said mercilessly. "You will walk behind me and only talk if I let you. I promise you will get used to it."

I clenched my hand around my fork, trying not to lose my patience.

"If you knew me, you would understand that I don't know how to shut up for a single minute."

"If you knew me, you would understand that you have no choice."

"I still have a choice," I said, dropping the cutlery onto my plate. "I'll annul this stupidity."

Rafael kept eating as if I hadn't said anything, and my protest didn't bother him, making my blood boil with anger.

"I'll give your arrogance a month," he said. "I promise I'll teach you how to be a proper Ettezi woman."

I got up, throwing my napkin on the table.

"I know my father ordered this wedding, but you should know that I disagree with this *shit*, and I'm not going to change just because I'll be your wife."

Rafael finally looked me in the eyes, "The word wife does not exist in our language. You are an accessory to the family to reproduce, and if it is so difficult for you to understand—"

"You are a pig," I interrupted in disgust, "and I won't marry you. Now get out of my room!"

Rafael calmly drank his wine and got up from his chair.

I thought I already knew hell, but hell was about to begin.

I will never forget that night. Rafael said, "Leave us," to all the servants, and I stayed alone with him in my room for hours that felt an eternity. I couldn't defend myself—he was so strong. Trying to push him away from me was no different than punching a brick wall.

Rafael did terrible things to me, and nobody came to help, no matter how many times I cried for help.

I was crawling, trying to catch the clothes he ripped me off when he pulled me by my legs and dragged me back to him, because he wasn't done. Rafael beat me until he made me vomit what little I'd eaten for dinner.

"I'll leave your pretty face intact this time," he told me, grabbing me by the neck so that I would look him in the eye. "You need to look presentable in the morning for the wedding."

He released me and stepped over me to the door.

"I recommend that you learn to stay quiet, Laila," he said before leaving, looking at me as if I were his property. "For your sake, I was soft with you this time."

I don't know how such a brutal beating was considered light since I couldn't get up from the floor. Until my maids came in to help me get dressed in clothes that weren't torn.

If there was one thing I understood after that night, I had to find a way out of this hell or die trying.

That night, I slept between groans of pain, knowing that I had to wake up to face the worst day of my life: my wedding day.

"I can save you from that misfortune," a voice told me as I slept.

It was the first time Tiara spoke to me directly. It wasn't just a nightmare like when I was a child. It was real, as if she were flesh and blood.

I was in the middle of a destroyed and terrifying corridor. I didn't dare move anywhere, pressing myself flat against the wall.

"How?" I asked, but I didn't hear an answer. "Tell me how!"

I didn't care about hurting people—I just wanted to destroy my father, Rafael, all of Ettezi, and everyone who allowed the king to ruin my home and family. I was full of hate.

She appeared in front of me. Tiara was the most horrifying thing I have ever seen—as if the darkness had created her. The hair looked like a weightless moving mist and her eyes—

I held my breath as her yellow eyes, as big as an owl's, looked into my soul.

"Fwejo komzwme," she whispered to me as if several voices were speaking at once.

"What?"

"Fwego konzume," she repeated. "*You'll* say it when you're ready..."

"I don't understand."

"Magic will set you free from everyone and everything."

I waited for a better explanation, but instead, I woke up when my sister called out my name. I was already late for the wedding, even though I hardly felt like I'd slept for a moment.

I sat in bed, seeing the wedding gown in front of me, held up by two servants. My sister had arranged a tray of jelly tarts, and my brother came out of nowhere with a box in his hand, which I assumed held the crown I would wear over my veil.

I stayed frozen in bed, looking at everything slowly, analyzing whether it was real.

"The faster you get married, the faster we go," said my sweet little sister. My wedding could be my undoing, but it was her salvation for her. Knowing that I would take her from our violent father sounded better than what awaited her if she stayed.

"They say their warriors are better than ours," said my brother. "Do you think they'll let me join?"

I hugged my knees with my arms, trying to breathe in through my nose and out through my mouth. I was having a panic attack and was trying to cover it up for them. I buried my forehead in my knees and began to hyperventilate. By the gods, I couldn't control myself.

I was trying to focus on what my two little siblings were saying to each other as if being banished was salvation when it wasn't. This was my home, and it was taken from us.

"Lala," my sister called me by my nickname. She'd been calling me like that since she learned to speak, and it stayed like that forever. "You're going to be late."

I raised my face with more anger than fear.

"Leave me alone with my siblings," I demanded through clenched teeth.

I felt every terrible emotion all at once. My heart was going to explode.

"The queen orders us to—" the servant tried to explain.

"Didn't you hear me?" I yelled with all the hostility I could muster. "Get out!" I scared my siblings, but I kept shouting. "Get out, damn it!"

The servant left, and I stayed with my siblings alone at last.

I wiped my sister's tears, and I smiled at her. The most deformed smile I can provide. "Now, you two will help me dress up, understand?"

I wanted to be with them once more. I didn't want anyone to dress me or touch me. I just wanted to enjoy one more moment with the people I loved, even if it was in hollow silence.

My sister gasped in shock when I took off my clothes, and she saw my bruises all over my torso and back. Even the bed had blood stains. I didn't explain or say anything. I simply prepared myself with their help as best we could, and we left.

I think my siblings expected me to say something. A goodbye, maybe a hug, but I could barely move. I couldn't speak because of the pain in my body. I simply looked at them through the veil, gave them a sad smile, and entered the throne room amid tears that soaked my cheek and neck.

It was filled with people from all over the union. But I didn't look at anyone as I walked across the carpet covered with the petals of our kingdom flower.

Rafael waited in front of the colossal throne, and the damn queen had the book in her hand to marry us.

I stopped halfway down the hall and bit my lip with a sob. It wasn't until my father reached my side that he took my arm and helped me continue.

"Please," I cried.

"It will be over soon," was all he replied.

He left me at the altar, my siblings in the front row, and my father next to his queen. I couldn't breathe, couldn't stop sobbing, and didn't want to look at Rafael.

The ceremony began, but something caught my attention. The book the queen was reading on the podium was upside down. I wondered if she hadn't noticed. She was with her eyes closed, giving a prayer to the god Krea.

"Read it, Laila, read it," Tiara whispered.

I looked for her everywhere but didn't see anyone around me.

The book was in my direction, and I could read the exact words Tiara told me in my sleep.

I got closer to the book, ready to say it.

"There will be no turning back," I heard Tiara's voice.

When I looked up, the queen had been replaced by the hideous image of Tiara.

Nervously I looked around me, noticing that time had stopped. The silence was drowning me. I had to decide now. Marry Rafael or trust this strange sorceress.

"I don't care," I mumble.

Tiara smiled, and I shivered.

"Say it and give me a drop of your blood," she said and gave me a knife.

I cut my own hand without making a single noise. I couldn't feel anything anymore.

I raised my hand and placed it on the book, leaving my blood print.

"What are you doing?" Rafael asked me.

I repeatedly blinked, realizing that Rafael was looking at me without understanding. Time was no longer stopped. People began to stand up out of curiosity as to why the ceremony had stopped.

Blood began to drip from the book onto the floor. My heart was racing so hard it showed in my heavy breathing.

Tiara was no longer in front of me, but I could feel her presence glued to my neck.

"Say it, now," Tiara said in my ear.

This time, the sky thundered loudly, and the wind began to open the windows scaring the crowd. I could hear people running by the sudden change of weather.

I thought I would have to say it several times to be effective, but I took a deep breath, closed my eyes, and courageously said, "Fwejo komzwme."

There was a second of silence, and then, I fell to my knees amid a cry of pain. I didn't try to stop it. I surrendered to the magic. The fire from the torches crawled across the floor, reaching me, and covering me from head to foot, creating scales in my skin. My yellow eyes scared everyone around me, and my dragon roar was heard all the way to the shore.

I was huge. I was unstoppable. I was out of control, and I didn't care. I let the monster inside me take control and burn everything.

The windows shattered, the ceiling began to collapse, people crowded the exit trying to get out all at once, and I consumed them all.

I destroyed the castle so quickly that I hardly remember more than fire, screams, and explosions.

I burned the flowers, the altar, and the garden, but I wasn't satisfied. I had to fly to the sky because I was looking for someone—I was looking for Rafael.

I knew where the coward was going and couldn't allow my tormentor to escape. I spotted Rafael and his guards fleeing toward the pier.

I swooped down and bit into the sail of Ettezi's ship and destroyed the deck while being mercilessly attacked by arrows. I felt no pain, only immense fury when I finally confronted the damned Rafael.

As the ship sank and his warriors threw themselves overboard, I landed on the vessel and roared in front of him. We stared at each other for an instant that felt like eternal, enjoying the fear that paralyzed him. This made him drop the bow and arrow and fall to his knees to await his end.

I didn't burn him. He was already injured by my flames.

I caught him with my teeth, and I chewed and chewed until there was nothing left of him.

I became bestial as if my human instincts had utterly shut down.

When I woke up, I was in the middle of dead bodies inside the castle. No one in the castle survived.

The night and the smoke covered the sky. My body was dressed in ashes and blood, confused at if all that happened was real or a nightmare.

I put on the first cloak I could find and run, but I fell because of weakness. I called my siblings, and I crawled through every corridor of the castle, but all there was death and silence. I held onto the wall and bellowed, clawing at my face in despair as I realized it was all real. It was driving me crazy. I needed to find my brothers. I needed to—

I found them near the altar, in the ceremony room.

I couldn't get close to them. They were dead, consumed by my fire, with my sweet brother hugging my sister, trying to protect her from my fire.

I covered my mouth, and a horrible sob consumed me.

I did that.

"You destroy everything you touch," I heard a voice near me, "but it wasn't your fault."

"Father?" I called, trying to find him.

I peeked into the hall, finding my father leaning out of the destroyed arch. What was once a bridge was now a precipice.

"Father, step away from the edge," I yelled in my weak voice, holding onto the wall to be able to walk.

He turned to me, and I gasped when I saw half of his face entirely burned.

"I was weak," he said, looking at me as if he were saying goodbye. "I will never allow the monster to touch me again."

I opened my eyes in surprise, realizing that the one who was looking at me and crying was my father. My real father. I wanted to hug him and cry and find a way to understand all this chaos. Together.

My scream got stuck in my throat as my father closed his eyes and dropped off the cliff. I yelled his name and covered my eyes, sobbing.

I never left the ruins. That first night I just hugged my dead siblings and cried until I lost consciousness.

The Kingdom of Andebeck had fallen.

The few brave warriors who dared approach the ruins and tried to attack me were consumed in seconds, creating the legend most feared by all the kingdoms.

I learned to live with the consequences of my action, not because I wanted to, but because no matter how much I tried, I couldn't die.

Now I can control the beast better, or Andebeck would've been dust already. But what's the point? The only people I would have wanted to save are dead.

I didn't get a chance to say goodbye.

I didn't get to tell them how much I loved them.

I wish I could turn back in time and have the self-control to let them ride on my back and get them out of this damn realm.

That is the true story of the curse of Andebeck.

CHAPTER 29

"Omhet," Laila whispered. "Please, talk to me."

I had my face hidden in my hands that were on the table. I was breathing heavily. I had to calm down. I wanted to show Laila that I could manage everything she just told me, but by Krea, I couldn't even breathe normally.

I don't know how Rafael had looked like, but what I saw in my mind was Karl abusing Laila, and I hated him like I never thought I could hate someone. Ironically more than I already hated him.

I hated him and everyone—this kingdom, Laila's father, and Tiara.

"I-I need a second," I said, getting up from the table.

I went up the steps two at a time and through the corridors more haste than I should have because I felt suffocated. I finally made it to the library, just so I could go out on the balcony and breathe. I loudly gasped as if searching for air but not finding enough.

"By heavens," I exhaled all the contained air, clenching my hands on the railing.

The legend I knew had always been a lie. I felt like I was going to throw up. I took a deep breath, closed my eyes, and tried to convince myself that seeking revenge wouldn't solve our problems.

"That's why the dragon destroyed everything at the festival in the city years ago," I spat out my words with contained anger, knowing that she was close by—she always was. "Because it was a bloody hypocrisy."

I turned around and found her leaning against the door, staring at the floor.

"Yes," she replied in a whisper.

Her arms were crossed, but I could tell she was trembling. Her voice was almost inaudible. This had been my fault—my emotions were making her lose control of hers. How could they hurt her so much? Where in hell was Tiara? Does she only appear in nightmares?

"There's something else I wanted to show you," she said from a distance.

Not today, by heaven—I can't take anymore, I wanted to yell, but I kept quiet.

Laila started walking without waiting for me. I had to take a deep breath and follow her.

I wanted to get Laila out of here, to take her away to distant lands where they couldn't find her. I want to protect her and fight whoever dared to hurt her. I'll take care of her during her nightmares and bake her tarts in the morning. I want to hide her from everything and everyone.

I was so overwhelmed by emotions that I forced my face to be expressionless to hide it.

I follow her earnestly at a reasonable distance. I needed a couple of days to process all of this. It hurt me so much to understand that all the competition would lead to killing her instead of helping her. It doesn't make sense!

We crossed to a different wing of the castle in silence. The east wing. It was one I hadn't visited before and was more destroyed than the other areas I'd seen. Here, the entire corridor wall was missing, and the connecting walls to the rooms were totally burned. I had to be careful where I stepped because the ground gave way as if it might break at any moment. It was the darkest wing in the entire castle, and the worst part was that I recognized it—this was the hallway from my first nightmare with Tiara, when her claws grabbed my head.

Laila winced as she pushed through a broken door. I crouched down to follow her and found myself in a large, dilapidated room.

I froze by the entrance. The carpet was burned, a gap in the ceiling and windows, cabinets that looked like they'd been smashed in, and fingernail marks on the door's wood. It looked like there had been a massacre in this room. I couldn't move from the arch.

"Laila," I barely whispered. "Where are we?"

Laila stood in the middle of the hallway. "This was the throne room." She said, and I felt the blood leave my face. "You wanted to know how to break the curse. Well, here is the answer to that."

I didn't answer. I think she saw how pale I'd turned.

Here she not only transformed for the first time but where thousands of dead were, including her siblings. There were still the remnants, even though there wasn't a single body. Here was where the terrible curse had been born.

"Omhet," she called me, and I looked at her at last. "We can come back at another time—"

"Show me how to break your curse, Laila Blume," I interrupted her.

She hesitated but slowly nodded. She kept walking to the throne, and I followed her, controlling my emotions as best as possible. I asked for this. I need to go through it, no matter what.

Laila didn't walk up to the throne but up to a podium, where there was a book on it. Interesting detail that everything was destroyed except that.

"This is the book that cursed me," I got closer, but when I saw Laila's blood, I immediately stopped. It looked—fresh. Not as if it had been a hundred years, but as if it had happened a couple of hours ago. "I need a couple of things, but we can do it together." She began to turn the pages with trembling fingers. "We need a rare stone, and if we build these arrows, that's all we need."

There was a drawing of black-tipped arrows on the page she was reading from. I didn't have to read too much to know this was dark magic.

"Some arrows?" I repeated, raising my eyebrows. I didn't like where this conversation was going.

"We need three," she continued. "And I want you to have them." I tried to interrupt, but she didn't allow me. "The scriptures say the arrows will consume even the most powerful magic, but only if you shoot at its weakest point—" She looked at me to see if I understood all that nonsense. "In other words, you have to do it to the dragon directly."

"Laila—" I didn't know what to say. I looked at the book, and then I looked at her.

She had just given me the key to winning the competition, and I was not even close to being relieved. Maybe I wouldn't need as much training or to win all the stations. I just needed to grab the arrows, aim well, and shoot—at *her*.

"You must shoot in the center of the heart," she continued. Her tone changed as her speech became faster. "It will consume the magic, and as soon as the magic leaves my body, you can end my life."

"Laila!" I yelled.

She turned to me, allowing me to see that she was afraid too. We fell silent for a second as we looked into each other's eyes. I didn't like how this conversation was going.

"You—you're asking me to kill you," I finally said. I didn't know until then that my heart could beat so hard it hurt to breathe.

Her voice was shaking when she responded, "It's okay," No, it's not. "I think this is the first time in my entire life that I feel ready to give up."

"Why do you want to give up now when I've only just met you?" I exploded.

"It's exactly because I finally met you," she said with a sad smile. "I trust you—" I shook my head firmly. "Omhet, you must win the competition—you must be the king and lead Andebeck with the purity you carry in your heart. I would be more than honored if you—"

"No," I interrupted and closed the book. "I heard enough."

I didn't want to have this conversation. My heart was racing, and my breathing was heavy. Why did it hurt so much? What had Laila Blume done to me?

"I'm not going to," I said, facing her. "I'm not going to kill you. I will fight Tiara, Marcus, my own king, and even you, but I will not give up. I can't—I can't. I'm sorry."

I turned to the door, but she grabbed my hand immediately. "Why not?" I would have answered if she hadn't gotten so close to my face. When I had her this close, she stole all my thoughts. "Would you rather let me burn Andebeck? Do you prefer that I kill everybody in winter?"

I closed my eyes, remembering the nightmare I had. In winter, hell would come to Andebeck if no one stopped the dragon.

"Look at me, Laila," I said, exhausted. "I am nobody."

"Don't say that, Omhet. Never say that again," she told me, getting angry.

"I've never killed anyone, and I won't start with you."

Seeing the look on her face hurt me so much that I took a step away from her. She squeezed my hands, causing me to swallow a hiss of pain as I felt my wound.

I could not do it anymore. I want—I *needed* to leave.

I could take everything else—the curse, the truth of what happened, the fact that Laila is the dragon, that she attacked me until I almost lost an arm—I can try to force myself to take everything except the last thing that she explained. I'm not going—I *can't* kill her.

"Omhet, you can't leave like this," she called me when she saw how I kept taking steps backward.

Nothing prepares me for this. On the contrary, I'd had failed so many times—to so many people. I can't do anything!

I can't have allies.

I can't keep the promise I made to my father.

I can't fulfill Cheikh's expectations.

And I cannot and *will* not end Laila's life.

I should have never left Glacier.

"I'm sorry, Princess," I said and pulled out of her grasp in one rough movement, "but you were wrong about me." I moved a little farther away. "I'm going back to Glacier today. I renounce you and this competition."

Without saying anything else, I walked away from her.

"Omhet!" she called, holding to the podium as if it were her support. "Please—please, you have to end my suffering. I can't shoot myself!"

I kept walking, leaving her in the throne room alone.

"Omhet!" she cried, followed by a sob.

I didn't even want to turn around because if I saw her, I knew I would run back to her.

So, I ran—

I ran away from Laila, feeling like the worst man in the world, knowing that I'd left her crying in the room, where the hell broke loose. The room where she'd lost her siblings and basically her life. It was the room where her damn curse began, which is why I could hear the dragon roar as Laila's emotion got the best of her, and she transformed.

CHAPTER 30

I was in Marcus's office, quiet, staring out the window. My clothes were haggard from the rain, dried blood from my injured arm, and poorly treated sores. I must have looked broken inside and out, which is why I didn't defend myself when Geronimo and Brenda were arguing with my three guardians. My guardians discussed blaming them for my injury and humiliation. Brenda and Geronimo tried to shout over all my faults, demanding more punishment or kicking me out of the competition. I don't know—I wasn't paying attention to them.

I stayed on the couch, listening without really listening, envisioning what Laila had experienced over and over again—a princess who was a dragon. A prince who beat her. A mad king who murdered her mother. A sorceress who destroyed a kingdom just by appearing in nightmares. And a request that was impossible for a failure like me to accomplish. I usually never allow myself to be so pessimistic, but this morning, I was inconsolable.

"Can you all leave me alone with Prince Omhet?" asked Marcus, interrupting everyone.

At that moment, I woke up, seeing Brenda and Geronimo choke on their own words as he stopped them roughly.

"Prince," asked Cheikh, glaring at the minister and his sister, a quiet soul at his side.

I nodded without saying a word. Cheikh sighed and signaled Lucas and Shin. It was the first time I noticed the hesitation in my guardians. They were so worried about me that I must admit it surprised me. I didn't know they were capable of being concerned.

"We'll be by the door," said Cheikh, loud enough to be considered a warning.

They all left but one.

Marcus looked at Lois, who was standing beside him. She was looking at me as if she were analyzing everything about me. She seemed anxious to know what had happened to me.

"Leave us, please," he said to her.

Even if she tried to look calm, I could see the tension in her eyes.

After a moment, she nodded and left Marcus's office.

Silence reigned for almost a minute, making the place feel uncomfortable. I have never wished so bad that I had my string bracelet. I wanted to fiddle with it in my fingers, to put my mind on something that would give me peace with such a simple thing. I noticed a floor clock. The click-clock sound was driving me insane. Then I heard the wind flopping the curtains. Marcus constantly hitting the table with his pen. Then a loud roar before spitting fire into my arm—

Laila screamed for help while Karl—no, Rafael beat her like a fucking animal.

Laila screamed for my help while I fled like a coward.

I could hear everything, and it was so damn loud.

I was mainly staring at nothing. Could I not silence my mind for a moment? I felt like I wanted to run out of this maddening kingdom.

"I've never seen you quiet in the time I've known you," Marcus began carefully. "I know something happened to you—"

"I quit," I said out of the blue, cutting him off. I dared to look at him at last, seeing his confused expression. "I do not want to be here."

Marcus straightened up. I was sure that of all the things he had expected to come out of my lips first, that wasn't it. He looked at my arm covered with dirty bandages that didn't completely hide a burn that clearly needed to be treated with urgency. He probably wanted me to explain so many things, but I didn't care—I preferred to leave him in the dark.

"I guess the roar we heard and your injured hand had something to do with this decision," he commented, pointing to my arm.

"It was an accident," *she didn't mean to—*

"I don't want to hear any more lies," he interrupted me, but he didn't seem angry. Instead, he seemed patient. "I know more secrets than you can imagine, and I think it's time for both of us to stop this charade. I know you must have a good reason for lying so much—sneaking out every opportunity, wanting to run over every leader and disappoint the kingdom you love so much—and I think that reason is Laila Blume."

He knew she was alive—of course, he knew.

I looked at him thoughtfully, for once not even bothering to hide it.

"I quit," I repeated in a controlled but stiff voice. "I have nothing else to talk about."

Marcus sighed, looking disappointed. I could tell he was trying to figure out what happened in all those hours I disappeared and why I returned so differently. He couldn't know, and I would never tell or confirm it. It doesn't matter how close he is to the truth. We had two completely different interests—he wanted what was best for his kingdom, and I wanted what was best for Laila, and it seemed like the two of us were at opposite poles.

"Prince Omhet, you can tell me anything. Your secrets are safe with me," he insisted with a calm smile. "Can you tell me what happened?"

I got up and went to the door, feeling defeated.

"Get my things ready and arrange for a carriage. I'll go home on the first train."

"You can't just leave the competition like this. There are protocols to follow—"

"Watch me," I interrupted him and closed the door without waiting for a response.

I immediately stopped in the hallway as I stepped out because not only were my guardians in the hall waiting for me but everyone else.

It was crowded with Lois, Geronimo, Brenda, Khloe, Karl, Alexander, Pierre, Alanis—the rest of the courts and even part of the palace staff.

They all wanted answerers from me.

It hurt to know that I never managed to make allies in the right way. The only real ally I'd found was fighting a dragon right now—my dear Laila, abandoned once more by me. I shivered and looked down as I started walking through the crowd toward my bedroom. I had to get ready to leave.

"We heard the beast again, little one," Karl spoke, and I clenched my fists. Immediately regretting it when I felt my injured hand. He was the last realm I wanted to hear from right now. "You've been to the ruins."

I kept walking, holding my injured arm to my chest.

"Were you able to find any weakness?" Alexander asked.

All the representatives were following me. I couldn't even feel my guardian close. I quickened my pace.

"Look at him—he's a total disaster. The weakness is him," Karl answered with derision.

"Don't start," defended Khloe. "Look at his arm. Omhet, you need a doctor now."

"What he needs is to stop provoking the beast, or we'll go into battle before the week is over," Sani pressed in a concerned tone.

"Ez kletym, moz matal!" bellowed the Or-Mua court in the old language.

"No one needs to die," said the Rustilla court to Or-Mua comment. "What we need to know is what the hell happened."

"If the prince doesn't start talking, we're going to die," the Zalinna court representative argued, trying to get closer. "Say something, pol pewz!"

I stopped half stairs and turned around. It was strange to have the full attention of all the representatives at the bottom of the beautiful stairs. The man from Zalinna court was dressed in bright colors and watched us like this was a fun spectacle. The woman from Or-Mua looked like she was dressed from nature, with branches in her hair and lips stained in black. The guy from Rustilla was a man who always wore a hat, with a thin mustache but a thick cigar. The young woman from Nova Cerise has her hair white as snow and a magic stone on each side of her face. Pierre with his bow like he was married to it. Sani with her colorful headscarf. And Daonna court was a short and quiet woman, who I can barely remember because she's calm, timid, and only talks to the Nova Cerise court.

I had wanted to meet and be part of them, but now it was too late.

"I'm sorry," I said. "But there are secrets that are better to give up than to face. Good luck to all. You all are going to need it."

"You can't leave like this," someone yelled, but there were so many of them that I couldn't find who. "What is going on? We deserve to know."

"It's the least you can do," another shout.

"Omhet," Alexander called me this time. When I looked at him, I hesitated. I couldn't lie to him too.

From the end of the corridor, Marcus came out of the office and gave me a warning look. A man who created this competition, knowing perfectly well that Laila was alive. And the gods know what else he knows.

"Ask the minister. If anyone has lied to you, it's him, not me," they all turned to him, but Marcus didn't look at anything or anyone but me as his gaze darkened. "Excuse me," I concluded and fled up the stairs.

I used a public telephone and inserted so many coins that it seemed ridiculous. It was expensive to make a call to my kingdom, but I'd rather be there at the train station than in the palace surrounded by questions I couldn't answer. Not even my guardians knew what had happened.

The phone rang more than expected, making me a little impatient because the call was expensive to make, and I was wasting time waiting for somebody to answer.

"Glacier Kingdom, Annally on the phone. Please say your permission code."

"Is my name enough?" I asked, biting back my smile.

I heard a loud gasp, and then Annally began to speak in a tangled way in the old language. I tried to tell her to control herself, I didn't have much time, but the call went silent. I leaned back from the phone, scratching my head impatiently, looking out the glass door at people passing from side to side and trains lining up on the rails. I had to hurry, and I don't know if Annally had hung up.

"Hello?"

When I heard my sister's voice, I let my eyes close in relief.

"I just wanted to hear a familiar voice. I missed you all," I said, knowing that my call was about to be cut off. "I'm coming home."

"Cheikh told us, but he didn't explain further. What have they done to you, Ahnani? I'm going to Andebeck with you and kick their ass."

I laughed. I missed being with Estefania so much that it brought my face back to life.

"I'll tell you everything when I get back," I promised. "I called to find out how the king is doing. I want to prepare myself mentally."

There was a pause so pronounced that I thought the call had dropped.

"The minister of Andebeck called him, and he disappeared since then. I don't think I'd ever seen him so furious."

Marcus, you son of a bitch, I thought, shaking my leg nervously. So, Marcus took the lead and exposed me before I could say anything.

My father was going to kill me.

Cheikh rapped on the door with his knuckles—my train was here.

"Okay, I'll see you in three days."

Estefania sighed. "Whatever happened, Omhet, I know you did what you thought was right, and no one can ever fault you for that," she said softly.

The thing is, this time, I'm not sure I did the right thing, I thought, looking down at my bandaged hand. I was barely able to move my fingers. Before leaving the palace, I had visited the infirmary, and they had dressed my wounds in medicine and gauze. But when Laila put her compresses on me and cared for me, I felt better than Andebeck's nurses did.

I didn't want to imagine Estefania's face when I told her everything that had happened in a little over a month.

"See you at home, dear," I said.

I hung up and listened as the phone gave back a single coin from all the ones I had put in. I left the coin where it was. I stepped out of the phone booth, and all the sounds hit me at once—the screech of the train, the engineer at the door in his striped uniform, people running with their bags, and others shrieking as they said goodbye to their loved ones with emotions that broke whoever listened to them.

It was busier than ever due to the sudden roars of the dragon, causing many to try to evacuate the city in a panic. I couldn't even see the station signs correctly as people were frantically milling about.

Cheikh had to grab me by the good arm and escort me as if I were an important person. Well, I was, but it was funny to see how the protocols were activated in my guardians because of a scenario as unpredictable as this avalanche of people desperately looking for their trains.

There was a private car toward the front of the train, where people tried to get in, but the driver was arguing fervently to move away from the door. The car had been reversed solely for my guardians and me, but desperate passengers were trying to enter.

"Everybody here is overreacting," Shin complained, crossing his arms. "If the dragon wanted them dead, they would already be dead."

"Explain that to them—I dare you," I said, trying to make a joke, but it came out sounding like an insult.

Cheikh took out his pocket watch and sighed impatiently. The line did not want to give away, and the driver kept explaining that the train was already full.

"Should we intervene?" Lucas asked. "We can get these cretins out in seconds."

"Leave them," said Shin in a bored tone. "If they find out that the car is being kept empty for the prince, they will burn his other arm."

I rolled my eyes. I wasn't in the mood for his jokes.

Everything had become complicated for me, and it got out of hand so quickly that it was scary. I couldn't believe how bad I wanted to leave. Coward, I yelled at myself, but I shuddered every time I closed my eyes and saw myself taking a bow and arrow to kill her. Not all of us were born with the capacity to kill a person—most of us are born with the desire to help. That was what I felt the first time I saw her sad and desolate eyes—a great desperation to be alive, to break the curse, and to have that freedom taken from her at such a young age. I fell into a web of despair at the sight of her. I wanted to save her more than anything in this world. It was my nature, my duty, and my honor to be able to help. I would even risk my life, but not hers. It wasn't in me—For Krea, I just couldn't do it.

I missed Glacier like never before.

Cheikh pushed his way to the front of the train and tried to show our passports to the conductor to get us in. People insulted him and demanded that he go stand in line, like everyone else. No matter how much they mentioned me on the radio or saw me in the newspaper, I was not popular among the other kingdoms. They did not recognize that Cheikh was wearing an official royal guard uniform, and several started arguing with him.

"This is taking forever," Lucas said, and he hung one of the backpacks on my bad arm. I groaned, glaring at him. "Sorry," he said in a rush as he began to walk through the crowd, trying to reach Cheikh.

"So," Shin whispered, now that no one was going to be able to hear him, "You gave up."

I didn't look at him.

"I'm surprised to hear more disappointment than relief in your voice," I said without emotion. "Have you had a change of heart?"

He snorted. "Part of me is happy that I'm going to stop being a guardian and go back to being a general, but—" he sighed, looking frustrated. "Something tells me this is wrong."

"Everything in this place is wrong, but who am I to try to fix it?"

"Omhet Guillermo Espinho of Glacier," he said. I thought he was joking, but when I looked at him, he seemed serious. "The most stubborn idiot in the world."

I almost smiled, but then I heard a shout and saw that someone had tried to hit Cheikh as they pushed forward. Cheikh and Lucas were in trouble.

"Prince, it's now or never," Lucas shouted above the crowd. "If we take five more minutes, they'll give your car away."

I looked at Shin.

"I'd let the five minutes go by just to see Cheikh drag them out by the hair."

Shin finally laughed at one of my jokes.

I picked up the bags with Shin, and when I started to push people to get into the car, I heard someone shout my name, but it was lost in the screech of the train. I didn't stop but looked at Shin, then my other two guardians, making sure they weren't the ones who had called me. I thought maybe I'd imagined it.

Again, I heard my name—this time more clearly. I discarded the idea that It had been imaginary when Shin also stopped to look back.

I froze in the middle of the crowded platform and looked up, seeing Cheikh hurrying me with his arm movement, Lucas trying to make way for me, and Shin looking for what he had heard, just like me.

Many times, I had told Estefania tales before she went to sleep. Usually, the stories begin with, "Once upon a time, there was a tall, handsome, and strong knight who bravely faced the dragon." Sometimes the knights were firstborn, heirs to the throne, poetic, and often sang for the maiden. So, when he put on his armor to face the beast, it was the dragon that was afraid of him. Every night, I saw her eyes light up in excitement, making her jump on the bed instead of putting her to sleep. She didn't know that I took refuge in those stories and her room, fleeing from a creature that was neither a beast nor a dragon but my older brother.

Those adventures seemed to happen in every story except mine.

In my case, I didn't know of battle. I was the fourth son and didn't even know what bravery was. Therefore, the one who ran away was me.

"Omhet," Shin called. I looked at him, paralyzed in the sea of people. "Please, move."

"But where to?" I asked desperately.

Shin looked at Cheikh, who was getting off the car. He looked red with rage while trying to get back to us. He couldn't understand why we were taking so long, and the train was about to leave.

A few long and eternal weeks ago, I swore that I had made the biggest mistake of my life when I asked to volunteer. My insecurity and ignorance had left me unprepared for everything I faced. But if I had one thing going for me, it was stubbornness.

That's why, when I heard her shout again, I reacted.

Hearing her voice made me realize that I wasn't trying to run away from her but from my fears. Her past and fate had utterly paralyzed me, but her voice made me realize it wasn't enough. She woke me up, and now I was pushing people away from my guardians and my doubts.

"Laila!" I called with all my might.

I stood in the middle of the crowd as they relentlessly pushed me.

I heard her answer, but I couldn't even tell from where. I had to run and climb onto one of the carts that were used to carry suitcases. The porter yelled at me, but I ignored him, looking around, about to lose my balance. I got down, ran a couple more steps, and then climbed on a bench, shouting her name with every breath I held. My heart was beating so hard I felt like it would explode if I didn't find her.

The train screeched, and I saw the crowd begin to pour into the cart that should have been mine. Another scream sounded from the train on the other side of the tracks shouting, "All aboard!" and I felt like I would lose my mind if I didn't find her.

I was about to scream when I saw something unusual. In the stampede of people, there was a gap where traffic flow was interrupted as if something was on the ground.

For heaven's sake, I found her.

Exhaling with relief, I threw myself off the bench and ran toward her, pushing hard, stepping over bags until I stumbled, groaning as I hurt my hand again and again, but I didn't stop. I couldn't, I wouldn't—not again.

When I finally got to her, I fell on my knees in front of her.

"Laila," I called desperately.

She was crouched on the ground, holding her head with closed eyes. For heaven's sake, I'm too late.

Apparently, there were so many emotions inside her head that she looked like she might lose control of the beast inside her, which meant that she would become a dragon in front of everyone.

I gasped, nervous. Laila had to get out of here, now! Her cream-lined dress would shred into a thousand pieces as soon as she began her transformation—not to mention all the people who would die around us.

"Laila," I called to her, completely nervous. Without asking permission, I grabbed her face and lifted her gaze until she met mine. Her eyes were watery, as if she had been crying. She looked terrified. "Are you crazy? I—I can't believe you're here."

Laila lifted her hand and gently placed it on top of mine. She was boiling from the heat.

"You can't go, please," she begged me, looking at me desperately. "You are the only one who has given me hope after *so*—so long. You can't leave like this! What kind of prince are you?"

I laughed nervously, caressing her face with my thumb with the most eminent tenderness. I didn't know that I would feel relieved to see her again—like returning home, one I didn't knew I had.

"Laila, I can't kill you," I told her with a devastating voice. "Ask me for anything, except that—"

"Stay," she interrupted me. "I'm not asking you to kill me but stay," she moaned and hugged herself, trembling. She was about to transform. "At least until the day of the competition."

It seemed fair and might give me enough time to find a solution. But what if I couldn't find it? What if, in the end, the curse claimed her life?

"That's enough for now," I whispered, answering all my questions.

Laila closed her eyes, and at the same time, a painful moan escaped her lips. I had run out of time to get her out of here.

"Laila, please, stay with me!" I begged her, shaking her by her shoulders.

She moaned, nervous, trying to control herself, but the more anxious, scared, and sad she felt, the more she lost control.

She had to find a way to make all those emotions disappear entirely. I had to make her feel differently—something positive, something that would make her come out of her trance.

So, kneeling where I was, surrounded by many people, I firmly grasped Laila's face. She couldn't open her eyes, but she didn't need them to be open to hear me.

"Laila," I whispered as softly as a caress. I didn't dare to say anything else—I just tried one last crazy idea.

My heart raced at what I would do, and I exhaled slowly, bracing myself. I had to hurry before I could get this strange idea out of my mind. So, I slowly moved my face closer to her, not taking my eyes off her lips. I admit that as I approached her, I felt an avalanche of insecurities, causing me to stop inches from her lips.

She opened her eyes weakly in confusion.

I thought about moving away when her gaze caught me, but I didn't stop.

I couldn't be shy. I had to finish what I—almost—started, for the people around me, right? Because it was all about distracting her—nothing more.

Sure, my mind replied with harsh sarcasm. Even I doubted what the real reason was. Hell, I didn't care. I had gotten to where she was. Because of that, all the words were lost in the back of my mind.

A shiver ran through me as I felt my lips touch her.

Laila gasped. I know she hadn't expected me to do something like that. I was afraid she would try to get away from me, so I held her tighter as I buried my fingers in her hair. Damn, I didn't recognize myself. I could feel the roughness of my fingers but the softness and tenderness of my lips, as if I were afraid of offending or going too far. I thought she might get angrier, but instead, I felt her skin start to cool down, and her hands rested on my shoulders.

That's it! I waited for her to push me hard. Maybe she would even slap me.

Her hands moved to my chest and closed on my shirt. I wondered what was going through her mind, but when I tried to break from the kiss, she pulled me by my shirt back to her lips, kissing me more insistently. I wanted to laugh in disbelief—was this really happening in front of everyone? I could not believe it. However, I allowed myself to finally enjoy the moment.

I let go of her hair, just to caress her face, and melt into her, as if the rest of the people didn't exist anymore and it was just the two of us in the middle of such a huge station.

We were surrounded by people who probably looked at us as if we were out of place, without having the slightest idea that this kiss had saved their lives.

When we managed to separate, we looked at each other differently, as if there had been an explosion inside of us that we had inadvertently repressed. Because of that, I exhaled slowly, looking into her emerald eyes as if for the first time. I was supposed to find the courage to fulfill her last request, but on the contrary, I was convinced now that I would defend her from the entire Union when the time of battle came.

"I'm staying," I whispered, unable to release her face from my hands. "But we need to find another solution to break the curse."

"And if it doesn't work, then—" she didn't complete the sentence, but I nodded with difficulty.

"Until winter," I agreed.

"You'll stay until winter," she agreed and smiled.

I was surprised when she kissed my cheek and hugged me tight, but more surprised that I returned it as if I had been expecting it.

"Thank you," she whispered, and I felt the blossoming hope in her voice.

I kissed her hair fondly but couldn't answer her. She shouldn't thank me—not yet. I knew ending her curse by being killed was better for her than living with it indefinitely, but it hurt so much to think about. For now, I accepted it, squeezing her in my arms, waiting to take care of her as well as I could.

The line of people began to open up into a wide, sprawling path in front of me, causing me to look up and meet someone's gaze. He froze when he saw me.

I released Laila in surprise, and when she turned and looked at him, she knew who he was without me having to say anything. It was kind of obvious, anyway. The noise was diminishing out of respect, the guards were behind him, and the people got out of the way as if he were a king.

I got up, holding Laila's hand tight.

"So, that's him," she whispered, watching as he stopped as if she were a ghost.

"Grand Minister Marcus Blume," I said. "Which means, it's time for you to go."

Laila glanced at me, then at Marcus, who was now giving orders to his guards that I couldn't hear. His expression was so controlled that I couldn't read it.

"Laila, now," I ordered, but she squeezed my hand tighter.

"I don't want to leave you alone."

"Don't worry, Princess," Cheikh answered as he stood beside her, with his hand on the grip of his sword. Lucas stopped by my side, and finally, Shin stepped almost in front of me. "He won't be alone."

Laila looked at me once more. "I'll wait for you."

I smiled widely. "I'll see you soon."

"Do you promise?" her voice trembled, afraid to let me go.

"Have I ever stopped bothering you with my presence?"

She almost smiled, but I could see an internal struggle in her eyes as she finally let go of my hand. I didn't say anything else as I let her run through the crowd, away from Marcus and me.

"Now this just got interesting," Shin said, sounding excited for the first time.

"On guard—and no matter what, don't walk away from your prince," Cheikh ordered when Marcus was almost upon us.

I straightened up and prepared myself for whatever consequence might come my way.

"I'm ready," I said.

I looked at Marcus with bravery I didn't know I had and waited to face him.

The real competition had just begun.

ACKNOWLEDGMENTS

The first person I want to thank is the person reading this sentence. Thank you. After reading my entire book up to this point. I want you to know that if I had been asked in my teens if I was ever going to let someone read my book, I would have laughed at them, because the fear I had of sharing my stories was one that I struggled with, but that no longer binds me. Thank you for reading the most special book in my life, my talent, and part of my heart. Thank you. Thank you. Thank you.

When I dedicated this story to my parents at the beginning of the book because they believed in me before I did, I wasn't exaggerating. My mother was the one who gave me my first typewriter when I was four years old, who fixed my stories for me when I was in fourth grade, and who read every story I wrote as if it were a best-seller. She made me believe that I was a writer when I didn't even know how to write properly. And my dad never stopped asking me "when are you going to publish your book?" but, I gave him a thousand excuses. When I decided to enroll in my psychology degree, I remember that he asked me a thousand times, "Are you sure? why don't you pick something like literature?" I can assure you there hasn't been a moment in my life that I don't have him on top of me. Because they knew me better than myself. Because they knew that in me there was a dream that slept and cried waiting to be taken out. Without them, I wouldn't have made it.

As if that were not enough, I married the most stubborn man in the world. My Sam. He loves me, with everything and my crazy side. My friend, my assistant, my co-editor, my beta-reader, my guide, the one who breaks my writing blocks, the one who challenges me to not just be a writer, but the best version I can give. You are the conscience that reminds me of who I am and the flame that inspires me to never stop writing about love.

To my TikTok followers, because without knowing me, they have decided to follow me, and month after month they have given me words of encouragement to not give up. Who knew that there could be people who don't know your name, haven't even read a page and inspire you to keep going? You were my pillars, thank you.

And to my friend Alice. Your words are my motto and I use them every day. "Small progress is still progress." For being the first to laugh and cry with my characters. For being the first to fall in love, to make the first fanfictions. For being the first to read about the prince who fell in love with the dragon.

Gracias.

The Twelve Terrirories

- **KINGDOMS**

Andebeck: Marcus

Glacier: Omhet

Ettezi: Karl & Khloe

Atsoc: Alexander

Puerto: Escondido Alanis

- **COURTS**

Sierra: Adaza Sani

Nordem: Pierre

Nova Cerise: Odette

Daonna: Vitya

Zalinna: Ivar

Or-Mua: Malin

Rustilla: Andreus

ABOUT AUTHOR

JERRY R. M.

Jerry is a writer who was born and lived until her adulthood in Puerto Rico. She loves traveling and reading fantasy stories as much as she loves her cat and coffee. Influenced by fairy tales from an early age and dreaming of seeing the world, she devoted herself to writing since fourth grade. At first, she hid literature as a hobby, which slowly began to take up more and more space in her heart. She finished her bachelor's degree in psychology and halfway through her master's degree her studies were interrupted by the 2020 pandemic. In that year she lost her job, her studies, and her home and decided to move from New York to Texas.

Eventually, she had to make the decision to return to finish her studies.

Or realize her dreams.

Almost three years later, she published her first book.

And she never thought that she could be so happy.

To find out more about the author, please visit:

Website: www.jerryrm.com

Email: jerry.r.m.writer@gmail.com

Instagram: jerry_r.m_writer